Doña Inés vs. Oblivion

THE PEGASUS PRIZE FOR LITERATURE

DOÑA INÉS VS. OBLIVION

a novel

ANA TERESA TORRES

TRANSLATED BY GREGORY RABASSA

LOUISIANA STATE UNIVERSITY PRESS

BATON ROUGE   1999

Copyright © 1992 by Ana Teresa Torres
Translation © 1999 by Louisiana State University Press
Originally published as *Doña Inés contra el olvido* in 1992 by Monte Avila Editores in Caracas
Manufactured in the United States of America
First printing
08   07   06   05   04   03   02   01   00   99
5   4   3   2   1

Designer: Amanda McDonald Scallan
Typeface: Bembo and Serlio LH
Typesetter: Coghill Composition

Library of Congress Cataloging-in-Publication Data

Torres, Ana Teresa, 1945–
    [Doña Inés contra el olvido. English]
    Doña Inés vs. oblivion : a novel / Ana Teresa Torres ; translated
by Gregory Rabassa.
        p.   cm. — (The Pegasus prize for literature)
    ISBN 0-8071-2476-1 (alk. paper)
    I. Title.   II. Series.
PQ8550.3.06753D6613   1999
863—dc21   99-15676
                                                                CIP

The paper in this book meets the guidelines for permanence and durability of the Committee on
Production Guidelines for Book Longevity of the Council on Library Resources. ♾

PUBLISHER'S NOTE

The Mobil Pegasus Prize for Literature, created by Mobil Corporation in 1977, recognizes distinguished works of fiction from countries
whose literature merits wider exposure in the rest of the world. *Doña
Inés vs. Oblivion,* winner of the 1998 Venezuelan competition, is by
Ana Teresa Torres. The novel was originally published in Caracas in
1992 by Monte Avila, Venezuela's state-owned publishing firm.

The competition drew more than a hundred entries and generated
considerable national excitement, for contemporary Venezuelan fiction has not received the international acclaim of other Latin American nations such as Mexico, Peru, Colombia, and Brazil. An indepen-
dent jury of distinguished literary figures chose this novel. The jury
was advised by former Venezuelan President Ramón J. Velázquez, a
historian by training and perhaps the most respected political figure
in the country; poet and critic José Ramón Medina, who also heads
Venezuela's prestigious Ayacucho Library; and Pedro Díaz Seijas,
critic and academic who is a member of the Venezuelan Academy of
Language. The actual jury included Oscar Rodríguez Ortiz, a critic,
editor, and professor of literature; Luz Marina Rivas, language professor at the Central University of Venezuela; Roberto Lovera de Sola,
a critic and essayist; Carlos Pacheco, professor of letters at Simón
Bolívar University; and critic Osvaldo Larrazábal.

A former practicing psychotherapist and current cultural correspondent of the Caracas daily *El Universal,* Ana Teresa Torres has won assorted national awards for her fiction. Her other works include *Exile in Time, Vague Disappearances,* and *Malena of Five Worlds.* She spent more than twenty years in clinical psychology practice and academic teaching and now writes full time. She lives in her native Caracas with her son and daughter. Torres is the first woman to win the Mobil Pegasus Prize since Keri Hulme of New Zealand won it in 1985 for *The Bone People.*

Steeped firmly in the Latin American tradition of magical realism and historical fiction, *Doña Inés vs. Oblivion* is a narrative that covers three hundred years, beginning in 1663. The narrator is Caracas aristocrat Doña Inés Villegas y Solórzano, and she is obsessed with securing title to a piece of jungle land. The legal battle goes on for centuries, and Doña Inés continues talking long after her death in 1781. But while seemingly surreal, the tale is rooted in reality, based on an actual Venezuelan court case that was resolved only in the late 1980s. The prime narrative force is the battle between the white heirs of Doña Inés and the black and mulatto descendants of her husband and a slave woman. But the real centerpiece of *Doña Inés* is Venezuela itself—from forgotten colonial outpost, to one of the bases of Simón Bolívar's independence war, to a land almost obliterated by earthquake in 1824, to the scene of a procession of battling political movements leading to the oil-rich nation of modern times. And most important, the winning novel completes the historical-fictional mosaic of Latin America begun by writers such as Carlos Fuentes in Mexico and Gabriel García Márquez in Colombia.

The novel was translated by Gregory Rabassa, renowned translator of two Nobel Prize winners and the previous Mobil Pegasus Prize winner *A God Strolling in the Cool of the Evening,* by Mário de Carvalho, published in English in 1997. Equally adept in Spanish and Portuguese, Rabassa translated García Márquez's *One Hundred Years of Solitude,* as well as Nobel winner Miguel Angel Asturiás' *Mulata.*

We wish to express our appreciation to Mobil Corporation, which established the Pegasus Prize for Literature and provides for the translation into English of the works the award honors.

For my son
Gastón Miguel Carvallo

Contents

PART ONE

1715–1835

DOÑA INÉS AMONG THE BRIEFS

(1715–1732)

My life has been a passage through slow mornings, long days that time ran through sluggishly as I supervised the work of the slave women, watching them sweep the flagstones in the courtyard, polish the floor tiles and the glazed wall mosaics I'd had brought from Andalusia, gather the fallen leaves from the lemon tree, and water the guava tree in the yard; embroidering a point or two on a mantle or taking a turn through the kitchen to taste the soup and see that everything was as it should be before Alejandro's arrival and asking him during lunch what had been discussed at the council, what the price for cacao was and whether the ship carrying it had sunk. Sleeping an unhurried siesta later when the heat grew stronger and preparing myself for the gracious reception of visitors, giving orders and overseeing the preparation of sweetmeats and teas served on the porcelain plates and gilded glasses that I had had imported from France, waiting for the ladies to arrive and then for the slave girls to take their cloaks in the entranceway, sitting in the parlor with my daughters, conversing, inquiring about the health of our people, commenting on how heavy the winter rains had been, speaking of husbands off on their plantations, of processions, or of the party the governor was giving to ingratiate himself with us; and at the appointed hour the slave girls returned with the cloaks in a basket, and we said good-bye until soon again or until

Sunday in the cathedral, where we aristocrats would be together, dressed in black and covered with capes as a sign of our privilege, escorted by two slave girls, one to chase away beggars and the other to spread a small rug over the dry brick floor of the church. At dusk all assembling, children and slaves, to recite the holy rosary in the chapel, dining in silence, and while Alejandro went over the accounts that the plantation administrator showed him, and I was playing solitaire, the children were already asleep and the crickets could be heard in the courtyard.

Now all of them have left me alone. Where are the ten children from my fifteen births? Nicolás, Alejandro, Mariana, Manuela, Antonio, Isabel, Félix, Teresa, José Ramón, Francisca. That weeping I hear, is it one of my dead children? Diego, Catalina, Juan José, Felipe, Sebastián. They've all deserted me; I'm alone, Alejandro. I'm left only with the rustle of papers against each other as I search for the title deeds I've lost, the ones my father certified in 1663. Where are those titles? Where have the files gone? I can't find them in the bedroom cabinets or in the desk in your room or by ransacking the drawers of my dresser or dumping the thread from my sewing basket or digging in the corners of the chest or snooping under the rugs or shaking the damask curtains. Where are they, those hundreds of pages? They are spinning and swirling around my head, yet I can't find them. Royal letters patent, decrees, provisions and rulings, official writs, letters and envelopes, briefs, pleas and allegations. Papers and more papers, Alejandro. All that work the scribes put in, all that ink, all that dust stored away; someday the rats will come and greedily gobble these bundles of parchment, the cockroaches will be frightened out of the cracks in the floor tiles and will leave their shit sticking to the margins, their dark smudges appearing everywhere, unmistakable, and even the signature of the king will be stained. Time, Alejandro, will erase my complaints, and my efforts will disappear, but I want my voice to remain, because I've seen all and heard all, and I'll go on searching for my titles, even if the dust from the files strangles me and I'm asphyxiated by these old pages, even if deciphering this hen-scratching costs my last rays of light and the final strainings of memory dissolve my intent to establish a chronology for the papers so the scribe can come and get his inkwells out, dip his quill, and bear witness to that memory; I want to dictate my story, which is scattered among my recollections and the documents because my past is in them along with the history of many others. My name will appear here a thousand times: Inés Villegas y Solórzano; and yours, Alejandro Martínez de Villegas y Blanco; and yours, Juan del Rosario Villegas, to which I always attach the notation *my freedman,* so you'll know it, so you won't forget it, not even when you're dead. Here I am, lying in bed, from where I call in vain to the slave women to come and put the sheets that smell of urine out in the sun; between the linen robe and the muslin pillowcases, under the feathers in the pillows, there the papers are hiding, I sleep with them, and as soon as I wake up I look at them and start my job of untangling them all over again until finally, at some moment when I won't know whether it's day or night, I'll have finished my task and they'll all be in order.

What are you saying, Alejandro? I can barely hear you, speak up, you know I'm deaf and you're doing it on purpose. Don't you want me to hear you? What are you laughing at? Are you trying to tell me that I'm just like the titles, just a loose piece of paper blown away by time, and that I'm searching for documents good only for lighting the fire or for me to wipe my ass with—by myself, because the slave girls have left me alone? Are you trying to tell me it's useless to squat down and bend my back, sweeping my hand under beds, lifting rugs, digging into the crannies of dressers and chests to find the history I've lost? Well, even so, I'm going to keep on combing my sparse white hair, sharpening my foggy eyes, with my wrinkled hands trembling, taking care of my carcass so it won't crumble into dust shut up in this animal's den that my room has become and that I'll never leave until I in turn have been changed into a paper phantom.

Now I've got to look for my titles, our titles, the ones my father certified in 1663, in order to put my chronicle together. You're probably thinking I won't find them because my eyes are worn out, that there isn't enough light around me. Where are my glasses? I don't know where I left them. Maybe I should open the windows; I'm not sure whether it's dawn or dusk, and I can sleep just the same in light or in dark, eyes open or closed, and it makes no difference to me whether I'm hearing the Angelus bells of noontime or nightfall, because the shutters are closed so the brightness won't blind me or the dew harm me. My memory conjures up the same faces, the same bodies, the same names: I feel them and smell them, they accompany me, they harass me, they don't give me a moment's peace. Sometimes I think the shadows that surround me are hiding the papers, that they know where they are but are deliberately saying they don't so I'll go on looking forever; but it doesn't matter, I'll win out over them, I've got all the time in the world to give to the hunt for my titles. I'll lift the last roofing tile and the last tile on the floor, I'll dismantle all the door and window frames, pull out all the bricks, remove all the columns, and if necessary I'll demolish my house, because I know they're somewhere, and I'm ready for all the centuries to come raining down until they appear. Time has ceased to interest me; its movements don't bother me anymore because I died a long time ago.

And where are you, Juan del Rosario? You've sneaked away so I won't see you hiding the papers from me. You've come back to take them away, haven't you? Because you do know where they are. Or are you going to deny that you know the hiding places in this house better than I do? Weren't you born in it? Or is my memory bad? Are you not the little boy who used to run around in the servants' courtyard at the rear? Aren't you the one who would bring the jug of water to the kitchen? The one who wallowed with the pigs and chased the hens? The one who would lie in the shade of the guava tree to spin tops with my sons? It was you, and you know it quite well, don't lie to me, you lying black bastard. Tell him not to lie to me, Alejandro, wasn't he your son? I remember very well the mother of this child you made me take on as a houseboy; I can see her as if it were yesterday, putting on your poultices, serving your tea, and massaging the soreness out of the hand you'd twisted when you fell off your horse, I can hear her praying the paternoster backward at night to invoke Mandinga, the devil, I spy on her when she paces about the kitchen while the other black women are asleep and recites her incantations there and prepares potions to control people's wills. Do you think I couldn't pick out her voice when she talked to the witches? Our Lady of Guidance, whom I placed on the ridge of the roof to frighten them off, was of no use. From when she was twelve I began locking her up at night, because I recognized the evil in her already at that age, and even so she would get out, she'd find the key or Mandinga would bring it to her and she'd release herself. I knew your mother inside out, Juan del Rosario. Do you think she didn't know how to defy all the laws and decrees and ignore the rules, not worrying about the fact that servant girls were forbidden to go out at night? She seemed to be waiting all year for Carnival or Saint John's Day, and it meant very little to her that Bishop Escalona had condemned the wily, crafty liberties that are taken in games and dances, in snares by both sexes, hand contact, rude and indecent actions—and dangerous even when they stayed within the bounds of propriety. She would go out and daub passersby with coal tar and flour, but it wasn't tricks with water and paint that occupied her attention, no, not at all, what she craved were little pranks and cavortings and games of hide-and-seek. She did a good job of getting around the orders of the commissioner of the Holy Office, who had absolutely forbidden, both in the countryside and on the outskirts of town, skits and kite-flying, fandangos and dances, and processions with overdecorated images of saints, and superstitious practices at the wakes of dead babies, where it was all lewd solicitations, adultery, incest, fornication, defiance, fights, and other pernicious acts. But she, no matter how securely I locked her up, would be concentrating on where the fandango was coming from and would spend her time dancing and hooting.

The son of the cat catches the rat. I know you well, Juan del Rosario; even if you're lurking in the corners I can see you quite well, although I can barely see anything anymore; I can smell you, though you're far away, and can hear your voice quite clearly despite the deafness that used to make the slave girls laugh at me and pretend to be speaking when they were only miming words. That white splotch is your teeth laughing too. How old are you now, Juan del Rosario? I can see that you're fifteen, maybe twenty, and that you're back from Barlovento, where your father sent you, following my advice because I told him you had none of the skills of a craftsman and that here you'd end up being a house servant with no trade, and that he should take you to the plantation, where in time you'd make a good overseer. Then you come back and go around spreading the word that your master, Don Alejandro, your master and your godfather, told you that in the Curiepe Valley there was a lot of uncleared royal land and that he himself didn't know the boundaries of his holdings. Is that true, Alejandro? Did you tell him to go there with other blacks to clear the land and set up a plantation and that the Curiepe Valley, after your death, would belong to them? I don't believe it, Alejandro. Tell me if you promised that. You're quite mistaken, Juan del Rosario, if you believed his word; what you alleged in your briefs is nothing but a pack of lies. Who was going to believe those fairy tales? The High Court in Santo Domingo? The one in Santa Fe? The viceroy? How uppity can a black man get—to write to the king! Weren't you just that bold? Here's your first supplicatory brief from 1715. Do you want me to read it to you?

> . . . *with the care and fervor of the aforesaid supplicants, which leads them to be loyal vassals, and with the large number of free men of color that we are with no place to settle, it would be good defense and a hindrance against enemies were Your Majesty inclined to give us permission to establish a village at the site of Sabana de Oro and a port in the cove of Higuerote . . .*

Here your name and title appear: Captain of the Free Colored Company of the Militia Battalion of Caracas. Who gave you that rank? It could only have occurred to a mad barbarian like Cañas y Merino. What a governor you saw fit to send us, Philip V! A ruffian with his face sliced down the middle by a scimitar slash he got from the Moors in Oran. Do you know, Philip V, what he did for recreation in his spare hours, which was most of the time because, with all the hate and ill will he felt for us aristocrats, he mostly avoided government house? Well, he could find no better fun than to tie pots to the tails of cats and organize horse races with prizes for the riders who killed the most cats with their whips; and when he couldn't find cats he went after chickens, burying them with only their heads showing so he could ride along on horseback and decapitate them with his sword. That was how he devoted his time to all the many problems of the province of Venezuela, and then at night he would soothe his lust with mulatto women. But that wasn't enough for you, you bandit, you had the audacity to abduct a girl from a prominent family and besmirch her forever on the bank of the Guaire. Our patience ran out, and we sent you back. I never heard any more about you, Cañas y Merino, but I'm sure you were killed in Spain or that you rotted away in some jail. Well, that was the one, he and nobody else, who granted my houseboy and freedman Juan del Rosario Villegas the title of Captain of the Free Colored. Quite another thing was the logic and good judgment of Don Alberto de Bertodano, who viewed with Olympian disdain the ridiculous brief that petitioned and planned for the establishment of a village tight up against our plantation. Since when have blacks founded villages here? Both Alejandro and I are equally the great-grandchildren of Don Francisco Maldonado de Almendáriz, an hidalgo from Villacastín, and grandchildren of the conquistador and captain Don Pedro de Villegas, a "son of nothing" but the founder of several towns in this province, and we have amply proven our services to the Crown and our clean and worthy blood, yet even so we had to suffer the affront of that smuggler governor Betancourt y Castro, who conceived the wild idea of giving Juan del Rosario permission to seek recognition of the lands and confirmation of the title of Royal Founder that Cañas y Merino had awarded him. Recognize what and how? Wait until I find the deeds, which have disappeared because I've guarded them too closely, but I'm sure I have them, and I can recite them from memory. They said

I have and possess lands and a valley called Curiepe that are two leagues upstream from Codera Cape on the cove called Higuerote.

Isn't it true, Alejandro, that this is how the titles that Porras y Toledo confirmed for my father read? I can see you, Alejandro, when you left with my brother-in-law Francisco on your way to call at the government house office of Portales y Meneses (weren't you district magistrate?) and present an allegation against that uppity black bastard who did nothing but submit plea after plea. Didn't he have the cheek to write directly to the king? So it wasn't all that much for him to send a new brief to the viceroy in Santa Fe. I told you plenty of times, Alejandro, never to trust a viceroy who showed his insolence and abuse of power by ordering you deprived of the privilege of magistrate and threatened you with jail, a fine, and seizure if you didn't accept the shyster Alvarez de Abreu, who with all the law he knew could only come up with the idea of giving new permission to Juan del Rosario to gather as many recalcitrant blacks as he could find and go to Curiepe to clear my land. I can still hear the sound in the valley of their voices and machetes—supported and protected by the viceroy's having read their brief, bolstered by the idea that Portales had to execute the writ. And there they stayed while Portales resolved his doubts, sometimes for us, sometimes against. Portales thought he could just ignore the council; how mistaken he was. It was necessary to arrest him, and we held him in custody until he came to his senses, and when he did, there was nothing for him to do but take away from Juan del Rosario that rash recognition he'd given in order to cover up smuggling.

I can't find them; I look through drawers and empty them out, I get down on my hands and knees under the beds, I lift up rugs, and I don't see the titles, but they were there, of course they were there. I can see you clearly, Alejandro, on the day you went to present them once and for all to Portales, to convince him that he should give orders to Captain Juan Joseph de Espinosa to destroy the village and bring the blacks to Caracas. Juan del Rosario, you liar, you played crazy and said you were sick in order not to acknowledge the ruling, but I know very well that your followers hid you and that you told them to accept the orders but not to carry them out, because in the long run they would win the lawsuit, because you were going to keep on writing. And when the royal decrees reached you, you felt bloated with pride, on the point of thinking you'd beaten us. Decrees from the king in your name—my, my!—all that remained was for you to stroll through Caracas with an umbrella and a cane, for you to think you were white. But in the meantime Espinosa's soldiers fulfilled their mission and set fire to the village; the sixteen houses burned and collapsed along the two streets. You'd even built a church—well, that shack of mud and palm leaves with a wooden cross, that chapel you'd dedicated to the Virgin of Altagracia and Saints Joseph and John, was turned into a torch. You lying little black bastard, did you think that

I, who've known you since you were a child, you and your mother, was going to believe that you had any faith in the virgin and the saints? That trick could only serve to delude their Catholic Majesties that you and the other blacks were devoutly waiting for the visits of the parish priest from Capaya, but there it was, in ashes, and stubborn as you were, you sent a new petition to the governor, this time with a ruling from the public prosecutor that the magistrates were in disobedience of the courts, the viceroy, and the king himself; and since that was more than enough to make Espinosa's soldiers withdraw, the blacks could clean up the rubble and raise their houses again, and I had to write another allegation:

> *And nevertheless they have not desisted and moved off, but rather by rebuilding what was demolished they are in stubborn and notorious disobedience, rebellion, and defiance, and as rebels have acted with no respect or reverence whatever.*

Do you remember? I have it in my hand; some of the lines have been smudged or the lack of light prevents me from reading it clearly, but listen, here it says:

> *of the rash attempt by the black Juan del Rosario, my houseboy, freed by my hand; the aforesaid black tried to settle some people of his color on my property. For that purpose they petitioned the viceroy, who ceded them the site of Sabana de Oro, two leagues distant from the Curiepe Valley, and when a plea was made to this government the blacks went beyond the fact and against the law, without the Curiepe Valley being named or having been named, and the aforementioned despoilment, which is an indication of their sinister guile, can be verified.*

From here on there are several paragraphs I can't make out, but I imagine that they explain the folly of establishing in such a remote place and so far from the vigilance of the authorities a village of untrustworthy blacks, and I end up asking for an order of reproof and apprehension for their having disregarded the order of abandonment—because, after the burning, the sixty-six people stayed on there (there were sixty-six, weren't there, Juan del Rosario?), I have counted them from the roster of the priest from Capaya, whom you got to come in an underhanded way, making him think he was coming at my behest. Well, he was just doing his duty, and besides, didn't you go about wailing that you didn't have a church, and didn't you give the hamlet the pompous name of Nuestra Señora de Altagracia y San Joseph de la Nueva Sevilla de Curiepe? Captain-Populator, that's what you wanted to be, but you saw how Portales took the appointment away when he came cowering out of jail in Santa Fe, from which he wasn't saved by the hollering of that sanctimonious Bishop Escalona, who, on top of it all, made us place saints in niches at every streetcorner and say the rosary at all hours, determined as he was to turn the city into a convent.

Was Portales the one who disguised himself as a monk to escape the council's wrath? Oh, no, that was Lope Carrillo. The governors we knew were so numerous that it's hard to keep them straight. Do you remember Lope Carrillo, Alejandro, or had you died already? Instead of busying himself with the problems that afflicted us, Don Lope, who had certainly been waiting more years than anybody for the job he finally got, brought suit against everyone. Who would ever know why he got it into his head that canons couldn't carry red or green umbrellas to protect themselves from the sun, couldn't have acolytes with surplices and caps lift their trains to spare them from the filth of the street when there was a procession. But the canons are bothered a great deal by the heat or they've got bad tempers, so on Palm Sunday there was a great to-do and people went out into the street more for the tumult and yelling than for the saints; the guard intervened and dispersed the priests, who didn't let the controversy pass until they filed an action and Don Lope had to leave for La Guaira dressed as a monk and with no one to hold up his train.

What was I talking about, Juan del Rosario? I'm losing the thread, involved as I am in these briefs. How many did we write? One for you, one for me, another for you, another for me. There wasn't a moment in which we were quiet; we were listened to by the magistrate of the council, the governors, the High Court of Santa Fe, the High Court of Santo Domingo, the viceroy of the New Kingdom of Granada, and, finally, since the snake is killed at its head, we went to the Council of the Indies and to the king himself. I missed you a lot when you died; your stubbornness and your challenge were the measure of my pride. What's the matter, why don't you answer me, why don't I hear your loud voice in the courtyard? In this solitude I seem to see you playing along the porches with my children, and I hear myself calling you, mingling your name with theirs to come in for your snack and your chocolate. Those shouts from Nicolás are because you fell off the top of the wall trying to reach a bird's nest, and I'm the woman who cleans your wound and brings into the servants' courtyard the liver-salt poultices to bring down the swelling. Yes, my houseboy and my freedman, you must remember the days of your childhood, when you were trembling with fever from smallpox and I had them take you to the doctor because I feared for your life; and you must remember when I told your father—wasn't Alejandro your father?—not to sell you because Alejandrito and Nicolás had fun with you. Yes, my houseboy and my freedman, you must remember the day you were born and I picked you up, a scrap of flesh filthy with blood and excrement, and wrapped you in a sheet and washed you, and I showed you to everybody and picked out your name. And this is how you've paid me back, you uppity little black boy, saying that the lands are yours. Yours how and since when? You've got nothing—do you hear me?—nothing that I haven't given you. Nothing that hasn't come from my generosity and my power, you ragged black bastard. I carried you naked in my arms the day you were born, and I could have drowned you in our well with no remorse or punishment; you even owe me your mother, the laziest and most disrespectful slave woman I've ever had, and more than once I wanted to sell her, get rid of her, but I didn't because I was sorry for you, didn't want you to be left an orphan, and I agreed to let Alejandro give you a shack on the other side of the Anauco gorge so you would have a place to live when you left my house—but for you to boast about your father, to proclaim to the world that those lands were yours and that he gave them to you as your inheritance? That I couldn't tolerate, Juan del Rosario. Owner of my birthright? Of lands given freely? Grandson of conquistadors? Sower of villages? If you had asked me for a piece of my plantation I would have given it, the way I dressed you in my sons' clothing, the way I had you taught to read and write by their teachers, the way I let you hide in my skirts when you cried at night, confused and afraid of ghosts . . . but *Founder*? No, that's not how you do things, my houseboy and my freedman. That's how you made me show who can growl the loudest and have succeeded in making me furious over the centuries. That's why I've devoted myself to bringing suit against you. Do you remember this document? It's the Royal Compulsory Provision of the Royal High Court of Santo Domingo of 1726. The procurator finds, to your favor, that in this whole legal tangle the one most damaged is His Majesty, because the village of Curiepe is of great use to the Crown, it will serve as a defense against English pirates and a bastion in preventing smuggling by the Dutch from Curaçao and, most of all, a refuge for so many loyal vassals who come seeking religious doctrine, because it seems that the blacks of Curaçao, the ones called Loangos, come to these shores because they want to be Christians. I challenged that in my allegation: who do they think they are, telling me that those foreign blacks are loyal vassals? They ran away to Barlovento because we Spaniards treated them better, and besides, I have the makeup of your villagers quite clear in my mind, and I know by name the ones who were born here and the ones who came in illegally. You yourself paid the consequences of an alliance with them, because they not only tried to displace the native blacks who initiated this lawsuit, but they took away the little parcel of land you'd left to your only daughter. Yes, in that decree of the High Court of Santo Domingo it asks that the briefs be remitted, that the blacks remain in the area, and that Portales be fined for his misconduct in burning the village. Look, Portales, you did the right thing by sailing off to Spain and doing it fast; things hadn't gone too well for you around here. When that royal decree arrived, I found out only later; they didn't give me notification, to my detriment— surely you don't imagine, Juan del Rosario, that I wouldn't have an attorney to answer the court. I waited two years, and when the verdict was handed down—I have it here, from 1728—I asked that it be revised. Do you know what the judges and the procurators in Santo Domingo replied? They returned only 117½ pesos to me as a settlement because the Curiepe Valley had never been confirmed or settled. One hundred seventeen and a half pesos! Did you think you could mollify me with that amount, Philip V? Did you think I was some white-trash woman selling olive oil in a tavern? You were very mistaken, my Lord King, if you thought this lawsuit was the kind that could be settled with 117¹/₂ pesos. I asked for the decision to be reconsidered, and I kept waiting; I couldn't let it stay that way, Juan del Rosario, you know that quite well because you know me. Didn't I bring you up in my home, and weren't you my houseboy? That blockheaded business of their paying my costs, which the Royal High Court sent to keep me happy—it didn't even come close to my figure, so I told the judges who heard the case that they hadn't heard too well; and since it was obviously necessary for me to shout louder, I had recourse to the Council of the Indies and filed suit in their Hall of Justice. Was there any hope? Well, I kept on hoping and waiting, and in 1731—look here—I received a royal decree, as is proper, authorizing a new act of dispossession. Oh, but then I came up against García de la Torre, who was already pretty much an enemy of ours, and as soon as he received his staff of office, he rushed to the defense of the Guipuzcoana Company. How many doubloons a year did they pay you to establish that monopoly? Some said a thousand, others said two thousand. You, too, García de la Torre, you told me to wait, that you were all tied up with the revolt of Andresote's black Indians in Yaracuy; that was your excuse for not taking up my writ of dispossession. All right, I answered you then. And my wait was an evil omen for you because, just look, they accused you of smuggling and sent Lardizábal as investigating judge. You placed all the royal charters on top of your head and swore to obey your king and liege lord, but you were lost, García de la Torre. Another one who dressed up in monk's clothes and hid in a monastery until he found a schooner to take him back to Spain. And you, Lardizábal, look what I told you, that you don't know these blacks, that it's one thing to bring down a governor and another to deal with these people. When you went in with your men, they left, making you think they'd been frightened because they remembered when Portales burned their homes. I told you not to believe them, but you paid me no attention, only babbled the nonsense you'd thought up to keep them docile: that I pay them for the improvements they'd made and put a pledge in writing, all of which I ignored. In the meantime they stayed in the area, working their small plots and waiting for me to be distracted so they could seize their chance to return. Years of truce, during which I let time pass.

R E Q U I E M

The sound of the double-tolling bell comes down the street. Under the canopy the priest, followed by four monks and four acolytes, reaches the door of the house; curious neighbors open their windows, and torches light his way. Voices giving orders, making suggestions, and intoning prayers can be heard echoing off the cobblestones of the narrow street as the confraternities arrive and pass through the vestibule into the courtyard. Present are those of All Souls, Holy Sacrament, Our Lady of Mercy, and Our Lady of Mount Carmel. It is cold by the window, dawn is just breaking, and one can see the shadows of their vestments, purple-and-maroon, blue-and-white, black-and-white, habits and candles, attendants chanting solemnly as they accompany the priest when he begins the office for the dead by the dining-room table. A flock of beggars is wailing loudly at the door, asking for alms for his eternal peace. What is today, Alejandro? Is it the day of your death? I can see you in your best clothes, a black velvet jacket with silver buttons, an olive-green taffeta underjacket, batiste knee-breeches, lace cuffs, a gauze bow tie, and Sevillian stockings with Brittany gaiters and cordovan shoes. I see you stretched out, a long candle at each bedpost, the shadow of the canopy on your face, your skin and the veins of your head transparent, your powdered wig under the tricorn hat with heron-plume embroidery, and at your waist your sword, covered by the tassel-trimmed serge cape. Inside the house, the weeping mingles with a rhythmic sound that ceases every so often, letting the response be heard, and then picks up again as the women busy themselves in the kitchen and the men, moved by the night's warmth, talk in the courtyard. Two slaves come forward and pick up the lifeless body, place it in the coffin, lift the casket and carry it to the dining room, where the priest, the monks, and the acolytes have assembled. The women cover themselves with their black shawls and in a single voice recite *The Mysteries of the Grief of the Passion and Death of Our Lord Jesus Christ.* The slave women close the windows on the inquisitive people who ask who's died, and they shroud the pictures and mirrors with purple cloth, and then, kneeling, they join in the prayers of the rosary, which will go on until daybreak.

I don't want to see, on the bed, your naked corpse veiled by a cotton cloth, your thin legs sticking up under the linen sheets, or the slave women changing the cold compresses on your forehead, or the male slaves picking up your inert body, tying your jaw closed, and arranging your hands to hold the cross over your chest. I don't want you to be in that uncovered box, Alejandro, or for them to jostle you in transit. I don't want to listen to the response or the prayers or see the members of the confraternities, torches in hand and heads bare, leave in a double row, or to remain sitting here surrounded by my daughters and relatives while my sons lift up your coffin and your funeral procession goes off toward the cathedral and is lost in the distant light that illuminates the lonely street. I don't want you to die, Alejandro. You were beautiful, Alejandro, you were handsome. Didn't I ever tell you that? Wasn't I allowed to, or didn't I dare? But, yes, I'm sure that at some time, in the half-light of dawn as the sun slipped in through the curtains to disperse the cold of the last traces of night, I moved closer and told you that you were handsome as I felt the sleepy warmth of your skin. I didn't like to smell the sweat of black women on your body. Did you think I was asleep, oblivious, when you would leave our room at night and knock on the door of the servants' quarters? Was it you or was it the devil who sprang the lock for Juan del Rosario's mother, whom I so zealously kept under guard? But it doesn't matter much in the end, so long as you confess that under the linen sheets you also tenderly left your seed between my legs. Or was it a lie? Did you only love the purity of my lineage, our being close relatives, and honor the maintenance of customs? Tell me it wasn't so, don't be mean; tell me my body was also food for your desires and that I, too, tempted you in the shade of the guava tree. We were children, and we played along the colonnades of my father's house; you put your hand in my brassiere to feel my breasts, which were just emerging. We were cousins, and you would look me up and down with impunity and your feet would brush mine under the table when the whole family lunched together. We were adolescents, and it was your steps that could be heard at nightfall when you tossed pebbles at my window to have one last look at me before you left. You can forget it if you want, but you can't take away my memory of the smell of your skin when we were married in the cathedral, and that night I came to know your strength and your drive. How many days have passed since then, Alejandro? Shut up in this bedroom, using my last vestiges of sight to scrutinize my papers, condemned to hear only the raindrops of the downpour, I get to thinking that the day of my own death has passed without my realizing it. Can that be possible? When you died, did you know you were dying or just that you were being dressed in a fine silk jacket and letting yourself be turned over and back in the hands of the slaves who were wrapping you in your shroud? If only someone would talk to me in this silence. You've left me all alone, Alejandro, and you, Juan del Rosario, contradict me, argue with me. Whenever I read one of your briefs I would find myself: with every new pretension that occurred to you, I became more sure of myself; with every aim you put in writing, my resistance grew more determined; with every issue you disputed with me, the more I saw right on my side; with every tract of land you tried to occupy, the firmer I became in my possession. What's that I'm hearing? They're the bells of my last rites. Who called the priest without my permission? It must be the slave women, trying to make me believe I'm dead so I'll let myself be carried off. They wish for me to die so they can dance and celebrate. Why don't they exercise their right to put themselves up for sale and look for a new owner? Not one of them does it.

They'd rather stay here, where I no longer give them any work, though it's true that sometimes—lost in my thoughts the way I am, not knowing whether it's day or night, sitting here among my papers in a black silk nightgown, my nails as long as a hawk's talons because I won't let anyone cut them, my hair like a scraggly white head-scarf because I won't let anyone put it up—I ring my little bell in the middle of the night to make them prepare some sweets and tarts. I touch my arms and don't have enough light to tell if they're the dead branches of a tree or made of cork, which looks hard but crumbles. I touch my eyes and don't know if the shadows I can only get a hint of are bodies in the room or if it's only an interior half-shadow, because I've stopped looking outside forever. I touch my ears so I can tell whether the sound that reaches me is the rumble of my own body or is the water beating on the window. Can it be that all this time has passed, Alejandro, and we haven't noticed it? What day is today? They're selling bulls for the dead today, and I must go to the church of the Conceptionist Sisters, must have the slave girls come quietly to dress me. Where are they? They're not bringing my underthings and brassiere. Have them come to hook up my taffeta bodice and put on my short silk jacket, bring my petticoats and the gown of Toledo silk, the one with black and white flowers, because today is a day of mourning, and have them cover my head with the velvet scarf decorated with a small silver knife and tuck black duck feathers into my hat. Hurry with my slippers, gloves, and fan! The flies on the street will swarm all over me if I don't shoo them off. Have those lazybones hurry up, bring my hand chair! I can't lose a minute; the officials go from the main square to the nuns' chapel at nine o'clock sharp. What time is it? I'm late, they're already gathering up the bundles of bulls and the procession is threading its way to the cathedral. I want to buy a bull, Alejandro, and I want them to inscribe your name on it so it will open the doors of Paradise for you. In spite of your many sins, may the Lord have mercy on your soul and give you eternal rest, pardon your faults and erase your mistakes. Are the slave women laughing at me because I'm shouting at them to hurry up and get me out to the procession? Or are you the one laughing, Juan del Rosario? In this solitude the voices of my memory get all mixed up, and the only coherent thing that guides me is the chronology of my lawsuit. But what's the matter with you that you don't answer me? Didn't I teach you to come at the sound of my voice? Didn't I tell your father that you'd be my houseboy and always obey me? So why don't you come now? Listen, Juan del Rosario, I'm talking to you! I don't hear your loud voice in the courtyard playing with Alejandrito and Nicolás, and instead I hear the *cumaco, mina,* and *curbeta* drums of the blacks who, gorged on cane liquor, are weeping for you, beseeching Saint John for food and health, good rain and sunshine at the proper times, agility for escape, and resistance to anger. They're praying to you so you'll continue protecting them from heaven. You've died, Juan del Rosario. The confraternity of blacks is coming out, the one of Saint John that the blacks called Taris founded, the one to which you paid seven pesos and five reals in order to be a redeemed brother and, upon your death, to have a coffin, rites, and solemn accompaniment. It's passing through the street, and every so often they ring the bell; nobody follows, no one pleads for alms, no one asks who died, they go by night and in silence to bury you in the church of San Mauricio, and from my window I can hear the brief tolling that announces your burial. I didn't want your death, just as you didn't want mine; we wanted each other alive, ceaselessly spying, sniffing each other out. Now Curiepe will be abandoned to a long silence; the cane and adobe huts will remain, but without a soul, there'll be the church with its priest but not a single body to kneel on its dirt floor. The village seems to have died, disappeared with you. The truce won't last long. You'll be pleased to know that I've got the urge to write again; you understand, if you'd been alive we wouldn't have left the high courts in peace during these years that have remained blank. In 1742 I petitioned the king once more—you too had grown old by now, Philip V—and I got a royal decree in my favor, but you didn't read that one, Juan del Rosario, nor you either, Alejandro. They started this legal wrangling with me and then went to sleep. Pay attention to me, I'm writing my chronicle.

THE COLONIAL SIESTA

(1743–1766)

Doesn't it wake you up, Alejandro, that noise, that deep thunder climbing through the mountain fog two thumps at a time and through the valley? What are those crazy people doing, bringing their carts and mules, flooding the streets, shouting, all in such a rush? From Santiago to Trinchera, from Atalaya del Gavilán to Caleta, the cannon shots are booming, and they've set fire to the Castellano in the harbor. Wake up, Alejandro, the whole city's in flight, and you're sleeping in your fine silk jacket as if nothing were happening. The English are attacking us. What can those sly devils have been thinking, that this land doesn't belong to anyone? Just when we have some respite from pirates and buccaneers, now it's the English fleet itself, nineteen ships strong, that's pounding the fortifications of La Guaira. All day and for part of the night our artillery has answered, and when darkness falls over the cove, sailing out to engage the distant foe will be the ship *Almirante,* with seventy guns, the ship *Capitana,* and two more, which, having cut their moorings, are running away through the firing that's lighting up the sea. Damaged, in bad shape, the English won't give up, and they point their ships toward Puerto Cabello, where Marshal Zuloaga is waiting to drive them off: they can swim away or go by any means they can, because they've taken a lot of shelling. Why does this land call down the wrath of God, Alejandro?

Why have they nicknamed it the Fortunate Land when misfortune hasn't given us any surcease? How could it have occurred to Columbus that he'd reached Paradise? Where's the El Dorado that some stupid chroniclers have described? If it isn't one thing it's another: if on the one hand they happen to send us a decent governor, on the other they saddle us with the Guipuzcoana Company, which bleeds us dry; when there are no heavy rains to ruin the harvest, there's an earthquake, and houses come tumbling down; if the pirates stop laying waste to us, the English bombard us; the year when there's no typhoid, smallpox and yellow fever plague us; and when everything seems peaceful, some blacks revolt and burn a plantation. I'm not so foolish as to think that everything is a matter of ordering the slave girls to serve chocolate in silver mugs or sending the houseboy to inquire about the neighbors' health so he can tell me people are ill. How many epidemics have we survived? Ever since I was a girl I can remember hearing the frightened voices of the slaves: they say there's smallpox, they say people have the vomits, that there's scabies, there's leprosy, there's talk of lepers wandering the outskirts of the city looking for a place to build shacks and settle, tired of being pelted with stones and driven away while people throw pieces of bread to them from the windows; they say troops have gone out to round them up and move them far off while they build them a hospice; they say that at night the wind carries the stinking smoke from consumptives' clothes being burned and that there's no more room in the hospitals, even with mattresses in the hallways, and that the sick awaken with a single shriek because in the darkness their bodies get mixed into the piles of corpses. I remember my parents preparing to go to the plantations to get away from the plagues and to isolate us from the putrefaction that strikes us down every so often. When Ricardos's troops were laid low by fever, it was whispered that it was punishment from Saint Rosalie for having established their quarters in her convent; neighbors said that at night they could hear the nuns asking for their cells back, the same as during the time when they were screaming because bearded men with horns on their heads were touching them; and the neighbors were sure that the torches and lights that could be seen were nothing but the lashes of fire with which the saint was fighting the soldiers, because they were the only ones dying. A punishment for you, Ricardos. Weren't you the one who tried so hard to defend the Guipuzcoana? For every doubloon they paid you to look after their interests, you buried a man who'd died from the fever, and in that way we might have seen the whole city drop, one by one, if you hadn't withdrawn the soldiers from the convent so you wouldn't die, too, and all Caracas be food for the buzzards. I didn't want to catch the plague, Alejandro, that's why I ordered the slave women to double-bar the door, and had it become necessary we would have eaten the grass growing in the courtyard and slaughtered the horses rather than leaving to die on the floor of the charity hospital, listening to the wails of the prostitutes being devoured by yellow fever and the howls of the madwomen who also had the plague and were shaking the bars of their cages for someone to give them something to eat. To die, Alejandro, bled by smelly barbers, when I should be here, immersed in my papers and looking for the document that proves me right! This brief I sent you in 1752, Felipe Ricardos. I read it here in faint ink:

> *The irreparable damages and injuries being caused by the aforesaid people of color, with the matter reaching the point of impeding or opposing the planting that my own sons are attempting to do on their aforesaid lands . . .*

They were claiming? I was claiming, I was the one giving them no letup, continuing the struggle I'd started along with Alejandro and Francisco, my brother-in-law, so that the blacks would stop their clearing and move off to no less than fifteen leagues from the sea. But what could my sons have been thinking when they settled the lawsuit, saying it wasn't giving them any profit but only vexation and worries? To divide their inheritance, sell the portions in I don't know how many parts so that the litigation would keep growing until it made up a thick jungle of parchments—suits and countersuits to such a degree that there wasn't an attorney who could find a path or a judge who knew what to say, either here or in the Council of the Indies itself. They did it in such a way that there wasn't any room, even in this house, for all the papers churned up by those lawsuits, and my resolve grew weak. Then, regretful and with his tail between his legs, my son Nicolás came to claim his right of primogeniture in our newly founded high court. Are you laughing, Juan del Rosario? I can hear your laughter mocking me, can hear you thinking that I'm powerless, with all the owners the land has now, but you won't be unscathed by my sons' stupid decision, either, I want you to know that your blacks have also gone to court, and they no longer recognize your son-in-law as Captain-Populator.

They appealed my document of 1752. Fine; but I made one thing clear to Ricardos, and it's that I was not going to pay for the improvements except to the old men, the first ones who arrived with you, whose names I know quite well. Though the light I have left is nothing but a white blur that holds on for moments while with my fingertips I recognize the names of the original settlers, and though I'm sure their eyes are just as blurry as mine and their hands just as gnarled, those are the only ones I'm going to pay, I told Ricardos. Where did a bunch of blacks who invaded the plantation get the nerve to come and ask me to reimburse them for improvements? And do you know, Juan del Rosario, what it occurred to them to ask for as well? Permission to turn the lean-to of cane and mud that served as village church into a building with adobe walls. And that dunce Machado y Luna, in order to ingratiate himself, thought it was fine to give them his episcopal permission because the blacks promised that if there weren't funds to build it, they would take up a collection themselves. Since they enjoyed the services of a chaplain, they evidently wanted to boast a cathedral. That was that boob Machado y Luna's affair, but you know quite well, Juan del Rosario, that it was a ruse on the part of the blacks, a trick left over from what you'd taught them, and what they wanted was to build up the church so they could establish their settlement more solidly. You, who know me, wouldn't think that I let them do so without opposition. Hadn't I left Remírez de Estenoz speechless with that business of the Guipuzcoana? You would have enjoyed that, Alejandro! They built a house opposite ours so that when I opened my windows the structure loomed up and blocked the view of the mountain as well as cutting off the breeze. I went there myself to tell them that it should have only one story, like all the others, and they answered that if it bothered me they wouldn't build a second floor. They thought a few days would be enough time for me to forget. When I heard the noise of the masons again and complained once more, the workers answered that they didn't know anything about it: they had orders to put up another floor, and that's what they were doing. Do you know what I thought to do? Well, I sent word to the administrator of the Chacao plantation to come to the city and to bring no fewer than thirty slaves with bags of stones, and the gang of them went out and hurled the stones and any rubble and fallen bricks they found. The masons defended themselves with their mallets, throwing rulers and plumbs and buckets of mortar until the scaffolding was knocked down and both sides turned to hand-to-hand combat. When there wasn't a man left standing, I went over to collect my slaves, some of whom were hurt, and I had them carried into the house to have their wounds taken care of; others, unfortunately, were dead. After the uproar, Remírez put in an appearance to ask what had happened. A joke, governor, I answered him, a silly quarrel that broke out because my slaves threw some stones at the masons and they thought it was a fight and answered back with their mallets. A joke I wanted to play on the Guipuzcoana for having gone back on its word, and you can see now that the joke rebounded on me, I'm the injured one because I've even lost my best foreman. Since the Basques didn't force that second floor on me, I can assure you, Juan del Rosario, that a lot of rain is going to fall before your blacks will see their church with adobe walls. Despite my influence as a woman of importance, my attorneys met resistance from the Church, and that was why they couldn't block Machado y Luna's permission or stop the diocese of Caracas from giving the trespassers three images, the Virgin of Altagracia, Saint Joseph, and the Christ Child, as replacements for the paintings lost in 1721 when, at my request, Captain-General Diego de Portales y Meneses ordered the hut with a cross torn down and the village destroyed. Still, churchly permission notwithstanding, your blacks remained in the same state as before, because Machado y Luna was more a man of words than of action; for many years all they could do was plead that they wanted an adobe church and one set farther back from the river because with every flood the water inundated their chapel and months would pass, even a whole winter, before it was possible to celebrate mass in it. I asked Alejandro many times to take me to see the village you founded, the shack you consecrated for a church, the shade trees you planted; you know I never left my house, never left these four streets where people of my station live, the ones I visited and who visited me. I would have liked to see with my own eyes the lands we were disputing, but Alejandro never wanted to let me, the trip wasn't advisable for a woman always giving birth or about to, so from child to child the opportunity passed.

Bishop Mariano Martí, on his pastoral visit to the valleys of Barlovento in 1784, ordered the walls erected. When he visited Curiepe he found a settlement of some fifty houses right along the riverbank and a church with a single nave made of cane and with mud walls and roofed with palm leaves, without a baptistry to hold the holy water, which was kept in a basin in a chest in the sacristy, and containing a niche with two poorly dressed figures that he ordered repaired and cleaned because in that state they wouldn't inspire any devotion, the floor unpaved except for where the priest stood, the door in very bad shape, and for an altar a brick platform sheathed with wood on which two Brittany altar-cloths with lace borders survived along with a mantle of worn embroidered silk on which rested the yard-tall tabernacle, which was made of partly carved wood, painted and silverplated and decked with a fraying veil. The bishop concluded that the church's deterioration and dirtiness made it unfit for His Divine Majesty; he then looked for a foundation that could be hauled to where your blacks had intended to build during the time of Machado y Luna, and he arranged for work on the church to be begun right there, ordering also that a cemetery be set up, since there wasn't one. He was concerned when he found out that the plantation owners refused to pay the stipends and perquisites for bread, wine, and wax, some citing the burden of the maintenance of their slaves and others demurring because they worked with free people to whom they owed wages; and in that way nobody would pledge himself for parish duties. Bishop Martí tried to correct that vice and the many others he found, because it hadn't escaped his ecclesiastical eyes that the blacks who attended mass were few and that except for an occasional old woman, they didn't fulfill their obligations or show any devotion, virtue, or regularity regarding the sacraments, something I knew quite well without any need to get onto a donkey like poor Don Mariano, to spend days on the road bouncing through mudholes and nights in huts without a floor; but he—like Saint Thomas, and you had to grant him that—tirelessly covered the whole province for several years, checking up and writing things down. The moral irregularities he found sapped his spirit when he came to see that his lieutenants could be of no use in taming and bringing into Christian life the black women, both slave and free—especially the latter, who were now going about on their own—and he was able to see, therefore, that all the people were indulging a passion for dancing at baptisms and wakes and were ready to take advantage of the eve of any feast day to do so, even though they would wake up afterward sleepy and weary and, as might be expected, little inclined to fulfill their religious duties. He was disappointed, in short, by the failure of talks and admonitions by the parish priests to prevent that dancing and to get people to come to mass—weekly for those who lived near the church, every two weeks for those two to four leagues away, and at least once every month or two for those who had to cross swollen rivers because they lived more than ten leagues away—and he ordered that if necessary for the good of these people's souls, the priests should not hesitate to impose punishment on transgressors by having them jailed. But he was very downcast when he became aware that his lieutenants frequently sought solace with the colored women and that parish priests themselves were not celebrating mass because they were preoccupied with their own affairs, spending parish money on their crops, and he even came to learn that more than one of them had been living in sin. By 1791 the work hadn't been finished despite the bishop's request that the four thousand pesos for construction be apportioned among the plantation owners, who were rightly opposed to squandering their money on that silly building; and all that had been built were the walls, with no doors, and part of the roof. Finally, in 1806, the Blessed Sacrament was enthroned and its confraternity founded, but God willed for that church always to be a target for disaster, and in the earthquake of 1812 seven yards of eaves fell off, tiles were dislodged, its two ceiling fans fell, and the sacristy lost its roof; escaping damage were Our Lady of Altagracia, Our Lord Saint Joseph, and the Christ Child, called the Christ Child of Curiepe, as well as the tabernacle and the lectern, which were also left intact.

And the fact is that earthquakes don't spare Spaniards or Canary Islanders, mulattoes or blacks. It was good, Solano, you who like accounts to be clear, that you made a list of the churches shaken by the tremors of 1766, because when a stone falls here it stays fallen until the end of time, but by recording it in writing we'll at least be able to remember: the cathedral, San Jacinto, La Merced, San Francisco, the Conceptionist Sisters, the Carmelites, San Pablo, Altagracia, Candelaria, Santa Rosalía, and San Lázaro. Solano had to interrupt his swanky social gatherings in order to walk through the cemetery with Bishop Díez Madroñero and the notables, had to distribute food on the streets, arrange for priests to be able to enter houses without asking and give extreme unction to those who'd already died, and to have slaves dig trenches by Santa Rosalía where the corpses could be piled—so many that they didn't take a count or even try to put names on the graves, since all of Caracas was one big tomb, an uninhabited city from which all who could had fled. People slept in the street so they wouldn't be crushed by bricks falling from the churches when the earth rumbled; frightened souls were screaming in front of this very house, and you could hear the servants' shrieks as they took refuge in the court and the backyard.

Wake up, Alejandro; wake up from the siesta, because it's all over. I'm alone in this house, and the afternoon has become oppressive, threatening rain. I have one unfulfilled desire; I wish you had taken me to Spain sometime to listen to sacred music in a great cathedral . . . but you never wanted to, and I've never been farther away than the Chacao plantation. These fallen stones belong to me, and the four rivers that traverse the city, and this narrow valley belongs to me, and the mist that clings to Avila Mountain belongs to me, and those ragged blacks belong to me. Do you hear me too, Juan del Rosario, my freedman? They are mine, and belonging to me are the cacao groves of Curiepe, they belong to me forever; belonging to me are Sabana de Oro and Higuerote Cove, they belong to me because that's what the titles say. Help me look for them, you stubborn little black bastard, because you're a living part of this search too. I have the right granted me by the past and you the one granted by the future; you'll soon see that time will erase both of us completely, but I'll keep searching because it's my will that we should remain in people's memory.

All the names that have been flitting by, all the letters of the alphabet in these papers, all the authorities we've been appealing to, Juan del Rosario, all the faraway kings whose funerals and coronations we've commemorated, deaths and births, rites and eulogies, and who, on the other side of the ocean, never heard us! Today the authorities are filing out for a grand parade to mark the proclamation of Charles III as king. What keeps you so busy, Alejandro, that you don't get up and join the column? All the notables are out on the street. What are you doing that you don't put on your tricorn hat of a magistrate and councilman of the Illustrious Court of Caracas? There go Governor and Captain General Remírez de Estenoz, his excellency Bishop Díez Madroñero, magistrates and councilmen, the quartermaster general of the army, members of the exchequer's court, the king's deputy, military units, employees of the finance ministry, scribes, and anyone from A to Z who is considered worthy of marching. Alejandro, aren't you going to make an offering the way you did when Ferdinand VI took the throne—providing a banquet on the main square, with a rich display of hams, cheeses, and cassavas so the crowd can eat its fill? Even a statue that poured wine out of its breasts, to the consternation of churchmen who saw in it the work of the devil to get the people drunk. Alejandro, get up and listen to the music that's filling the streets, see the boys passing doing the sword dance, followed by bugles, guitars, violins, and shawms. When has anyone ever seen such pomp! There are all kinds of celebrations—processions, bullfights, jousts, races of cats wearing ribbons, dancing; stages have been set up on every square to put on plays and skits, and masked revelers are going all through the city scattering confetti and streamers. The mulattoes' association is staging a religious play on a platform with a silk curtain; that of the blacks is performing panegyric sketches for His Majesty; that of the shopkeepers is parading on caparisoned horses; and you can hear the whooping and clapping until early morning, the laughter and the calls, and the whole city is bright with torches and illuminations. They say the celebrations were set for three days but that there was such frolic and merrymaking that nobody paid any attention to the calendar and they lasted more than five. Five days at least of revelry in this poor forgotten province that didn't have the wealth of Peru or the grandeur of New Spain, five days at least in this obscure village on these four paved blocks in the middle of woods and snakes.

What are you doing, Alejandro, are you still sleeping your siesta? I've got to tell you about the trip two blacks from Curiepe made to Madrid to the court of Charles III. You don't believe it? I wasn't imagining things; it was hard to believe, but I can assure you that Charles III, King of Spain and the West Indies, in the year 1763 received in audience Joseph Colmenares and Juan Pedro Barrios or Barreto, inhabitants of Nuestra Señora de Altagracia y San Joseph de la Nueva Sevilla de Curiepe, subjects from the province of Venezuela on the coast of Terra Firma.

The waves rose up over the ship, higher than the bridge, and fell with a roar onto the wooden planking that creaked and threatened to break loose. The sailors furled the sails and the masts swayed in the wind, the shouted instructions of the officers could hardly be heard; the rudder didn't respond to tugs, and the crew was begging God to keep the frigate afloat until the storm died down. The few passengers, tied to the masts with strong ropes, were trying to resist the reeling that at any moment could fling them overboard. Soaked by rain and sea, they helped the cabin boys bail the water that was flooding the deck. The ship could break up in an instant and take on water, with no hope of anyone's reaching land in the lifeboats. The dark sky prevented them from seeing that they were only a short distance from St. Thomas; and only at dawn, when the wind had died down and the clouds evaporated, did a sailor spot the island. The captain ordered them to head in for refuge and to set about repairing the storm damage before they could resume sail for Cadiz. The frigate spent ten days at St. Thomas, and passengers and crew couldn't believe it when under a calming sun they sank their feet into the warm sand and refreshed their dried lips with the coconut milk from trees that bordered the beach. The mishap was costing them ten days, but that wasn't so bad, since the crossing usually took two months in any case. Time was needed to make the broken masts and torn sails seaworthy again. When the captain, though fearful that the winds might not be favorable, ordered their departure, the sailors celebrated the fact that their lives had been spared, and the night before they left filled up with all the rum their bodies could hold until they fell down dead drunk. They weighed anchor at dawn on a peaceful blue sea that was so clear the coral could be seen. The chaplain, gathering everyone on deck, conducted a thanksgiving mass, and an amateur actor who was among the few passengers recited poetry and enlivened everyone by singing songs where the men joined in the chorus. The weak wind only let them go a short way before it finally abated, and night fell over a dead calm that left them gently floating. The crew, still hung over, fell into a deep sleep, and the ten or twelve passengers, including the chaplain and the surgeon, lay down in a heap on deck, fleeing the stuffy air of the hold. A fortunate few managed to string hammocks from the battens and cover themselves with blankets; others had rescued a still-damp mattress, and three of them were dozing on it. No one heard the faint sound of a lighter slowly approaching. Without giving them any time to realize what was happening, the pirates tossed up their boarding ropes and burst onto the deck. In minutes they took over the cargo and divested the passengers of their belongings. The latter were so surprised that they couldn't tell whether they were having a nightmare. A cabin boy who tried to hold onto a silver coin he had secreted in a kerchief fell bleeding in the midst of the brutal shouts of the corsairs, who ordered their victims into the hold before they left.

Joseph Antonio Colmenares, captain of the village of Curiepe, and Juan Barreto, the oldest inhabitant, looked at each other without saying a word. Just when they thought they had been saved from the storm that left them numb with fear, they found themselves with empty pockets, robbed of the little money the village had collected to send them to Spain to speak to the king. They hadn't foreseen that any more misfortunes could befall them. They listened in silence to the heated words the captain and the boatswain were exchanging with the crew. The captain, weary of adversities, wanted to return to La Guaira, since a voyage with no cargo meant no profit. The boatswain backed him; the Guipuzcoana was paying them not for crossing the ocean but for the goods they had been carrying. The sailors, on the other hand, didn't want to go back. They'd been away from home for several months already, and their pay would be the same, cargo or not. The pilot sided with the crew and refused to turn back. Captain and boatswain had no choice but to yield, and, cursing their bad luck, they pointed the prow toward the Canary Islands. The two blacks didn't know what to feel, didn't know whether they should be glad to be continuing or sorry they hadn't gone back to La Guaira. They'd sailed to ask for an audience with the king, and they brought with them as their only means of access a letter recommending them to Joaquín Guadalupe—a black from Caracas, the servant of a prominent duke in Madrid—and some money that the villagers had managed to scrape together. Stripped by the raid of the English pirates, they had nothing left but a gold coin that Joseph Antonio took out of his rectum as he winked at the old man.

They arrived at the port of Cadiz one morning in December with no further calamities, after much searching managed to join up with a carter who was driving a team of mules to Madrid, and crossing mountains and plains they discovered something they had given little thought to: cold, the icy cold that came over them and that they could only succeed in warding off with a blanket—which, along with the hammock, was their only baggage. With the letter of introduction for Guadalupe and a piece of paper with the address of the duke's palace, they confronted the embarrassment of eyes that were startled by their skin color, ears that listened mockingly to their accent and scant vocabulary, confronted the fear of finding themselves among such tall buildings and so many people in a city of carriages, promenades, streets, and corners that they kept getting confused. Joseph Antonio Colmenares was afraid that the old man, worn out, shivering from the cold, with nothing in his stomach and blighted with fear, wouldn't live to reach the duke's house, where they hoped Guadalupe would offer them something to eat and a patch of floor on which to sleep.

But they got there, Alejandro, they got there and the duke took pity on their misery and referred them to an attorney who agreed to take care of them and obtain for them a few minutes' audience, which I imagine they attended with more fright than they'd felt in the middle of the storm. Didn't you have anything better to do, Charles III, than to give an audience to those blacks from Curiepe? Did you powder your wig so you could sit and hear their plea? Did you weep with compassion when they told you about their lawsuits with Doña Inés Villegas y Solórzano? Did they explain to you that they'd been faithful vassals, had defended the Barlovento coast from pirates and put an end to smuggling? Were you greatly concerned about smuggling, Charles III? Didn't you know that it was your governors and your quarter-masters who were behind it? Oh, no! You didn't know anything except that these people believed in God and the Church of Rome, had built a chapel, baptized their children, and celebrated the feast days of their saints. Didn't they bring a drum so that you could get excited too and dance along with them the way they do at wakes? No, you were there with sober mien on a boring afternoon when they placed before your royal person their many tribulations, the ravages they were victims of, the hard work they'd put in, and the improvements they'd made, or lamented how their letters hadn't reached you or mine had reached you first, so they, loyal subjects, had come in person to ask, beg, implore Your Majesty to listen to their entreaties, hear their pleas, read their briefs and documents, from the first one, the supplicatory brief that Juan del Rosario wrote to your august father, Philip V, in 1715, soliciting permission to settle the site of Sabana de Oro along Higuerote Cove, lands unfamiliar to you but that they'd been inhabiting and working from 1715 until then, 1763, day after day, despite the complaints initiated by Doña Inés and her husband,

Don Alejandro, and their multiple descendants (because they'd divided up the inheritance to cause even more turmoil) lands that they refused to cultivate but wanted to maintain fallow and in their possession, alleging titles put together in 1663. Were you weary of study, or was it a bad afternoon for hunting, Charles III, that you stayed there listening to that string of lies? Where did they get the idea that we didn't want to cultivate? They took advantage of the fact that you knew nothing about cacao except that you liked chocolate, and you didn't understand that not all the land is cultivated and that cacao grows in the shade. Five thousand sacks a year is what my trees produce, if you think that constitutes fallow land; and I don't *allege* the titles, I *have* them, and they confirm my ownership. But there you were, listening to that gibberish, listening to the blacks saying that several royal decrees had given them the rights, but others had taken them away and that they no longer knew whom to turn to or what to do to save their fields, because they found them confiscated, and Doña Inés, refusing to pay their claims, and had ignored the document of guaranty she was made to sign; she insisted that she would only pay the first settlers, and since so much time had passed, the original ones were almost all dead, among them Juan del Rosario, who was First Captain-Populator and Captain of the Free Colored Militia of Caracas.

You would have had to come in person, Charles III, rowing or swimming, for me to pay the blacks of Curiepe for improvements. You would have had to come with the document of guaranty in your hand and knock on the door of my house on the corner of San Jacinto for me to sit down and chat with you about that old matter and explain to you who the blacks of Curiepe are. But there they are, wailing about all the misfortunes that have befallen them, before His Majesty, beseeching his patience to hear them and reading all the many documents that testify to their right, and pleading for him to decide this lawsuit in his royal person, since they said it gave them no rest and was limiting their opportunity and sapping their effort to serve the Crown better. Am I to believe that you read all the briefs the blacks and I had sent back and forth over all these years? Including the ones I've kept here and the ones resting in the Council of the Indies, there must be enough to paper all the walls of Oriente Palace. You signed a decree for them so you could wriggle out of the mess, and you didn't measure the consequences. Didn't you see the mark of the pillory on Joseph Colmenares, a runaway who'd escaped from some plantation? Did he tell you how we colonial whites were cruel and mistreated them? Well, you should have taken off your wig and come to your senses.

I can see them arriving, Alejandro, I know very well who they are: Barreto came to Curiepe with Juan del Rosario, I can see him opening his toothless mouth and laughing like a child, so old and arthritic that he almost makes me feel pity; and the other one, Joseph Colmenares, was born right there. I can see them now, bundled on deck with the piece of blanket they've got left, hiding the king's decree under their armpits, freezing to death as the chaplain says prayers for a dead sailor who's been tied to a cannonball for ballast and will be dropped into the sea, and despite everything they're laughing, they're returning in triumph because the king—just imagine!—has received them. They're eating soggy biscuits and dry seeds they crack with their teeth and that make them all the thirstier, surrounded by all that water and the smell of stinking barrels. The dead sailor is the second one they've dumped into the sea, one from dysentery and the other from a gangrenous leg, but there they go, laughing and betting, because the officers have decided to organize a cockfight to combat the boredom of a long and windless night.

Can you imagine, Juan del Rosario, Solano's face when Joseph Colmenares and Juan Barreto appeared to tell him that they were back from Spain with a royal decree in their favor? Scribe, fetch me a lamp, because there's hardly any light here for me to make out what I'm reading, yes, 1763, Charles III says:

> And you are not to impede the aforesaid blacks from removing from the village in question the possessions they may have nor from dismantling their huts and taking their things to the location that has been assigned them for their new settlement.

So I shouldn't interfere with them and they shouldn't interfere with me? I can only tell you one thing, Charles III, and it's that this is not the end of the matter, because we aristocrats have had it with the Crown up to the crown of our heads.

If You Don't Want Me

(1789–1810)

And you, Charles IV, they kept telling you, but everything went in one ear and out the other. Didn't the news from Caracas reach you? Hadn't you been told by your captain general, Carbonell Pinto Vigo y Correa, who even with such a long name never tired of signing it to letters that informed you about conspiracies and intrigues on the part of your superintendents and counselors, who'd split into factions, with some of them writing to you and others sending letters to Godoy? Hadn't a certain Marquis de Campo Alange had the insolence to tell you, invoking your Catholic name, that you shouldn't vex your sovereign attention with such irrelevant matters? So keep your silent sovereign attention for other affairs, because you don't know the half of what's going on here, and you only think about our existence when María Luisa gets a taste for some chocolate. Well, while you were having a snack with snooty duchesses and bragging about offering the princes of Europe the best cocoa in the world, something besides chocolate was boiling under this hot sun. Events that are of great interest to the French have taken place, and refugee blacks from Haiti have even told ours that they're guillotining queens in Paris and talking *liberty, equality, and fraternity* now. Gossips have been saying that you've caught the wind from France, too, and that's why you're finishing the century with that little proclamation of yours that everyone calls *Thanks for the Getting.* We protested, but your sovereign attention was elsewhere; we protested again, but it was too late. Who's going to appeal to an abdicated king? According to that decree, in order to be white all you have to do is pay for the privilege; tell me, if it's so easy to change color, why don't you do yourself a favor and turn black? You did a fine job, just what we aristocrats needed to make us fly into a fury—three centuries of keeping the blacks at bay, and you pitch everything overboard with a stroke of the pen; three centuries of watching over our daughters and their virtue and pretending not to notice our husbands, who must have derived some kind of pleasure from sleeping with black women . . . all that just so rights can now be bought like going to a store. Take Juan del Rosario—I don't have many doubts left about his origins, and may God in his glory have forgiven Alejandro—he bears my surname because it's the custom to give it to slaves, but he's never gone beyond being a free black, and that because he was freed by me, because I was sick and tired of feeding so many mouths and having him standing there, a lazy houseboy who couldn't even run errands properly and whose main job was to play hide-and-seek with my sons—Alejandro's godson, yes, but besides that connection, more binding in the eyes of heaven than of earth, he had no other. In 1789 you fired up the blacks' imagination by handing down the royal rescript called the Caroline Black Code; I don't know whether you or your father wrote it, but even before it they went around claiming that the King of Spain had emancipated them and that we colonial whites had stashed the document away. Didn't you get the news that a black man called Cocofío, a marketplace charlatan, was going through the countryside spreading the rumor that the Black Code existed and that we were feigning ignorance? If they'd known how to read, they would have found out about the nonsense you'd invented to make them think that you were the one leading the French Revolution; you said we should instruct them in religion, well, that's been done, as far as is appropriate for them; that we should feed and clothe them, and don't you think we've already done that? That they should work only from sunup to sundown, and no longer. Do you think cacao is picked at night? And, to top off your lordly generosity, you instructed that punishment by imprisonment, shackles, or whip should be regulated and no more than twenty-five lashes given, and that those be administered with an instrument that causes no serious contusions or flow of blood. Don't you know that it's quite expensive to maintain a slave if the blows miss their mark? No, you probably don't. You probably imagine that the slaves come to us at the snap of a finger, the way your lackeys do. Well, you should be aware that here, too, no matter how miraculous this America may be, women take nine months to give birth and fifteen years at least must pass before you're old enough to bring in a crop . . . not to mention the ones who die when they're still small or who hurt a hand with a machete or are bitten by a snake. Here, just so you know, the only ones punished are the ones caught in outlaw bands or fomenting trouble, or when the overseer gets worked up because he's tired of looking for them when they're fishing in the river or getting drunk with the women. Or do you think that the missionary priests have been able to convince them that sex is a sin? Here almost nothing is a sin, Charles IV. Didn't you know that the authorities have confessed that despite their active efforts to eliminate infidels and chastise them for the damages and enormous excesses they've committed, it hasn't been possible because the thickets where these evil people live are impenetrable and they're the only ones who can get through because they were brought up in those same woods and still live scattered all through them? These do get punished without pity—a hundred lashes, hard labor, confinement on the plantation except to fulfill religious duties (which is what must gall them the most), and having the upper part of the left ear cut off so that a person missing that piece can't fool anyone and be hired as a field hand on some other plantation. More than once the landowners of Curiepe have asked the Royal High Court for energetic action against the runaways, because ours are the most rebellious, and poor Carbonell kept asking for help and was turned down every time. It was no use speaking of the dangers on Saint John's Eve, when rebel blacks would come into settlements with an eye to having a good time and dancing but afterward would draw their machetes and leave a bloodbath behind them. He tried to tell you, the desert prophet Carbonell did, that in addition to the blacks' insurrection, Gual y España's conspiracy was taking shape in La Guaira; and he wrote a long letter informing you of the arbitrary acts of your servants and the uneasiness of the colonial establishment, predicting the events that would take place later—and when he despaired of your listening to him, he only asked for you to recall him to Spain because he was old and poor. There's no deaf man worse than the one who refuses to hear. You left him to die here, and you waited for news when it was too late. The fact is, we inhabitants of Caracas are restive, are troublemakers by nature. You tell him that, Vicente Emparan.

What a pity, Alejandro, that you didn't hear or see him out on the balcony of government house with the look of someone who is resigning when in fact he was *being* resigned, as he left floating in the air forever that high-sounding phrase: *If you don't want me, then I don't want to govern either.* Oh, Vicente Emparan! So many governors, and you'll be the last, the only one schoolchildren will remember. You did Spain no favor by bouncing the ball back and forth, with Ferdinand today, with Bonaparte tomorrow, and in that back-and-forth we took you at your word on that final Maundy Thursday of 1810. You ran out of government house to confession, and rightly so, because you'd lost the empire. How could you expect that dull murmur to reach you, Alejandro, that underground river that was spreading out, slipping along, filling hitherto silent throats with hate! When we thought we'd die of boredom and impotence in this forgotten captaincy, poorly served and worse governed, a brig arrived in La Guaira sent by Victor Hugues, Imperial Commissioner of France, informing us that our king was Joseph Bonaparte. You should have seen the confusion among the Spaniards, inclined to accept the French and trying to suppress the dissenters, but to complicate things all the more, the *Serpent* and an English frigate, the *Acasta,* dropped anchor in La Guaira with the mission of informing us that the Spanish people had risen up against the usurper and established a legitimate junta in Seville. You would have taken part in that farrago of secret meetings with the most distinguished colonials of the time, would have witnessed the bafflement of Emparan—harried by the insurgencies, the conspiracies, the proposals, as he tried to win the colored people over; convincing them that the ideas of the aristocrats were not for them; uncertain about falling into a trap, not daring to back Ferdinand when the Supreme Junta for the Preservation of his Rights was declared and then backing him when the junta declared itself in revolt; jailing people haphazardly; waiting in vain for a Napoleonic army to arrive and straighten things out in Spanish America. I know you would have wanted to take your saber with the silver hilt and leap on your horse to follow Colonel Bolívar, our cousin, and you would have trembled at the roar of the cannons from La Vela de Coro to Güiria, from Apure to the port of La Guaira, as the shout arose that woke up the whole captaincy. We inhabitants of Caracas have been denounced as rebels by the junta of Seville, and we are at war with Spain. What are you doing, sleeping like a dolt? You're a doltish dead man, Alejandro. Have you got lost, perhaps, and can't find the way back? Or are you rolling around with the black women there? At this decisive moment I won't be so nasty as to throw your sins back on you. Are you snoring drowsily while your grandsons take leave of their wives and children and go off to become heroes? I'm sure that if you'd put in an appearance when you should have, your signature—as a prominent figure—would have been scrawled on the Article of Independence. Do you know what's been going on, or haven't you realized it, in spite of my shouting? Well, it so happens that we uncaged this monster one day, and from then on nothing has been the same: the earth was round, the sea didn't pour off the end of the world, the sun never set, there was a multiplication of colors, the imaginations of chroniclers were inflamed by grandly feathered birds, endless rivers, hidden treasures, infinite beaches; astronomers, botanists, and zoologists threw away their books because they were incomplete, theologians sat down again to discuss the sex of angels, financial advisers to the courts of Europe had to add their figures all over again, all because on the other side of the ocean a dream of invention had opened up that kept kings and princes awake, tortured the doctrinaire, troubled popes, exacerbated the sensuality of poets, shifted the center of the world, and offered the disinherited a new body for seduction and greed; and none of this amounts to anything, Alejandro, as in this village of Santiago de León de Caracas now, in these dusty streets squeezed into a narrow valley, right here, around the corner, almost across from our house, the denizens are shouting to Emparan to leave. Do you know what's happened, Alejandro? Well, the empire has crumbled. It was already rotten, you say? Probably so. Napoleon gave us a hand? I don't deny it. Like every other dream it will end up corrupted, they'll make fun of us and we'll try to cover the shame of our nakedness with our hands, but we've brought the phantom of freedom to light, and it will travel all over the world, and the seats that Europe is sitting in will start to creak again.

A CHRONICLE OF WAR

(1810–1814)

It smells of gunpowder and the scorched flesh of Spaniards and Canary Islanders, of white colonials and riffraff, of blacks and halfbreeds, of mulattoes and quadroons, of octoroons, black Indians, redheaded blacks, and throwbacks. Nobody will be left untouched here. Didn't they want equality? Well, now they have their chance, with this slaughter nothing will ever be known about any of them, I don't just mean the one who gave them birth but the one who gave them death. The decks have been cleared, and everyone who goes around with a grudge or is chasing some hope will fight to the death, and in this tumult where only we aristocrats know where we're headed, and we're prepared to perish, as we shall in fact perish, not a stone will be left standing, whole families will go under, and the hooves of horses will ride roughshod over everything, laying waste wherever they tread. Juan del Rosario, go to the window and see the men on their way to enlist in the patriot armies, see the women selling their last belongings in order to equip them; stop running up and down the courtyard and come here, you insolent houseboy, a day didn't pass when, if I sent you to buy a quarter-pound of sugarloaf or a yard of cloth, you didn't filch a few pennies on me. Look outside so you can see the great fight that took place here; stop hiding in the shade of the trees and come here, my houseboy and freedman, come over here,

Captain of the Black Militia, because I have a story to tell you, everything you don't know and haven't been able to see about your blacks from Barlovento. Sit down beside Alejandro, wasn't he your father? Don't try to hide it, Alejandro, because in this final hour we're not up to any lies. Isn't it true, Alejandro, that when he was just a child you took him to Curiepe Valley and gave him a mare so he could learn to ride the length of it? And isn't it true that you were proud of his courage and dash when he was a boy, and you taught him to use pistols? The four male children that I gave birth to weren't enough for you, you wanted to scatter your seed and feel like another God, creator of the universe, progenitor of races—well, you'd probably like to know now what happened to the land you promised him and what's left of yours, what remains of the forty-three slaves and eighty-seven free peasants who picked your cacao. I'll tell you: nothing's left of them. In 1792 the Royal High Court of Caracas handed down a ruling confirming our rights in the agreements, but it was a royal decision, and there are no kings anymore because we deposed them. And you probably want to know, Juan del Rosario, what became of the blacks you worked so hard to settle—well, I can tell you too: nothing's left of them. Your documents and briefs have gone with the wind, the ink you used has faded away, and—so you can be ashamed once and for all—your people have all revolted and are roving about cheering Ferdinand VII. Can you believe it? They've turned their backs on you and become royalists. That's how it is, because in this fuss somebody's told them that their hopes for equality will be better served if they remain loyal to the Crown, and they've risen up in defense of the supreme rights of King Ferdinand.

Weren't you the presumptuous one (as your name so clearly shows), Narciso Coll y Prat, you who went about explaining to the blacks of Barlovento that we colonial whites were a Frenchified bunch, followers of atheistic and Masonic enlightened despotism, and that they should defend the king because that's what God wanted. Stop fooling around, Don Narciso! Your explanation has worked out fine for you. You promised them the protection of the Crown, the Virgin, and the saints, and what happened? I could have told you if you'd asked me, but, oh no, you know everything—so it turned out that they got out of hand, and you've had to preach them another sermon, scurrying up and down the valleys and disbanding slave groups since all they want is to kill whites in any way they can and they don't understand much about enlightenment, and you beg them in every conceivable way to join the Spanish troops and not make war on their own. When they heard the shooting they armed themselves as best they could, with machetes, stones, and hoes, and they've formed an army without a name that wreaks havoc wherever it goes—steals, plunders, rapes, and kills. They've made your flesh crawl and your hair stand on end, isn't that so? A recollection of the recent butchery in Haiti came to your mind, and you were afraid that if the blacks caught you in an unguarded moment they'd tie you to a hitching post in the square, without a biretta, without any archbishop's ring, and they would whip you until you lost consciousness, with no God to help you or King of Spain to come and hold back the machete that would slice open your neck. You did well; these are not people to take lightly. You managed to bring a few of them under control, but you had more than four thousand royalists left, and when those four thousand started marching toward Caracas, royalists' and patriots' hands trembled. What did you write then, Don Narciso, in that Bulletin on Independence?

those slaves, although they have risen up in favor of Your Majesty, now claim to be free by virtue of martial law itself, which is nonsense . . .

Nonsense, is it? But the damage has already been done; you've persuaded the royalist plantation owners—and there are plenty of them—to go about their property handing out gifts to get the blacks to rise up on their side, and you've convinced them that it doesn't matter that Bolívar has issued an edict ordering them to suppress the slaves and the slaves to submit to their masters. The chaos has cut off supplies to General Francisco de Miranda, and with no other way out, and attacked by Domingo Monteverde, he surrendered. Plantation owners, royalist and patriot alike, have been abandoning their lands, and a week doesn't go by without killings. One poor fool even gave the blacks a pair of mules and a brace of bronze and silver pistols and was left wailing and lamenting that they'd sacked his plantation and killed his wife. Administrators and overseers in the areas all around have taken flight or been massacred on the spot on a night when royalist blacks surprised them.

News has reached Caracas, Alejandro, from Julián Cayetano, our grandson Francisco's administrator, that everybody has run away and the only ones still on the plantation are old people and cripples, women and small children, and that he himself is terrified of being murdered at any time by some band of outlaws. He reports that he sleeps with his machete in one hand and a pistol in the other, with one eye half-open and with his ears on the alert for the slightest sound, and that wavering between escaping or staying, he decided to stay because he couldn't think of anyplace to go. Wherever he looked he found the ravages left by the flaming torches of runaway slaves from the woods, hungry and shabby, who would fall on settlements, destroying everything with blood and fire, and after them General Arismendi's soldiers, killing without pity every recalcitrant black they found, chasing them relentlessly into the jungle until they caught one, whose head they would cut off and parade around on a stake as a warning to vagrant peasants, slaves, freedmen, and any other miserable soul who was led by royalist voices to oppose the patriot armies. That, Juan del Rosario, is what the land we've been in litigation over has turned into. Do you think the royal decrees we were waiting for over the years are worth anything now? That land doesn't belong to anyone, it's all devastated, and a dark night has fallen over the bones of those who fell amid the groves, with no graves, no crosses.

Where were you, Don Narciso, on Saint John's Eve, 1812, when the blacks rose up in the name of Ferdinand VII? You'd taken refuge in Caracas, isn't that so? You didn't want to see the bloodbath you'd left behind. And where were you on Maundy Thursday of that same year? What did you do after the cathedral tower collapsed and the clock stopped at the moment of the tremor? Did you mimic your predecessor, Don Mauro de Tovar, who shook his slippers and said: *I don't even want the dust of Caracas*? Where were you that night, you great theologian, when you invented that humbug about the earthquake being God's punishment for challenging the king? Where were you so that no piece of rubble fell on you while you harangued the terror-stricken people of Caracas to convince them that in addition to being degutted by nature they should have to bear witness to the divine wrath? Welcome to history, Narciso Coll y Prat: books will name you as one of the causes of the loss of the first republic.

That day, Alejandro, we were mortified; the ground was trembling, all over the republic the houses and church steeples were falling; the city reeked of open sores, singed flesh, the stench of corpses, was infested with the filthy odor of the lepers who'd come out of their hospice, of poxed and plague-ridden people scrambling to shelter in houses that were barred to them; the city was teeming with bandits and desperate people knocking at the doors of the rich, coming in by tens and twenties; and the noise, Alejandro, that dull rumble, like dammed-up water pouring out; the ground was breaking apart, and its moan was joined by the bells tolling for the dead and the cries of the people following the priests who took to the streets to implore God for mercy and the confraternity members, who went along in processions with their crosses held high, making fearful shouts: "God is punishing us, God is condemning us for having challenged the king."

And I was here, Alejandro, locked up in my corpse, my eyes astonished and ears bewildered, looking on helplessly as Isabel, my grandson Francisco's widow, was shaking all over, and shaking inside her was Francisco's posthumous fruit; speaking to her without her being able to hear my voice, seeing her defenseless, surrounded by children and a few weeping servants, I tore my throat raw as if my words could reach her: *Close the windows, Isabel, have them cover the well so those pestilential fumes won't get in here, and don't let those crazy people get close to the windows, throw them some bread, throw it far so they won't stick their swollen lips up against the gratings.* The city's rotten, overflowing with rot, the shaken land is draining its sinkholes, the streams are flooded and bridges and drains broken, snakes are all around and coming down from the mountain. A slave tells her: "Ma'am, I killed a snake in the courtyard. That's a bad sign, ma'am, a snake in the house of a pregnant woman, people who know things like that say that if it bites there's nothing you can do." Don't pay any attention, Isabel— what do they know about it, there aren't any bad signs, just bad times, don't listen to that hogwash. There comes another one to tell her: "Ma'am, the quake knocked down San Jacinto and La Merced, the earth is angry and is punishing sins, they say it's the fault of the masters because they've offended the king; pray to the Virgin of Carmel, ma'am, there are children still breathing under the rubble, they say that in a house not far from here a woman pulled so hard on her son's arm to get him out that the arm came off." There's no rest for the soldiers gathering the dead, and they've ordered a big pyre built in front of the cathedral to burn them before they decompose. Ashen bodies, Alejandro, all coated with dust, their eyes open, cold foreheads, piled one atop another and trampled by the frightened horses. Caracas is a city of desiccated bodies under the fallen stones, their hands sticking out of the ruins, hair tangled in window gratings, whimpers blotted out by the roar of the mountain. The world is coming down on top of us in this forgotten village, this hamlet lost in the vastness of the earth, where we've invented freedom. Now it's raining; it starts slowly, and little by little a heavy downpour comes, cleansing the putrid air. Close the doors and windows, Isabel, tell your slaves and your children they're better off shut in while the rain clears up the night and the earth calms down. The house is still standing, it has endured, and remaining inside you is that spongy hope you're sheltering and that is mine and yours, Alejandro.

Signs of Isabel's imminent delivery came at night. Emeterio, a big lad, the son of a house slave, ran to the Caridad Hospital to get a doctor, but there were so many plague sufferers and sick people left from the earthquake months before that he couldn't find one, and with no science available it occurred to him to stop at the Franciscan monastery. Isabel was lying on the bed, naked, sweating, panting. When the priest entered, a slave woman covered her with the sheets. Fray Antonio kneeled beside her and spoke: "Pray with me, my child, let us ask Our Lady of Good Fortune to assist you to have a fortunate childbirth like hers." I couldn't tell how much time had passed, but I do know that the day was dawning when a midwife was finally found, and a short time later a cry was heard from among the bloody sheets. Fray Antonio had not seen many births, but he had seen many deaths, and when he lifted up that small, purplish creature he said: "Isabel, these are not the times for festivities, nor do you have any more relatives to expect for the baptism, so let us perform it right now."

And I was there, Alejandro, a guest without their knowing it, when they bathed the baby girl and dressed her in swaddling clothes and poured water from the jug into a silver punch bowl; and I was listening when Daría, a slave brought from the plantation, held her in her arms and Fray Antonio pronounced: "I baptize thee Isabel Francisca María de la Purificación, in the name of the Father and of the Son and of the Holy Ghost." I was there when Fray Antonio, moved by Isabel's distress, promised that he would visit her every afternoon after services and together they would pray to God for the health of the child and of the country.

And the child lived. It comforts me to hear her playing in the courtyard while the black woman sings *Malembe, Malembe, don't you cry, Saint John's gone but he'll be back by and by.* The rain leaves puddles there, and Daría is leaning back in her rocking chair with the little girl in her lap. Isabel is teaching her sons to write, since they have no school in these crumbly years. Daría has never seen writing from close by. From her life on the plantation she remembers seeing a piece of paper with script on it only once, a yellowish sheet overrun with marks that said nothing to her, but that said to others: *Daría, property of Don Francisco Martínez de Villegas, born on the plantation La Trinidad, area of Curiepe, dark-skinned, some twenty years of age, good temperament, full set of teeth, fertile womb.* She's worth, if they were to sell her (but they won't sell her), three hundred pesos. Daría watches Isabel bending over the table while Juan Bautista and Francisquito scribble and their mother, with a heron quill, makes flourishes. The little girl cries, and the black woman raises her up to her breast and soothes her with a lot of words that she doesn't know how to write: "Doña Isabel, tell me, ma'am, how do I say sugarplum, little birdie, smart girl, the black girl picks you up, the black girl puts you to bed. Could you write it out for me, ma'am, what the words I'm saying are like?" Isabel takes her hand and guides it to trace out Daría's name. "Don't you believe that all white women know how to write, Daría; writing isn't an activity for women. I promise to teach you when the war's over."

Alejandro, why can't they give us a chance for peace? Why can't I be calm and contemplate this scene that I wish could be the last my eyes take in? Why do I have to listen now to the ravings of that wild man José Tomás Boves, promising freedom and land to blacks who defend the Crown and murder their masters? Haven't I heard of that savage Asturian who's taken on the war as something personal and is fighting us with our men, our horses, and our rifles? Why couldn't the ship bringing him here as a child have sunk? Why do I have to wait so long for them to kill him? Hasn't the sound of his hatred and the clatter of his horses crossing the plains to Caracas reached you? He wants to tear us out by the roots and slaughter everyone he finds, whether defenseless women, children, old people, or slaves; he wants to enter my city, my street, and my house, and I won't have it, do you hear me, I won't allow those men to set foot in my family home, I want him to know that this house belongs to me and my descendants, has since time immemorial, and you've got to appear, Alejandro, and defend this house where we've all been born and where we've died. It's necessary for us to be tranquil in death, and I can't be if I know that Boves's men are urinating in the courtyard of my house on the corner of San Jacinto. Are you a man, Alejandro, can you see that Isabel and her three children are vulnerable and that my house is desolate, abandoned, and battered? Can't you see Isabel scrambling about like a madwoman, trying to stow her belongings in trunks? Can't you see her weeping, genuflecting at the prie-dieu for the last time, begging God for the grace to let them arrive alive at the end of the crazy journey our cousin General Bolívar is going to make with the unfortunate citizens of Caracas, evacuating the town before Boves's blood-cries appear in it and he torches what's left? Can't you hear her moaning when she lifts her little girl into her arms out of the crib and wraps her with her cloak and they climb into the cart that Emeterio is getting ready? Can't you see Juan Bautista and Francisquito loading the trunks and boxes and Daría filling the jugs with the water she's been able to draw from the well? Can't you see them turning the corner of San Jacinto and heading toward the main square to join the unlucky refugees who make up the caravan that's following Bolívar east to Barcelona? The ghosts are left behind here, Alejandro, what remains is the darkness of an empty city, inhabited by those who aren't even capable of making an attempt; our name ends here, our blood, our life, because that woman and those children are our only continuation, and they have no other choice than to await death in the courtyard or to seek it farther on, along the forest trail. Alejandro, tell me why we started this war. All my grandchildren are dead—some in the fighting, others from disease, others shipwrecked as they tried to flee to the Antilles; all of them have perished, and I'm alone here again, lost among the legal papers that attest to who I am and how much I own, tracing over them with my fingers in order to make out the words, covering my ears because I don't want to hear the cries and lamentations of those who've lingered behind. I should like to know now the reason for my having borne ten children in fifteen births. Alejandro, I need a new son immediately, right here in the main room of my abandoned house, to continue your seed. I don't care about your lust, I want your descent, and since all I have left is my voice, I'll stay on to tell about the destruction. Listen from out of my deep memory to the fate of our line.

It's six o'clock on the morning of July 7, 1814, and dawn is beginning to break in the valley. The slow, unlikely caravan is leaving the main square, forming an endless, tottering line of wheels and horses that stretches off into the distance. More than twenty thousand people make up the withdrawal that is following General Bolívar to Barcelona. Women, children, house slaves, victims of smallpox and malaria, men too old for war, all have managed as best they can to reach some cart or to walk, and they're leaving behind a village of invalids and cripples to the bloodlust of Boves's soldiers. They pass through the plantation canefields and string out along the trail to the east. The morning is still chilly, and Daría snugs her cloak around the sleeping baby girl, who searches with her lips for the breasts that had been feeding her until a short time ago. Isabel closes her eyes and doesn't think about much, the world is collapsing all around her and she doesn't know what to say to herself; she's a patriot, she's a blueblood, she's the owner of devastated plantations and the now-darkened body of a dead man. She sits between her sons, and the jostling of the cart makes her lean sometimes toward one boy, sometimes the other—who are ashamed at not being old enough to fight and half-frightened because they are still children. Daría, across from her mistress, doesn't think they've ever been so close; never before have her legs brushed against Doña Isabel's knees, never before have their skirts mingled, never before has her smell been overwhelmed by the aroma of the soap with which Doña Isabel washed her face in the basin one last time before forsaking her house on the corner of San Jacinto. Daría, with her dim eyes, accepts without blinking the strong sun that's now rising up to the height of the mountains; she stares straight ahead and finds no answers in her confused heart.

The horses and the shouts halting them can be heard, the hens tied to the staves of the carts, the voices of men issuing orders and leading the animals to the river. The wagons keep creaking to a standstill, and the women and children get off the road to squat in the high grass to relieve their bowels. Daría holds the basin for Doña Isabel to urinate in, and then she does the same for herself. Never before did the slave girl imagine the intimacy of necessities that has mingled their waste. They eat and drink in silence, secretly, so that the sick and hungry won't come close. They scrimp on their water because it's a long way to Barcelona, and Daría eats as she rocks Isabel, who is crying, sweltering in her own sweat. Juan Bautista, the elder son, has gone with Emeterio over to the river, where the men leading the caravan have contradictory news: some shout that they have to hurry, that Boves will be pursuing them; others shout no, that he'll stay in Caracas to take over the city. The boy comes back all flustered, and his explanations, mixed with Emeterio's, can't be understood. He sits beside his mother again, and as they start up once more, a breath of cool air lessens the sting of the hot afternoon sun.

Isabel tries to nod off, which is impossible; her slight, bony hand caresses a tiny rosary with which she prays intermittently, and her sons respond sometimes but not others because they've fallen asleep. She tries to think of something that will calm her, but they're all bad memories, which makes her shrink all the more in the face of circumstances . . . and pushes her even further away from any hope. If she thinks of Caracas, all that comes is the dull rumble of the earth opening up, the stench of corpses burned in the streets, and the plaintive wails of the crowd on the night when the houses came tumbling down. If it's the war, about the men she let go, three brothers and a husband, all she has left are heroes. If it's her fortune, she touches the pouch under her skirts in which she carries eighty pesos of silver, a gold chain, and a topaz pin. If it's the house, shuttered windows and an abandoned courtyard where snakes must be coming in. She tries to go beyond that, casting about for other images, and she thinks about her mother playing the guitar in the shade of the courtyard while she and her brothers hunt lizards in the shrubbery; she thinks about her father's library—she barely knew him, but it calms her to remember his books and the desk where she sees him seated; she thinks about her wedding in the cathedral and about one last and hurried night of love that ends with the squeak of boots going off and about Isabel's crying as she wakes and asks to be fed. Daría has fallen asleep, and Isabel takes the child in her arms to give her something to drink while she tries to sing a lullaby that's interrupted by shouts outside and the noise of a cart that's overturned; the horse runs off, dragging it, and bodies are dumped onto the road. Under a wheel, a child lies in agony, smeared with dirt; it isn't possible to tell its sex until a woman lying on the ground cries out: "My son, my son, get him out of there." The men are afraid the horses will spook and follow the one that's run away; some carts stop, and the people get out to look. "They're dead," someone says, "push them aside so the wagons can get by, there's no time to bury them." "What about the child?" another voice asks: "The child's alive." "He'll die soon enough, there's nothing to be done." The caravan continues on its way, and on top of the parched earth, between the dusty trail and the jungle that devours it, there remain the wheel, the trapped body, and a woman who strokes it from time to time, looking for its head among the wreckage of wood and scooping out a hollow in the ground with her hands.

When night falls they halt. They stop a few steps away from an almost vacant settlement where a few freedmen live in two or three houses and some runaway slaves sleep in the open. The noise of the caravan has drawn them to the road, and they timidly approach to ask questions, but it's the others who want information. Whether to rest.

Whether to press on in the dark. If they stop they can be easily overtaken by Boves's troops, fresh men and on horseback; if they move on they'll run the risk of getting lost, and the greater one of the wagons breaking down. The fatigue of the weak irritates those who still have hopes and strength. They build a bonfire and pass around bottles of cane liquor. Others wander off and look in the shadows for some skirts where they can let their semen and their fear flow off; there are more than fifty women to each man, not counting those trembling with fever who can't even get down out of the wagons to take care of their needs. Pestilence invades the night, and some who can't bear their thirst have drunk from puddles and flooded their stomachs with dysentery. The stench and the wailing of the children will betray them more than any tracks the wheels are leaving behind. Isabel tries to say her rosary again, and Daría responds, almost inaudibly—it's just the sound of two women consoling each other with words that go back and forth and are only spoken because they can't communicate their thoughts.

When they go forward, Daría begins to recognize the countryside of her childhood, the lands of Barlovento where she was born and grew up, where she had two children who died, the second born at the same time as Isabel, so they brought Daría in to take advantage of her milk before her huge breasts dried up—and therefore almost without any time to pray for the little angel, they took her to Caracas in the same cart that's bouncing along now and on which Emeterio takes every opportunity to tighten the bolts on the wheels. Daría catches a soft whiff of banana trees, a smell that reaches her despite the filth enveloping the caravan; she goes along feeling a heat that doesn't crush her but pacifies her, and she begins to wonder how far away the plantation is, how far away the blacks are who saw her born. Out of her fear and fatigue she's drawing a strength she didn't know she had, breathing in the night, and the sounds begin to spawn a feeling of security that she never had leaving the city; looking at the downcast face of Doña Isabel, her mistress, she starts comparing her strong arms, her muscular legs, starts thinking that maybe, if it became necessary, she could run, that maybe, if necessary, she could sleep several nights in the jungle, could even reach the place where the blacks who saw her born are.

Isabel, on the other hand, is suffering from a terror that arrives with the same rapidity as the night, which has fallen without warning. All the places she knows have been left behind, the whole world that's her world, the small city where no more than twenty thousand people remain, those four streets, that cathedral, that square, and a few half-ruined churches. The only sound she can imagine is that of a few hens in the backyard and, from time to time, that of carriages along the narrow streets or the nickering of the horses when the groom unhitches them in the stable. The only children she's heard cry are her brothers, back in her youth, or her own children chasing each other along the arcades. Her only knowledge of illness has to do with the silence of slave women hauling jugs of water up to her father's room as he trembles under the sheets while her mother changes the cold compresses on his forehead and the doctor bleeds him. The only men she knows are her uncles, her brothers, her cousins and second cousins, her husband, and her slaves. The only poor people she knows are the ones who were sleeping huddled against the walls of the monasteries when, wearing a black mantilla, she went out to mass in the cathedral on Sundays escorted by two black women, who chased them away. Her only grief was the night of her father's funeral, sitting on the window ledge while the cortege departed. The only fear she remembers is the beginning of her blood rites: the blood of a young girl, the blood of deflowering, the blood that runs down her legs when the first head opens her uterus and she hears the cries of joy all through the house, "It's a boy, it's a boy," and a murmur from the family drinking coffee and brandy in celebration of the well-born child. But all that world has disappeared now, demolished by the earthquake, buried with the bones of her brothers and her husband; now she's alone in this cart with her three children and Daría, fleeing into the night on their way east, following General Bolívar. None of the stage she trod for thirty years exists anymore, and she, beside Daría, their feet touching, the slave's still white skirt brushing hers, lost amid the men's shouting and the endless weeping of the children, can't recognize herself, can't conceive of herself as anything but a body next to other bodies that bounce along, abused, over stones and crude trails.

The men yell to get underway again, and the swaying line of carts awakens. Isabel comes out of the short nap she was able to manage during the halt. She hesitates before opening her eyes and ears again. She had a blank, empty nightmare, and all she can see in her mind is something that keeps turning and turning. As they get back onto the road, the weary wheels of the covered wagons are rolling; the carts are crammed with people, up to twelve in each, legs hanging out, naked feet, bleary eyes. Suddenly the rain pours down; in a few minutes the road is a quagmire, and the bodies look like one single torn shirt stuck to the staves of the carts. Blinded by the rain, the men driving the animals can scarcely be heard shouting in the uproar, "Wait till the cloudburst passes!" The answer is heard, "We haven't got time, we haven't got time, let those who can keep going." Some wagons have forged ahead, breaking off from the rest like the detached segments of a worm, and others have remained mired in the mud: whips crack over the horses, who are straining in an impossible effort; men, women, and children get out to push, the wheels seem nailed down permanently, refusing to turn—overcome by terror, the ones who have lost their carts to the muck try to invade the others'. "There's no room, there's no room for so many people, we've got two families here already, there's no room for any more." The women grapple with each other, the ones on the ground try to climb up and the ones above try to push them away. "Take my child, for the love of God, take my child." Emeterio and Juan Bautista have taken on two women, a girl and an elderly one who had difficulty clambering on and who, once up, collapsed against the trunks and let herself fall limp, as if she'd attained salvation. The girl, shivering under tattered clothing, runs her hand over her head and tries to wipe away the water that's running down her dirty, yellowish braids. "This cart's empty"—and before Emeterio can stop them, more than a dozen people pounce, throwing off trunks and boxes to make room for themselves. Francisquito picks up a shotgun and screams: "I'll kill anyone who gets in here!" With his thin, quivering body, he has the look of a child hero. "There's no room for anybody here; go climb into the other one." Isabel watches the trunks as they fall, exposing to the rain the ruffled skirts, open bodices, taffeta shawls, lace mantillas, muslin wraps, silk capes, Brittany camisoles and petticoats, damask doublets, Irish linen sheets, Rouen fabric, batiste underskirts, fringed underdrawers and jackets, cambric shirts and vests, fans, linen table-cloths—nothing but a jumble in the mud of the roadway now, stomped by horses and torn by wheels as they pass. Looking at her last belongings and bursting into laughter, she says: "Daría, just think of all the time we spent folding everything so it would fit." Daría looks at her but isn't sure about laughing; she doesn't understand her laugh. "They were very pretty things," she answers after a time. "What does it matter what they were; they'll never be worn again. The only thing that matters now is for it to stop raining." When the water ceases coming down, left on the road are the ruts of those wagons that have managed to continue and a cargo of aching, exhausted bodies that were cast aside, a bunch of people who climbed off and are staggering into the woods, shouting, almost naked, not knowing where they're going, and gently, gently lying on top of each other, waiting for the sun to dry them and the breeze to relax them.

Isabel is so drained that when she dozes from time to time she awakens with a start because she doesn't know whether she's asleep or dead. The pain in her back tells her she's alive, briefly she recovers an awareness of herself, but she immediately succumbs to the nightmare about something that keeps turning and turning—discovering again that she's trundling along in a cart on the way to Barcelona, and she wonders again if she did the right thing in following Fray Antonio's advice, if she shouldn't have stayed behind to die at home. The memory of the priest comforts her for a moment, for that man was her father, her brother, her husband, her friend, her doctor, the only person who, besides her children and her slaves, stood by her during those shattering days. She would have liked to hear him again soothing her soul with his words, but Fray Antonio refused to go; he wanted to stay with the ones who weren't even capable of making an attempt to flee.

Long live his Majesty Ferdinand VII, long live General Boves, death to the whites, long live the blacks, take out your tools, cut off their heads, plant your seeds! María, crouching, looks up, and her eyes get lost in the darkness as she tries to recognize the blacks who are shouting. Isabel, hiding on the floor, hugs her sons and trembles. The night has fallen silent, and all that can be heard are the echoing shouts: *Torches high, death to the whites, blacks plant your seeds, live and you'll see,* followed by random shots into the woods. There is an exchange of fire, and the women and children break into shrieks.

A man leaps into the cart, and his eyes meet María's. He has a machete in hand, and his fly is open; he drags Doña Isabel onto the road, and when he gets on top of her, María, from the rear, accosts him: "Stop it, Ceferino." They look each other up and down, recognize each other. "Don't hurt her, Ceferino. I'm María, you remember me, I'm María." María remembers Ceferino, can see him as a child playing in the doorway of the slave quarters; she can see his sadness when the men throw his mother's corpse into the ground and turn him over to María's mother to be taken care of; she can see him as a boy killing snakes and tarantulas; she can see him as a man working in the cacao groves, his body strong and sweaty, lying in the shade drinking cane liquor with the others, talking about things that women don't understand; she can see him escaping with the others to an outlaw band, losing himself in the forest, a renegade, full of pure hate, sleeping in the dark, eating the animals he can kill; she can see him in her memory lifting up her skirts while she jumps and runs away and laughs, and she can see herself telling her mother: "Ceferino is after me, Ceferino is chasing me."

"Remember me, I'm María. Don't hurt my lady." Isabel is prone on the ground. She doesn't want to move; she doesn't know if the shadow of the black man is still over her. She closes her eyes so as not to know. Time is passing, but she can't measure it. The royalist blacks are going to kill us, she thinks. And then nothing. She can still detect his smell nearby; she thinks she would rather die, be run through by the machete, giving him her blood, and be left in a small red puddle that in seconds would be absorbed by the damp earth, and in just one more bit of dampness leave the constancy of her life there—than to give him a moment of pleasure. To die among the many who've already been dumped beside the road, mingling her bones with all those that the buzzards are pecking at, leaving her life and her children forever, before she would let the black man believe, say, think, or imagine a pleasure that would give him revenge. No one will remember her death, it will be lost among the ever so many deaths and it will be impossible to find her; she prefers complete absence, annihilation, to surviving in his mind. She hears Daría's voice calling her, helping her get up again. The children are inside, crying. The women's screams have ceased, and bursts of rifle fire can be heard from time to time; the soldiers have scattered the attackers and started up the caravan again. Many carts are left in a jumble in the forest, overturned, with no one to right them. The bodies of the fallen horses lie with those of the men, and as the buzzards gather to eat their remains, the people left standing shoo them off and continue on their way.

Daría hugs Isabel between her breasts and calms her crying, giving her slow spoonfuls of water. Everything is silent now, all that can be heard are the sounds of the animals, and she chases off the cloud of mosquitoes that keep biting the little girl's legs. She looks at the dead being left behind, the bodies mixed in with earth and mud, the women who have stayed in the woods to bury their children, the little yellow corpses tossed from the carts because the breasts to feed them have dried up; she sees them lying on their backs, sockets empty of the eyes that have been pecked out; she looks at the elderly and the sick who've been pushed out so they don't infect those who are still healthy with their stench and putrescence; she looks at that man who has a worm-ridden hand, who with the other grasps at the stave of a retreating wagon. Daría remembers Ceferino's words before she saw him disappear into the woods, his wild eyes. "Don't stay with them, they'll never get there. It's two days' walk to Curiepe, maybe three; you're strong, Daría, you'll make it." "But my mistress, the children, it's too far, we haven't got any water, a lot of people have died of fever. How can I abandon them, how can I run away all by myself?" "Don't be afraid, walk, walk, when you get into the woods carry a pot to catch the rain, don't drink from puddles, only what falls. You've got to leave before you get to the coast; it'll be too late then, you'll never get there, they'll die of thirst in the sand. Now, Daría, now, run now, leap out, nobody will see you. Go to Curiepe with your brothers, stay there with them and I'll come back and make you a lot of children, because the masters are going to lose the war, you'll see, black girl, they're going to die, every last one of them, and never again will the overseer holler at me, 'Get to work, you lazy nigger,' never again is he going to whip me, 'Mulatto bastard.' Do you know how much you're worth?" "Three hundred pesos is what I'm worth, Julián Cayetano told me when they sent me to Caracas. 'You're worth three hundred pesos,' he told me, 'if they sold you, but they won't sell you.' "

Daría hasn't made a decision in twenty years; in twenty years she's never said: *I want, I desire, I propose.* In twenty years no one has ever said to her: *What do you want, what do you propose, where are you going?* Her hands have worked, her body has bent and bowed, her lips have answered respectfully the questions that others have posed, her bare feet have walked over the ground and have crossed in silence courtyards and porchways, the rugs covering the parlor and the anteroom; her eyes have caressed the branches drooping gently from the columns of the courtyard, her hands have stroked the dark and solemn furniture of the dining room, her eyes have contemplated the static eyes of a gentleman portrayed on a framed canvas that hangs on the wall of the study, her voice has sung soft and somber lullabies to baby Isabel, sitting beside the cradle that rocks to the same rhythm with which her hands stroke the little hands; her teeth have opened in a smile while her heavy, round breasts have been tipped into the baby's mouth, pouring out the juicy whiteness they hold. But never before has she made a decision.

The rain comes pounding down and soaks her dress, which was white when she left Caracas. In tatters now, the gingham skirt and lace-trimmed blouse, her hem-stitched cloak, stained with mud, have the same cast as her skin. She shields the child's head with the cloak to protect her from the water driving against them, and she listens to the downpour. Why does it rain so much in this place? Why is God punishing them with all this rain? She looks at the calluses on her feet, the soles hardened by going barefoot, the muscles of her legs, and she thinks about Ceferino. She thinks that she'll get there, exhausted, frightened, but she'll get to the blacks who saw her born and they'll take her in, care for her, lay her down on a hide and swathe her body with plantain leaves until her wounds heal, until the scabs close, and they'll bring her salt and water to settle her stomach and let her sleep until she recovers.

In memory she runs through the whole path before her and tries to untangle the jungle surrounding them. Doña Isabel is sleeping with her arms around her sons. Emeterio is dozing, hunched over his knees. She leaps out, she leaps out now, hearing Ceferino's voice: *It'll be too late afterward, leap out now.* Daría looks at Doña Isabel and would like to ask her an impossible question. If she speaks, Doña Isabel will say no; if she doesn't say anything, her mistress will never forgive her, will hunt her down and whip her to death.

How could you know, Daría, illiterate black woman, if your mistress will understand that this caravan is heading toward certain death and that they're already specters lost in time? How could you know, black woman worth three hundred pesos, black woman the descendant of Taris, coal-black, born here, how to interpret the principles of justice of that woman sleeping in a wagon full of ghosts? How could you know, black woman with a full set of teeth, a fertile womb, a twenty-year-old black woman, what they'll write about you? You, who only scribbled something one day when Isabel took that hand of yours that gathered leaves, washed floors, warmed pots, ironed lace— and guided it over a piece of paper and, with the heron quill in her hand, wrote your name for the first time. How could you know the meaning of history? How could you know that I'm waiting for it to be you who'll carry my hope in your arms? How could you know how to read in Isabel's sleeping eyes whether you should leap out or stay with her to her death? You couldn't know, and, not knowing, you leap out.

She jumps out with her eyes on the marshes and bubbling mud-holes ready to swallow her forever, and she's afraid. The gullies and ravines of the mountains are there, waiting for her unsteady, bleeding feet, which trip over rocks and roots, her weary eyes and her skinned hands, which part the branches and thick leaves, going forward, always forward, thinking that at any moment her body will plunge into a hollow, her body will roll and smash against tree trunks, her body will sink in the muck and her hands will flail in the air, gasping for an impossible freedom. She feels the weight of the child clinging to her, her right arm holds her while the other is raised and bent like a shield of flesh in order to fend off the thorns; she listens to her constant rhythmic sobbing—the child cries, cries all the time—and Daría, depending on the extent of her fatigue, runs, bounds, slows down, and rests against a tree, blows away the mosquitoes that encircle the little girl's face, stops to let a snake slip by, repeats the prayer of incantation: *Blessed and glorious be our holy Saint Benedict and Saint Paul and Saint Pantaleón. Deliver me from all rabid and poisonous animals by the grace and glory that the Lord gave you at the hour of your death. Walk on straw and tread on wild snakes and come to me gently as my Lord to the feet of the saint at the side of the cross. Jesus, amen.* She closes her eyes and wraps the child in her torn cloak, protects her with her shadow, and sleeps, lets herself drift off, not knowing for how long, not knowing how many nights, with no memories of herself. Daría makes herself keep going while her exhausted body pants against the child's; she no longer knows where they're going or where they've come from, whether the spirals in her dream are the same as the turns around the mountain that descend gradually to the valley of Curiepe, and suddenly she wakes up because the sun is warming their bodies and she opens her eyes and picks up the child and brings her close to her heart to see if she's still breathing; with her tongue Daría cleans the infant's face, reddened by the heat and swollen from the underbrush, and her eyes brighten when, like a happy dream that takes away her numbness, the cacao groves spanning the valley appear.

She takes up a more leisurely pace, all those days to get there, all the suns and all the moons, until perhaps she'll come upon the houses of mud and palm leaves and the blacks who saw her born; but fear has left her now, she looks restlessly around as if there were a bird circling her and fluttering in front of her, as if there were a snake biting her and paralyzing her forever, she looks for whatever it is in her vision, opening and closing her eyes as if there were a curtain darkening her sight, she looks into her body as if there were a hand tearing her open;

but fear is no longer in her, she can't find it. She tries to see her soul from outside then, to see if she feels cold or night in it, to see if it feels broken or collapsed to her, and she touches herself all over, and, inside, Ceferino tells her, *You'll get there, Daría, you're strong, you'll get there.* She remembers his excited eyes fastening on her in the night, amidst the shots and the smell of gunpowder and the anguished screams of the wounded, who are falling on all sides onto Doña Isabel's clothing, which is all spattered with mud and looks like an illuminated splotch. Daría gets up and shakes the remnants of her skirts and cloak and resumes walking, because now she knows where she's going, all she has to do is keep on, not lose sight of hope, and wander the cacao groves until she hears a voice, until someone hears her calls. She remembers Ceferino's words—*Don't drink from puddles, only what falls*—and Daría looks up, waiting for a cloudburst, but the sky opens up splendidly, blue and white, and the noonday sun pounds them mercilessly. The child has given up crying, and Daría feels that all she's carrying in her arms is a small bundle; she talks to her, sings with a hoarse voice snippets of a lament, "Saint John is leaving, next year, Isabelita, Isabelona, Saint John will come back, your black girl carries you, your black girl puts you to sleep." Isabel seems to be sleeping, but Daría knows it's not a peaceful sleep, she runs her finger over the lips that have been split by the sun and over the swollen belly, and the child is no longer crying, no longer sweating, sometimes she opens her mouth and a dry tongue and lips try wearily to make the movement of suckling. Daría wets them with hers, also parched, and tries to make saliva as they touch each other like pieces of threadbare cloth. She continues on, slower, more uncertain, searching for shade, slackening her pace even more until she finally lies down and, placing Isabel on her cloak, goes back to sleep and asks Our Lord Jesus Christ—who the priest said died on the cross in a faraway place, very far from here, where there are also palm trees and sand and sunshine, very far away, very far away, where the three kings went to adore the King who reigned over blacks and whites—and she prays to Our Lord Jesus Christ, the Virgin Mary's son who died on the cross to forgive our sins and came to save us all and said that where He was going everyone would enter, black and white, all the same, and she closes her eyes because only now that she's so close, now that she can almost hear the voice of the overseer and the singing in the houses at night, now that she can almost see them, see the blacks who saw her born, only now does she believe that they'll make it there.

The sun relents a little, and Daría half-opens her eyes, stretches her way-weary muscles, and gazes at the clouds for a while. She feels for Isabel with her hand, runs it over the tiny body and stops at the heart; she can still feel a soft flutter under the skin, a weak, living throb. Under the branches sheltering them, Daría scrutinizes the sky as if expecting a sign, and there, over her head, she discovers the leaves that are chewed for kidney trouble, the leaves the old women taught her to distinguish from the ones chewed for vomiting, for fever, for bleeding, for unwanted births, for relieving pain in people who are dying. And she pulls them off violently and chews them with fury, spits them out, and chews and spits them out again, and lies down once more beside the child until the leaves that are chewed for kidney trouble take effect. Daría, squatting, cups her hands to receive a stream of her own liquid, drinks it, collects some more, and slowly passes it to the mouth of the little girl, who also sucks it in; she repeats the procedure several times until, empty and exhausted, she rests. The child in her arms starts to wail again, and a few droplets of sweat reappear on her face while her hand starts searching for the nipples. Daría, standing, starts walking and doesn't intend to stop until she gets to the blacks who saw her born, until she hears voices calling to her, until she sees women swarming around her, saying "It's Daría, it's Daría with Doña Isabel's little girl." And Daría turns the child over to other hands and hears her own voice telling Julián Cayetano, the administrator: "I ran away with her; she's the child of my mistress, Doña Isabel." She lets herself be led by all the people coming out to greet her and lets them lay her down on a hide, and she drinks water until she falls asleep.

LAMENT FOR THE DESTRUCTION OF

CARACAS

Here I am in my tattered silk nightdress, hair hanging loose, dirty, smelly, sequestered in my room, letting the dust from the holes in the roof fall on me, letting the rainstorms soak me and the sun dry me. Here I am, Alejandro, crying out at death, weeping for my corpses. First I must weep for our grandson Francisco, the son of Nicolás, who fell in a gully and is only one in a pile of thousands of bodies, the earth covering their bones, their bent legs like scribblings, a thin thread of blood on his forehead, and he's only one body thrown onto the road from a horse that gallops off without a rider. And I must also weep for his wife, Isabel Madriz, who left Caracas on July 7, 1814, in the caravan of ghosts led by General Bolívar. (How could I not be in mourning, Alejandro, because they've torn my lineage out of my womb? And you ask me who died. You're a stupid dead man, Alejandro, you're a useless dead man, a dead man abandoned to his own death.) I must cry for that woman, her face yellow and thin from fever, who is thirty years old and looks fifty, with her trembling body, her lost eyes seeking the light that's beginning to filter in from the distant sea. A nameless husk who reached the end of her journey to die completely. I must listen to her incoherent words, her broken mumbling as she tries to say something to a woman who has come to give her water. I must listen to how she asks about Daría, the slave girl who accompanied her in the withdrawal, and keeps repeating: "Daría, Daría, where are you? Where's my little girl? Tell me if you got away, tell me if you took the little girl with you, I don't see her anymore. Is there anyone who's seen her, anyone who's seen the slave who was traveling with me? Ever since the night when the royalist blacks attacked us I haven't seen her anymore. Where's General Bolívar? General Bolívar's going to save us, we're following him to the coast, some ships are waiting and will rescue us." I must feel her chills, the salt taste she has in her mouth, the salt spume of the sea, and look with her at the ships in the distance. I too must ask if anyone has seen Daría, a strong black woman, about twenty years old, wearing a white cloak and with a scar on her right hand between the index and middle fingers, and who's carrying a little girl of about two in her arms. I must ask if anyone has seen her run away into the woods with the girl, because Isabel wants to know if she has anything left in the world. I must be with her when the men throw that boy from the cart because he stinks from being dead several days. I have to roar with rage, Alejandro, when those men grab Francisquito and toss him into the mire while they hold back Isabel, who's screaming for him. Tell me, Alejandro, who those people are who dare do a thing like that; what do they know of life and death, dumping him onto the compost pile like that—if you're a man, tell them he's mine and that I want to take him and give him proper burial, but I can't, I must stay with Isabel, who is left defeated and undone when the cart rattles on, leaving one more among so many bodies, that of Francisquito, the only body left to her because Juan Bautista's fell onto the trail days before, clutching a shotgun that someone quickly snatched away. I must feel the quivering of her hands and hear her moan as she asks that unknown woman who wished to be with her in her death to retrieve from her bodice a small inkwell and a quill wrapped in a sheet of crumpled paper, because she has to write a letter, and I must listen while she dictates meaningless words to a woman who doesn't know how to write: "Say this, 'To my daughter Isabel,' write this, 'To my daughter Isabel' . . .'" And there her words stop, there her flight comes to an end, because she can't flee any farther, she needs to crawl into death's corner because she no longer recognizes herself, is confronted instead only by her creaking bones and afflicted skin. I must be there, Alejandro, when that anonymous woman closes her staring eyes, shrouds her with her own cloak, and folds her hand, in which there's a piece of paper, a letter without any text. I can feel the soft breeze blowing between them and can see Isabel's hair moving above her hardened, ashen face when the last shreds of the caravan finally reach the east and greet the dawn on the coast between Píritu and Barcelona. You ask who died? The world, Alejandro, the world we used to have. Can you see what's left of my house? Come closer, look over our ruins with me. I spend my days and nights stroking these battered bricks, putting my hands into the holes that history has punched in them; look out through the gratings of my windows that give a view of the courtyard; go through the entranceway, there are the fragments of the tiles I had brought from Andalusia; use your foot to push aside the shards of mosaic so you can go through the passageway that joins the courtyard to the entrance, and there you'll find weeds devouring the flagstones, and by the font where the birds used to drink you'll smell the urine left by Boves's men. My house has been a refuge for indigents, the wounded, a latrine for soldiers; the traces of their filth still cling to the walls of my porchways. Go into the empty rooms, and there, where our children were born, you'll see what's left of the wrecked furniture, the shreds of the damask curtains, the pieces of tables and armchairs, the broken cabinets and torn rugs. Continue on to the parlor, where I used to sit after siesta and receive the Mijares and Madriz women, my lady cousins the Solórzanos, your lady cousins the Blancos; listen to the murmur of our laughter and our chatting, the monotony of our conversations, which were, nevertheless, our only entertainment. There we'd speculate about our daughters' marriages, criticize the governors, make fun of the bishops, we'd complain about the laziness of our slave women, and sometimes, too, we'd share reminiscences of lost husbands, daughters dead in childbirth, wastrel sons. There, Alejandro, we'd live our little aristocracy and weave a world we thought was forever. Kneel down in the chapel where we baptized our children, celebrated communion, and said the rosary; the tabernacle is open and the gold trim ripped away; only the legs of the prie-dieu remain, along with a few one-armed and one-legged statuettes. Go into the kitchen, where once my slave women prepared corn stew, roasts, crullers, puddings, meringues; now rats cavort across the rubble, and if you come to the end of my lot you'll encounter the wilderness that has invaded the servants' benches; the well is caked with mud, and the well jar from which water used to pour out over the clean stone is in pieces. This is the sum total of what we have left, and I'm weeping, Alejandro, because it was everything.

Why shouldn't I tremble with rage and desperation? We've won the war and lost all we had. I've remained alone in this house of ashes that shelters the corpses of my memory, and I have to dress in mourning and weep for my ruins. Wherever you go you'll find the debris from what once were churches and convents—we were never rich, never built grand monuments, but those churches were our testimony, and now what you see are open doors, askew walls, toppled steeples and bell towers; we never knew the pomp and elegance of other provinces, our city was an obscure village, poorly paved, with cramped streets and snakes and vermin dodging through the bricks and the detritus; we never had a grand cathedral to show off, instead had one that looked more like a village chapel than anything else, but our history took place there and now there it is, its belfry damaged and its clock stopped at the hour of the earthquake of 1812, which marked the beginning of our destruction. The years have passed, and there haven't been any hands to reassemble the stones that shook loose that day or to rebuild the fallen houses, because Caracas is a city of ghosts. Look at the unfortunates wandering aimlessly through the streets and sleeping nestled in doorways and on the ground in the squares, ragged shadows that beg for alms at convents and parish churches, converted into hospitals now, by whose doors hungry peasants gather, pleading to be thrown a bit of food; look at those dogs fighting over the remains of unburied bodies from San Pablo and La Misericordia, and those men you see dragging themselves along on boards, showing their stumps, their blind eyes, their amputated feet— these, Alejandro, are the veterans of our great and final battle of Carabobo. Smell the corpses of the ones who've died tonight or last night of disease—smallpox, tuberculosis—and whose death was nothing but a slipping down the wall that supported them as they held out their filthy hands to the generosity of passersby. Look at this city, which is ours, anchored in this narrow valley, which we made ours in spite of its afflictions, this city that we loved for its warm days, its cool nights, its clear sky, its majestic mountain, the clarity of its thousand little streams, its remote small-town charm, its streetcorners with absurd names that made visitors laugh, its small taverns, its narrow shops run by Canary Islanders, the bustle of its people, who were always proud, noisy, irreverent, and trouble-making, a combination of insolent colonials, refractory blacks, and upstart mulattoes. It was in this village, Alejandro, that America invented liberation, and now I can tell you that we are liberated corpses and there isn't a single family in all the republic that isn't in mourning. And you ask me who died? Look at this city of ours, then, turned into a dungheap of beggars and madmen shouting on streetcorners, of women and children starving, and setting off to the outskirts to hunt birds with stones; and take a good look, because when darkness falls, only a few lanterns will light the way—for bandits who rob the inhabitants of their measly belongings. Only I can see in the dark, because my eyes died a long time ago and, as the eyes of a corpse, they take pleasure in contemplating corpses; I'm the only one who doesn't shake with fear and hunger and wait for the crowing of the cock for this morass to light up again. I'm here to record the end of the war that we undertook and to sing its victory, and despite my misery I cherish the hope that someday someone will come and rebuild the house and that someday I'll find the titles that have been lost to me.

In the Shade of Cacao

(1814–1834)

Do you, Juan del Rosario, want to hear about the lands of Curiepe? Mine, and don't you forget it, the ones Philip IV confirmed in the name of my father in 1663. If your eyes can't reach that far, I'm here to inform you, because mine can. Are you laughing at me, you insolent houseboy that I freed? Do you think I'm pursuing my titles in vain, since my possessions are now vacant and have been promised to the masters of the republic? I'm quite aware that I don't have any men to defend them from hungry peasants, soldiers without a pension, usurers and creditors, from anyone who thinks it suits him to settle on them—but don't get too happy, because the only ones of your people still there are women and old men; your royalist blacks have run off into the woods, and their roving bands are nothing but whitened bones drying in the sun, buzzard bait. Nothing belongs to anyone now, and all that's left of what used to be the plantation house are the traces of brick floor that show where it once stood; but listen carefully, because I hold its whole history in the secret places of my memory.

Julián Cayetano couldn't have been more than twelve years old when my grandson Francisco picked him to be administrator. They'd known each other since infancy, and since they were almost the same age, it wasn't strange that when Francisco visited the plantation he would escape from under his father's eyes and together with Julián would ride horseback over the trails, ford rivers, and then lie on the sands of Higuerote Cove and splash in the surf until the sun was at its height. More than once, when asked, Francisco had brought along some book with which to practice the reading that Julián Cayetano, slowly, syllable by syllable, was beginning to master. "When I grow up," Francisco promised, "and I'm master of this plantation, you're going to be my administrator"—and that was what he did. My grandson didn't agree with the recommendation of Governor Guevara Vasconcelos, who urged landowners to name only white men as administrators for fear of complicity with runaway blacks in the outlaw settlements. "Those people don't know anything about the country," Francisco had told Julián Cayetano: "The slaves hide in the groves on them and they, afraid of snakes, don't dare go into the woods, they don't know how to walk through the underbrush and can't stand the heat and the thirst, all they know is how to keep accounts and tie slaves to a stake or put them in stocks so that later on they won't be any good for work. You're going to be my administrator, and this will be the richest plantation in Barlovento." The bond between them grew even stronger when Francisco was around sixteen and came down with smallpox, and in his condition, with the fever that was sapping him, they couldn't think of any way to get him to Caracas; so Julián had come along with his mother, the slave Críspula, and for several days and nights she nursed Francisco and daubed his face with Dutch tallow and lemon juice and wrapped his torso in plantain leaves with the greatest care and patience in order to prevent the pustules from marking his skin forever.

When he was manumitted and made administrator of the most extensive plantation of Barlovento, 143 slaves and 87 free laborers were under his orders, picking more than five thousand sacks of cacao a year along the length and breadth of two leagues of forest and cacao groves. He would arise at four in the morning and once on his feet would awaken the overseers and ring the bell so that everyone would get up and say a third of the rosary; by daybreak, work had already been parceled out, and after the blacks had eaten, chores were assigned: full tasks for men and women between ages fifteen and fifty, half-tasks for elderly males and for women who were pregnant or had given birth, quarter-tasks for children; allotting them time afterward to tend to their own plots until sunset; he would ring the bell again to summon them to prayer and call their names to check if they were all there or if they'd wandered off to get drunk or have fun with women in nearby settlements. Once a month he would go to Capaya with Florencio, the head overseer, to buy cane liquor to clean boils, grease for blisters, candles, soap, flour, yards of Brittany fabric for clothing and shrouds, shovels and hoes to replace broken ones. And when, in summer, the merry time of Saint John's Day came and the rain let up, he would go with all the people to Higuerote to bathe the saint and get him drunk and then to bathe everybody and everything—people, weapons, work tools—and to sing and toast the fertility of the women and the land, and there was no scarcity of revelers who thought they saw the dove of the Holy Ghost crossing the broad sky, descending over them to heal illnesses and sins, to ward off sores, tumors, smallpox, syphilis, tetanus, poisonous bites, machete cuts, and the evil eye. He was the first to pay a call on someone who was ill or a woman having difficulty in childbirth, and he was the only one who dared approach the isolation house, where those with incurable and contagious diseases were all crowded in. He would be quite upset by the lieutenant's visits to impress upon him that as administrator he should put a stop to irregularities, because other landowners were complaining that blacks under his charge had been stealing fruit, or, if not that, the lieutenant would want him to look into concerns that his honor the parish priest had about the free mulattoes living in sin with slave women and would demand that he see that they were not missing at curfew, would further demand that he proscribe the practice and place them under arrest; and if his honor the priest didn't appear in person to object on this count, he would about the paltry attendance of blacks at Sunday services, because Julián's lack of vigilance in that regard went against the wishes of the king for them to be educated in Christian doctrine and according to the Holy Gospels. Julián Cayetano would close his ears to the recommendations; his only interest was that the sacks had been properly counted, that there hadn't been a decrease in the harvest, and that the underbrush was cleared on schedule. Very few blacks on the plantation held any rancor toward him. There was one, however, whose name would put him into a sweat: Ceferino. Ever since Ceferino went to the outlaw group, Julián Cayetano hadn't had a peaceful night's sleep; he had punished that one brutally, making his back bleed, leaving him in the stocks for days on cassava and water, making him walk in leg irons and kneel before him howling with pain. Ceferino had run away when war broke out, and no one in the village had seen him again, though a peasant said he'd been recognized in Tacarigua. Someone heard he was organizing a rebel faction near Caucagua, another that he'd been spotted near Capaya, but what was certain was that no one could be sure of the exact place where he could be found, much less confirm that he'd died. Julián Cayetano never overcame the fear of seeing him running half-naked, teeth gleaming in the night, looking to give his former tormentor a well-aimed blow, to make his head roll with the blade of his machete. Ceferino was always lying in ambush for him, never forgiving a single one of the lashes, a solitary drop of blood, waiting for the day of Julián Cayetano's infirmity so he could take death's opportunity away and give himself that pleasure; Julián Cayetano would have liked to die first, so that Ceferino's only vengeance, when he came, would be to piss on his grave.

Since more momentous events had put a halt to his functions as administrator, Julián Cayetano dedicated a good part of his time to the care of the church and his duties as a senior brother in the confraternity of the Blessed Sacrament, and it wasn't strange to see him with his wife, Juana Solórzano, bringing out the children who would go in there to play, he driving off the goats that were sleeping on the altar or she sweeping away their excrement so the congregants could hear mass with dignity, or chasing out the pigs with a whip, and one time she had all she could handle in struggling with a mule who balked at leaving the holy place, then bolted out of the church with the altar-cloths in its mouth, eating them as if they were fodder, and kicking over the altar-stone and candlesticks. In the sacristy he'd kept the things he was able to salvage from the ruins of the plantation house, and he would be able to list them from memory when someone came to reclaim them: a small trunk inlaid with mother-of-pearl; a cedar chest with its lock intact, but lacking the key; an image of Our Lady of Mount Carmel a yard-and-a-half high, missing the hands; a yacca-wood bed, with lathe-turned posts but no hangings; a damaged leather chair and three cowhide stools, two in good shape, one missing a leg. He only kept for himself, because he was sure Francisco would have given them to him, some things he considered of questionable value: five Talavera china bowls, seven glazed dishes, and a cedar wardrobe—short one drawer, which Juana Solórzano had given to Daría. The spoils from others that constituted their wealth, dishes and bowls he never used and a wardrobe he would only allow to be touched when it was dusted—remembrances of when Francisco had inherited the plantation from my son Nicolás and had promised Julián Cayetano that after fifteen years he would be owner of a small twenty-acre spread as payment for his work.

Who would have thought in 1802—how could Julián Cayetano have imagined that we were going to declare war on the King of Spain? Who could have told him at that time that Francisco, far from being the owner of the richest plantation in Barlovento, would be changed into a corpse on horseback; who could have anticipated all that when he ordered Daría to move to Caracas to be wet nurse for the child expected by Doña Isabel and Don Francisco, the latter already dust by the side of the road, and who could have foreseen that two years later Daría would knock at the door of his house and fall into the arms of her sister, Juana Solórzano? For several days they looked after Isabel's tiny body, which was giving off blood and green vomit, and Juana administered little sips of cinnamon water until the fever broke and the little girl recovered and grew up alongside Daría and the children that she was having. No one, not God Himself, could have envisioned so many things happening so fast. And so Isabel, the daughter of my grandson Francisco, was reared in the shade of cacao.

Time was passing; we were winning the war, Alejandro, but I was despairing as to whether that little girl would ever come back, it seemed to me then that she would die the way she'd been born, in solitude and silence, and that only my memory would record her existence. In a warped and battered drawer that her sister Juana Solórzano had given her, a relic of the old wardrobe from the plantation house, Daría kept the last threads of the cloak she wore that July 7, 1814, a date lost now in the smoke and dust of war; she'd preserved these rags for the future—as evidence, as proof, as a keepsake of the legitimacy of her act. All that remained of that fateful leap was those shreds of cloth and the tiny slip of a girl who was living with her, surrounded by three of Daría's own children—hers and Ceferino's some said, the mulatto Juan de Dios's according to others; but in the end it didn't matter to anyone, they were blacks born of her slave womb, and someday someone would come to claim them, would come to rebuild the demolished house and once more start cultivating the cacao groves, which were still harvested from time to time, for their own benefit, by those who had remained in Curiepe; someday, perhaps, Ceferino would also return, or maybe he too was a shade adrift in the forest and his bones were blanching in the sun and his amputated hands were scrabbling under the ground. Daría knew without being told that Doña Isabel had died, and Juan Bautista and Francisquito too, she knew they hadn't reached Barcelona and that even if they had they would have perished. Her fear of punishment for her act of rebellion, for the decision without consultation, had been subsiding, and she was sure that when her mistress awoke and saw that Daría had fled with the infant, she'd understood the act and had thanked her from heaven. Daría waited in vain for someone to come from Caracas to reclaim Isabel, and after ten years passed in silence, she feared that no one would ever come. The mule drivers who very sporadically brought and took away goods said Caracas was nothing but a wasteland, and Daría was afraid that Fray Antonio had disappeared too. If he had died, who would believe her, a slave, who said she'd saved the daughter of Don Francisco Martínez de Villegas? She remembered Doña Isabel's words in the cart: "If I die, take care of her, because I haven't got anyone else left in the world." Daría could not in her heart distinguish Isabel from her own children, and the idea of giving her up was a torment; if God had wished for her to rescue the child, maybe it was because she was to keep Isabel forever— returning her to what seemed to be a void struck Daría as impossible, unbearable. Still, when in 1824 the announcement came that General

Bolívar had defeated the Spaniards, Daría understood that, after ten years, the time had come. She made a small roll of clothes, sold the balance of her small crop, and asked Julián Cayetano to find a mule driver for her because she was going to Caracas to return the girl. And one morning she told Isabel to get dressed quickly, and during all the days of the trip, riding in a cart among sacks of cacao, Daría explained her plans and consoled the tears of the child, who refused to accept this incomprehensible separation.

Daría, squeezing in her hands the remains of the open-weave cloak that only a slave woman in an important house could have worn, blurted out her story to Fray Antonio, who was disconcerted by the presence of this black woman and a white girl who'd knocked at the door of the monastery of San Francisco one day. His eyes bleary and tiny behind his wrinkles, his hair white and sparse, looking in his surplice like a slim blue post bent over from weariness, he listened to Daría's plea: "You remember, Father, don't you remember? It's Daría, Doña Isabel's slave. I've come back with my little girl; this is the daughter of Doña Isabel and Don Francisco, may they be in heaven. I was in Curiepe. I ran away with her when we were going through the woods. I took her to the plantation. You have to tell them, Father, because they won't believe me. Say hello to Father, child, he's the one who threw water on you. Remember, Father, don't you remember? You have to write it down because they'll all believe you, sir, write it nice and clear that she's the child of Doña Isabel and Don Francisco."

All my bones were shaking, Alejandro, while Fray Antonio questioned Daría, trying to find out if she was lying, setting traps to catch her in a contradiction, searching in her eyes and her voice for the certainty of the truth; but her tale was as clean as a January sky and as clear and cool as a river coming down off the mountain, and he believed her. Here it is, I've kept the document, the proof that our lineage hasn't been snapped off, that history hasn't split us in two, that a girl of twelve, shut up in a convent for indigent children, for those without a stipend, is waiting there for the day of her majority or matrimony, and that she's the thread of continuity and survives us. Write, scribe, Fray Antonio's testimony:

I, Antonio González, friar of the monastery of San Francisco in this city of Caracas, swear that on July 20, 1812, I did baptize and place oil and chrism on a girl named Isabel Francisca María de la Purificación in the house of her parents, Francisco Martínez de Villegas and Isabel Madriz, deceased, and as the cathedral had been damaged by the recent earthquake, I recorded the baptism in the baptismal book of the parish of Altagracia, but those books were lost in the destruction of the war. I now attest that there has come to this monastery a slave by the name of Daría, belonging to the Martínez de Villegas family, with a white girl, age twelve, who has been under her care, and I am of the belief that this is the selfsame child that I baptized on her day of birth and that today, May 23, 1824, I place under my guardianship in the School for Poor Girls.

When Isabel crossed the threshold of the school, Daría ran off, fleeing the cries that kept resounding in her ears and the arms that wouldn't let go of her. But that pain was necessary, Alejandro, so Isabel could be restored to her proper status. Daría went back to Curiepe in a cart going inland; she lay on empty sacks, looking at the patterns of the clouds as they dissolved in the clear space only to cluster together again later, foreshadowing a rainstorm, and as she was getting soaked through and was returning to her house of mud and palm leaves, to her shack, to her broken drawer, to her work, to her own children, to sit at the door with the other women and watch the sunset, she hoped that someday she would hear of Isabel again. She would fill with joy when, once a year, a carter would deliver a letter and she would run to Julián Cayetano's small farm for him to read it to her:

Dearest Daría, it pains me so much to be here and not know anything about you or Venancio, Miguel, and Josefina. Tell them to behave themselves. I am learning a lot of things and the teachers are nice to me but I feel so alone. Fray Antonio comes to visit me on Sundays but he's gotten so old and he falls asleep during his visits. He tells me that before he dies he wants to do his duty by me and find me a husband, but there are so few young men who've survived the war. He says that I need a husband in order to get back my lands, which are many and

have all been taken over. How are you? If you get sick, come to Cara-
cas, because there are doctors who will cure you. Tell Julián to write a
few lines for you so I can know about you and how you are. Hugs and
kisses, Isabel.

And then she made Julián Cayetano write:

To my child Isabel. I am well and the little ones too. Pay attention to
Fray Antonio because he knows a lot of things. We've had a good crop
of bananas and I've done well selling them. Keep well and I'm well
here. Daría.

So much time had passed during which the plantation existed in
name only that Julián Cayetano couldn't believe it when they came
to tell him on his farm that some gentlemen from Caracas were there.
Breathless from running, he passed the row of houses shouting "The
owners are here, the owners have come back," and he reached the
front of the church, where four men—three in civilian clothes, their
shirt fronts sweaty under their frock coats, and one in military uniform—had set up an improvised table. People crowded around the
strangers and listened in silence to his honor the judge, who read a
long document in which it was established that La Trinidad plantation, located in the valley of Curiepe, two leagues above Cape Codera on Higuerote Cove, belonged to the holdings of Isabel Francisca
Martínez Madriz, wife of José Manuel Blanco, citizen and resident of
Caracas and twenty-three years of age, Doña Isabel having inherited
it from her father, Francisco Martínez de Villegas, and the latter from
Nicolás Martínez de Villegas, and the latter from his parents, who established it by royal grant (you and I, Alejandro); and that Don José
Manuel Blanco was coming to work it again and wanted to alert his
servants that they should not recognize as owner anyone who might
arrive with such a fancy, because the court had decreed the legitimacy
of his wife's rights. Furthermore, the lieutenant of the jurisdiction of
Capaya explained that he had orders from the government to remove
from the premises anyone who was not a slave or employee there, and
his honor the judge reminded them that General Páez had decreed
that slaves and peasants be held on the land and that those slaves who

wished to purchase their freedom should give half of their cost to the Council of Manumission, who would turn it over to their owners with the other half.

José Manuel Blanco called Julián Cayetano, confirmed him as administrator, and asked him to come forward to the scribe's table to provide an inventory of slaves and possessions that remained, and to list the births that had taken place. Julián Cayetano, taking off his hat, recited: "Many have died, and others have run off; those still here are Juan de Dios, mulatto, aged forty; Gregorio Taumaturgo, dark black, twenty-two; Basilio, sixty-one, sick with tetanus; Juana Antonia, fifty, Basilio's wife; Faustino Farfán, eighteen, with a bad leg; María Reyes, twenty-eight, Faustino's wife, and their two infant sons, Nepomuceno and Pascual; José Eladio, free mulatto, thirty-one, missing three fingers on one hand, and his sisters—María Trinidad, twenty, who gave birth to a dead son a while back, and Blasina, no births; Marcos, black, forty-two, missing an eye, and his son José Isabel, fourteen, whose wife ran away on him; Daría, black, forty-five, and her three children, Venancio, sixteen, Miguel, fourteen, and Josefina, eleven; and, at your service, Julián Cayetano, fifty-two, and my wife, Juana Solórzano, black slave, sister of the Daría just mentioned, and a son we have, born six months ago, Andrés Cayetano. Of the remaining possessions, the house, as you can see, was burned, all that's left is the brick floor and a wall or two, and I've kept in the church the other things that were saved, and there aren't many."

While José Manuel Blanco and the judge gathered up the writings from the table and conferred with each other, Julián Cayetano waited, hat in hand, to approach: here at last was the moment of promises. He had a long talk with José Manuel, and the scribe jotted down his request as follows:

I respectfully request from your excellency a letter of freedom in the name of Juana Solórzano, who is my legal wife, as stated in the parish records, and in that of my son, Andrés Cayetano, six months old, for which I submit 280 pesos for the mother and 50 for the child; and, furthermore, I explain that not having been able during these years because of the absence of the legal owners to establish before a scribe the wishes of my former master, Don Francisco Martínez de Villegas (whom God keep in his glory), who graciously freed me, I now ask that there be recognized for me in a registry document the ownership of a small plantation of twenty acres of trees, bordered on the east by the lowlands of Aguasal, on the west by the trail that comes out at the bridge, on the north by the San José plantation, and on the south by the highway to Higuerote—which homestead, as recompense for fifteen years of work as administrator of La Trinidad plantation, he promised me in the year 1802, and more than fifteen years have passed because at this date they number thirty-three.

They signed, and José Manuel had Daría summoned. Down the street came a woman followed by two boys and a little girl. "Isabel is waiting for you in Caracas," José Manuel told her; "I didn't want to bring her, so she wouldn't have to undergo the hardships of the trip, but she told me very firmly not to return without you, and for you to bring your children or leave them on the plantation, whichever suits you best. This is for you." He handed her her certificate of freedom. Amid the murmurs of the dispersing crowd, Daría listened to his words, and then went back home with the document in hand. Darkness was falling over the village, and she lighted some candles. She spent the whole night in discussion with her sons, and at daylight the calls of Julián Cayetano and Juana Solórzano found them still awake. "Daría, Don José Manuel says to hurry up, they're leaving." Daría hugged them, comforted her sister, who was crying, and kissed her sons. "I'm going to Caracas, and I'm taking Josefina," she said. "I'm leaving the two boys so they can work with you." Running, she caught up with José Manuel's carts as they were entering the road. When they disappeared from view, Julián Cayetano went back to his house, sat in the doorway, poured himself a mug of cane liquor, and said to his wife: "Juana Solórzano, I'm a citizen. I was born the slave of Don Nicolás, was freed by Don Francisco. I can read and write, I'm a married man, and now I have a useful skill and I'm a landowner; when the government holds elections I'll be able to vote. Have a drink with me, black girl, because that little bugger of yours is going to be a citizen too."

And here I am, Alejandro, haunting the nooks and alcoves of my house on the corner of San Jacinto, happy to see that they've cleaned the stains and painted the walls, looking at its new curtains and the mosaics all back in place, delighted to hear the water gurgling up out of the well once more and dancing in the courtyard fountain, pleased to take my ease in the shade of the guava tree and to bask in the half-light that comes from my porchways. Despite all the events and calamities, here I am searching for my titles, stooped over, rummaging in chests, climbing up to examine the tops of wardrobes in this house that Isabel has filled with children again. Here I am, Juan del Rosario, in spite of my spite. I've come to the end of the war we started to watch how Isabel is sifting and reviving the ashes of what once was ours. I've suffered twenty-five years of contemplating my ruined groves, twenty-five years of losses and abandonments, of arson and looting, of flights and revolts, twenty-five years of burying my corpses, and now, in 1835, out of ten children I'm left with a single little girl. Twenty-five years of waiting until, after three years of litigation for its rights, José Manuel Blanco arrived to reclaim my plantation. This really is funny, my houseboy and my freedman; three years of wrangling to make them believe the word of Fray Antonio, of battling impostors who say they're my relatives and heirs; three years of confrontations with those who've called themselves creditors of the republic—speculators who took the land in trust from fraudulent owners, last-minute patriots who usurped it, soldiers without pensions who claimed it as booty, decorated colonels whom it suited to settle there, doing reckless cutting in order to carve out a few acres for themselves—and it will take another twenty-five years to pay the interest of the usurers. The plantation's splendor will never return; never again will the aroma of cacao envelop my possessions, never again will the carpet of beans form a road so long that it seems to me as if it might reach around the world. Write, scribe: I am a creditor of the republic; I award myself this honor and this disillusion.

PART TWO

1846–1935

DOÑA INÉS AMONG LIBERALS

(1846–1899)

They invented liberalism, Alejandro, it was invented by a gentleman named Antonio Leocadio Guzmán, the son of a sergeant in the queen's grenadiers who happened to marry a cousin of General Bolívar. And the world isn't what it used to be; so many changes have taken place that I don't understand it anymore. Now they're calling us oligarchs and themselves liberals. What's the difference? I don't know, Alejandro, I haven't got the mind to grasp it; you know I'm an uneducated woman who only learned how to read and scribble a few clumsy bits, all my writing has been done by scribes, and I never held in my hands more than two or three of the books in my father's library: a vocabulary by Nebrija, the *Qualities and Death of the Glorious Patriarch Saint Joseph,* a volume by a certain Cristóbal Lozano on *The Loneliness of Life and the Disillusionment of the World,* and you can stop counting there. It wasn't my mission to fathom the politics of men, but to keep an eye on the work of my slaves, tend to my ten children, perpetuate my line and give it roots in this province, preserve my heritage, watch over my legitimate holdings, and defend my purity of blood; so how can you come around asking me what liberals are? I can tell you that all they've done is dream up promises, and in that they outstrip the ones who came before. This disputed land, Alejandro, was the first false promise. And you're to blame, too, you promised Juan del Rosario, your misbegotten son, a tract you had left over because it wasn't usable and hadn't been cleared, and you already know the years of ink and litigation it's cost me to make sure that promise was in vain. You inherited the habit of promising things that our grandparents passed on to you; other people were also promised things—adventurers, profiteers, the ones who came to load themselves down with glory and with gold and who found only a cursed and bedeviled land. During the war this country was a grab bag of promises, and afterward there wasn't a person who didn't feel he deserved his recompense, and came to collect it in the rubble . . . and what did they find? More promises. In the aftermath, since General Bolívar—having fallen sick, and sadder than a cemetery cypress because there was no way of governing in this wild spree—went to Colombia, there's been a torrent of rallying cries, slogans, mutinies, mobs, insurrections, uprisings, and disturbances, and all that's happened seems to me to be nothing but indescribable chaos and agitation. There's also been a deluge of books, pamphlets, magazines, and newspapers, and I've searched in them for what learned people have to offer me, an ignorant woman, as an explanation of this commotion; but neither in the *Notes for the True History of the Revolution of March 1858,* nor in the editorials in *El Sol de la Justicia* or *El Eco del Pueblo,* to mention only a few, have I discovered anything. I even tried to understand the *Statement Presented by the Liberal Meeting of Caracas to All Liberal Men and Circles of Venezuela,* and nothing there either. I've seen that fellow who had more than ten peasants among his counselors rise to the top, and a long list of generals whose names it would be impossible for me to remember ascend, decline, and die. I've seen the ghosts of landowners killed in the fighting, some by the government, others by the opposition, seen former slaves joining forces in guerrilla bands to slaughter landowners, seen landowners recruiting former slaves to murder other landowners, seen former slaves named leaders of ragtag armies and promoted to colonel, seen popular leaders inciting peasants to rise up and kill landowners, and seen peasants converted into landowners, after which they dubbed themselves generals to justify their campaigns to slay popular leaders. I've seen villages, churches, and prairies burned, water for cattle poisoned, statues knocked down, deaths from cholera and malaria, cheering for generals and then a call for their heads, the alternation of conservatives and federalists in seven-year, five-year, two-year elections, acclamations and removals, monuments erected and blown up, a surge of legalist, continuist, legitimist, vindicating, liberating, restoring, blue, yellow, and every other color revolutions, and, I repeat, I haven't understood a thing. Only that slavery was abolished when there were no longer any slaves because that wartime promise was not fulfilled until the middle of the century.

What's cacao selling for? Idiot, I'm trying to explain that the country is falling into anarchy, and you wake up asking nonsense like that. When José Manuel Blanco, the husband of our great-granddaughter Isabel, went back to Curiepe to set up the plantation again, I thought things were back on track, but what use now is the document that attests to his rights to the plantation? One more piece of paper to wipe my ass with, more parchment to chase away rats with, more manuscripts to cover my bones and fill my stinking ragbag. Copy, scribe; in 1834 the court orders:

> Don José Manuel Blanco, legal spouse of Doña Isabel Martínez Madriz, has presented proofs that said Isabel Martínez is the legitimate daughter of Francisco Martínez de Villegas, deceased, former owner of La Trinidad plantation, located in the vicinity of Curiepe, and thus is affirmed in a registry document that the property in its entirety belongs to her as his only heir.

Do you see, Juan del Rosario? They found in my favor again; our people rebuilt the foundations, replanted the groves, and when the trees began to grow, Alejandro, the liberal wind roared like a hurricane across my lands and the cacao leaves were scattered in the air. They burned the plantation house down again, do you hear me? They burned the trees again and destroyed the plantings. Why didn't I call the governor to send some lieutenant to mete out justice? Now, how thickheaded can you be? Do you think we're still in the times of Portales y Meneses, when all you had to do was cross the street, don your tricorn hat, and knock on the door of government house? Haven't I been telling you that there aren't any governors to give orders or lieutenants to execute them or slaves to obey them? Nor are there any courts to read my briefs; justice is taken into a person's own hand, and I have no hands.

Haven't you heard of Ezequiel Zamora, a tavernkeeper from Villa de Cura, a redhead, and his people, threatening to mount an assault on Caracas and to kill all whites, all the rich, and all those who know how to read? Haven't you heard his cry of *Free Land and Free Men?* Well, that's funny, because in 1846 his voice brought half the republic to its feet, and like a river overflowing its banks, thousands of poor people spread over the plains, with ragamuffins joining them in every village, every settlement all up and down the country, making up not one but hundreds of vagrant armies. A handful of them, an offshoot armed with lances, machetes, shotguns, and hoes, headed for the coast, going into the Capaya mountains, and they came upon my plantation. How could they help finding it, since they were under the command of the former slave Ceferino? How could Ceferino not know the path to my plantation, since he'd been born on it, since he still bore the mark of the irons Julián Cayetano had put on his ankles? He was coming to fulfill his vow that one day he'd see Julián Cayetano at his feet. I can understand *him,* Alejandro, because I, too, know how to store up hate. I, too, know how to bide time; I can see Ceferino saving himself for that dark day in 1846 when the antislavery insurrection that was pumped up by the stupid preaching and speeches of that pen-pusher Antonio Leocadio permitted him to reach the land where he'd been born, to nose around the groves he'd planted once, feel the softness of the air, hear from afar the singing of the blacks at night, breathe in the smell of Julián Cayetano's blood, and then, at last, to exact vengeance.

Hearing the cries of the workers as they tried to defend themselves, Julián Cayetano came out, unaware, and he fell right there by the breezeway of the plantation house. There lay his face, his forehead split by a machete blow, in a welter of blood that soaked his open shirt and his pants, his machete fallen by his side, before the twelve-year-old eyes of his son Andrés Cayetano and the interminable weeping and wailing of the former slave Juana Solórzano, who threw herself onto his inert body, trying to staunch with some rags the blood that was pouring out. Moments later José Manuel Blanco, unarmed, was brought down by a lance. Then Ceferino's confederates threw torches onto the house, smashed the furniture, tossed the papers kept in the office into the air, emptied the wardrobes, ground pieces of mirrors into the floor. They set fire to the kitchen and destroyed ladles, pots, stove, work tools, brick flooring, the woodwork of the porch, roof tiles, adobe walls, jugs, grindstone—and it was all one great funeral pyre that kept burning long after they had disappeared into the woods again. The women—who had hidden, trembling on their knees—and the surviving workers helped pick up the corpses, and right there, a few steps from what had been the plantation house, they buried José Manuel Blanco and Julián Cayetano.

Are you silent? Haven't you anything to say to me? And you, Juan del Rosario, are you laughing now? Can't you understand why blacks are killing blacks? Because there's too much hate stored up and choked back for anyone to know where it's come from or where it might go. You're thinking it's time for me to be quiet, and that I should burn my papers, too, along with extinguishing my voice, because there's no reason for me to keep pawing through my title deeds anymore. Well, that's not the way it is; I've got to stay here, cached in the cave that's my room now, my fleshless bones draped with the tatters from my linen sheets, so I can be with my great-granddaughter Isabel and see the day when Juana Solórzano appeared in Caracas, dressed all in black, black skirt and blouse, black kerchief tied around her head, holding the hand of her twelve-year-old son, to bring Isabel the news that their husbands' ashes had been buried side by side and that the plantation was abandoned because the workers who'd survived had taken to the woods. I have to continue talking so that you'll know how she sold off half of my four-windowed house, how she gathered her daughters together to make cakes and candy to sell for public charity, and how she looked for husbands for them and a tutor for her son, José Francisco, who'd just been born. I must stay with her until her death in her destiny as a poor, solitary, worn-out widow, she who'd been a little girl brought back to life from among the dead. I must watch her going with Daría to the market and haggling over the price of vegetables, must watch the two of them sitting in the coolness of the courtyard in the evening mending clothes while Isabel's eldest daughter gives piano lessons to more favored girls. Don't think I'm surprised by her poverty, Alejandro, or that it humiliates me—this is a city of poor people, and fifty years after the earthquake of 1812 the rubble still hasn't been cleared, the nights are unilluminated and the few coaches splatter the mud when it rains—but don't think, either, that I've forgotten that I own and possess some land that's two leagues from Cape Codera, on Higuerote Cove; to keep on hoping is simply my profession.

And now I will dictate the story of Andrés Cayetano, the life of a small-time cacao-gatherer who stayed on in Curiepe with his mother, Juana Solórzano, to cultivate the twenty acres of trees that my grandson Francisco promised his father as payment for his work as administrator. Hear me well, Alejandro, because it's a story that involves you. I'll start it in 1859, during a winter that brought a river flood that was long remembered.

When Andrés Cayetano kicked open the door of the church, the goats clustered under the altar gave a start, a pig grunted, and the drunkard who'd taken refuge from the flood and was sleeping on the altar snored on. Andrés Cayetano went over, jumping across the puddles of water, and with his sandal swept away the excrement the goats had left. *This is nothing but a jungle fit for snakes,* he thought. The chairs and the few remaining benches were floating; the mud was up to the niches of the Virgin of Altagracia and Saint Joseph. In water up to his knees, he waded into the sacristy; from the cabinet he took the candlesticks, the cross used in processions, a cape of silver and gold with thin fringes, and a few yards of silk satin for the ceremonial hoods, which were soaked through. *This is nothing but a mudhole,* he thought again. He could see his father come out of the church wearing a purple tunic and carrying a candle as head brother of the confraternity, and behind him the table on which the bearers were carrying the image of Jesus on the Mount of Olives; he saw the procession marching slowly and stopping at the first corner; the musicians played, and then the parade resumed its pace, pausing at every turn until they went all through the village. He saw his father put the images away, dance and recite poetry, drink and sing until he fell down, overcome by sleep; he heard him say, You've got more than ten thousand trees, when I die you'll have your little plantation there, your mama's old now and you were the only one born, defend that land that cost me a lifetime to get. There are more than ten thousand trees, Andrés Cayetano, look on them as if they were your children, learn to recognize them, run your hand over them until you learn to say *This tree is mine.*

This is nothing but ruin, Andrés Cayetano thought one more time.

It had rained for a week without surcease—growing stronger, half letting up, pouring out of the sky again. The village was a phantom place of muck, a dark blur in the middle of the woods, and the mud-coated men fought against the wrathful current. The river overflowed its banks and wiped out everything it found in its path, filling every rill or hollow and leaving ponds everywhere. It dragged along with it fenceposts, earth, stones, pieces of houses, animals, children. For two days Andrés Cayetano waded alongside the others, searching for the bodies of his children; some corpses appeared, but not his. He left the church, went back home empty-handed, and told his wife: "Nothing." He rolled up his drenched pant legs, and his wife wordlessly watched him take out two clean pairs of pants, cotton underwear, three shirts, and some boots, watched him hitch his machete to his waist and clean his shotgun. From a drawer in his father's cedar wardrobe he withdrew several coins, counted them, and laid half on his wife's skirt. He went out and threw a blanket on the horse. His mother, Juana Solórzano, heard the animal whinny and came to the door: "Your papa planted them many times," she said; "the seedlings can be planted after winter passes." Andrés Cayetano fastened the shotgun to the saddle and said, "I'm never going to plant again; see if you can get some money for masses out of them," and from astride his horse he shouted, "Keep Papa's things for me, the wardrobe and the plates!"

He dug in his heels and went off at a half-trot, disappearing into a dust cloud, going for days, killing birds and limpets for food, sleeping in the open at night, crossing plains, hiding from guerrilla bands when he heard war whoops and gunfire. In every village he passed it was the same, some leader had risen in revolt and recruited men to follow him; it was 1859, and the federalists had gone to war against the conservatives. The whole land seemed equally inhospitable to him, and it had been two weeks since he left Curiepe, meandering with no particular direction in mind.

In the distance he caught sight of a group of houses, and he headed the animal, which was goaded by thirst, that way; it was a tiny settlement, forlorn on the plains; on its dry dirt square there was only one business open, and a huge rain tree provided the only shade. He went into the tavern and asked for a glass of cane liquor from the child who was serving the few customers. He discovered that the boy was the son of the washerwoman on the ranch, who lived with the foreman, and that rebels had killed the owner not long before. And that was how he came to appear before the widow Doña Amparo Tejera de la Mota; she asked if he knew anything about herding cattle, and he answered no; if he had any experience in buying and selling cattle, and he answered no; if he would like to help the administrator in counting and sorting the cattle, paying workers their wages, and handling the sale of cheese, and he answered yes. Then the widow Amparo Tejera de la Mota read him a contract she drew up herself; it stated that his percentage of the earnings would be one-fifth, and she asked him to sign it, and when he printed *Andrés Cayetano* and stopped, he saw that Doña Amparo wanted more than his first names, so without thinking too much about it he improvised *Sánchez*. Andrés Cayetano Sánchez proved to the widow Amparo Tejera de la Mota that with time he could get to be her trusted assistant and confidant, and when the administrator died, he took over, having learned enough to drive the cattle and negotiate the best price with buyers, discuss what size scale to use and calculate the herd's weight in the pastures, carry merchandise for sale, and supervise the maintenance work; he even had the leisure to go to Valencia, wearing half-boots and a vest and watch chain, and court the daughter of Vicente Escobar, the proprietor of a small print shop, and marry her and start a family in the house he bought two blocks off the square once time had erased the flood and the search in the river for the corpses of the children he'd had with a woman who'd also been expunged from his memory. Memories that had only one day of resurrection, when, years later, he appeared in Curiepe with two laborers and a covered wagon and sought out the house where his mother, Juana Solórzano, was still sweeping, and she picked up her broom to gaze at him for a long time and say: "So you've come back." Andrés Cayetano took off his boots and lay down in the hammock, and when he awoke, Juana Solórzano brought him coffee and corn cakes, and then she made him go with her to where the plantation house had stood and where his father was buried, and the two of them prayed beside the wooden cross.

José Francisco Blanco, Isabel's son, was a grown man now and had pledged himself to start things moving at the plantation again—though he'd only recovered a small fraction, not even half of what La Trinidad had once been—but because of a lack of means with which to rebuild the house, when he came to Curiepe he would sleep in Juana Solórzano's, and as payment he would give her a few pesos, on which she lived. When Andrés Cayetano returned to Curiepe, his mother tried to coax him to wait for José Francisco, who would surely be appearing at any moment, because the beans were dry, and he would come with the carters to take them away; but Andrés Cayetano told her no, he'd only come to visit her and—this was why he'd brought a wagon and two workers—to retrieve his father's things, because now he had a house and a new wife. And when the workers had loaded the cedar wardrobe and the plates that had been stored away for years and never used, Juana Solórzano gave her son a long hug and said good-bye: "Now I know that I'll never see you again."

The wardrobe was enthroned in the parlor, and Griselda Escobar cleaned and carefully stowed away the five ceramic Talavera bowls and six glazed plates (one of the seven plates had, over the years, been broken); on its side she nailed up the picture of their wedding day, he with cravat and frock coat and she with silk bodice and a crown of orange blossoms; and, one year after another, she appended tintypes of the three girls that were born, whose fleeting existence was memorialized and extended only in those carved wooden frames. When Manuel Andrés Cayetano was born, Andrés told Griselda, "We're not going to put up a picture of this one because it's unlucky," and Manuel escaped the fevers that would be stirred up with the start of the rainy season, and the only one whose picture wasn't put up was the survivor, because Griselda Escobar died too, and Andrés alleviated his loneliness in afternoon palaver with the druggist, the civil chief, and the butcher, gathering in the tavern to review, like scholars thumbing through biblical texts, the deeds of Ezequiel Zamora and the stories about the revolutionary priest Simón Pedro, and to retell, with minimal changes of detail, how the guerrilla leader Espinoza, about to execute some oligarchs, had asked him if there might not be some liberals among them, and Father Simón had satisfied his scruples by saying, "Oh, shit, how can we tell in this darkness, just shoot and let Saint Peter sort them out"; or to be saddened by the glorious last years of General Pullido, a great leader of the revolution, who was left loony in his house with four colonnades in Barinas, with nothing else to do but toss crumbs to the pigeons. Manuel had a son, Dominguito, and Andrés Cayetano, old now, liked to show his grandson the books Griselda Escobar had inherited from her father's print shop, and he would comment about the illustrations and relate fragments of conversations with his friends, which were now considered national history: he especially relished telling the boy about the night when Ezequiel Zamora himself, General of the Sovereign People, had knocked at the door of Andrés's house, asking for refuge, and they'd spent several hours, all night, talking—a short time before the conservative oligarchs killed Zamora; or if it wasn't that, about Stubby Hernández's bravery, and even about Andrés's own when, more than once, he'd grabbed his pistol to go up against rebels who'd invaded the ranch to steal cattle. But in all his stories he omitted any memory that had to do with his life up to the age of twenty-four, with his life until 1858, which had been banished from his mind and only appeared when he was alone, staring at the ceiling, scratching the floor with his bare feet, lying in his hammock smoking, and he would, through the astonished eyes of the twelve-year-old he had been, again see the bloody face of Julián Cayetano. Andrés didn't like to remember, "because there's nothing good behind," he would say when Dominguito would ask: "Behind everything there are people who've gone away; behind everything there's one big cemetery, son, a long good-bye from people passing. When I die, you sell this house and start another life, far away from this village that's so small." He didn't like to tell his grandson things about his family, but once in a while he'd mention in passing that his father's name was Julián Cayetano and he'd been administrator of a cacao plantation in Barlovento, and that his mother, Juana Solórzano, had been a slave on the plantation, but that was so long ago, so very long ago, that not even he remembered: things lost in history. Then he would sink into his meditations and say, "Go out and play, Dominguito, leave me by myself, we old people like to be alone." Andrés Cayetano was very sad thinking about his grandson; he felt old, exhausted, and he couldn't find anyone to entrust him to when he died. He didn't know that Dominguito's destiny was to meet up with a general.

"Don't shoot him; that boy's all right."

Hair disheveled, eyes yellow with fear, barefoot, and clutching a weapon between his shirt and his chest, Dominguito crawls along the ground near the boots of the soldier aiming his rifle at him. The whole village gathers; it is rumored that the general's troops are going to kill a boy who was caught stealing chickens. The old men appear on the square, which at that hour of early afternoon is bursting with light; the women are hiding among the sandbox trees, and the children are waiting, frightened. It's been a long time since any rebels passed through, and they haven't killed anybody like *this,* in plain view of everyone. Ever since Manuel, Dominguito's father, had surprised Gregoria, the boy's mother, with another man, ever since then no crime had been recorded here. He gave it to them just like that, point-blank, and left the bed sodden with the pair's blood; then he shouldered his rifle and rode into the plains to serve with General Hernández. Responsible witnesses saw him leave the house, dragging his feet in his straw sandals, saw him put on his hat and then climb on a skinny horse and set off at a gallop, never to return, getting lost forever, not wanting to come back to the village even when dead. He was casting off his shame there, to be buried along with his victims, she with her naked breasts hanging out over her blouse and he with his member dangling from his fly; he hadn't even taken off his pants. Dirty whore.

Old Andrés Cayetano, without exchanging a word with his son, knew what had happened four doors down; he heard the shots, and he went out into the street to see Manuel mount his horse, and, not saying anything, he let his son go, and when the dust had settled he walked to the house and found the child crying in the yard, all alone and defenseless to stop the stray dogs that were licking his face; he was tied to a pole of the chicken pen by a rope that abraded his ankles as he tried to squirm loose. Andrés picked the child up in his arms and went back up the street and told old Rosa Margarita, "Give him a bath, he's all covered with dirt," and the old woman put him in a tub of sun-warmed water and scrubbed off the chicken shit clinging to his skin and dressed him in an old shirt, cutting the sleeves shorter; then she fried some plantains for him and set him in her own bed to sleep; when it was night the old man went out again and located the civil chief and told him, "Old friend, go take a look in my son's house, where the authorities are needed, and see what took place there in an evil hour." And he shut himself up for several days with old Rosa Margarita and the child, because he said that until the funeral was over he wouldn't open the door again, and so the retinue passed—it consisted of only a few women, relatives of Gregoria's, who came from her village to accompany her, and some children who ran behind to see if anyone would throw them alms, but nobody did—and none of the three saw it.

So Dominguito grew up with the two old people, and Andrés Cayetano, who only wanted to await death now, had a kind of second life, and he would walk the woods with the boy, and he taught him how to hunt with the shotgun he kept in the wardrobe; and since the school was so far away, in the morning Andrés would sit at the kitchen table and, while he had his coffee, would dictate sentences for Dominguito to write, and later he went to Valencia and bought a few books and more pencils and erasers, and they would spend the whole morning at lessons; in the afternoon they would go out to the square, and the old man would sit in the tavern for a while, and when he'd had a lot to drink, Dominguito would tug on his arm and lead him home, and that was how they lived, quite happy, and, above all, not mentioning anything that would remind them of the past. But there was no dearth of people who told Dominguito that his mother hadn't died in the hospital as he thought, and that it wasn't true that his papa had been killed fighting alongside Stubby Hernández, and they would laugh, and, along with the laughter, out would come the fact that his mama had died of something else, because though they were small and ignorant they knew the power of truth. Dominguito never questioned his grandfather, and only once did he ask Rosa Margarita to accompany him to the cemetery, and the two slunk out very timidly when the old man was sleeping his siesta; walking past the stones, they reached the niche, and Rosa Margarita took a handkerchief out of her skirt pocket and ran it over the stone to remove the dust, and Dominguito was able to read *Gregoria Luna* inscribed there and engrave the name in his memory, and, without tears or further comment, he said to Rosa Margarita that they'd visited her now and they'd better go before Grandfather woke up. Soundlessly they slipped into the house through the back way at the moment when the old man began calling them, but he never caught on to anything; they had dinner as always and said good night.

No one knew exactly where old Rosa Margarita had come from. She'd arrived at the house one day and never left. She would get up when it was still dark and dust the wardrobe, which still ruled its corner of the main room, would open its doors and stroke the valuable china cups that rested there as the survivors of a past prosperity— "Chinaware from Spain," the old man would say, "from where my papa had his little plantation." She would polish the portraits that hung on the wall, do a little sweeping with no great aim or order, certain that the dust would soon blanket the concrete floor again; she would run a rag over the table and chairs, then use the iron that smoked from the wick inside it, and prepare coffee before the old man arose. She always dressed in black, petticoat and blouse, and no one ever saw her hair or knew if she was bald, because she never removed the kerchief that was knotted tightly around her forehead, as taut as her yellow skin, which was like paper stretched over her protruding cheekbones; over her eyes, sunk in dark tunnels; and her thin lips, which rarely parted to show her few teeth. Her almost weightless body would float from the main room to the old man's bedroom, from the kitchen to her own quarters, some poorly joined planks by the backyard. Dominguito slept in a hammock in the main room, and from there he would watch her slip about, appear or disappear, with her acid old-woman smell and her stiff hands, flitting among objects or sometimes squatting with the agility of a young woman. Rosa Margarita never volunteered her age, and no one ever asked her. She would suddenly rise up out of the darkness, and her shadow would loom alongside the stove, but just as quickly she might be sitting in the backyard throwing corn to the chickens, or leaning over the washtub scouring clothes. She could cloister herself in her room for hours or wander through the village in the blazing sun, when all the houses had their doors closed and the only stragglers in the square were the dogs sleeping in the shade of the trees. She could spend days in an almost complete muteness or go through the entire morning babbling proverbs and gibberish—"What's the priest's is for the Church, what's the priest's is for the Church, what's the priest's is for the Church"—and she would only stop when Dominguito yelled at her, "Shut up, old woman, you're driving people crazy." "Crazy people, crazy people were the other people, crazy people are for the crazy house," she'd say, and then lapse into a peeved silence that would last for days or weeks. "There's no talking here," she would answer if the old man asked her about her taciturnity.

Dominguito didn't like sleeping with her; that's why, when he grew older, he asked his grandfather's permission to use the hammock in the main room, and Andrés told him he could, since everything there, which wasn't very much, would be his; the boy didn't like her smell of funeral flowers, didn't like to feel her birdlike bones under the black cloth, and if he only bent them in his hand they would crunch like a dried toad. He didn't like when she would laugh to herself or would sit in the yard and keep repeating, "How many chickens are there, how many chickens are left, how many chickens have died, more whorish than a hen, more whorish than a hen." He didn't like to hear her when she would shut herself inside her planks with a tub of water and splash around for a good while until she emerged the same black clothes and exuding the same rancid, acidic smell of a rotting plantain, which filled the whole house. He didn't like to think that old Rosa Margarita had been the only female presence he knew, and he didn't like to see, through the doorways of their houses, other children sitting around with young and pretty women, full-bodied mulatto women with hearty laughs; then he would run out, would sprint far off, and in the woods would lie down and look at the sky and the white clouds and fondle his member until he made it gush. He would spend hours there, watching the buzzards circle and musing: he would imagine his father in a uniform, his chest full of medals, lame in one leg because he'd been wounded in glorious battle, and General José Manuel Hernández called him by name and honored him in front of all the troops; his father rose to captain, to colonel, to general, and he would come back to the village and take Dominguito away, and the boy would gallop off on horseback with his father in front of everybody.

He'd rummaged all through the house, into the most remote corners, in search of a picture of his mother, but it had been in vain. Not in the wardrobe, not in the drawers of his grandfather's nightstand, not in the chinks between the shelves where he kept his clothes could he find any trace of that woman, who must, however, have existed. Once he got as far as his parents' former residence. The door was nailed shut with a crossbeam, just the way it had been for years; no one had ever wanted to buy the house, "People have their ways," his grandfather said when Dominguito asked, "Why don't you sell the other house? We could pick up a few pesos." By breaking down the door that opened onto the deserted backyard, he was able to get in without opening the windows, which he was reluctant to do for fear of being discovered. He pored over every inch without finding what he was looking for. The house was empty, denuded; dust covered the floor, and a weak light filtered in through the cracks; a solitary double bed occupied the center of the bedroom, but nowhere was there a trace, a single hint that could say anything about its former occupants. Dominguito left the house and fled into the woods to stretch out on the ground, and he imagined for himself a white woman wearing elegant silk skirts and an embroidered bodice, her hair in a stylish bun and with a fan in her hand, like the pictures in his grandfather's books.

He saw her get out of a horse-drawn carriage while a young soldier came forward to help her down.

When old Andrés Cayetano died, the boy wandered about through those woods without rhyme or reason, like a lost soul. He would go out at dusk and spend the night outside without old Rosa Margarita's being able to find him. She paced up and down the street, shouting, until people opened their windows and doused her with pots of cold water to make her be quiet. "Crazy old woman," they said. Sometimes he would sneak in the back door of a house at siesta time and carry off eggs or a chicken and, if seen, run into the woods, where they couldn't catch him; at other times he would drop in at the tavern, and his grandfather's old friends would take pity on him and invite him to have a drink, treat him like a man, and see if that would straighten him out. The civil chief had scolded him and warned that if he persisted in his vagrant ways, he would end up in jail. The priest, when he came every other month or so to say mass and perform baptisms, asked about Dominguito and promised he would find him work as a farmhand in order to make a man of him, but Dominguito promised them both that he would change, and then went back to his thieving forays. At night he would bar the doors and rifle through the drawers of the wardrobe, and he wouldn't let old Rosa Margarita in even to dust.

In that way he reached the age of fifteen in 1899, when General Cipriano Castro passed through, winning skirmishes and defeating his enemies on the way to Caracas, and the whole village was in a frenzy when they found out that the revolutionary troops were camping in the area on their triumphant march from the Andes. Dominguito watched the soldiers enter, heard the general read a libertarian proclamation on the square to the puzzled multitudes, and saw the people come forward with food and water for the troops' sustenance. Without giving it much thought, he went over to them and nosed around a bit until he found the right moment, grabbed a chicken by the neck, and ran off. A soldier spotted him and, moving quite rapidly, caught him, knocked him down, seized the chicken, and cursed him. Dominguito remained on the ground, looking at him blankly, and then he finally got up and walked slowly to his house, went into the main room, opened the wardrobe, took out the shotgun with which his grandfather had taught him how to hunt, and went back in search of the soldier. When he found him, he raised the weapon and shot but missed. Men grabbed him from behind and dragged him onto the square and left him lying on the ground; the soldier ran after and aimed his rifle at him. The general, having been informed of the disturbance, came out, and he approached Dominguito in person to ask for his version of what had happened, and Dominguito told him. Then the general turned toward his soldiers and commanded, "Don't shoot him; that boy's all right," and then he asked, "What's your name?"

"Domingo Sánchez at your service, General, sir."

And Don Cipriano ordered: "Get a mule and a bedroll for this boy; he's coming with me to Caracas."

Dominguito dressed as a soldier and left the village without even saying good-bye.

EPITAPH FOR GENERAL JOAQUÍN CRESPO

Did you see, Alejandro, that strapping young lad in hemp sandals and rolled-up cowboy pants as he slung on his shotgun and mounted the mule that Cipriano Castro gave him? Can't you see him prodding the animal with his toenails, ready for anything and following that sallow man from the Andes, who has the size and lechery of a monkey, as he pursues the Restoration? Can't you see him in the column of sixty coming from Táchira on their way to Caracas to inaugurate the century with the Andean dynasty? Liberalism didn't work out, Alejandro, and they had to invent dictatorship. The Andeans thought that instead of having so many generals that they sprang up like weeds and squabbled among themselves to see who was in charge, it would be better to decide on just one. Now they say that Cipriano Castro is the last of the liberals, and that under his power the fighting will come to an end; but it hasn't been his power that's brought us peace, it's been attrition, because with malaria and all the killing there is scarcely a man still standing, and they've conscripted so many, just like the little chicken bandit, and when they finished with the men they started drafting children, equipping them so that from a distance they'd look like full-fledged soldiers. I don't give a hoot for Cipriano Castro. I have a deep contempt for him, though I must confess that even I am amused by his impudence as I watch him take off his frock coat and, dancing a jig atop his desk, declare war on the Germans; but there's one thing I hate just as much as I do governors, and that's liberalism. And there's something I hate still more than liberalism in general, and it's Joaquín Crespo in particular. Rancors and animosities are jumbled in my memory; that's why when I saw Dominguito, the grandson of Andrés Cayetano, leap onto the back of a mule, changed into a soldier, I couldn't help remembering you, Joaquín Crespo. Didn't they spirit you off in the same way when a troop of rebels passed through your village and the leader, whoever he was, saw your strong figure and bold courage and took you away with him? From a raw peasant recruit you rose to be a general and entered Caracas in triumph—fortune smiled on you after you escaped your obscure origins—but sometimes the smile turns into a frown, and that's what I've been anticipating ever since June 5, 1884; since that day I've been waiting for April 17, 1898, to arrive, to see you encamped in Sabana de Arce, confident in your troops and your victory and patrolling up and down the plains looking for José Manuel Hernández, who had it in for you because he'd won the election and you, great liberal leader, cheated him out of it. Isn't that the way it was, Joaquín Crespo? Weren't you cheated too? Didn't you take refuge on your ranch in Totumo, gnawing at your liver in rage against Guzmán, a leader and comrade of yours, the Civilizing Autocrat, the Regenerator of the Nation, the Illustrious American, when he ousted you from power? Isn't it true that you got the idea to go along with Velutini and concoct an invasion from the Antilles, and that after being brought to the rotunda under arrest you slyly agreed to return to your lands, there to await a more opportune occasion to declare that your duty as a citizen, a liberal, and a soldier of the republic obliged you to start a revolution, and someone whispered in your ear that you should call it "legalist"? How did you inspire your peasants to be ready to die for legalism? Did you give them some of Ño'Leandro's tacamahac sap to drink, the potion prepared by your father, the witch doctor of Parapara de Ortiz—the drink that cures all ills, past and future? That tacamahac must really be good, Joaquín Crespo, for those starving peasants to get on their mules and put their lives at stake for that trick of legalism you invented so you could be master of the great plantation called Venezuela. That's why they flock after the liberal promise and follow you as they've followed and will follow so many others and are with you today: the day of your death.

I want to see you, Joaquín Crespo, I want to enjoy this moment when, in the silence of the plains, you prick your bumpkin ears and catch the sound of firing; your blood boils, gunpowder and the neighing of horses excite you—you're a brave man, nobody doubts that. You go tearing over the plains after Stubby Hernández without encountering him; the peasants admire him, venerate him, pray for him, and nobody gives you any information, all you've got to find him with are your ears and your nose. Finally you hear the shooting, your Colonel Elías Maduro has run into some fighting on the Carmelera ranch; you extend your gaze far out, dismount your mule, ask them to saddle your Peruvian horse, and there you go, your Panama hat and white cloak floating over your shoulders, in open country, crossing the weave of the plain. In the distance is Carmelera, and the soldiers shout to you, "They're in the grove, General." What a great moment, Joaquín Crespo! You're bursting with pleasure at this turn of events. "Let's give them a good fight right here," they say you told your second-in-command. You don't calculate the danger; prudence doesn't hold you back; you don't realize that your cloak billowing in the wind, your white horse galloping over patches of straw, your Herculean figure on a spurred animal in open country, are not likely to escape their notice; that would be quite a bit to ask of luck. Mad for glory, intoxicated by the odor of gunpowder, you approach the grove . . . and there they were, ready to ambush you. What soldier couldn't have thought it up? High in a tall rain tree, hidden in its foliage, Joaquín Crespo, were José Manuel Hernández's men, and before you could fire a shot, a bullet came down from the treetop and went in beneath your right shoulderblade and came out behind your right lung. And you writhed on the ground there, your tunic sopping with blood, your pants stained with earth; your Panama hat flew off, and your white cloak was trampled under the horses' hooves. The clash went on for several hours and—just look at the irony—your General Ramón Guerra defeated Hernández, routed his forces, and killed half of the seven hundred peasants he'd managed to recruit. You won the battle, Joaquín Crespo, but you'll never know it, and I'm waiting for you in Caracas, you fat-bellied, kinky-haired, fat-lipped, short-legged mulatto, waiting for you to arrive in triumph, dead, to tell you that your horse was left in the Carmelera grove alone, bucking under a rain tree. I'm waiting for you while your corpse sways in the bottom of a hammock strung between two horses. They've taken off your tunic and boots in order to lessen the weight of your inanimate body; your white shirt is soaked with blood that's already dried and begun to stink; your white pants are mud-smirched and your fly stained with urine; your face is ashen, and your eyes are closed, your men are withdrawing, sweating from the heat of the plains, and they carry you on foot to Acarigua in a stretcher, and you're already getting cold, it's ninety-eight degrees in the shade and you're frozen stiff. Your tunic with two holes is draped over the back of the horse, Joaquín Crespo, two singed holes that the bullet left, and hanging from the saddle are your boots and sword, and you're bobbing along in the hammock like a child, curled up and quiet, fast asleep and rocking to the canter of the horses. The doctors Capriles are assembled in Acarigua, but not to heal you, to open your belly rather. They're preparing the solutions and salts, washing the syringes; they're spreading a sheet over the mortician's table and readying pails, basins, and flasks to wash your entrails; they're cutting open your chest and your stomach, from top to bottom, like a cow's, in order to fill the thoracic and abdominal cavity with alcohol; they're removing the intestine to inject it and are steeping the stomach and bladder in preservatives; they're carefully bathing, one by one, all of your viscera, your orifices, and your skin. They're bleaching your organs, which turn whitish, yellowish, soft, like crumbling algae, and then they'll stain them to restore their col- oration and submerge them in clay-filtered water in glass jars. They're soaking your bones; they're going to remove the flesh and fat from them, boiling them, treating them with benzene until they're free of tissue, and then they'll stuff you with sawdust like an empty doll so you'll be firm and plump, the way you used to be, so they can put your tunic and pants back on. They're going to sew up all the gashes they've made, and in that way you'll be whole again, dressed in an immaculate glowing uniform, like a statue, and placed in a new coffin of wood and zinc that they're making so you can travel by train—a worm that rolls along, whistles, belches smoke, and goes at an unheard-of speed, much faster than horses and carriages. All of Europe has been crisscrossed by railroads for a long time now, but we're so poor that we travel by muleback. And nobody's interested in cacao anymore; now we sell coffee. That's why we're so poor, because we always produce things that are only good for a snack, and yet how elegant are the names the Europeans have given our trains: *The Quebrada Railway, Land, and Copper Company; The Guanta Railway, Harbor, and Coal Trust.* And do you know what your train is called, Joaquín Crespo? You're going to travel on *The South-Western of Venezuela Barquisimeto Railway.* But first they're going to transport you from Acarigua to Barquisimeto in the old-fashioned way, your casket on a cart, and when you reach Barquisimeto you'll find the military escort that is waiting in formation to place you in the railway car; and little by little, bouncing about, you'll see how much fun rail travel is. You're going from Barquisimeto to Tucacas. You'll have a look at the sea, Joaquín Crespo; there's the settlement of Tucacas, the planking of the pier, and the fishermen waving to you from among the mangrove swamps. Let yourself be carried off like a dazzled child listening to a story about swashbuckling pirates; there, a few steps from the beach, is Morgan's house with its shattered bay windows like empty eyes looking for the sea, the house where they say he used to stash treasure after his raids, and across from it the sailors are gathered, surprised at being spectators of such a sad event, they're lifting the coffin of General Joaquín Crespo to place it on the dock to wait for the warship that has been sent for you. You're going to sail the waters of the Caribbean until you reach the port of La Guaira, all that's left is to board the launch and cross the shallows up to the anchorage; see how clear the water is, how the coral seems to sway under the wake of the oars; enjoy it, there's no hurry, the ship won't leave without you, and neither will I, having sat on my window bench ever since June 5, 1884.

What happened on June 5, 1884? Oh, Alejandro, you don't know anything. What corner have you been hiding in all these years while I haven't stirred a single day from my house, where I've remained ever since the day of your death? Can this be my punishment, Juan del Rosario, for having ordered them to burn your village during the time of Portales? Could God have condemned me to search till infinity for the titles of possession without unearthing them? The deeds from 1663, Alejandro, the ones that Philip IV gave my father and that you confirmed. Can God have forgotten me, forsaken in this house forever, obliged to watch the destiny of my history, subjected to knowing about so many events without being able to take part in them? All I have today, May 1, 1898, is the joy of revenge. Today, Alejandro, I'm stationed at the window of my house on the corner of San Jacinto like an Arab by the door of his tent, waiting for the carcass of Joaquín Crespo to pass my door. You mean you don't know that Joaquín Crespo is our enemy? I'll explain it to you. When our great-great-grandson José Francisco Blanco returned to the ruined plantation, powerless, eaten alive by usurious debts, and restored a piece of it, an insignificant remnant of what once was our estate, he hacked away the underbrush again and replanted the groves, and when the trees were already full-grown and I seemed to be able to hear the rustling of their leaves from here and to enjoy the cool of their shade, the winds of progress whipped through and uprooted them. Joaquín Crespo swept through and wanted to play with trains. What did he do? He gave my lands to the Dutch so they could establish the *Carenero Railway and Navigation Company,* just the way you hear it; they were his lands, not mine, he told them, and to make it so all he had to do was issue a decree of expropriation and promise José Francisco that he would be indemnified. And I'm still waiting, Joaquín Crespo, today, as your funeral procession reaches Caracas, for you to settle accounts—to tell me how much you owe me and explain how it is that my lands are not mine but yours and that you can give them to anyone you please. How can you remain impassive, Alejandro? They've built a railroad, its rails slicing through my plantings; they've cut down my shade, they blight my harvest with the infernal smoke that this awful machine gives off, and my great-great-grandson José Francisco has no other course than to retire to Caracas in defeat and relinquish forever that plantation, which he now says he doesn't even want to remember. And your people are affected, Juan del Rosario, because the train's whistle shrieks through their farmland, too, and they've been set to digging ditches and moving rails and cars with the promise that the train will carry their harvest to the coast and they'll be a part of progress too. I hope the train has a wreck, Joaquín Crespo, I hope you never get to play with your cars again, I hope the forest gobbles up the track.

Listen, Alejandro, the ship has just dropped anchor in La Guaira. What a reception! They've designated a body of officers to render him military honors, and there are bugle flourishes while they unload the coffin and set it on a carriage drawn by four white horses that will take it to the railroad station; now they're going to climb the mountain, to ascend slowly over bridges and gullies. It's a long way, I never traveled it by train; right now I'd like to be a happy little girl dressed in lace and crinolines, looking out the coach windows to see the sea from up high, taking out a handkerchief to wave it in the distance. We never got on a train, Alejandro; we never had as much fun as that! What a pity that we weren't children of the century of progress and steam engines! We were like brother and sister, and I can hear our laughter when, playing blindman's buff, my sisters and I blindfolded you and spun you around; I can still remember when, on your tenth birthday, the pieces from the piñata flew off and I, so greedy to pick up my candy, was hit in the face, and you were upset and dropped the stick and your tears mingled with mine. How I wish we could feel the whirl of crossing that huge mountain together, going through tunnels and skirting precipices. In that way I could make up for my fear when my father made me a present of a mare, you lifted me up with your handsome arms and I clutched you about the waist, and together like that we took a long ride up the Camino de los Españoles. But I mustn't get lost in useless reveries now that I'm here on watch, sitting by the grillwork of my window waiting for the announced funeral cortege of General Joaquín Crespo, the Hero of Fulfilled Duty, senator in Congress, president of the state of Guárico, minister of war and navy, Chief of the General Staff of the States of the South, twice president of the republic, leader of the legalist revolution.

How distant, Joaquín Crespo, are the days when they sang you a Te Deum for the success of the Sacred National Cause; how lost is that moment in which you entered Caracas in victory! The heaviest rain in history was falling, it wet your uniform, the plumes on the horses, and your mustache, but you were unfazed; when they complained that you too were a continuist, you had a touch of humor, came up with the only joke known to be heard from you—you said, *On the day we entered, the downpour washed away all slogans.* Slogans, Alejandro, have been like slips of paper set out in the elements, but every one of them has had the allure of the tacamahac tree, promising the power to cure all ills; and since none of them has cured anything, the storm washes them away, but there's always someone to invent another. After they'd shouted *Free Land and Free Men, Down with Slavery, Long Live the Federation, Death to Whites and Those Who Can Read and Write,* along came Guzmán, who turned out to be enlightened, and he said *Long Live Regeneration*; and Crespo, a Legalist; and Castro, a Restorer, who proposed *New Men, New Ideals, and New Procedures*; and Gómez, a Rehabilitator, and he established *Union, Peace, and Work.* We've had no shortage of slogans; but sadly, it always rains, and—perhaps this is part of nature's wisdom—they're always washed away. The same way, Joaquín Crespo, that those days were washed away, the ones when they hung your portrait in the Club Paraíso and all Caracas society outdid one another in paying homage to the leader; the newspapers were full of fancy praise, and, so you wouldn't lose your habits of a plainsman, they offered you and Jacinta barbecues on plantations, and they pitched the pictures of your predecessor out the window, and you passed judgment on those who'd lost power. And the same thing keeps going on, Alejandro: it immediately rains, it always rains on that magnificent day when they make a triumphant entry, and the water flushes away the catchphrases. But a thousand years can pass, and never washed away for me will be the day when Joaquín Crespo arrived on the train from La Guaira and they carried him his house in Santa Inés to lie in state for a day and a night. Today is the great day when they put him on a gun-carriage drawn by two horses with black plumes, and his last parade through Caracas starts.

How sorry I am, Alejandro, not to be alive and able to enjoy how beautiful the city is! I had never thought it possible to see so much both by day and night. Caracas has such modern things now! A gas-light on every corner, not the darkness that scared me as a child and—though I learned to live with it—always made me feel afraid and alone when the last lamp was extinguished. Guzmán Blanco gave us the telephone, and it's no longer necessary to send a houseboy to inquire about the neighbors or to announce visits. The streets look cleaner, and there are carriages and horsecars driven by men in French-style uniforms. In fact, everything has been done up in Gallic style because Guzmán fancies himself Napoleon III, and as a consequence decided that his generals, his horses, and his city would look better if they wore the best Empire style. You'd get lost, Alejandro, if you tried to reach government house, tricorn hat on your head and staff in your hand, because they've knocked down the arcade of the market Ricardos built, and in the center of the square they've put up an equestrian statue of Bolívar that was brought from Germany, and it's surrounded by four forged-iron fountains; there are a lot of other squares, I can count them up to ten, and more than fifteen bridges, including the one erected in the time of Charles III. They built the Capitol on the site of the Conceptionist Sisters' convent. Do you remember how we used to buy bulls for the dead there? And on the ruins of the Merced convent there's the Plaza Falcón; over the vestiges of the charity hospital, Carabobo Park spreads out; where San Jacinto church used to be, a huge market's been set up, and dozens of vendors bring carts there to sell flowers, fruit, birds, and vegetables; and where San Pablo stood, an impressive theater has been built . . . but what I thank Guzmán most for is that at last they've removed the debris of the earthquake of 1812, and the cathedral clock strikes the hour at the proper time again. Oh, how I'd like to go out with a fan and gloves and my hair in ringlets, dressed in laces and wearing a bustle! You don't think it's right for women to venture out at night now? I never would have imagined that after six o'clock I would be able to leave my house and sit on a bench in the square to listen to a band concert, and that afterward you might take me by the arm to the opera or to a swanky ball to dance waltzes and polkas, or that in the morning I could take a walk without any slave women and go shopping in stores that import their clothing from Madrid and Paris, and without dirtying my shoes in the mud.

I must get back to the funeral cortege, which is passing the corner of La Torre now, and the wonderful moment is approaching when the gun-carriage with Joaquín Crespo's casket will go by the corner of San Jacinto, and from my window I will toss him a white carnation, yes, I'll throw him a flower so that the horses will trample it the way he trampled my possessions. They say that the lead horse, all alone and marking the step, is his Peruvian mount, and now it's passing Jesuitas, then Tienda Honda, and now they're in front of the Pantheon—the Pantheon, Alejandro, is the Church of the Holy Trinity, but that's not where they're going to inter him—I can hear the echo of the cannons, the bugle calls, the trumpets, the drums, and the horns, the funeral march played by the military band, tributes from three battalions of infantry, two of artillery, a squad of cavalry; flanking the gun-carriage is the Perennial Guard, and when silence falls, all the people pour into the street and follow him to the cemetery to give him burial in his mausoleum, which, with posterity in mind, he had built in a style worthy of a pharaoh. Your children will indeed be talked about, Joaquín Crespo, but when they drop dead they'll have nowhere to be laid to rest. I'm not going along with you; even without seeing, I'm sure they're burying you, and I retreat from my window, close the blinds, and let the shadows reassert themselves over my porchways as the half-light of dusk settles into my courtyard and brings out a shadow from the lemon tree. I shut myself in the corridor and gather up my papers, briefs, writs, dispatches, all traces of my litigation, adding the decree of expropriation that you signed on June 5, 1884, and I wait, Joaquín Crespo, I wait for the march of time. Now you're dead too, and you can wait with me; sit down here beside me, next to Alejandro, and Juan del Rosario, and my children, and my grandchildren, and my great-grandchildren, and my great-great-grandchildren. I know very well that in 1908 a daughter of yours will make an appearance, selling a parcel of what you expropriated; so in addition to granting my lands to the Dutch, it seemed perfectly all right to you to set aside a little morsel for yourself. That's the least of it, a pittance, I have the document and know that it wasn't many acres. Take a note, scribe: General Joaquín Crespo owes Doña Inés Villegas y Solórzano some property and a valley, Curiepe by name, which lie two leagues above Cape Codera on the cove called Higuerote. When I find my titles, the last inch of land—do you hear me, Joaquín Crespo?—the last grain of dust that rises up from my possessions will return to being mine.

THE VENUS OF SAN JUAN

(1900–1905)

You'll be hearing about him again, Alejandro, but for now I'm going to forget about Joaquín Crespo so I can continue telling you the story of the living: the story of that strapping lad who entered Caracas behind Cipriano Castro with the smell of manure still clinging to his clothes. I have to follow his steps because his life has to do with mine, and I won't turn him loose until it's over. You don't understand why that peasant, the grandson of a freedman on the plantation, is any concern of mine? Then you haven't understood anything of how circumstances have been reversed. So listen carefully, you deaf dead man, listen to that child barking on streetcorners:

> *The Metropolitan Circus announces a special performance in honor of the unvanquished army of the revolution. The famous trapeze artist Yamila on the Russian rings, the trained dogs from China, and the juggling act of the clown Salpicón.*

Domingo Sánchez, promoted to captain for his valiant conduct in the battle of Tocuyito, where he fought the way someone who has nothing to lose fights, arrived in Caracas with the army of the *Ever-Victorious and Undefeated General,* and his jaw dropped with his first glimpse of a city. He was given leave and, wasting no time, left the barracks and went out for a breath of fresh air; and there you have him, traipsing through the streets, dazzled and happy, with a few pennies' pay in his pocket and a pair of too-tight boots, slowly dragging his feet through the square in San Jacinto. In the early-morning hours, sitting on a bench among the trees and streetlamps, he watches the carters unload their goods from donkey trains and oxcarts, the peddlers open up their shops and stalls—offering the public kiosks full of flowers and fruits, selling stamps and postcards, birds, monkeys, goats and dogs, curative branches—and the men engaged in animated business colloquies. He stops at a postcard stall and asks the price of some landscapes of places unknown to him, women dressed as odalisques in strange positions, soldiers sporting shining epaulets and magnificent swords; he buys one that shows a woman sitting on a silk cushion, her eyes behind a veil, and with a diadem of pearls in her hair. He puts it—worn and soiled, its edges dog-eared—inside his jacket, and he probably thinks he owns something quite precious, a well-kept secret, because he looks all around to see if anyone is observing him as he buys it. But no one is paying any attention, the crowd is now milling around two men who are announcing the Chinese charade; I'm the only one watching as he goes over, too, like another curious child, with the other people rushing to the stall where they're laying out the cards with pictures of animals, and while one man collects the bets, the other plucks out the balls that indicate the winners. Domingo spent a good while taking in the show before he dared gamble a few coins; he quickly lost them and withdrew as new faces came up to try their luck. That was how he spent the day, walking around and gawking, sitting down to rest or quenching his thirst with some oranges and appeasing his hunger with a penny's worth of bread, absorbed in what seemed to him a huge city, exploring alleys, reading the signs on shops and boarding houses, coming upon elegant ladies with fans, low-cut patent-leather boots, and face powder; and fine gentlemen, their hair combed with pomade, who wore starched collars and top hats; barefoot children; servant girls in a hurry; carters; skeletal figures wrapped in shreds of clothing; crippled men hauling themselves along on makeshift wooden skids; women ringed by skinny, dirty children begging for alms; faces emaciated by malaria and scurvy. The handbills for the celebrated Metropolitan Circus lured him in to laugh a little at the stunts of the clown Salpicón, and he sat down on some boards to see the exploits of the female acrobat, who looked fearful and sweaty. He'd never been to a circus—maybe he remembered his grandfather's promise of a trip to the capital someday, sometime, and now that time had arrived and he had no one to tell about it; he only knew of old Rosa Margarita, and he certainly couldn't have had any desire to share it with her. When night fell he was still perched on a wooden chair in the Plaza Bolívar; the military band was playing tunes chosen from the "March of Cadiz" and then, as the finale, "The Blue Danube Waltz," which was applauded, after which the people left the square and withdrew to their homes amid the silence of the night. Captain Domingo Sánchez returned to the barracks alone, and, without talking to anyone, he shed his uncomfortable boots and uniform and, lying on his cot, thought, *Tomorrow I'm going to tell the colonel that these boots are no good for me.*

The soldiers were bored in the city that some thought invaded and others restored. For a time internal quarrels seemed to have quieted down; they were like cloudbursts, sudden onslaughts that immediately gave way to the sun. The general had forgotten about the glory days and lost interest in that body of insurgents who had crossed the country in triumph. Things being what they were, Domingo Sánchez got no more promotions and was assigned unimportant, routine, and almost domestic duties—accompanying the general's wife on her social visits and supervising the cleaning of the barracks; he even followed such orders as taking the Great Railroad to make sure everything was shipshape at the presidential house in Macuto for when the general would go there for a change of air and a few days' respite from his feverish disputes with international powers. Day by day the fame of the battle of Tocuyito, where Domingo had stood out as a national hero, was eroding in everybody's memory, even in his own, and he already felt far removed from emulating the valiant actions of his father riding with General Hernández—his father, the peasant soldier equipped with only a shotgun, and who spurred his animal with his bare feet. Domingo Sánchez was being converted into a city man without a city, and he was enjoying himself at evening soirées at the Teatro Caracas, where the general's wife went to see zarzuelas. On several occasions he had done guard duty, stationed until the wee hours outside the great festivities of Villa Zoila, and from a distance he studied the movements of the ladies and gentlemen, the polkas and the contredanses, oversaw the masked balls where coquettes from the Directoire alternated with musketeers and hussars while he, Sánchez, bone-tired and sleepy, waited for dawn finally to break and the cocks to crow so the important people would consider the party at an end. He also attended the celebrations of national holidays, the high point of which was always the lighting of the luminous fountains of El Calvario; and among his military cronies, amid laughter and crude jokes, a bottle of rum circulating, he'd doubtless remarked about the furtive comings and goings of the general when a coach and escort would whisk him away from a side door of the Palace of Government. But to Domingo Sánchez, none of that talk was anything but bluster—somebody else's fun, a wild release for other people—and for all his dreams of glory, he found himself awakening again and again in ill humor and with a headache after nocturnal visits to the merry brothels of San Juan and the Arab ladies of Camino Nuevo. From Caño Amarillo to Catia and from Horno Negro to Monte de Piedad, there wasn't one bordello that Domingo Sánchez wasn't familiar with, but his place of preference was the one with the façade of a boarding house but whose real business could be recognized in a small sign that read, in the light of the small streetlamp, *The Venus of San Juan.*

I'd heard, Alejandro, of the dissolute life of the women of Nueva Cádiz who lived in sin, actresses and chanteuses who came from Andalusia to entertain lonely men and who didn't hesitate to have a good time with sailors as well as with prominent gentlemen, not disdaining clerics, and I'd also heard about the dances in the slums of Caracas that the local magistrates cracked down on in order to put an end to rowdiness and carousing; about the ordinances for the jailing of scandalous and vagrant white women in the Caridad hospice and the correctional facility for lascivious and disorderly slave and free black women who had no known occupation and who strolled about so shamelessly and did themselves up with the greatest elegance (and I also knew about the important women who were taken into custody for having disgraced their husbands), but in all my life I never thought I could be witness to so many lewd acts as I had to observe when I followed the footsteps of Captain Domingo Sánchez. Next to his, your escapades with Juan del Rosario's mother were child's play. Though he didn't pay much, he was always well received; perhaps those starving peasant girls were weary of entertaining dolled-up old rakes who tried to make characters from *The Arabian Nights* out of them. He, on the other hand, treated them in a straightforward way, didn't ask for any complicated rituals or try to demand a lot for the little he gave them, and he would go with one or another, depending on who was free, and they evidently also liked his youth and his timidity. He would tell little anecdotes of life at the palace, some true, others (most of them, I imagine, fanciful) heard secondhand, and the women in turn would tell stories about the private lives of all the gentlemen who passed through there, so that it might be said that among them they were weaving together the secrets of small dignitaries and even those of a few notables. When the posh clientele headed home, or if some rich bigshot ordered the parlor closed, they would all gather in the kitchen with the madam, have some beer and rum, and if he'd been paid, Domingo Sánchez would order brandy while they cooked something, and they would laugh and chat until dawn; most of all he simply kept company with them, and on holidays or when the girls weren't in shape for work, they would go out walking with him and he'd invite them for ice cream at La Francia pastry shop, and he'd also do little favors for them—recommend a son or nephew for the army, obtain a loan, or take to the doctor any one of them who suspected she was sick.

You think it's beneath my dignity to be witnessing such goings-on? Oh, Alejandro, I feel embarrassed too in telling you about them; things are taking place here that I imagine are much more sordid than the ones described in the forbidden book—I don't know how it ever slipped into the province—that though written in English was known in Spanish as *The Pleasures of Love*. Coming to this brothel, Alejandro, are the most distinguished men of Caracas, because the madam has the reputation of being very strict in her selection, and she therefore assures them the greatest protection against the French disease, the one they now call syphilis; these gentlemen appear with a password, leave their hats and canes in the vestibule, order a snack of pastries and champagne, and prepare for the women to flounce by—though I don't see what the point of these parades is, since they're always the same women, with rarely anyone new. They like to see the girls undress and sit on their laps, or dance in their underwear as they crank the phonograph while the men stroke their goatees and mustaches; after choosing among them, these customers climb up to the bedrooms, where some limit themselves to the acts that nature intended, but others, Alejandro, want scenes I'd guessed only occurred in the Old Testament, and that there triggered the well-deserved wrath of God and extermination by his angels. There's one woman, called the Turk because she has very Arab-looking eyes—and who says she was born in Melilla, though I think her way of talking gives her away as someone from our own eastern shores—whose specialty is knowing how to use her mouth for filthy things, and she is, without a doubt, among those most sought after; another, nicknamed Salomé, likes to have them kneel down and—lo and behold!—men, whom I always thought were so dominating, like that humiliation too; there's still another one, with a bad eye, who will accept sodomy, and from what I can make out, this causes her to be held in high esteem. The proprietress, the one they call madam or Madame Ninón, is Lucía Chuecos, an Andean woman on in years, and I don't want you to think badly of me for this, Alejandro, but she seems to me a kindhearted woman, because she treats the girls as if she were their mother: looks after their health, speaks to them tenderly at times and sternly at other times, and despite her depravity turns away a lot of miserable girls who come looking for work and recommends that they seek some worthier trade. The mystery I haven't been able to fathom is the love and care she gives to a young servant girl named Magdalena. She's between thirteen and fifteen years old but already showing the unmistakable signs of future development. In her dark eyes there's a combination of innocence (that fleeting moment!) and of insinuation. Her job is to get rid of the dirty water from the washstands and the basins every morning; to make the beds and cover them with the oft-mended cretonne bedspreads; to pick up the stockings and brassieres strewn on the floor, the petticoats and skirts, the blouses hanging from hooks on the wall; to clean the enameled iron receptacle for douches; to pass a rag over the night tables, empty the ashtrays, rinse out the glasses with diluted alcohol still in them; to put the bureaus in order and arrange once more hairpins, combs, brushes, perfumed soap, and here and there a half-empty flask of perfume, plus coral powder for the teeth, black powder for the eyebrows, white powder for the neck, red powder for the lips, pink powder for the cheeks, puffs and compacts, pencils to bring out beauty marks, and small boxes of ribbons and creams; to sweep the two small downstairs parlors, arrange the chairs, and scrub the floors of what is the private salon for the girls of *The Venus of San Juan*. Her life is split between the hurly-burly of neighborhood streets and the upkeep of the house. In the morning she greets milkmen and bakers, washerwomen and pressers, knife-sharpeners and shoe repairmen, children hawking sweets and meat tarts; she listens to the women's complaints, helps the Turk darn stockings, Salomé cure her pockmarks, Estrellita (a rather stout Canary Islander) alter some clothes for a son she has somewhere; she accompanies the madam to the market and haggles with the food vendors, listens to the older woman's stories and lamentations, and tells her from time to time, "Madame Ninón, today you look prettier than the girls," waiting for a smile of thanks for her sweetness from that wrinkled face and portly body. That child, Magdalena, admires the madam, sees her as much more refined than the girls, listens to her chatting with them as she dispenses advice, her opinions on various matters of life and death, the weaknesses and the attributes of men, reminiscences of past times and forecasts about those yet to come; and Magdalena, who can barely scrawl her name and quickly figures on her fingers how much is due the milkman, feels plunged into what seems to her a deep well of wisdom. But there's more, there's also her eternal gratitude toward old Lucía for having given her a home, food, and work, for having brought her from her village, for having taught her the rudiments of reading and writing, all this largess for reasons Magdalena doesn't understand, and that she has asked about on some mornings while the girls are sleeping—Madame Ninón, in her wisdom, maintains a strict regimen of social hygiene: eight hours of work, eight of diversion, and eight of rest—"Why, Missy Lucía, did you summon me to Caracas?" and she always gets the same answer: "Because it was my duty." Since Magdalena was prettier than the prostitutes and could have been what would be called a gold mine, why the madam remained so zealously protective of her place and role in *The Venus of San Juan* is a mystery: "You're not here to be degraded," she said. "The others, when they arrived, already wanted to work at this; nobody gets corrupted here." Day after day the same response, and Magdalena realizes that she'll never learn much more, and if she closes her eyes at night and ponders her brief past in the village, she won't find anything there to resolve the mystery either. She knows she was brought up in a family that wasn't hers, with a last name that wasn't hers either, if she had one at all, and she was accustomed to being thankful that life had gone along being good to her ever since she could remember, because the woman who took care of her was a good friend of her mama, and she only remembers that once a man came by, strong, large, Indian-looking, to visit her, and her godmother said *Go on, say hello,* and she greeted him, and he gave her a decorative comb of fake tortoiseshell. Once she asked the madam about that man: "How should I know?" she retorted. "Do a good job watering those shrubs; they're drying out."

And sometimes Lucía tries to make her confess something: "What's going on between you and Captain Sánchez?"

"Nothing, Missy Lucía, we just like to pass the time together."

"You be careful, child, that passing time together doesn't make a one-day flower out of you. Find someone who's not such a womanizer."

Magdalena limited herself to smiling meekly at Captain Sánchez when he left the place at dawn. She worked during the day, and at five in the afternoon, when the first customers dropped by, she would disappear into the rear of the house, which, separated from the rest by some grillwork, consisted of a small courtyard with some wicker chairs and a few hens and functioned as the private salon, to which no outsider had access. Once activity began in the house, Magdalena had strict orders not to venture beyond the grillwork, and only when that part was empty again could she circulate freely through the two small reception parlors and the bedrooms on the upper floor. Domingo Sán-chez wasn't a stranger to her, and on a few occasions he'd slipped her a box of chocolates or flask of perfume as a gift that Magdalena was very dubious about accepting, and she would refuse sometimes be-cause the madam, who knew quite well where things got their start, had quite emphatically forbidden her to accept gifts. It was obvious to Domingo that Magdalena, for reasons unknown to him, wasn't des-tined to be part of the business, and that only made his desire grow; he was infuriated by the presence of a protected virgin in a place where all the women took part in debaucheries. A few of their jokes carried a double meaning that indicated that his wants were under-stood but wouldn't be granted, and he made other hints, but the madam, most unyielding in her role of priestess in charge of the vestal, would say: "Just look at Captain Sánchez, the way he complicates life for himself; with so many pretty girls he concentrates on the one who's not for him." And she would go on joking and laughing to let it be understood that this one strict prohibition would in no way cast a pall over the party, as long as they all knew their places.

Nonetheless, Domingo Sánchez thought otherwise. During the very brief conversations he and Magdalena had as he began leaving later and later and she started work earlier, he came to understand that her origins were similar to his, and he remembered with a certain nos-talgia a childhood in the country, far from the hubbub. Captain Sán-chez began to fondle an idea that occurred to him now and again dur-ing the long nights in the barracks when, lying on his cot, he saw his life as a frenzy of events that was leading nowhere. He sometimes wondered what had become of old Rosa Margarita—whether she was dead, whether anyone had accompanied her to her burial, or whether she was still in his grandfather's house, swaddled in her black cloth, smelling rancid and talking to the chickens. He felt a mixture of re-pentance and hate as he brought her memory back. He also felt a heavy weight when he thought about his grandfather—he would hear Andrés Cayetano's voice, *Make a good man out of yourself, far away from this village*—but what aspirations and what destiny were there left for Domingo since the general, who'd called him into his service in such an epic way, had now forgotten him? Only on very rare occasions did

Domingo see him now, when the general deigned to visit the barracks; on those occasions, he would venture to say, "I'm Domingo Sánchez, General, sir," and the general stared off into space and, with a slight bob of the head, went on inspecting the troops with his sunken, wandering eyes—the result, the soldiers said, of the wild life he was leading. No, no hope remained for Domingo Sánchez; and at times he would entertain the fantasy of giving up what he thought was a heroic undertaking, and he daydreamed about the easeful comforts of going into business and establishing an honorable home with some young girl who, taken by his uniform, would strike up a conversation with him during the Sunday band concert. Maybe with a good girl, a girl like Magdalena, he'd be able to start all over again, sell his grandfather's house and set up some little enterprise now that he'd absorbed something about the commercial world from listening to the women at *The Venus of San Juan* and taking part in the conclaves of the vendors from the Linares passageway. He would listen to them grumble about the hardships under the dictatorship, and the words would reach him from a world that was foreign to him; monopolies, monopolies in cattle and the sale of meat, in rum, flour, cigarettes, matches, the cornering of the market in milk and eggs, boosting the price of business licenses in order to pay the army's expenses and to bankroll the festivals, especially the fêtes and balls with which the general had himself acclaimed all through the republic. Those were the ones, then, the lawyers and magnates, the owners of the houses Domingo Sánchez dreamed about, houses decorated with carved wood and broad balustrades, houses with well-cared-for gardens adorned with statues; people on whom he'd spied when he accompanied the general's wife, people who danced until the early hours of the morning, the ones who had a grand good time while he stood guard duty in the garden—they were the same ones, then, that the shopkeepers ranted about and said had ruined the country.

Early one morning when he was leaving the narrow house in San Juan and the lamplighter was going through the neighborhood putting out the kerosene streetlights, Domingo Sánchez spotted Magdalena's face behind the grillwork. He went back over and they started one of their quick tête-à-têtes, their ears sharpened so as not to be caught by the madam, and Magdalena arranged her first love tryst: "Tomorrow there's going to be a big party; they're going to close the place to customers, they say the general's coming. Nobody will notice if I'm not here, and we can go out walking."

Domingo Sánchez was happy again. Just as he did on the day of his arrival in Caracas, he roamed through the streets and squares; he took Magdalena to San Jacinto, bought her oranges and shredded mangoes; he gave her a cristofué bird that she promised to take good care of until the day of her death; they gazed at the prints and post-cards, which Magdalena had never seen, and they bet in the animal lottery without winning anything. They sat down on benches and watched the children playing around them, and he told her that he was already a man of the age to have a child and she blushed and covered her face; they went to see a puppet show set up on the Plaza Bolívar, and Domingo Sánchez ran his hand over her neck and whispered in her ear, and Magdalena sensed that something was happening between them that was different from what the San Juan girls talked about, and she laughed at what the puppets were saying, but it wasn't really for that but from the simple happiness of having discovered what a love tryst was about. When it got dark, Captain Sánchez proposed going to a small hotel not far from the house, and Magdalena gave in, but she stipulated *everything except that,* and he told her all right, and they spent some time on the bed hugging and caressing each other under the light of the gas lamp, doing everything except that.

That night Magdalena, so as not to make any sound, took off the high heels the Turk had loaned her and kissed Domingo Sánchez good night. When she was climbing the stairs, trying to pass unnoticed, the party was at its height. All the lights had been turned on, and the girls, nude except for G-strings, were sitting on the frayed little velvet chairs and laughing hard. The Turk was cranking the phonograph and singing and dancing. Magdalena's stealthy steps were discovered, however, and the general got up from an armchair and asked the madam, "What about that girl? Why didn't you show her to me?"

The madam made a quick signal to Magdalena and, pouring the

general a glass of champagne, lied: "That girl's my niece, and she's just passing through, because she's been quite sick. I don't recommend her, General."

And the following week Magdalena told Domingo Sánchez what had happened when she sneaked into the San Juan house after their first date.

Do prostitutes know what men want? I'd always thought they sought such women out in order to satisfy their bestiality, but now I wonder if the whore's attraction doesn't rest in her readiness to go along with anything dark and unknown; I'd always thought these women were libertines with unbridled appetites, but from having seen and listened to them I've come to understand that they ply their trade with coldness, and that there isn't much pleasure for them. Did Juan del Rosario's mother know your desires, Alejandro, or was it just a matter of offering her body for pleasure the way you use your hands for work? I would have liked, or I'd like now and didn't know then, to be that coveted body for you and know your secret, but how could I have even thought of submitting to the humiliation of asking you what there was in her that I couldn't give you! *Lock her up and punish her,* that was the only thought I had, *Sell her or send her away*; I couldn't think of any other way to stop you, nights, when you thought I was sleeping, from knocking on the door to the servants' quarters. My mother hadn't prepared me for anything but to receive your seed, and you—let me tell you, now that so much time has passed—were a bad teacher. Maybe you figured that our congress wasn't a love tryst, and as a man you knew how fleeting the act would be . . . or you preferred to conceal your secrets from me so I wouldn't imagine myself their owner. I forgive you, Alejandro, because I loved that serene intimacy of ours too. It was seeing the illusion of that child, Magdalena, that made me hark back to that afternoon when you got up to leave and we heard my mother's voice calling me, and just at the moment when our words were stumbling over each other and our hands were touching in a gesture of good-bye, the limits that held us back broke—and it was a rainy day, and it got suddenly dark when, in the courtyard, we stole our first clandestine kiss.

But I don't want to defile my memories by mixing them with the rotten tricks of that scoundrel. Captain Sánchez wasn't sure what he should do. He'd seen more than a few soldiers carried out under a shroud after days of fever and dysentery, sick from eating bags of rotten alligator pears, moldy kidney beans, tainted meat. He was luckier; he could save his allotment for rations and eat with the officers, but he aspired to a promotion to colonel, and it was never forthcoming, and he began to despair of rising in the army. By scrimping here, asking for a loan there, and playing up to the madam, maybe he could cajole her into letting him marry Magdalena; he'd rent a frock coat and buy his bride a colored percale gown. He went over his friendships. A tavernkeeper had proposed going into partnership because the son-in-law who used to help him had died; it was a fine business and would be all the more so if they could obtain a license to open a bottling plant—but where would he, Domingo Sánchez, get the money to buy in? Then he remembered the house of his grandfather, Andrés Cayetano; he would return to the village and sell it off. And the ownership papers, where could his grandfather have put them? Maybe in the wardrobe in the main room or buried under the floor tiles; maybe held closely by old Rosa Margarita, who certainly must still be there, retired in the backyard to her room made of planks, in which case he'd have to take her to an insane asylum and leave her there forever. If he sold the house, which seemed to him now like a hovel, everything would change: he could be partners with the saloonkeeper and buy the license; there were people around who owed him favors; and for better or for worse, wasn't he a captain in the restoration army?

The family of that little soldier who was dying from poverty, and Domingo advised them to come and get him . . . but no, they wouldn't do—what influence could those destitute people have? He had gone to a loan shark to pawn some cheap imitation jewelry for the Turk, but what could she do for him? Well, she might be of some help, if he asked her what big cheeses visited her bed. On a piece of paper, he jotted down with a pencil stub the names of possible benefactors: the soldier's family, the Turk, the owner of a restaurant on the Linares passageway—didn't he have a son with the reputation of being a revolutionary? Hadn't the boy been held under arrest at the prefecture? And if Domingo hadn't interceded with the colonel, wouldn't they have sent him to San Carlos castle? There he would have rotted away and never been heard from again. That was a man who owed Domingo a big debt, and besides, he was in business. And the madam herself: hadn't he got rid of a health inspection for her? The police might have closed down her business had they found that syphilitic girl there, the one old Lucía had missed in spite of her sharp and shrewd questions to gauge the health of her employees. *Lucía Chuecos,* he wrote down on his list. Then the name of the general appeared on the paper: if he considered that valor in battle as a favor . . . but the general doesn't remember that anymore, Domingo thought—it has to be a more recent favor.

The officers convened in the barracks were talking in loud voices and drinking. Captain Sánchez got up and thoughtlessly let himself be seen; one of them called him over, and they made room for him. They prattled on about everything and nothing, but then the conversation took an interesting turn. They were remarking that it would soon be the general's birthday, and that all his ministers were scrambling around, eagerly looking for a present that would please him. There were no longer any women in the city who caught his eye.

"A virgin!" one shouted with a great guffaw. "What the general wants is a virgin."

And they all went on with their chortling and foul jokes. He listened in silence. "Why so serious, Dominguito?" his colonel asked, and Domingo felt a tightening of rage at hearing himself called Dominguito again.

"He's probably thinking about finding a doll for the general," another laughed.

And they joked some more. "This shithead? All this shithead knows are whores, isn't that so? Watch out that they don't give you some disease, Captain."

Domingo couldn't endure any more of this raillery. He withdrew without taking his leave, left them to their chatting. Lying on his cot, he was turning over an idea that had sprung into his mind. The idea, like a wild animal, was attacking him, biting him, challenging him, snorting at him furiously, ripping him to pieces, leaving him impotent, hounded by its force. He closed his eyes in order to chase it away; for moments it disappeared, and the night was dark and lonely without his thoughts. He managed to sleep, and once more, like a torturer who'd decided to torment him to the very end, it returned to assail and unhinge him. Sometimes with a force like an impulse that must be executed immediately, like an imposition that is impossible to escape, and sometimes surreptitiously, like a drop of water that seeps into a person slowly until it ends up soaking him to the bone, or a current of wind that insinuates itself into a room little by little, turning it cold, the same idea was rooting its way into his plans.

The next morning Domingo woke up with body aches and chills. He went to the doctor's office and sat down to wait. Passing in front of him were yellowish men with parchment flesh, all skin and bones, unshaven, their eyes gleaming with fever, their faces sweaty, their hunched bodies wrapped in flimsy coverlets, their fingers like quivering sticks. Finally it was his turn. The doctor examined him silently and quickly, said, "It's nothing, don't be concerned; it's not the fever, it's a passing cold. I haven't got anything to give you. Take a good shot of rum and wait for the trouble to pass." He shouted, "Next!" Domingo Sánchez left the office and told his colonel he was ill. He spent the whole day burrowed under blankets, dozing, and darkness was falling, catching him unawares, when a man with a lamp in his hand came and woke him up. "How's it going, Sánchez?" "Not too well," he answered. "Not too well? What more do you want? Everybody knows about it. The general asked for you, said he wanted to pay you back for the present." "I didn't give him anything," said Domingo, and he retreated beneath the blanket again.

He woke up and shook his head to dispel the nightmare. He'd dreamed he was sick with malaria, that he was lying on his cot and the colonel came to tell him that the general was going about asking for him, that they all knew about it, that everybody knew about it. He threw some water on his face to jolt himself wide awake, got dressed, and went out to check the orders of the day. In celebration of the general's happy birthday, there was to be a talked-about party that evening at the home of a minister. Captain Sánchez was assigned to escort the general's wife home when the ball was over; the general's personal guard would remain at the ready in case there was some special visit afterward.

A special visit, for example, to the bar called *Bosque de Bolonia,* given that pompous name, perhaps, because it was built in the form of a kiosk and because, with its secluded and private location in some gardens across from a shady little square, it was reminiscent of a courtly Paris. The coach with two horses, followed by a small escort, set off in that direction around twelve o'clock, after all society had paid its respects to the general at the minister's residence. The general's distinguished spouse would stay on a while longer to give the guests the impression that the festivities were still in full swing, and once more the small orchestra attacked the waltz "El Tocuyo" as the couples whirled by.

"Try a champagne so you'll know what's good," they said to Captain Sánchez as, sitting on the steps of the main terrace, he sipped a cup of coffee. Domingo wet his lips. "I don't like it; I'd rather have brandy," he said, and handed it back with a brusque gesture. An hour passed, maybe two; the party was never ending, they would dance until dawn. He was nodding sleepily when he violently awakened: the general's wife was leaving. A murmur of people approached with her, taking their leave at the door while the guard made ready to escort her home. Afterward Captain Sánchez headed for the barracks, but suddenly he changed direction and made the coachman loan him the victoria.

"If they fire me, it'll be your fault."

"Do what I tell you and you won't be sorry, I know how to repay a favor." He whipped the horses furiously, without stopping for an instant, through the dark and silent streets until he arrived in front of the house.

He pounded on the door. The madam—half-asleep, wearing slippers, her nightgown covered by a poncho—opened it.

"You're crazy, Sánchez, everybody's asleep here."

He shoved her aside and went in, barking through the grating: "I came to get you; come with me."

He put her into the carriage and once more whipped the horses until they got to the *Bosque de Bolonia.* Along the way he was talking to her: "You don't have to do anything; let him do it to you."

In the victoria, trembling under her nightgown from the cold,

Magdalena listened mutely. She had watched Domingo climb down, but she couldn't follow the conversation between him and the aide. They were two shadows gesticulating; from the coach all that could be discerned were two dress swords chafing against leggings. Finally Domingo Sánchez came back and helped her down. He walked her through the inner gardens until he reached the door of the kiosk. On one side was a parlor furnished with red velvet chairs and gilded tables on which there were still some half-empty glasses to be cleared; on the other side, a closed door kept the interior in silence. The aide and Domingo Sánchez resumed their discussion. Magdalena was listening to them, but fear wouldn't let her grasp the meaning of what they were saying.

"Tell him I'm bringing the girl from San Juan. Tell him that; the general knows who she is. Tell him it's a birthday present. If you don't want to, I'll leave, and nothing's happened."

The other man seemed skeptical, time was slipping away, and Domingo Sánchez, losing heart about succeeding with his idea, made a half-turn and, grabbing Magdalena fiercely by the arm, was leaving hurriedly when a voice was heard from inside.

"The general's asking for another bottle. You can go in now, but remember, we go fifty-fifty." A few minutes passed, and the man came back, took Magdalena by the hand, and led her to an empty bedroom. She sat down on a large bed and looked around at the mirrors, the basin on the marble tabletop, and a bottle of champagne with two glasses.

"How old are you?" the aide asked. Magdalena didn't answer. "Are you sure you're a virgin?" he asked once more, and still she held her tongue.

Outside, the aide spoke to Domingo. "So, what are you going to ask for in return for this present, Sánchez?"

"What I want is a license to open a bottling plant," he replied in a low voice.

The aide started laughing, laughing, and Domingo Sánchez, not knowing what to do, tried feebly to laugh along with him as dawn caught a staggering old man taking off his pants, and a girl seated on a bed shielded her breasts with her arms.

DOMINGUITO FINDS ANOTHER
GENERAL
(1905–1929)

You still don't understand, Alejandro, why I insist on telling you the story of that swine? You think it's not like me to concern myself with fornication and base goings-on? I couldn't have imagined either, for the life of me, that I would be eavesdropping on soldiers' conversations, and I never thought my memory would be plagued with such miserable episodes. You say that you don't even want to remember Andrés Cayetano's grandson, and all you're interested in is whether or not I've found the titles? You're a forgetful dead man, Alejandro, like all the rest—like you, Dominguito, who went along through life purging your memory until you forgot yourself. You no longer remember Don Cipriano or the boots that pinched your feet when you were a peasant recruit, you no longer smell of mules and gunpowder, and you've also cast off the smell of the girl you made a present of on his birthday, and what you got in recompense for his drunken spree and his misconduct. What a surprise, Domingo Sánchez, when overnight you found yourself become head pimp! Such drive you had as you changed professions and learned how to canvass the run-down neighborhoods of the city in a door-to-door search for some miserable person with a daughter or a sister to rent out! If I hadn't known you since you were a child and hadn't followed you step by step, it would have shocked me, as it did your lady friends in San Juan, to see you resigning from the glorious army of the restoration in order to dedicate yourself so earnestly to the most lucrative of commercial activities; instead of standing the way you used to, stationed in front of the grillwork, waiting for the general's wife to leave the garden party or evening of dancing, you yourself began to be invited to soirées, began—gradually, little by little—to be recognized as you went along the downtown streets, tipping your hat courteously in Las Gradillas, and finally you rose high up in the scheme of things and were accepted into the Concordia Club, where other gentlemen hobnobbed with you and invited you to a game of poker or billiards, where, in addition to spicy anecdotes about the wanton behavior of certain fine ladies, attention was paid to business deals transacted under the new motto of the Worthy Chief of the Nation: *Union, Peace, and Work.* Perhaps you felt a bit alone and strange in the mansion you bought yourself a few blocks from my house, and, accustomed to your uniform ever since that distant day when the general gave you a soldier's garb and you put on boots instead of hemp sandals, you got lost rummaging through the clothes you kept in that high wardrobe: so many pressed trousers, so many silk shirts, so many floppy ties, so many patent-leather shoes, even a set of tails with a vest. Tired of serving yourself mugs of water and coffee or sharing the rum in bottle stores, you learned to drink the best brandy in fine glasses delivered on a silver tray by attentive servants; and, sick of getting up to the bugle's reveille, you liked to take your time now, having a leisurely breakfast and dressing slowly until it was time to open your commercial and export offices. How you've come up in the world, Domingo Sánchez! But tell me one thing: you gave the lewd monkey food for his lust; and his chum and successor, the greedy peasant, what did you give him? Have you forgotten that too? My, what a bad memory you have! Don't worry, I'm here to refresh it for you; memory, Dominguito, is my strong point. Do you remember the date 1920, perhaps, when Mr. Domingo Sánchez Luna had a bad night?

He'd awakened several times to drink some water because his thirst was strangling him, and he opened the windows, hoping the coolness of the early morning would come in. Maybe he'd had one drink too many, maybe he was worried about the loans he wanted to propose to the general, maybe he was just tired, but he hadn't slept well that night, couldn't manage slumber with his accustomed ease: he'd dreamt about old Rosa Margarita, he saw her clearly, sitting in the backyard talking to the chickens; suddenly the old woman got up from her stool and wrung the neck of a hen, and blood was dripping and wetting the ground. He'd awakened all agitated, had lighted a cigar and poured himself a glass of water from the pitcher that was resting on a showy little English table. He didn't want to recall old Rosa Margarita, not even in his dreams, not even in an image that, like an old photograph, would vanish as soon as he opened his eyes. He'd wiped the slate clean and started over again, and that was the way he wanted to live from now on. Old Rosa Margarita was only a bad dream, a fragment of someone else's past, one that belonged to Dominguito, a sad, crazy, barefoot little boy with pants torn at the knees, a white shirt tied around his waist—a child he'd known once, dashing through the woods, killing birds with stones, chasing dogs to tie a can to their tails, hunting skunks and possums, sitting in the tavern with men of the village, holding the hand of an old man with a tired gait who would don a pair of gray pants and a worn vest on feast days and take out a watch chain to confirm once more by the church clock that his watch was slow; a child who rocked in the hammock while old Andrés Cayetano smoked and chatted and read him stories from some book or other about the old days of independence, or spoke about the grandeur of General Ezequiel Zamora. Old Rosa Margarita belonged to that child's memory: she was the one who'd gone with him to uncover a name inscribed on a small niche in the cemetery, and also the one who'd walked with him behind the old man's funeral procession—which, indeed, had been a memorable occasion, the entire village was there and the priest had come, and the mayor, and all the men from the surrounding area, and all the women wore black and sat down in the house and had been praying, running their hands over their heads. But old Rosa Margarita had died completely now, because she only existed for a child named Dominguito, who'd also died completely, who'd been erased by the dust of the road to Caracas. And Magdalena, too, was entirely dead to him—Magdalena, a girl he'd known in a house in San Juan with two windows and a mosaic vestibule and a small courtyard where, glimpsed through the fretwork of the connecting gate, her petite form could be seen watering the shrubs: a girl he'd known at a false boardinghouse over whose doorway a lamp illuminated the notice *Beds for rent for fine gentlemen* and an iron sign that read *The Venus of San Juan.*

Magdalena had gone away, faded from memory: it was a slow, incremental vanishing, or maybe a quick, solid blow had dislodged her forever. As in a trick photograph, she'd been elided from the picture where once she appeared with the girls from San Juan, all in a row, some crouching in front and others standing behind with the madam on a day when they were celebrating Captain Sánchez's birthday or maybe Christmas or the new year. Magdalena had perished in a distant adolescence, in an abandoned age, and her dark eyes and curly hair no longer existed; nor had she ever been anything but a tiny shadow singing snatches from a zarzuela in the courtyard, cleaning the house of Madame Ninón, Lucía Chuecos, the madam. Magdalena was the ghost that sometimes accompanied Captain Domingo Sánchez, also dead and buried, to an afternoon band concert, on a morning stroll through the Plaza de San Jacinto, on a day's outing on the La Guaira railroad—a memory that sometimes smelled of salt in the breeze through the uvero trees. But now she was completely dead, as much so as poor Captain Sánchez, and maybe they were making love in some crook of the Macuto seawall; maybe dawn would catch them in a narrow boardinghouse bed, doing *everything except that.* Maybe somebody remembered the meeting of those two hesitant and uncertain bodies who were discovering each other for the first time and had the custom of making love trysts. Magdalena wouldn't be coming anymore, nor would he be going back to the house of the girls in San Juan. Now that he was ensconced amid the Persian rugs that adorned his parlor under the crystal chandeliers, with the orchids in a Chinese vase, the Empire cupboards, the Queen Victoria chairs, the broad gilt mirrors, the damask drapes, the alabaster lamps, the carved-wood end tables, the grandfather clock, and the little modernist statues on marble bases, it was useless for Mr. Domingo Sánchez Luna to search for the husk of a girl called Magdalena, of uncertain surname, more on loan than documented, born in a village of unknown name, brought to Caracas by a gust of wind that blew in that direction; Magdalena had been consigned to Captain Domingo Sánchez's lost file, and, since that file had been purposely misplaced, she had no opportunity for survival. But *I* remember her, Dominguito, I'm not going to do you the favor of forgetting her, and when you least expect it you're going to bump into my memory.

He finally woke up. He had a frugal breakfast of a cup of black coffee, and while he read the newspapers the barber used his strop to hone the ivory-handled razors that bore the initials *D. S. L.* engraved in curly, flowery lines of gold, and the barber was commenting about news items, incidents, rumors that were making the rounds of cliques and backbiters. So engrossed was he in his gabbing that his hand slipped and he gave Mr. Sánchez Luna a slight nick on the chin. The latter cursed, and the barber outdid himself with apologies and praise for the patience shown by Mr. Sánchez Luna, whom he'd known for so many years and had had the honor to shave every morning, except on those days when the gentleman showed the traces of a heavy night out and the servant sent the barber away because his master didn't want to be bothered. But that morning Domingo Sánchez was in a hurry, and in no mood for stories and gossip, for he'd obtained an audience with the new general to discuss important matters. He had a tingling inside. Would the new general have forgotten that he'd served the old general? Everybody said his memory was infallible, that in the recesses of his mind he kept the name and status of anyone who had reason to be remembered and that just as a rancher can recognize his cows by the color of their hide and can also determine the cows whose offspring they were, the general, in like manner, knew the origin of every calf who grazed in his government of rehabilitation. Could that memory hold any reason for Domingo's being looked upon unfavorably? He didn't know, couldn't be sure, but the barber's scratch seemed a bad omen. It had been so long already since the old general had left with his wife for other shores that no one mentioned his name anymore except to insult it, and he, Domingo Sánchez, had taken great care not to remind anyone of the marvelous day when he'd entered Caracas with the *Ever-Victorious and Undefeated General.* Nor would he have any reason to divulge the mistake or the curiosity that brought him down to La Guaira to watch the smoke from the stack of the ship taking the general into exile as it steamed into the distance. No one had seen him take leave of the general in the company of Dominguito, a brave boy who stole chickens and who challenged the troops of the restoration, no less. But with Dominguito dead, who would recall the admiration of a village boy for that undefeated army? Not he, of course, and he was hoping fervently that the new general wouldn't either. If he remembered it with bitterness, would he have allowed Domingo's business to prosper? Hadn't he permitted Domingo to grow under his purview, without suggesting anything but also without any conditions? Absolutely—had the general wanted to cut him down, there were ample opportunities; either the leader had forgotten about it, or it didn't make any difference to him. Domingo called for his car, and slowly they made their way to the Palace of Government, the chauffeur weaving through the still-inexperienced pedestrians, blowing the horn to warn the people riding donkeys and driving carts. The general received Domingo punctually and for only a few minutes. He listened to his long-winded speech with an apparently distracted air and answered with monosyllables from time to time. Finally the general took his leave and promised to let Domingo know as soon as he'd consulted with his ministers. Then he had a brief chat with a close aide, figured out what steps to take, and he could hear in his head some old anecdote, one of the few in which Captain Domingo Sánchez had played a main role in bygone times. "I don't think so, General," an advisor had said then: "Take those loans away; there are a lot of people to give them to who can serve you better." "Don't kill him, that boy's all right," the general answered. After a brief wait in the outer office, Mr. Domingo Sánchez was called back in, and the general told him that a man of his qualities and business acumen should take on other responsibilities, and then Domingo Sánchez presented the little deals and inducements he had in hand, and the general offered him an official position. And it was as a minister, as a Distinguished Personage, that he left the office. He sent the chauffeur off and, in no hurry, got onto a streetcar and rode across the city to the Plaza Bolívar. He had so little time available, these days, to take a turn around on foot, sit under the trees, watch lovers having a photograph taken or children out of school frolicking in their white aprons; he liked to feel himself at liberty in the city, free of his several occupations, and for a moment he remembered the late Captain Sánchez, when he was on leave and counting the few coins in his pocket. Only rarely did Mr. Domingo Sánchez enjoy quiet hours like that at home, lounging in an iron chair in the courtyard. He lighted another cigar and ordered another beer while he perused the papers, and his eyes alighted on the news of ships sailing for Europe. He'd never been aboard one, only seen them from a distance when the late Captain Sánchez strolled along the seawall of Macuto, and also when, in the company of Dominguito, he went to make a mute and surreptitious farewell to the first general . . . but he'd never shared the pleasures that his new friends told him about: Paris, Madrid, Rome. Maybe now the moment had arrived for him to discover Europe, to saunter through the streets of the Old World, eat in its elegant restaurants, and take in spicy shows; maybe his colleagues noticed the absence of travel stories in his conversation, his being unable to bandy the names of fashionable places with them, even though he had a feeling of knowing those places from having heard them mentioned; maybe it was also the moment to settle down.

Domingo Sánchez needed a wife and couldn't find one. Sometimes he would invite a young girl and her respectable parents to a performance at the Municipal Theater, but he would yawn into his palm during the endless acts of the opera; on other occasions he would put in a brief appearance on the Avenida Paraíso on Sunday after mass. But he was bored, as if I didn't know! He missed his girlfriends from the house in San Juan and found nothing in the company of those insipid young ladies, who were constantly watched over from a distance or close at hand by their worried mothers. He couldn't command the delicate tone of their banter; he was unfamiliar with their customs, their turns of phrase, and their desires, and he would remain taciturn, stroking his goatee. He passed as a man withdrawn into himself, graying at the temples and with an interesting air, who only liked to shut himself in his library and lose himself in history books and chronicles . . . but those weren't appropriate themes for such young and vivacious women, who looked for romantic dialogues and an established domestic life. There were no few families ready to overlook his murky origins, and they gave him to understand that they would be satisfied to receive him; others, more snobbish and pretentious, forbade their daughters to accept the visits of a man in whom their sharp aristocratic eyes caught the tincture of people of color.

And the fact is there was something of everything, Alejandro, in that provincial Caracas of Gómez's time, divided between people who bore the grief of some shackled prisoner and those getting rich with the same speed as the oil bubbled up out of the earth. Did oil bubble up for us? No, Alejandro, nothing bubbled up for us. Now that the aroma of cacao has disappeared, José Francisco Blanco, my great-great-grandson, is only an old man who died penniless, once the owner of a plantation expropriated in the name of progress; and Belén, his daughter, orphaned at an early age, born of a second marriage, is a forgotten woman, the daughter of an old conservative whom nobody remembers or cares about. And Belén—this is all the more reason to forget her—is the widow of an anti-Gómez student, a revolutionary, a candidate for rotting away in the Rotunda if he hadn't managed through some trick of magic to escape and go off to die of tuberculosis in a sanatorium in Switzerland—though it would appear more likely that *she* was the one suffering from a contagious disease, because, really, what greater leprosy is there than that of bearing a surname that was so hateful to the general, a surname no one wanted to pronounce in order not to upset him, the way so many names that might irritate him were shunned. Miguel, her first husband, planned—such naiveté!—to overthrow General Gómez, but the person I'm going to talk about next is the man who, though for only a short time, saved his life.

León Bendelac Discovers

America

(1926–1935)

The brilliant light of the cove is momentarily soiled by smoke from the ship. Morning is beginning to spring its surprise on shore. Faces crowd up onto the deck—they, too, are yearning to discover the New World. The little islets are left in the wake. Eyes peep out at the dawn, try to look beyond the docks to glimpse what's offered there; in the distance, a movement of men is hinted at along what will be the entry roads—streets to go through, people with whom they will have to deal from now on. León Bendelac, leaning against the rail, is approaching a landscape that's not completely foreign to him: heat, palm trees, sun-browned bodies, the quick and silky talk of southern people. He's wearing a shabby dark suit and a broad-brimmed hat and carries a black leather suitcase that he refuses to let go of whether in sunshine or shade because it holds the first and only items he owns and with which he hopes to make his fortune. He is a silversmith by trade, and Spanish is his mother tongue, which lets him look a bit askance at the Tangierian Arabs, his companions in the crossing, whose gabble causes astonishment among the few fishermen they encounter as they leave the steamer. He slowly scouts out the small city with steps that try to be confident—stopping people on corners, asking questions—and at dusk he happens to arrive in front of a house with rooms for rent. Meticulously counting a few coins, suitcase in hand, he goes back to the dock and eats bananas as he watches the sea grow dark, as if now he is finally leaving the color of the Mediterranean and saying good-bye forever to a previous world. After sunset now, he lies on the bed after carefully hanging up the clothes he's taken off. The landlady has given him a candle stub, matches, and a pewter plate, and León Bendelac writes a first letter to his mother, telling her that he arrived all right, that it was a good trip, that he has a place to sleep, and that next morning he will start working and will write her again.

Leaving the downtown area, he arrives at the vague address described to him by the landlady, according to whom in a shack by the side of the highway there's a man who has a donkey for sale. Accustomed to more direct dealings between merchants who know what they're buying and selling, León isn't completely successful in getting down to business with this skinny, withered little old man who slowly sips coffee and from time to time flails at mosquitoes with his hat as he banters on and asks León where he's from, at other moments snapping back to the donkey as if he suddenly remembered its existence: "The donkey, yes, of course, it's for sale. What'll you give me for it? It's a good donkey, no, a bit thin, that he is, but this animal's got a lot of walk left for you," and the little man went back to his meandering questions: "So you came on the steamship that docked yesterday? Across all that ocean and from so far away! The people who go to sea here get to Cumaná and Margarita, to Trinidad—to Trinidad, yes sir, some of them get that far. Well, then, the donkey comes to twenty bolívares, I'm giving him to you because I need the money; he's a good donkey, but I've got another one. When he goes lazy on you, give it to him good; he'll turn to with that."

And, giving it good to the sad, gaunt animal, León Bendelac went off with twenty bolívares less and a donkey, and when he got back he asked the landlady's permission to tether it in the backyard. That night he wrote his mother again and told her he'd bought a donkey so he could reach the most distant settlements, because Barcelona was a small city, and there wasn't enough business, and they told him that almost nobody went out to sell things in the interior, and there was a great need there. The Arab in the bazaar called La Estrella would give him 1 percent of any merchandise sold, and León would be able to go about drumming up customers for himself.

In just a short while they all called him *The Turk,* and when they heard the little bell he'd set atop the donkey's head they would shout, "There comes Vendelá the Turk," and they would greet him cordially and ask, "Vendelá, what have you brought to sell, Vendelá?" And León Bendelac would offer them sugar and salt, needles, scissors, denim, cooking alcohol, tobacco; and for the wealthier ones laces, silks, and shoes. One day he sold the civil chief a wristwatch, which the man looked at suspiciously: "Are you sure this damned thing runs, Turk? Don't try to trick me, or I'll put you in jail." León Bendelac assured him that it was a Swiss watch of the finest quality, the latest thing from Europe, and would last a lifetime—always, of course, provided he took good care of it, because it had a very delicate mechanism. When León returned from trips to the settlements, he would sit in a dockside bar and have a glass of rum. He was lonely and far removed from the fishermen's conversations, except on those occasions when one, thankful for a good purchase, would say, "Turk, come join us and have yourself a snort." And León would sit down and listen to their endless merry chatter until he said good-night and thanked them for the invitation, finishing the day with another short letter to his mother in which he told her the few anecdotes he managed to come up with.

Bendelac the Turk, by dint of roving and making good use of his tongue, had bought a mule and could now cover the coast faster, followed by the old donkey carrying the merchandise. When he'd saved enough, he wanted to go as far as Cumaná and check on the trade with Trinidad; he might even venture a little beyond, for salt trading in Araya. The trip took a full day, and he was humping along, pondering how to get established, when he was startled by the sound of gunfire and the smell of powder. The peaceful provincial town had suddenly been turned into the flashpoint of a revolution, and he was frightened as he saw units of soldiers rush by and enter into combat with disembarking rebels. Wondering whether to hide or flee, he opted for the former, fearing that a stray bullet might find him; and he dragged the mule and donkey along, made them lie down and converted them into an improvised barricade while the shooting lasted. Shouts, bursts of smoke, calls for death to the dictator, wounded men, fallen horses, corpses that the terrified inhabitants carted away, curses—all this went on for several hours right before his eyes while León Bendelac lay on the ground, protected by the bodies of his animals, until night came to dampen the short battle, and he began to think about how he could escape the city. He lifted himself tentatively from his hiding place and immediately crouched back down when he heard a voice mingled with the moans of the wounded. Somebody was trying to get his attention from a window; squinting, he was able to make out a woman signaling to him. He didn't dare move, uncertain of her intention, and for a long time he held his position, pretending to be injured or dead; but the woman, wrapped in a dark cloak, had approached and with gestures was asking him to go with her. León Bendelac followed, unsure whether he was doing the right thing—but, unable to know if it was better to accept or decline, he clung to the woman's shadow against the wall and crept along the long street until they reached a door that was abruptly opened, and the two of them slipped into a house. Lying on a cot was a young man, his torso bound and a red stain growing between the folds of the bandages, which were sheets cut up for that purpose; he was sweating with fever. The woman, without any preamble, almost declaratively, said, "We want to know if you can take him to Barcelona."

León Bendelac was unable to react, scared and unnerved as he was. "On the donkey," the woman went on, "if you could carry him on your donkey. The soldiers will be back, and if they find him here they'll kill him. He can't go alone; he's too badly hurt."

She served León Bendelac a mug of rum until the color returned to his face, but still he had trouble getting a word out. "They'll find us and kill us," he finally said.

"I don't think they'll be back yet; there's still time. I'll show you a way out over a different road from the one you know. Outside the city you'll be safer. They won't be going to Barcelona; they know the revolutionaries are here, and they're just waiting for the sun to come up to attack again. The invasion was a failure," the woman said, "the weapons didn't get here; he"—she pointed to the wounded young man—"came from Caracas with some other revolutionaries; they were all killed. His name is Miguel, he's a student. We're fighting against the dictator, understand?"

León Bendelac understood, but it worried him, the idea of fleeing with the two animals and a man so weakened by pain and fever that he could barely stand.

"He'll die here for sure," the woman insisted. "If I go for a doctor they'll find out, and if he's not taken care of he'll die—and when they come they'll kill me and my children too."

Draped over the donkey and tied to it, following the steps of the mule Bendelac was riding, Miguel left Cumaná, and when the sun came up they were far away and safe. Using cloth from his merchandise as a coverlet, León was able to disguise the young man's body, and he waited for nightfall before entering the house. He laid Miguel, unconscious now, on the bed and went into the kitchen for a few minutes to drink a glass of water and meditate on the questions that were assaulting him. What should he do? Whom could he trust? Whom could he tell? He was on good terms with the doctor, but how to know which side he was on? Looking at the young man, León thought maybe it was too late to do much for him, but even so he left and knocked on the doctor's door. He explained briefly, without much detail, what it was all about, and together they returned to León Bendelac's house. It was a Friday, at sunset, and while the doctor extracted the bullet and cleaned the wound, León lighted a candle and prayed. He also wrote a letter to his mother laying out what had happened, but, thinking better of it, he tore it up just as carefully as he'd composed it and watched mutely as the bits of paper burned—until the doctor interrupted him, saying he'd done what he could and jotting down the names of some medicines it would be necessary to administer. The following morning León went to the pharmacy, and after placing his order he showed the woman there a fake bandage with which he'd swathed his hand, gave a long explanation of how the mule had kicked him, traitor mule who didn't recognize his master, the person who gave him his food.

★   ★   ★

Because he had few close friends, León Bendelac didn't expect anyone to come visiting and discover his secret that way. He headed out in the morning, leaving the wounded man water, food, and medicine on a table within reach, and he only returned at night, after his usual rounds. Together they read the newspapers, which had little or nothing to say about the failed uprising of the *Falke,* and Miguel, who was regaining his strength, explained his motives: his desire for freedom and justice; the jails and torture the tyrant had in store for his opponents; and the desolation in which the country found itself. They established a friendship up to a certain point, and León confided, for the first time since he'd arrived in Venezuela, a few of his memories and his reasons for having emigrated—but so far he'd only been able to subsist and send small savings to his mother, and that was why he'd thought about going to Cumaná, to see if he could do better. For the first time he began to consider Caracas, too. Miguel insisted he would have better opportunities there; there were rich people, some extraordinarily so, people who could buy jewelry, and his craft as a silversmith would put him in better stead there than in little Barcelona, where resources were so meager. But León Bendelac imagined Caracas to be a huge urban center where he would be lost. Besides, the smell of the sea was comforting to him; the fog at dawn and the breeze in the palms brought him a familiar feeling, transitory but sufficient, at times, to relieve his loneliness. Encouraged, he shared other confidences: sometimes he would let off steam in a small house of prostitution in the city's outskirts, but that didn't satisfy him—he wanted to get married, have children, settle down, and there was no Jewish woman thereabout. His mother wrote prodding letters in which she reminded him that he would soon be twenty-three and he should set up a household; he answered evasively, not daring to reveal the situation to her. The student also saw a solution; he talked about businesses downtown, where León would certainly make friends, meet marriageable young women. Caracas was beginning to grow in his thoughts, but even so he felt wracked by doubts. For better or worse he had a modest clientele here in Oriente; he was known in all the scattered villages in the interior, and in the city they respected and liked him, everybody greeted him, and he had the reputation of being an honest man. In the capital, who would he be? How could he open a way for himself?

When the young man was completely recovered, León Bendelac sadly said good-bye to him. For the first time since his immigration, León felt something close to friendship—he'd spoken to another man about his life and his hopes—and for the first time, too, somebody owed him something that wasn't for merchandise bought on credit. Miguel was going back to Caracas, hoping to leave for Europe from there to avoid the imprisonment that loomed if they found him. It wasn't likely that they would ever see each other again. He jotted a few lines and an address on a piece of paper: "If you ever decide to go to Caracas, look up this man. He's my father; I'll tell him about you, and he'll know how to thank you for saving my life." León cached the letter in the small chest where he kept his mementoes: his *khipa,* a ring of his father's, a small gold star of David, and a photograph of his mother. He closed the chest again and felt a pang as he drew close to the other man in a farewell embrace. That night he didn't wait for the fishermen's invitation, and without ado told the bar owner to serve a round of rum for everybody. "The Turk's buying! The Turk's buying!" they shouted happily, and León Bendelac, for the first time, drank until he forgot himself.

Before leaving for Caracas, León Bendelac said good-bye to his friends on the docks, the civil leader (who still had his wristwatch), the doctor, the pharmacist, and the Arab who owned La Estrella. He'd sold all his possessions and auctioned his merchandise in booths set up in the backyard of his house, a bargain sale that brought in everybody in Barcelona. Housewives and children took away, at a good price, fabrics, ribbons, bow ties, tallow candles, straw hats, and even a pair of two-toned shoes. Sitting in the empty house, from which the furniture had already disappeared, with the bureau drawers empty, León slowly set his clothes into a cardboard suitcase that he lashed to the back of the mule. He gathered his valuables in the black satchel and donned a dark suit, sweating under the jacket, in a pocket of which he carried the folded sheet of paper, a bit damp, that Miguel had given him a while back. He got on the animal and, spurring it, headed out of the city in a cloud of dust and at a swaying trot. "León, León, when are you coming back?" a girl shouted from a window, and León Bendelac smilingly waved good-bye with a noncommittal gesture, remembering that he'd sold her some flowered fabric for her sweet-sixteen dress. "León, León, when are you coming back?" It was a question he couldn't answer. Sometimes he thought that if nothing worked out, at least he had a place to come back to, and if everything went well maybe he'd return and buy a big house on the sea. This is what he wrote his mother: *I'm going to the capital, where there are more opportunities. Don't worry; I've got some friends who will help me,* and he touched the pocket where he kept the letter, concentrating his thoughts on the address that he'd memorized; he'd repeated it hundreds of times as he had coffee with the doctor. "Yes, of course, between Madrices and Ibarras, everybody knows the address—when you get to Caracas, go to the Plaza Bolívar, and they'll tell you how to get to it from there. It's close by; you can't miss it. Leave the mule tied up fast on the square (you must do that so nobody will steal it), get off, and walk in the direction of Ibarras; from there you go two blocks, and there you are." In all his imaginary peregrinations through the city he began at the Plaza Bolívar, and then he would go up and down the streets the doctor had described or he would trudge through the steep alleyways that extended the city toward the north of the narrow valley, where the Arab had told him there were brothels and houses where fun was to be had. "The synagogue? Hell!" That the doctor didn't know. "Ask someone when you get there—on the Plaza Bolívar, of course—ask someone there, and he'll know."

León Bendelac, squinting into the sun that was glimmering over the blue line of the sea, spent days crossing the sands of Tacarigua, trying to reach a village before nightfall overtook him without a place to sleep. It took days for the mule to climb Capaya Mountain, and despite the heat León shivered in the jungle solitude, his eye fixed on the rocks and precipices, happy when another traveler shouted good-day as they passed on the slender trail; days until he finally caught sight of the village of Guatire and had, for the first time since he'd left Barcelona, a peaceful night's sleep. By the following morning Caracas should be visible; the Plaza Bolívar would be there, waiting for him, and León Bendelac lay on his cot, listening to the night and resting his sore body before undertaking the last leg of his journey.

"Watch out, watch out, the bogeymen are coming!"

He hears loud yelling all around, sees an automobile pass, followed by several men on horseback who, whips in hand, are lashing out right and left without looking while women grab their children and wrap them up in their skirts.

"There goes the general."

Almost nobody dared pronounce his name, the doctor had already explained, lowering his voice. Discombobulated, León keeps watching the spectacle and doesn't realize that the mule, in the middle of the street, is impeding the caravan's passage.

"Get that mule out of there, you big shithead!" And before León Bendelac can react, the Andean cracks his whip twice at the animal, which, spooked, rears; León is unable to stop it from galloping off down the street with his load. León runs too, but he can't catch up, and, panting, he watches the mule disappear at high speed, carrying the suitcase that contains everything he owns, and as he bends to retrieve two or three items that dropped off during the mule's bouncing dash along the street, for the first time since arriving in Venezuela León Bendelac feels hatred. Satchel in hand, drying his tears of rage, he asks a passerby how to get to the block of Madrices to Ibarras.

Standing by the house's door, he tries to imagine the interior; he's not sure whether to ring the bell or use the knocker or wait until someone comes out. Finally, a woman toting an empty basket opens the door.

"What do you want?"

León Bendelac pronounces the name he's been repeating to himself for months.

"Who shall I say is asking for him?"

"I don't think my name will mean anything to him. I'm a friend of his son; I've got a letter."

The servant looks at him and, lowering her voice, with an air of mystery, answers: "Mr. Miguel's not here; he went over Europe way."

"What about his father?"

"They're not here either; they're on vacation in Los Chorros."

Los Chorros, Los Chorros—the name is turning about in his head, and he seems to recall the doctor's mentioning it once; the vacation homes of the privileged class.

"Is it very far?" he stammers.

"Well, a bit far, and unless it's urgent the master won't see you, because he's sick." Then, in a condescending way, she adds, "But I'm here if I can do anything for you."

Not much can be done for León Bendelac as he sits in a small boardinghouse room in La Pastora, with no change of clothing, counting his dwindling funds. He writes to his mother, telling her he arrived in Caracas all right, *My friends will take care of me; I'll write you as soon as I can;* and, having dusted off his shoes with a handkerchief, he goes into the street and asks where the post office is.

A carter has offered to take him to Los Chorros for the sum of five bolívares. León Bendelac doesn't know if he's going to lose his little reserve of money in this undertaking; he is weary of canvassing the city's hardware stores and offering his services, which are continually refused. He hasn't much of anything left, unless it's the hope that they'll return his favor; and, arguing with himself, he asserts that what he did at first out of fear metamorphosed into a gesture of friendship. He wheedled the address out of the servant woman by taking her to a band concert one afternoon and listening to her laughter and her prating without hearing anything. Afterward, he left her disappointed at the door; he courteously took his leave and promised to come back. Now, in the cart, he passes through country estates that surround the city and from time to time exchanges a few comments with the driver. It's a bright morning, and Mount Avila has been cleared of clouds by an early rainstorm and is showing its colors and prominence as it opens its arms to the valley while the cart winds between the smaller vacation homes, which are plagued with shadows and dampness. Among the trees the houses can be seen—an assortment of styles, those with long, low porchways and cane roofs mingling with ample French-style structures, several stories high, that have steps and balustrades across from small terraced gardens, and neoclassical sculptures sprinkled among rotundas and kiosks. The carter is in a hurry and drops León Bendelac off, hat in hand, in front of a grillwork gate behind which he can see a broad garden and, farther on, some leafy rubber trees. In the shade, in wicker chairs, a man with white hair is smoking a cigar and resting his goutish foot on a stool while a woman by his side seems to be reading a book. The gardener comes to ask the reason for his visit, and after a few moments comes back to report that the master is not feeling well and can't see him. León insists and, unfolding the celebrated letter, handing over his only identity paper, begs: "Please tell the gentleman I must see him."

Now, sitting across from the man and drinking a cup of coffee, he doesn't quite know how to formulate his request. "I need work. I'm a jeweler by profession, but in Barcelona there weren't many opportunities to practice it. Miguel spoke to me about the capital, said I'd be able to find work here. I wouldn't bother you if I'd been able to find something on my own, but it hasn't been that way. I sold everything I had, and I've spent my small savings on living expenses."

"Don't you think Salbic would be interested in this young man?" the gentleman asked his wife, who until then had remained out of the conversation. They conferred and reached the conclusion that he would, definitely: Salbic is the jeweler who can give him a job. "Tell them I sent you. My wife is a good customer—too good for my taste—but in this case that will work in your favor, young man."

León Bendelac bows several times, thanks them in every way possible and, ready to leave, asks timidly: "Is Miguel coming back to Caracas?"

"Miguel, Mr. Bendelac, died in Paris, and two weeks from now we're taking a ship to be with his widow. So, you see, illness can do more than the general can."

He returns on foot. Now and again he touches the card they gave him, his new passport to hope. Mount Avila takes on its bluish colors of evening: the mountain can be sad when it wants to be, he thinks, it's happy sometimes, misty at other times, can be stormy or foreboding; it's a living mountain. He remembers the student's face and bandaged chest, the bloodstain under the cut-up sheets; he tries to accelerate his pace before it grows dark. Back at the boardinghouse, he composes another letter: *My best friend died, but his parents are going to help me. Tomorrow I will put in an appearance at an important jewelry store, the most important one here. I'm sure they'll give me a job. I'm saddened by the death of my friend. He was a generous young man. I'll tell you about him later.*

"So you were born in Tangier," Salbic says, opening and closing the narrow drawers where he keeps his precious stones. "My grandparents came from Tangier, too, but my father went to France and there took up the jeweler's trade. It's a family trade. My father had a small business in the south. I've been here for several years. So, what brought you to these parts?"

León Bendelac gives vague answers about his commercial travels.

"Oriente. No, friend, there's nothing there yet—this is a poor, backward country—but you'll see, the oil business will change it completely. Keep in mind what I'm telling you; a few years from now, everything's going to be different." And he launches into a long discourse on economics and politics, to which León listens patiently, hoping that at some point his new possibilities will become concrete. He tries to steer the conversation toward more precise and practical matters, but Salbic seems to have found the listener he's been looking for over the years, and he's not about to give up the opportunity just like that. After a long while he says, "Lunchtime, my friend, and nobody's come in today. That's what this business is like. Days can go by without anything happening, but sometimes in just one morning there are enough good sales to produce a whole month's profits. Remember that we open at two—be punctual; punctuality on the job is the key to success." And without saying any more Salbic gets up, takes his jacket off the hook, and accompanies León to the door.

At two o'clock on the dot, León Bendelac was standing in front of the store, and that afternoon he worked for the first time on an order, some silver engagement rings.

"Excuse the rather personal question, but are you married?"

León shook his head and was about to give an extensive explanation of his travails, but Salbic resumed his monologue.

"A man should settle down, make a home, have children. If he doesn't have children, who'll take care of him in his old age? My wife and I have an only daughter, Dorita. Dora hasn't found a mate either, I mean a proper man that her mother and I would accept. It's not easy, Bendelac; it's not easy today to make a good marriage—I can see already that you've had the same problem. Are those rings ready? Let me see, yes, very good, very good. You've got a skilled pair of hands; this is fine work. Here we work honestly; we don't fool our customers, and that's why people come back. Take a look at the competition. Better prices? Yes, but how? They mix metals—and what about the cutting, the carving? They think what they have in their hands is glass. All you have to do is see the people who come here . . . how can I put it, only discriminating people come here, that is, those with good taste, who can appreciate—we're not sharpers here, you know, swindlers, it's a small clientele but one with impeccable taste. These are fine, Bendelac, you give them to the customer yourself; I've got to go out. I'll be back at closing time. If there's anything you don't know, call my wife and she'll explain it to you. Feel like one of the family."

And so, months later, León Bendelac had the honor of accompanying the Salbics to the synagogue to celebrate the new year and could dust off his *khipa,* which he'd kept carefully put away in his jewel box.

Belén was bored. Women today are flighty, Alejandro, did you know that women got bored? I never did; I didn't have time to. At Belén's age I'd already given birth to seven of my ten children, and she, on the other hand, has been fallow. My house and my inheritance were enough to keep me busy, and I never thought about any other distractions—and there weren't any of them anyway. I can sentimentally recall a day when the Mijares women invited the cathedral musicians, and they were playing a sonata in the private chapel. I told you then that my fondest desire was for you to take me to Spain to listen to sacred music, but it didn't seem convenient to you, or proper, to take such a long trip; and I also remember an innocent little skit put on in praise of Ferdinand VI—there were other spectacles that thrilled the rabble, like bullfights, cockfights, ribbons tied to cats, and fandangos in the slums, but these were forbidden to me.

Belén was bored. Too poor to live a merry widowhood in Paris, too distinguished to marry just anyone in Caracas, too young to accompany her mother in the sewing room, too old to find a husband of her class, she could not derive sufficient consolation from the memory of her husband, and she regretted her hasty marriage in Curaçao that sad and solemn day in the presence of their closest family, before leaving for Paris. She wanted to stand out at parties, travel to Europe again, give and attend receptions, make a show of her youth and beauty, and all she had left now as fun was helping her mother sew little baskets for indigent children or getting together some afternoons with women who wanted to read literature; at most she might attend a show at the Teatro Municipal with her sister Carlota and her brother-in-law or stroll in Caobos Park on Sunday. She had more than enough spark and enthusiasm to fill that empty house, which was run-down and leaky. (I had so many children that even with all the bedrooms, there never seemed to be enough room for me; and their laughter and joyful cries could always be heard in the courtyard and out back. Now, on the other hand, there's always silence, and sometimes I share her urge to run away from it.) Then Domingo Sánchez discovered Belén. Her timid look and her odd expressions caught his attention at a party she attended, chaperoned by her mother, at the Club Paraíso. It was still during the lifetime of General Gómez— 1928, the beginning of 1929. She was enveloped by a hush, and she aloofly accepted the courteous but distant greetings from the few families who honored the memory of her father, but avoided her husband's shadow. And he, outgoing, convivial, a gentleman, holding a glass of champagne and surrounded by fawners, went over to rescue her and requested the honor of dancing a paso doble with her— which caused a stupor on some faces and sparked hot whispering among the matrons, nervous coughs among the socialites. And she, with her thankful smile that seemed extraordinarily beautiful to him, accepted the paso doble and then a tango and a foxtrot. Then Domingo Sánchez, bowing respectfully to her mother, Doña Cristina, asked permission to visit them some afternoon. Oh, all the fancy manners you've picked up, Dominguito!

And all the humiliations I've had to bear while closeted in my bedroom, which is now the storage room; I've been a forced spectator of the unforgettable scenes of fine manners whenever he visited my house on the corner of San Jacinto! The coach house was converted into a garage, the chapel into a sewing room, the servants' courtyard into a place of business; but it still holds its own. I can still feel the coolness of the courtyard with its long porchways that have been cut in half, where Cristina, in a wicker easy chair, offers Dr. Sánchez Luna a glass of brandy and lays out before him the illustrious memories, remembrances of her husband when she didn't even know him and he owned a cacao plantation in Barlovento; and afterward, an obligatory moment, she takes him into the dining room to appreciate the painting, commissioned by José Francisco from a famous artist at the turn of the century, that commemorates the flight to Oriente of his mother, my great-granddaughter Isabel, when as an infant she escaped in the arms of a slave woman who was fleeing in terror through the jungle; and then he, Dr. Sánchez Luna, outdoes himself with praise. Wouldn't you have liked, Dominguito, to have told Doña Cristina that your grandfather, old Andrés Cayetano, was a cacao harvester on the largest plantation in Barlovento? But you didn't say anything; you were a mute child and you let Dr. Sánchez Luna stoically take in Doña Cristina's tales, and with the second glass of brandy her vituperations against Joaquín Crespo, the cause of all her late husband's sorrows, of his ruin, probably of his death, and in general of all the ills, past and present, of the country—the fault of the liberals. Why didn't you say anything there either, Captain Sánchez? Why didn't you tell her that you entered Caracas at fifteen, serving in the *Ever-Undefeated Invincible Army* of the last of the liberals, under the command of General Cipriano Castro, swaddling yourself in the yellow banners of the sacred liberal cause? You no longer remembered your old general, isn't that so? Now you only owed loyalty to your new general, and so you calmed Doña Cristina by explaining that thanks to Don Juan Vicente the civil wars have given way to peace, and the country has found better paths to follow under the motto of *Union, Peace, and Work.*

A day came when Doña Cristina pretended to leave them alone and spied from behind the door while Dr. Sánchez Luna and Belén chatted in the small parlor. When he took a solitaire out of his vest pocket, Cristina blew in like a whirlwind and said, "Belén, you can't accept gifts from a gentleman who's only paying a visit," and she pierced him with, "Dr. Sánchez, you know you're welcome in this house, but you've been visiting Belén for a long time now, and people talk." Then Dr. Sánchez Luna stood up and pompously declared, "But the fact is I've come today to ask Belén to marry me."

So the day arrived when his name became joined to mine, because Dr. Sánchez found a way to fill the dead space in himself that he despised. Plenty of people said Domingo's money had bought her, but that's not the way it was, Alejandro; it was her own flightiness, and that of her mother—not too bright a woman, I've got to admit—who would refer to her daughter's existence as *poor Belén's tragedy,* constantly comparing it to the life of Carlota, whose lot she judged as rife with excellent things. I expected more of Belén, I confess. You know that in our era widows married two or three times and that I was the daughter of my mother's second marriage; men used to die quite young, or else we women resisted illness more, I don't know—but I might have hoped more of her than going from her love of a hero husband to an alliance with a henchman of the powerful. I, who knew you in your youth, Domingo Sánchez, understand that the young captain in the Army of Restoration would have wanted Belén desperately and would have squired her to Las Palomas Park in Macuto to kiss her again and again under the grape arbors, but now, corpulent and fiftyish, you lack—among other things—hope; if she joined herself to you in order to continue on with life, you married her to feel you had companionship as you ended it. I, from my storeroom, have a long perspective, and I know that time will betray not only me but you, too, Domingo Sánchez; its labyrinths await you.

Domingo Sánchez smiles. Belén, in sports clothes for her golf lesson, looks like an adolescent overwhelmed by schoolwork.

"All these appointments! The dressmaker, the hairdresser, the visits of condolence, the new babies, the social-work committees, receptions. Domingo, I'm sick of your being a minister all the time—it's so tedious—you ought to find some other job."

He listens to her from far away while he reads the newspaper. He has a feeling of success, satisfaction.

"I'm going to the country club," she says. "Shall I expect you for lunch?"

"No, I won't be home until night. The general wants to see me today." Picking up his cane, he kisses her forehead.

Belén is left alone with her agitation over all the things to do. Vicenta is preparing a broth at a long counter.

"What are you cooking?"

"I'm making the chicken-and-corn stew the doctor likes so much. For dessert, crullers, or, if you want, a meringue."

"Vicenta, have you ever been in love?" The black woman lets out a guffaw and continues working. "So why don't you answer me? Haven't we known each other all our lives?"

"All our lives, yes, but I don't talk about those things with you." Vicenta laughs, covering her mouth, which is missing several teeth, with a hand. "If the doctor ever heard us—such a lack of respect! I never got married. When I was a girl I saw how much my mama suffered, and I thought *It's no good having the shade always coming from the same branch.*"

"And is it so easy your way?"

"You're different, Missy; you were brought up different. But let me get my work done, because you've got me jabbering, and if the doctor doesn't like his meal he gets mad."

"I'm having lunch at the club. I'll be home late. I've got to make a lot of stops today."

"What you should do is tell the doctor to give you a child. Women, if they don't have children, can't find anything to do."

"Don't be giving me any advice; I don't give you any." Belén leaves in a hurry.

Stretched out on the massage table, she let herself be lulled by the mutterings of the women, sweating in the steam bath or crying out at either the masseuse's pinches or the scale's treacheries. She accepted an invitation for a light lunch at poolside; most of all, she let time pass. Despite the innumerable engagements awaiting her—sometimes pleasurable and other times annoying, a duty imposed on her—Belén had the relentless feeling of having nothing to do, of making an effort to maintain a position, live up to a social rank . . . and fill an empty space inside. It seemed to her that she'd been repaid for her painful moments, and when she'd reached her limit—what her mother called the tragedy of poor Belén, comparing it with her sister Carlota's peaceful and harmonious existence—something like a miracle had happened, and her future had been restored to its former grandeur and rolled out before her as if it were a carpet just awaiting her step. And Belén had a grateful smile for her fate, and probably, she thought later, a necessary blind eye. With passing time she'd become disillusioned with herself; the boredom that was mounting in her despite her enviable circumstances was inexplicable, and her annoyance seemed to her a more censurable sin than any other, an unpardonable impiety that she tried to conceal from other people. She had the impression—against which she fought hard, yet it was insistent—that her life was running along without her, the impression of a deep gulf that separated her from herself forever, as if she were condemned to a permanent nostalgia for herself. And when she'd begun to accept that dizzy feeling of not recognizing herself in her gestures, her actions, her words, and as she struggled against the distressing sensation of lostness, she'd run into León Bendelac.

León was sinking into uncertainty. He couldn't help feeling proud when, as soon as he arrived home, his children would run to open the door and Dora would hug him as if she'd been eagerly anticipating his return from a long trip. Her companionship suffused dinnertime with warmth, as he told incidents from work and she brought out her inventory of the minor events in the immigrant colony. He'd thought himself happy, and had left behind his wistfulness for Barcelona on the sea; he thought that God had blessed his union, and he couldn't understand this explosion of his well-being. Every night when they turned out the lamp and kissed each other until the next day, in the light from the street that filtered through the venetian blinds and outlined Dora's body beside him, her hand clutching his, León would ask himself the same question and sink deep into his pillow, trying to go into a sound sleep. Every night since *she*'d entered the jewelry store for the first time, he would revisit the scene where his mistake had occurred, his undoing. Because he was convinced that he'd made an irremediable mistake. When she first rang the bell at *Salbic and Bendelac* and he came out from the back of the store, vexed at the interruption because he was overseeing the workers on a delicate engraving, Salbic had introduced him to Mrs. Belén Sánchez Luna and told him that, in Salbic's absence, León was to take care of her with the greatest solicitude. Mrs. Sánchez Luna had come to them because she wanted a new setting for the solitaire engagement ring her husband had given her. He turned to Belén, who was sitting across from the counter, thumbing casually through some French magazines he'd spread out, her face veiled so that her protruding lips could barely be seen; and there was no doubt that his mistake began there, when he indulged in that first dialogue of banal phrases and then the words of surprise with which they had recognized each other. When they came together in the strangeness of having fallen in love without knowing it.

When León Bendelac was invited to form a part of the intimate life of the Salbics, and Salbic, smoothly and with the same circumspection with which he polished his jewels, let it be understood that León and his daughter, Dora, would make an excellent couple, León finally had the joy of writing his mother with news of his approaching wedding; the memory of Miguel had remained back in the days in Barcelona, lost among the cloths and bottles of alcohol that he was selling on muleback at the time. His recollection had dimmed and receded, become a dark body that no longer said anything, but suddenly, when he saw her, it appeared before him. While the wounded man was recuperating, the two of them sat at a table lighted by an oil lamp, in long and cozy conversation; he'd begun to understand the history of the country where a quirk of fate had landed him, and as a part of Miguel's stories he'd known her, a frightened adolescent waiting for the student radical to return from his failed revolution so they could get married without delay and escape to Europe. And when León saw in her, alive, the description he'd heard so often of her face, her expressions, her laugh, Belén, like a pleased child who'd found a lost toy, had exclaimed, "Why, you're Bendelac!" And he, beside himself, trying to maintain a serious manner but verging on laughter, had answered, "Yes, ma'am, I'm León Bendelac, at your service"; and she'd laughed even more and then explained how she'd carried an image of him, would have been able to recognize him anywhere, his dark and curly hair, his very white skin, his rather short stature and Andalusian accent. And both of them had confessed the strange sense of feeling themselves united in a vanished tale in which Miguel, without knowing it, had brought them together.

That day León Bendelac sent the workers home early. Salbic had told him never to do that—*Son, keeping to schedule is the key to success*—but he trumped up an obscure reason for closing ahead of time. He roamed the streets without any desire to go home and began walking aimlessly through the blocks he'd come to know by heart, the imaginary route the doctor in Barcelona had taught him and that then had seemed like a labyrinth, but that now was his everyday landscape. Going up and down, letting himself be carried along by the promenading people, by the colors of the shops, by the electric signs that were starting to flicker on, by his own solitude, he reached the Plaza de la Candelaria. There he sat on a bench and watched the trees darken through the streetlights, and while he took in the bustle of the people strolling in front of the church in the coolness of dusk and listened to women calling to the children playing on the swings, he found himself bewildered. He'd gone into a crowded bar where patrons were shouting and passing glasses back and forth, had mingled among the unfamiliar throng, so many people who meant nothing to him, and from that day on he found himself possessed for the first time by a shameless desire. He'd returned home afterward, dragging his mistake along like a bundle. Dora was waiting for him, grave, worried, sad perhaps; he'd never come home so late. "I felt like taking a walk; don't be concerned. What's the news?" And together they'd sat down to listen to the war report from the BBC in London, its special broadcast to Latin America.

At first he'd felt befuddlement, fascination, which caused him to babble in her presence; he experienced a disturbing feeling that the only important thing in life was seeing her come into the jewelry store, a constant fear that at any moment she might break off her visit and go away, with no explanation or assurance of her return—as if her coming had been an unmotivated gift that could be snatched away in an instant, because she obeyed no laws or covenants except a desire to spend a few minutes there, to sit for a spell and thumb through design magazines, to question him about small details of his jejune life or tell him banal anecdotes from hers. León had begun to live an existence that was split in two: everything he was and had come to be on one side, everything he wanted to be on the other, and he couldn't measure the duration of those moments: sometimes they would seem extremely long, and the clock would show only half an hour, and other times too short, and the clock would show that two hours had elapsed. He'd entered a time that didn't have anything to do with his schedule—the alarm that awakened him as dawn began to break, the routine with which he placed the open or closed sign in the shop window, the hour of his lunch served punctually by Dora or of the joyful reception she and their children were waiting to give him, ready to tell him everything that had happened during the day. And then there was Belén's time, which didn't conform to any measurement known to him and would plunge him into an unknown vertigo.

The time that belonged to what he called for lack of other words his real life began to be insidiously transformed into a suffocating weight, a burden cobbled together by the rancor of a prisoner serving an unjust sentence, the bafflement of someone caught unawares on a foolish errand. He thought he should have fought to drive these temptations off and to settle down to his real destiny once more, his real affections, his real motives. Comforted by the recognition of his proper place, he'd ventured to comment to Dora about the frivolity of those women who only think about the dress they're going to wear or the jewel that will show them off, and, without realizing it, had brought up Belén's name with such frequency that Dora felt compelled to say that if that lady had enough money to be constantly ordering baubles and gifts, it was, quite the contrary, reason for being thankful, because that was what his business was there for. León had comprehended then that his incessant mentions of Mrs. Sánchez Luna, far from being a criticism of his customer, were instead an ingenious way of mentioning her, of feeling that when she was out of sight she still existed, of thinking about her, speaking her name, repeating it, even when the context made it the most inapposite thing. But he'd also understood that he better keep it to himself, bottle it up inside and wait in loneliness until she would appear again one day—and after that, with a tacit regularity that took on the character of complicity, every Tuesday from five to seven.

He had sketched of her face the portrait of a girl in love with a romantic hero. Yet the face sometimes showed a joy whose reasons were beyond him, and at other times a perplexing shadow overcame her, which made him uneasy. He would listen very attentively, trying to catch in her words some explanation for her presence, but Belén would leap from one subject to another without his being able to seize upon any clue. He'd come to understand that there was something forced about her marriage to Sánchez Luna, but she would immediately follow that innuendo with an expression of admiration for that man who was so famous for his reputation and wealth. León suspected at times that Belén's husband neglected her, but at any imputation of that she would straightaway praise her husband's virtues and marvel that he, so weighted down with obligations, always had time to cater to her. When León talked about his children he seemed to notice a disagreeable emptiness in her—this was a subject she wanted to avoid—so he preferred to leave them out of the dialogue, though at some moments they served to occupy a silence that was becoming unbearable for him. Because if anything tormented León in Belén's presence, it was not knowing what to say. He would let her carry the conversation, let her ask questions or relate familiar tales that were always a source of astonishment and curiosity for him, and he could never understand what attraction his company had for her. What could she see in him—this woman awash in blandishments and luxuries, besieged by all of Caracas high society, who saw in her a means of access to her husband's power? No matter how hard he tried to come up with an explanation, León found himself bereft of any attributes, lacking anything that could account for the regularity of her visits and, above all, the happiness they seemed to bring her. He also thought during moments of crude reflection that if Belén was seeking the favors of a lover, there must have been more than enough interested people, and of all his quandaries, the one León considered unsolvable was knowing what his role was. But he'd become accustomed to that uncertainty, for at the same time a certainty had settled in him, one of feeling himself irrevocably involved in an erroneous love.

Ever since that first day, when he should have said, *Mrs. Sánchez Luna, you have a lot of things to do, and so do I; you have to attend receptions and ceremonies in your duties as the wife of a minister, and I'm taken up with my work and my family.* But instead he'd agreed to make a setting for the solitaire, which, no matter how hard he tried, never satisfied her. Those frequent visits, which were more and more contrived, uncalled for, were when he should have said, *Mrs. Sánchez Luna, you don't need any more friendships, least of all one with your jeweler, and I have other obligations; I can't just devote myself to satisfying your whims.* But then he'd taken on some watches that always seemed slow and some baptism medallions for the countless children to whom Mrs. Sánchez Luna had to give them. Those afternoons that became prolonged and obliged him to concoct silly excuses for Dora were when he should have said, *Mrs. Sánchez Luna, I've got a lot to do, and not much time, and you should use your Tuesdays for formal visits.* But he'd acquiesced to releasing the workers early on Tuesdays and bringing in a bottle of sweet wine now and again. And, finally, he'd set up a small divan in the rear of the store and made the fundamental mistake from which it was now impossible to retreat. It was too late now: the business was prospering; his children were growing; Salbic was thinking about retiring; and all León Bendelac wanted was for it to be Tuesday.

His life had lost the effect of continuity. Between what he called his real life and his life with Belén, those two villages in his soul, there was no communicating bridge, and he would jump from one to the other, unable to choose. He reproached himself for being too weak to rein in a passion, a game, and every time he tried to, he failed utterly—sunk by the thought of what his life would be once this was cut off. He admitted defeat, acknowledged the intimate awareness that between him and Belén a current flowed that was his most incontestable truth, his surest affirmation, and he reached the deepest part of his desire. Ever since those solitary talks with Miguel in Barcelona, the image of an adolescent girl had seemed to trap León. Miguel's vivid words made her come alive, and yet those words were part of an inconclusive narration, had an evanescent character that tormented León; and even if the memory had been tamed over the course of time, her living presence, her yearned-for body, her recovered image confronted him with a force that was impossible to overcome without demolishing himself. He pictured an outcome whose details he left blank, because it was impossible for him to imagine a scenario where he and Belén got rid of all the ballast that constituted their circumstances; and together they discovered the absurdity of feeling themselves alike in the midst of such discord, and that way every minute that was stored away prefigured the definitive moments that would ensue. He understood that during the whole time his life limped on without Belén he might be up to his duties, but with an absence of interest in anything that wasn't she, and he would see himself amply rewarded when she was present. So from one week to the next, their meetings were separated and interrupted by the distractions of his real life, voices he hushed in order to remain in silent communion with her.

As other women bragged about their wealth, they flattered Belén—sometimes subtly, other times coarsely—exchanged gossip, and even divulged their troubles, but she felt herself infinitely superior, because she'd captured the joy that utter certainty awards. It seemed to her that there was no betrayal on her part: the woman she surrendered to León Bendelac was one Domingo Sánchez had never known, never desired, and, in short, never possessed. On the other hand, the woman that he loved, Mrs. Sánchez Luna, was always there for him, always tenderly attentive, never careless about any detail that might disgrace him. If they both coincided in the same body, she'd come to think it was mere chance and that she wasn't responsible, but she recognized that with time she'd ended up despising Mrs. Sánchez Luna, considering her tyrannical, lacking in compassion, judgmental, meanspirited, and, above all, the mistress of her life who could never be dethroned. But it wasn't in Belén's power to destroy her, annul her, or deprive her of her hold. She could only leave her from time to time to some formal visit while Belén ran off madly to meet *the*

Turk in the jewelry store . . . because that was the way Mrs. Sánchez Luna spoke of him, and so showed her disdain for what to Belén was the warmest and most intimate pleasure.

Mrs. Sánchez Luna and she had arrived at a cruel pact, a division of time—which seemed unjust and small-minded to Belén, but nights of weeping had convinced her that no better agreement existed, and Belén had learned to love her brief bliss and stretch it out until it seemed her whole life; she'd managed to convert the rest into a preparation and a memory, so that despite Mrs. Sánchez Luna, Belén succeeded in forging a kind of monopoly, and she'd trained herself to think about everything she would like to tell León the next Tuesday, even if she was enjoying a dinner and gossiping and laughing with the wives of other ministers—even while she was distributing baskets at the committee for social welfare, she was recalling everything he'd said to her the Tuesday before. All that was left for Mrs. Sánchez Luna, though this situation was devouring her with rage, was choosing her dress, discussing her coiffure with the hairdresser, being told by Minister Sánchez Luna what subjects to avoid and what deferences to offer—but when they returned from the party, fatigued, and Mrs. Sánchez Luna had undressed and turned out the light, Belén had the rest of the night to ponder León Bendelac.

Miguel's story of how León had saved him—which the newly-weds recounted during Miguel's final weeks, when they found themselves forced to speak about the past because the future was a closed subject—had always incited Belén's curiosity. The story seemed to insert that man into her life in a way that was mysterious and especially fraught with feeling. The name of León Bendelac was inscribed in her circumstances like that of a character that she would not only know someday but to whom, in some unknown but necessary way, she would be linked forever. And after events seemed to erase him, when she saw him for the first time in *Salbic and Bendelac* she was surprised at not having known for so long a time that he was there, working in the jewelry store—where it was more than probable he would be, since she knew that Miguel's father had given him a recommendation. And when she recognized him, as she stood before someone she felt so close to and so distant from at the same time, she had to admit to a confusion, an upset, as if her life was coming unbound, and all the years with Domingo Sánchez in a sensible and loving existence together seemed to crumble to nothing. If her visits began to be assiduous, if she conceded ordering more gifts than she needed and discovering that the setting for the solitaire had tiny defects, Belén couldn't help it; it seemed that in those short talks she'd gained a small corner for herself, a happy spark that turned out to be a ray of sunshine for her, one indispensable for a plant that was languishing. There was no reason for these furtive visits, but on the other hand no reason to break them off.

Belén decided that this space of joy, even if minuscule and hemmed in by so many hostile forces, was hers completely, and she wasn't about to give it up until circumstances did it in, until a final point put a halt to it—not a fading of her feelings, a notion that seemed impossible as she reveled in her secret little corner of pleasure. And so, for many a Tuesday, León Bendelac and the woman with the solitaire would meet from five to seven, neither a minute more nor a minute less; and unless for some exceptional event they never missed their appointment.

Customs must have changed a lot for something outrageous like that to happen? You find it strange that I tell my story without condemnation? Oh, Alejandro, what do you want me to tell you!? I feel disconcerted by all the changes that have taken place, and sometimes I lose my sense of things. I, too, am ashamed at seeing her rolling around in bed—what am I saying, *bed,* on the cot of that Turk—and then returning home with a smile that says *It wasn't me.* I also remember the case of that prominent woman whom I shan't name now so as not to stain her memory, but who for several months was the subject of a scandal when it was learned in Caracas that her husband had ordered her imprisoned, and only the pleas of her mother prevented such an affront . . . but they didn't prevent the daughter's children being taken away and her misbegotten offspring put into a convent; but so much time has passed, Alejandro, that I see cruelty in that punishment, and it happens that Belén's sin is at the same time my revenge. Yes, because I detest Domingo Sánchez, and I deplore his lack of memory. I haven't been able to forget that child, Magdalena, who was the basis for his rise and success; and on Tuesdays from five to seven, when I see Belén get dressed and quickly comb her hair to return to her husband, I say to myself, *The one is recompense for the other.* I should tell the scribe to expunge that whole episode because that shameless hussy humiliates you? It can't be done, Alejandro, because what's written stays written. Make a note, scribe: Domingo Sánchez has paid his debt to the women in the house in San Juan.

PART THREE

1935–1985

General Gómez died, Alejandro, the most difficult death in our history. The whole country spent days and days waiting for the general to urinate, and he didn't. He died of kidney trouble. The same as his comrade Don Cipriano, whom he'd dethroned; aged, uremic, surrounded by doctors and courtiers, without Dr. Bueno's succeeding in bringing about that momentous piss. December 18, 1935, dawned in a tomblike silence over the city; not a leaf was stirring, not a child crying, not a dog barking. Newsboys were peddling their papers sneakily, because they carried the news that Don Juan Vicente had died the day before, and no one dared buy them or read them for fear it was a trick and he was perched in his wicker chair, twirling his Kaiser mustache and laughing at the fools who'd believed the hoax. But he really had died. He was mourned by his 117 children and his 23 wives, he was mourned by his 10,000 horses and his 50,000 cows, he was mourned by his 18 plantations and his 32 ranches; but nobody else mourned him, and when everybody was sure that he'd died, they called him dictator and took away his title of Worthy. Did you grieve for him, Domingo Sánchez, his minister? No, why should you? He was still warm when you declared yourself part of the transition and began to go about seeing who would give you a job now that you were out of work. General Gómez died, Alejandro, and the country rejoiced. The jail doors were opened, and it seemed there'd been more people inside than out; newspapers were uncorked, and never had more ink been spilled; platforms were erected, and never had more speeches been delivered. And the fact was that General Gómez had stopped us from entering the twentieth century; the rest of the world was practically halfway through it, and we were barely on the doorstep . . . and now that it's come, I don't know whether to surrender to nostalgia or to this festival with which we're celebrating the demise of General Gómez—and avenues with traffic lights at the same time. Yes, Alejandro, I too am in the twentieth century; I too want to travel in an airplane, watch television, and take an antibiotic. They dropped the atomic bomb; the world is on fire everywhere, and people are arriving here from all countries, speaking all languages, and worshipping all gods. Just think of all the centuries that passed, and nobody came: a few voyagers to the Indies who strayed off course; four or five madmen, Lisboa, Depons, Humboldt, and Bonpland; and the Canary Islanders who planted vegetable gardens and sold hemp cord; and now the city's been filled up, and they no longer fear earthquakes, and houses are built with so many stories that you get dizzy looking out from them at the valley and the mountain. The valley always seemed so long to me, and it was just because I'd never crossed it from one end to the other—now I know that it only takes half an hour to do it. I'm completely out of my mind, you say, and ought to be locked up in Caridad Hospital? Oh, Alejandro! There's nothing left of Caridad Hospital, not even the dust. Some machines passed through and in one instant wiped out all my memories. There's no longer anything in Caracas I can call my own. They've knocked down all the houses I used to visit when I repaid the calls of the Madriz women, my cousins the Solórzanos, your cousins the Blancos. One by one, the homes that withstood earthquakes, revolutions, and Guzmán have fallen—and, though I know you won't believe me, Llaguno's too, Count Tovar's, Count San Javier's, the Carmelite convent, and General Bolívar's almost came down. They poured concrete over slabs and cobblestones, got rid of donkey carts, widened sidewalks, and strung electric wires up to the last alleys bordering the mountain, then paved its base and built new neighborhoods on the banks of the Anauco because it was necessary for the whole of the twentieth century to fit into the city. I realized then that for all these years I'd been in love with a nameless village.

Also, Domingo Sánchez demolished my house on the corner of San Jacinto. Why wasn't I able to stop him, the way I did when I stood up to the crafty people of the Guipuzcoana? Oh, Alejandro, how naive you are! You would have had to be present instead of turning about in my memory in order to persuade him not to do it. My lot was worth plenty of money, he said, but not its walls, which were adobe with the straw coming out when it rained; the house was suffocating in bus exhaust and engulfed by vendors' stalls, and the gentry no longer wanted to live amidst people of all different stripes. Each block was subdivided into a thousand pieces so it could accommodate more residents; buildings went up, businesses opened, and, in short, what you used to think was the center of the world was transmogrified into an unlivable place. Domingo Sánchez sold it to the highest bidder—just as he disposed of most of the furniture of Isabel, my great-granddaughter, because he said it was old and broken—and he raised himself a mansion where one of the sugar plantations that girdled the city used to be. I was very happy about the short time God gave him to enjoy it. Then I became an evicted ghost, a shade at the mercy of the elements. Yes, they separated me from my titles. I had to leave my house, poking around its cubbies for a last time before a huge stone ball smashed its walls, but I haven't abandoned the search; time will give them back to me. When I took refuge in Belén and Domingo Sánchez's house I realized how poor we'd been, because mine would have fit into theirs ten times over—I can't remember anybody in my time who had enough money to build on a whole block. I must confess that Belén, despite her marriage to that man of evil memory and the unpardonable indiscretions she committed with the jeweler, has been the consolation of my loneliness. When she dies I know that this house, too, will be abandoned; they'll leave the font behind, the same one that for many years was in my courtyard, and which, thanks to Belén, they brought along when they moved to the East End; they'll destroy the French-style pergola she had constructed so her nieces and nephew could play and have lunch there, and whose latticework is already in bad shape; they'll sell to a secondhand store the statue of a beggar boy who's smoking a cigar and has always lacked two fingers on his left hand—a modernist piece of junk that Domingo Sánchez had in his house downtown and that I've grown, over time, to like; they'll sell off cheap the Empire horrors that he bought and treasured so much, and I know that one day nothing will be left of what we have been.

The day came when Domingo Sánchez thought it was time to get to know Europe, or maybe he felt he'd already tolerated too much. Didn't he know quite well that Belén was tearing herself apart as she packed the bags for the happy journey he was laying out for her? Didn't he know all the details of her venturing out every Tuesday from five to seven to pay her formal visits? Hadn't his trustworthy underling advised him that the lady had so much interest in jewels that she spent one afternoon a week admiring them? And hadn't Domingo doubted her excessively innocent and unworried look, hadn't he been tempted many times to confront her with the evidence and humiliate her publicly with a divorce? Hadn't he had to stifle his anger many times so as not to insult her with words that would have scandalized the girls of *The Venus of San Juan*? But by then he'd learned— isn't that so, Dominguito?—how to act with the discretion of a proper bourgeois, and he planned a fictitious and impromptu pleasure trip. Very generous, he was taking along the whole family: her mother, her sister Carlota and brother-in-law Luis Villaverde and their four children. He did the proper thing; when important women slip up, it should be kept under wraps. I can confess now, too, that I erased a folly of my daughter Manuela without a trace when, on a trip to the Chacao plantation, I discovered her dallying with Juan Servando. I sold him, to the great anger of my son Nicolás, who raised a row with me because he thought very highly of Juan; her I immured for several months, until I was certain that her frivolity hadn't any consequences, and I told the houseboy to visit all the neighbors and tell them that they shouldn't appear at my house until further notice because I had a daughter with tertian fever. If Juan Servando had left a memento in her, I would certainly have sent her away to Barlovento to await the outcome, so I can understand Domingo Sánchez's trip, a vacation he didn't even look forward to: visiting monuments, getting to know museums, deluxe restaurants, stones left over from other centuries, gloomy churches, broad avenues, finally entering the order and harmony of European civilization—none of it engaging his interest one tiny bit. What Dominguito liked was activity, but his time had passed now; other people were the ones prospering, and all that remained for him was to grow old reading the newspaper or going off to live in France. He would be a rich mummy, leading a misplaced life with no point of reference, where everything—whether dying of the pulmonary edema that wracked him with an uncontainable morning cough or reserving a table in the best restaurant in Paris— would be the same to him. For Belén that sudden trip was the alarm bell she'd long been expecting, the one that announced the end of what she'd always thought was a fleeting gift whose end hung over her as though some cruel god had invited her to partake of happiness and simultaneously had warned her that its term was limited. Here was the victory of Mrs. Sánchez Luna, a triumph known ahead of time but obscured or overlooked in the passage of the days, in the impossible struggle to sustain a world built on a flimsy foundation. Shortly before leaving, Mrs. Sánchez Luna did her duty. With a thinly disguised rancor she obliged Belén to make a phone call to the jewelry store and advise León Bendelac that she would be coming at the usual hour but that he should be exceptionally careful to eliminate the presence of all employees and customers. Belén arrived alone in a taxi, wearing dark glasses and dressed in her cook's uniform, under which she was hiding a blouse León had given her. She arrived with her mind made up to fulfill the most hateful of the obligations imposed on her by Mrs. Sánchez Luna—not to weaken, not to betray the extent of her sorrow, to pretend a domination of the circumstances that she was far from feeling, trembling with the fear that some gesture on León's part would break down the solid mask she'd assumed. I felt proud, because Belén showed that under a veneer of sentimental foolishness, beneath her inconstancy, under a certain infantile behavior in her, there lived someone who, though suffering, didn't disregard her limits—someone with a sure knowledge of the role in which she was installed. Showing her lover that there was no shadow of doubt, that there was room for feelings but that they also had their place, could have broken her, but she'd been brought up not to show it. I don't see any merit in her determination, nor hypocrisy either—rather, only the inevitable, inexorable ending that had been assured from that very first day when she'd let a part of her life run along unchanneled.

Do you know what that scoundrel she'd shared her sin with proposed? That they run away, no less, that they take refuge in some village along the Barcelona coast, because he didn't feel up to telling his wife he wanted a divorce, and Domingo Sánchez would never grant one to Belén. He said that life was crumbling for him, he would fall apart without her—during all those years, time for him had contracted, had boiled down to the wait, always uncertain despite their routine, for Belén's appearance behind the glass door and his hearing the agreed-to signal (two rings, a pause, two rings) to get rid as soon as possible of any inopportune customer who might fritter away a single second of their rendezvous. He pleaded that the enjoyable and wicked moment where he felt a denial of all other people—his wife, his children, Salbic—had become an indispensable support for his enduring the intimate circle of long and boring family get-togethers, when he would look at the clock in exasperation, as if something were going to happen; during the copious Sunday lunches in which his wife and mother-in-law took great pains to please the men of the house; in exhausting evenings of parley with Salbic about collecting funds for the benefit of their war-refugee brethren; he would listen from a distance to the sounds of a life to which he belonged but that seemed to cease being when she rang the bell of the jewelry store and he saw her, radiant to his eyes, as happy as ever, ready to drink some sweet wine (which he never got to know whether she liked or not) and to tell him little remembrances, fragments between kisses, whispers, and starts when some sound threatened their secret. And the impending trip seemed alien and senseless to him, the same as that failed invasion from the *Falke* when he'd saved Miguel and entered our story. He was wounded, bitter, trying to recover Belén, who was getting away from him, asking him to wait, explaining that it was only a temporary sojourn, that he should understand her circumstances. Then he, saddened, shouted that he didn't know why he'd come to that country, why he'd saved Miguel, why he'd agreed to marry Dora, why he'd fallen in love with Belén. Everything was collapsing in impossible questions now. He had ascribed to a guilty conscience his many nights of bewilderment and agitation, but now he was coming to realize that he'd always had a foreboding of this farewell, which had been marked from the beginning, and that basically nothing unforeseeable had taken place, that events had developed in accord with circumstances, and he, only he, was to blame for not having understood them. All those years had been a passage, and he a suffering person in transit who'd tried to insinuate himself into a new place; and now life was looking to him like a space from which he'd been dislodged, an empty suit in which others thought he was living while he, naked, was lying on a beach of dark sand like an anonymous shipwreck victim whom others would try to revive. Dora wanted him to live so she could feed him, care for him, need him, and Belén so that he might serve as a happy hope that she had carefully laid away while she accompanied her husband around Europe. And he felt again like a frightened youth that a small English ship had brought from Trinidad, carrying a black suitcase and looking for a place to spend the night.

It's an embarrassment, what that man expected: for Belén to abandon her husband, who was going off to Europe with the whole family, in order to run away with a Jewish jeweler. Even so, I was afraid for a moment that his heartfelt speech might soften her weak nature and that she'd lapse into a mistake; for an instant, perhaps, her eyes doubted, for an instant her voice quavered. But it didn't turn out that way.

León Bendelac opened the door of his house. Dora wasn't there; she'd gone out with the children, and the rooms were empty, silent. He turned on the radio, turned it off again. The phone rang, and he thought it was Belén. It was Dora; she was at her mother's house, would spend the night there because she wasn't feeling well. León Bendelac lay down on the bed and was thankful for that absence, that respite. He recalled his altercation with Belén: there had been shouting, grieving complaining back and forth, and when night had come on—it was raining ceaselessly—approaching her in his car as she scurried into the darkness in the downpour, hearing the click of her heels mingling with the sound of the raindrops on the sidewalk, imagining her opening the door and disappearing forever from view. He closed his eyes and tried to recover her smell, her gestures; he didn't want to see empty furniture around him, a desert wasteland of voices and routines that would torment him from then on. He was sure, convinced inside, that finding him had been a decisive joy for Belén, but he was discovering now how much he hadn't comprehended; she had known how to hide from him what his place was. A feeling of absurdity crashed over him like a cloudburst, and he couldn't prevent it from leaving him flooded with an awareness that the next day would be one like any other. He did an unexpected thing. He went into the bathroom, shaved, and changed his clothes. He wrote a short note, and he went out at daybreak and got into a taxi that took him to the bus station, bought a one-way ticket, and, when night fell, he caught the salt whiff of the sea, an absolute emptiness, absolute peace. He was lost forever in the nothingness from which he'd come, and I breathed easefully because our history hadn't been altered by his presence.

When they'd all gone, I was afraid that any chronology would be useless, and since there would be no one to whom it could be passed on, my memory had reached its end. I felt so sad, Alejandro, seeing how they were leaving me all alone, thinking in my loneliness that it might be forever. I was forgetting then that they would be back soon, and it was (I think I can remember, though some dates and details are hard for me) in 1951—during the reign of the fifth general of the Andean dynasty—that they made their way back and once more went up the old highway from La Guaira, snaking around the mountain in the old Pontiac. I've kept the hazy image of their return like a photograph: the girls' white dresses, Francisco's cap, Cristina's veiled hat, Luis Villaverde's sweaty country jacket, Carlota's shirtdress—and Belén, so elegant in a yellow tailored suit with shoulder pads, signaling Martínez the chauffeur from the gangway . . . all of them shouting, as if in that way they could speed the slow pace of disembarkation, amid the smoke from the stack and the whistle's deep echo. It was as though in all that time I'd done nothing but wait for them to get back from Europe. And later came the clamor, the scrambling about, the incoherent orders to the servants, the arranging and disarranging of the house, the noisy commotion brought on by their return, which supplanted my loneliness with life once more. They came burdened with suitcases, satchels, boxes, and trunks, which were stacked in the shed of the customhouse and gave the appearance of belonging to a small circus troupe. The objects that began to be taken out seemed never to stop: Francisco brought a collection of lead soldiers, an electric train, and a Pekingese that barked nervously all through the house; the girls, a multitude of costumes—Alsatian, Breton, Tyrolean, Andalusian—and a wooden puppet theater that they set up in the pergola; Carlota, innumerable dresses and hatboxes; Belén, pieces of porcelain, Chinese vases, and a complete set of Rosenthal chinaware; and they also brought Domingo Sánchez, who had deteriorated into a reticent man who had difficulty walking, and who coughed constantly, swaying his big-bellied torso. I can't fix the year of his death exactly, but I can, to my delight, recall the picture of an unpleasant person that everyone had of him. "One of Gómez's flunkies, that's what he was," Luis Villaverde would say if asked his opinion. "And Castro's, too," Carlota would chime in. "An arriviste, corrupt," Luis continued. "And someone of a different class from ours," Cristina would stress. His funeral was ill-attended, only they and a sparse group of old friends. "Where are the people who used to besiege him before, asking for favors?" Luis asked. "I, who remembered him surrounded by sycophants, saw him buried in an absolute silence." But Domingo Sánchez, of course, had disappeared in Paris. What came back was a sickly, unknown old man who almost made me feel pity; when he was already quite ill they would seat him in the porchway, facing the garden so that he could take in the view of the mountain, and from time to time the servant girl would change his cuspidor. But the discomfort of seeing him once again didn't reduce in the slightest my pleasure as I recognized the merry and nimble way in which Belén introduced her three nieces and her nephew to that Caracas; I could observe without distractions when they took refuge in what they called, because of its leather chairs and hunting pictures, the English parlor, and they would have pillow fights and get smeared with chocolate as they listened to stories, legends, anecdotes, a catalog of reminiscences that Belén would narrate for them and maybe for herself too. Seeing her repeat the history I had lived both refreshed and sustained my memory—listening to her relate to those children, avid for terror and mystery, the escape of my great-granddaughter Isabel and the slave girl Daría, or how outlaws raided the plantation and massacred José Manuel Blanco and Julián Cayetano during the antislavery insurrection of 1846. Her voice, with its theatrical pauses and tones of wonder and alarm, put together an abridged national history for children, one in which I could re-create myself and feel that at least a part, even if a minor one, of my memories remained. The wall behind the chesterfield easy chairs was completely covered by the enormous painting that my great-great-grandson José Francisco had had done by a famous artist. Belén was on the sofa with Elena by her side, and María Luisa and María Cristina were on the rug. Francisco, still daubed with chocolate, was riding horseback on the arm of the sofa facing them. Or was it the opposite, with him the one sitting on the floor? No matter. That afternoon the tales followed one after another, thanks to Belén's unflagging imagination: they went on and on, a kind of oral explanation of the canvas.

"See the little girl?" Belén asked. "That was my grandma Isabel." "Why was she so small if she was your grandma?" María Cristina asked. "Well, because grandmas were little girls once, too. The painting shows Isabel in 1814, the year of the evacuation to Oriente. Haven't you studied that in school?" "I have, I have!" Elena shouted. "When the Liberator fled with the population of Caracas and the patriot army so they wouldn't be killed by Boves." "That's right, very good. Well, Isabel fled, too, with her mama, and she was a little girl then, a very little one, but then she grew up and had several children. The last was my papa, who was your grandpa José Francisco." "So why isn't your papa in the painting?" "Francisco, love, because he hadn't been born yet; he was born much later, but his mama, who's the little girl in the painting, told him how she was saved from the war by running away with the slave girl, who carried her to Barlovento, and he had this picture painted. But she'd died, you understand, when the picture was done she'd been dead for many years. This is the way the painter envisioned the slave girl running through the jungle, and I was the model he used for the little girl. Your grandpa wanted it painted because if Isabel had died, too, our family would have vanished. All her relatives died in the war." "A lot of people died in the War for Independence," Elena recited, "whole families—some died fighting, and others from hunger." "That's right," Belén finished, "and others because the blacks attacked plantations and killed everybody—that's how my grandfather, José Manuel, my papa's papa, died; but that was later, when the War for Independence was over." "And when did your papa die?" "My papa died when your mama and I were very young, because he married Grandma when he was kind of old; he'd been married before, but he was widowed and didn't have any children, and then he married my mama and we were born, but I barely remember him." "Now tell us how the ocelot was ready to eat them," María Luisa asked. "Then pay attention. The slave girl was hurrying along with the little girl in her arms, but she was tired, very tired from running through the jungle, and then she leaned against a tree to rest a little. She heard a growl, and she immediately realized that it was an ocelot, because she'd been born in the forest and knew the sounds of animals. She stayed very still, not moving a hair, clutching the child in her arms and covering her mouth so she wouldn't cry, because those wildcats have very sharp ears, and a keen sense of smell too. The animal got a whiff of them and began looking until he found them—don't cover your ears, María Cristina, nothing's happening, it's a story I'm telling—the ocelot stared at them and then climbed a tree and went away." "But how could your grandma tell all that if she was so small?" "Elena, she didn't remember it, but the slave girl told her about it when she was older; she lived with the slave until the war was over and the slave girl brought her back to Caracas." "Why did she do that? Didn't she love her?" "I imagine she did, that she loved her very much, because it would have been much easier to have run away all by herself than with the child on her back. She loved her a lot, because in those days slave women carried around the children, and they also gave babies milk when their mamas didn't have any; I imagine she understood that her duty was to take her back to Caracas. Now, if you want, I'll tell the story of the snake." "No, not that one," María Cristina shrieked. "Yes, yes, tell it": Francisco liked very much the part that produced horror in his sisters. Belén had put together a story according to which Daría and her tiny charge were asleep and a bushmaster slithered over their legs and coiled on the slave girl's breast, looking for warmth; suddenly Daría woke up, and without making a sound she grabbed it by the head and smashed it with a rock—since she'd grown up in the forest, she knew how to kill snakes. Francisco insisted that in a corner of the painting, where the hillock was, part of a snake's head could be seen; but, climbing on the sofa and trying as they could, his sisters couldn't spot it. Yet Belén backed him up: Francisquito was right, it could be seen. Francisco was her favorite, and he also responded to Belén's almost maternal affection.

Do you remember, Alejandro, the games and raucous fun of all our children? The only thing that quieted them was the arrival of the teacher, when they sat down at tables under the portico in the courtyard to start class. I can almost see the older ones now—Nicolás, Alejandrito, Antonio—dirty from chasing each other in the backyard with Juan del Rosario, washing their hands and faces and combing their hair, with their grammar books open on their knees, and the teacher unscrolling a map that was by then already an old, wrinkled piece of paper to show them with his pointer the borders of the province; and the older girls—Mariana, Manuela, Teresa—learning their numbers, because I didn't want them to be ignorant like me, and I insisted that at least they know how to add and subtract correctly. Watching Belén's nieces and nephew lets me share in the gaiety and terrors of childhood again and laugh at their pranks, as when María Cristina and Francisco, the youngest two, sit in the pergola in the garden and she makes him play with her dolls in exchange for her eating his spinach soup at lunch; or when, hiding from their mother's watchful eyes, Francisco tells her, "Show me your peepee place and I'll show you mine." María Cristina was a cheerful, silly child, but now she's developed into a model of seriousness and good manners. On Sundays she takes her children to mass, and she constantly organizes social affairs that she imagines will be of great interest to her husband, a rather uncouth moneybags; she's extremely alert to social proprieties down to their most picayune details, and she censures any comment she deems dangerous to the moral health of her family. Obsessive and tight-fisted in the management of her home, she's without doubt a paragon of virtue who seems to follow the precepts of Fray Luis de León, by which I was brought up; but there's nothing about her present personality that reminds me in any way of that darling bouncy little girl who on party days, along with her sisters, would dress in vests and patent-leather shoes, tie back her curly locks with a ribbon, and climb into the old Pontiac, pinching Francisco, who looked like a little man in blue trousers, a white shirt, and a bow tie.

I also enjoy eavesdropping on Belén and Carlota, who spend their time discussing and sometimes arguing over events that took place twenty years before. One afternoon, a while after the overthrow of Pérez Jiménez, the fifth and last of the generals, they were reading together a small column of items in the newspaper *Ultimas Noticias*:

A number of robberies, assaults, and other crimes were committed last night. The death of José Salbic, 76, a merchant, was discovered. He died as a consequence of a stab wound as he was preparing to close his small establishment. It is supposed that he was attacked during a robbery of cash and other items of value.

Belén gave a shudder that Carlota was unable to interpret, and Carlota insisted that León Bendelac, a person remembered so fondly by everyone, deserved a visit of condolence. Belén explained curtly that León and his wife no longer lived in Caracas; she could assure her of that because she'd been to the jewelry store not long before, and Salbic had told her. Belén, doggedly persisting in her mistakes, had of course gone back there after her return from Europe.

On the evening of his death, Salbic dragged his arthritic limbs from the rear of the store to the small counter. He'd put on slippers so he could shuffle along more easily. Bending over, he was examining the account books. He was selling the business. Located in a two-story building, the shop had become sandwiched between high-rises, and its name—inscribed in large silver letters, Salbic's pride—no longer stood out as the city's most distinguished jewelry store. It had gradually evolved into a variety store, and the beautiful silver objects, the fine watches, the delicate jewelry for society ladies, were giving way to necklaces of cultured pearls, imitation-gemstone earrings, baking dishes, towels and sheets, items of dubious taste that tried to look Murano, and even plastic toys imported from the United States—which, whether he liked it or not, sold very quickly and were the most sought-after merchandise. The well-known names that appeared in the newspapers no longer came, the ones who couldn't be born, have a birthday, or produce children without his knowing it and in some way being involved, putting a stamp of quality on the commemorative acts of a society to which he'd never belonged but to which he'd been quite close. Helped by his daughter, he took care of a transient clientele made up of housewives and office-workers who happened to pass by the shop and rested their harried glance on the signs, handwritten by Salbic, that announced huge reductions, special prices, great sales for August, and extraordinary offerings for Christmas. Some took advantage to ask to use the phone, and some women even wanted access to the bathroom for the urgent needs of their children while the mothers poked through the Christmas decorations—little glass pine trees painted green, angels, Santa Claus figurines, plastic myrtle leaves that hadn't been sold in the holiday season and were being liquidated at unheard-of prices that January.

He was at the counter, stooping over the account books that recorded, day by day, the rise and fall of what had been *Salbic and Bendelac, Jewelers and Silversmiths,* taking on the vain task of showing future buyers how efficiency and quality had been the hallmarks over the years of a business that closed only on Yom Kippur, Rosh Hashanah, and the anniversary of the death of the founder's wife. Despite his age he stayed in the store right up to the time marked on the sign and rebuffed his daughter's pleas to come home earlier. "It's a matter of ethics," he'd say. "Keeping to schedule is the key to success." He pored over the old books, and he could distinguish his script from the other man's perfectly, could trace in detail the exact moment when he'd allowed León Bendelac, as if he'd been Salbic's own son, to record the balances and enter in the book of orders deliveries and the dates when items arrived and were sold—along with the prices, which looked ridiculous twenty years later, but which at that time could only have been afforded by an affluent lady following the whim to enhance her beauty.

A pointless effort, his attempt to prove the former eminence of his shop through its books, because the prospective buyers, as the owners already of the adjoining buildings, didn't plan to continue the business in any way. They made him a miserable offer accompanied by a threat to open, precisely by his door, an underground parking garage that would block the way for his last customers, obliging them to make a detour. Who would stop to capitalize on the Turk's marvelous bargains? (Mr. Salbic, with the passage of time, had gone back to being *The Turk*.) The names to whom Salbic could have had recourse in the past had been replaced by others, new, different ones. The new rich ladies, who traveled by airplane to Europe and the United States, would have felt quite humiliated at wearing costume trinkets made in Caracas. Where now were those women who couldn't conceive of buying a piece of jewelry, having it cleaned or adjusted, anywhere but at Salbic's? All the anecdotes, all the secrets that had reached his ears while, sitting across from his counter, they chose a bracelet, looked at samples of earrings, or decided on a necklace. All the gentlemen who'd come discreetly to choose a gift, and all the times he'd laughed with León as they remarked on how the gentleman chose the official gift and the clandestine one at the same time. All the intrigues and amours that had been woven in that place, but Salbic had always said, "It's a professional matter, son. We just sell them; let them be the ones to know for whom they're buying them." Those nabobs had never appeared again in what now had turned into a cramped and uncomfortable little store, poorly located, with a stock that was worse every day. It had devolved into a bazaar stall, just one more shop among many others. Little by little the old customers had grown scarcer: once in a while, perhaps as a gesture of loyalty, some small order—a watch to be fixed, a baptism medallion to be made.

He could remember Mrs. Sánchez Luna perfectly: one of his most enthusiastic customers, a woman in love with jewelry. More than once he'd seen her come in, not feeling like buying anything, just to gaze at what new things he had. Women with that graciousness and elegance were few. Always so attentive to him when she would pass by some afternoon to browse. Always a pleasant word, inquiring about his wife's health, his grandchildren. The wife of a government minister, a woman with all that power and yet so simple, so unassuming—unlike the others, who were impertinent, vulgar, stuck-up. "New money, son," he would observe to León; "you have to be able to distinguish people of taste—yes, sir, people of taste. When she got married the first time, the diadem that held her veil was made here. Poor woman; her happiness was so short. Her husband was wanted by the police for political reasons. I think he died out of the country—tuberculosis. Take good care of her, León; her father was every inch a gentleman. He'd been quite rich, had plantations, a lot of land, lost it all." Mrs. Sánchez Luna, one of the few who had the generosity to come back; she bought a medal for her nephew's first communion. Though Salbic's hand shook and he didn't have the sure touch and precision of old, he'd engraved it himself. Mrs. Sánchez Luna had taken a great deal of interest in that medal; it was for her favorite nephew, she'd told him, "He's like a son to me, because I never had any." He could remember the name perfectly, Francisco Villaverde, and the date was, what, 1953, 1954? She wore all black, with the same grand dignity, still splendid in her mature beauty. She seemed to have nothing else to do, and he had so few customers to take care of. They'd chatted about old times, and he offered her a cup of tea and told her that his wife had died. She told him then that she was dressed in mourning for her husband, who'd returned quite ill from Paris, where they'd lived for several years. Dr. Sánchez Luna—how could Salbic forget him, a thorough gentleman; he came in person to pick out a diamond for his proposal of marriage to her. She still had it, yes, of course; Mrs. Sánchez Luna told him she would always keep that gift, a jewel of a kind they don't make anymore, a work of art. Such a discreet woman—only then did she touch upon the theme of León. She asked about him, and Salbic told the truth; she was the only one to whom he had dared open up. "He went away, Mrs. Sánchez Luna," he said laconically, with few details. "He went away, and we haven't heard anything more about him; men sometimes make strange decisions." And she'd understood his grief, did not try to soothe him with a foolish or clumsy phrase. "What a pity," she said, only that—"What a pity." But time had passed, and now not even Mrs. Sánchez Luna returned. She'd abandoned the old mansion downtown and, like all the rich people, had moved to the new developments in the East End. Mrs. Sánchez Luna had been lost like so many others, and there was no pastime left to him but to put his account books in order.

A fruitless effort, trying to use the figures to unravel what for him would continue being the mystery of León. If for any untutored observer a quick glance at the books was sufficient to observe the store's rise, how must it have been for him, who in just an instant could determine the index of profits that went with León's joining the business? First as a worker, then as supervisor, and finally as master and co-owner—as it should have been, since Salbic had figured from the first moment he saw him that León would be an excellent husband for Dora. Shouldn't a father look out for his children? Dora, a girl with many fine qualities and—why not say it?—not lacking in attractions, wasn't finding a husband; and León, a young immigrant without a father to protect and guide him. He'd been a kind father to them both, and they'd come together like a good brother and sister. More than the abandonment of Dora, what wounded Salbic most and was most inexplicable was León's betrayal, his stony silence.

Not a letter in all those years, not a word telling where he was. He'd vanished into thin air just as he'd appeared. Sometimes Salbic suspected that he'd gone back to Morocco; at other times some friend who'd been traveling would report that he might have recognized León on a street in Paris or London. Finally, when his wife was dying, Salbic had lied: "A letter came from León. He's in Curaçao. Dora and the children are going to see him. He's very sorry for what he made us suffer." To give her at least that consolation at the moment of her death; to let her die in peace, trusting in his words. The letters he'd sent to León's mother's old address had brought no reply; one came back with the stamp *Addressee Unknown*. He was pained by Dora's loneliness and the chill that had come down between them, the unspoken reproach with which they blamed each other for their error in judgment.

Salbic closed the books; it was getting dark. He would leave for the next day the completion of his accounting report, with which he wanted to demonstrate to someone what his business had been. He slowly took off his slippers and limped to the rear of the store to put on his shoes and jacket. He heard a noise, and when he drew back the curtain, two boys were facing him. They'd broken the glass in the door and effortlessly forced the lock. One of them was stuffing a bag with everything it could hold; the other, a switchblade in hand, kept watch over the old man. Few items were left in the drawers and on the shelves when they got ready to leave. With a facile movement, the boy twisted the old man's arm behind his back and sank the knife into his throat. They ran out.

Nothing was gained from the dictatorships either, and they had to invent democracy, Alejandro, I'd forgotten to tell you. It was devised by a gentleman named Rómulo Betancourt. Is he the same one who invented liberalism? Heavens no, what nonsense! That was somebody else. He didn't come in on horseback like Joaquín Crespo—no. How could you think such a thing, Alejandro? We're in the twentieth century, and there are lots of automobiles, and nobody rides horseback in the city anymore. As for democracy, I'll tell you briefly that just as I didn't understand liberalism, I can't grasp this either. Despite their progress, the same thing happened on the day the democrats entered as did with Joaquín Crespo: there was a cloudburst. It rained so much that slogans got stuck to the pavement again. Are Belén's family democrats? I really don't know. Domingo Sánchez is dead now, fortunately, and didn't have time to prosper from the political shift; but I knew him quite well, and there would have been no lack of opportunities if body and soul hadn't given out on him as soon as he got back. Belén and Carlota don't much follow politics. Democrats, or, rather, *Adecos*—that's the nickname they've given them—are what the husbands of Carlota's daughters have been, but I haven't followed their lives closely. As for Luis Villaverde, he's always been a rather skeptical man, a shadow lost in the depths of his large study, the room that's always inaccessible to the children at the end of the hall on the top floor, with a window, opening onto the garden, from which he would watch them play hide-and-seek, cops and robbers, and kick the can. When the children would ask, "What's your job, Dad?" Carlota would always answer, "What a question. Your father's a lawyer, and he's very busy, so don't make any noise." And he would sit in a leather armchair and examine papers tirelessly. The day came when Luis Villaverde died. I've become so used to death, Alejandro, maybe because I've stored up so many in my memory, that I love my corpses more than I do myself. I can't say that his loss was the greatest of griefs for me, but a flood of changes began then. Carlota and her three daughters wept, all clustered about the coffin while the priest's psalm and the response could be heard along with the murmur of voices, some praying in the parlor and others whispering in the hallway. Francisco, who must have been sixteen, wore dark glasses and sweated in his black suit as he got into the car that led the funeral procession. They returned home at dusk; the main parlor was still full of people, and Belén prepared cups of consommé in the kitchen. Francisco went upstairs, and I wanted to accompany him when he went into the room that had been shut ever since his father had been moved to the hospital. Solitary in the darkness, Francisco looked over the garden as the aroma of the jasmine that was entwined around the grillwork wafted in along with the persistent sound of the crickets. The garden was a dim square into which he wanted to plunge, to drown, to lose himself along with all his childhood, everything that was pressing him so much. He wanted to do it before dawn, so that everything would be left behind in the dark. It was decided that Elena would marry after the six months of mourning, with, under the circumstances, a modest reception; Belén would pay for a year at a boarding school in the United States for María Luisa and María Cristina; and, as for him, once he finished his preparatory schooling with the Jesuits, he would be a doctor, a lawyer, or an engineer. On his father's desk were an ivory ashtray, singed on the edges; the green leather desk set; the typewriter; an inkwell, never used; a letter knife; a set of pipes; a stamp for sealing wax, another with its inkpad; a card file; the silver clock engraved with his initials; and the keys to the files. Francisco tried the keys one by one until the piece of furniture, a cabinet of carved wood with leaves embossed on it, in terrible taste, slid open. The shelves were empty except for a folder on one of them. He'd hoped to find the cabinet full of documents, but it was bare, clean, except for a cockroach slipping through a crevice. He also found a certificate for the sale of some stock, a letter assuring a client that Luis was proceeding with a debt seizure, and a few other scattered papers with no headings on which Francisco was able to recognize his father's handwriting in marginal notes. Now there came to him a phrase he'd heard Belén let drop many times: "You haven't got a head for business, Luis; stop squandering the little that Carlota's got left." What had his father been busying himself with during all those long afternoons when his mother had led them to believe that he was scrutinizing complicated dockets and briefs? Now Francisco understood, with no doubt whatsoever, that all those years they'd been living on Belén's inheritance, and she, with her delicate and generous manner, had made sure neither he nor his sisters ever suspected that Luis Villaverde was only lounging in his study and whiling away time there until dinner was ready.

He wasn't pained by his father's failure, nor by the knowledge that he must now enter the middle class, but it vexed him to know that while his sisters and he were playing in the garden and his mother was keeping up the comedy of well-being with her friends, his father was marooned among empty sheets of paper, trying haplessly to recoup a fortune. It pained Francisco that he'd been treated like a child, that no one had ever confided the truth about the situation; it pained him that for all these years they'd been living, as if they hadn't known, off the fortune of Domingo Sánchez.

How did Domingo Sánchez get so rich? Alejandro, I've done nothing else but explain it to you. Didn't I tell you that he was always alert to who was in power so that he could get his hand in? Well, he dug a little into the meat monopoly, tapped into the liquor monopoly during the times of Cipriano Castro, and then there were the lucrative import licenses Juan Vicente Gómez gave him when the world was overflowing with new inventions; and in that way he got to be a stockholder in banks, the owner of textile factories and office buildings and sugar plantations that he sold off at a handsome price. But now there's so much money around that even Domingo Sánchez's bequest isn't worth all that much; there are people who are so rich, Alejandro, that his fortune, which had looked to me like that of an Oriental potentate, has been shrunk to merely a good living. But I've got to stop talking now. I can hear the bell being rung. It's Francisco, coming to pay Belén a visit.

DON HELIODORO'S GIFT

He goes along the porchway of black and white mosaic tiles; at the end there's a set of wicker furniture surrounded by drooping ferns that block the sun. Francisco sits down and lets himself be cloaked in the silence. It's the same furniture, the same ferns, the same afternoon calm that was abruptly shattered by his shouting and that of his sisters; it's the same slow afternoon as when they played hide-and-seek among the big house's generous share of nooks and crannies, and they would go to the second-floor bedrooms and there, lying on a bed with a heavy headboard, would invent scenes of terror. The shadows of the half-open windows enveloped them until Belén, after siesta, would invite them into the small English drawing room and serve them custard-apple juice and pastries she'd bought especially for them. Belén is all alone, a little dotty, in this house that was magnificent fifty years ago but that is full of leaks now, the old masonry kitchen dilapidated, most of the rooms closed up and smelling musty, the huge garden untended, bedded with leaves, with vines eating away at the faded and crumbling walls, and she, she herself lost in her abandoned spaces, of which only the portico and the English drawing room retain their previous appearance. She is hunched over, something in the hollows of her cheeks giving her a look of haunted past splendor, all prepared for her nephew's visit; she's dressed in light-colored clothing, her hair recently styled, wearing a discreet piece of jewelry to avoid the look of a shuffle-footed old woman that she has when alone—it all makes me feel so sad.

"Francisco, how happy I am to see you! You've forgotten me."

"I heard you were ill; they only told me yesterday."

"Nothing much, my love. A little shaky, but they gave me some pills, and I'm better now. Why haven't you come to see me? I can understand that life these days won't allow for visits, but it's been a long time since you came; and your sisters . . . don't even mention them. Well, since you've come, I'm not going to scold you now. Francisco, I want to talk to you for several reasons: first, because I haven't seen you for a long time; second, because I'm going to die. Yes, my love, don't say what you feel obliged to say"—she shushed him. "You're going to tell me I'm fine and I shouldn't think about such things, but the truth is I'm going on eighty-one; I've survived my own self, everybody's died, and you're not going to convince me I'm the exception. I open the newspaper, and I see funeral notices for the few people I still know, and this last scare I've had tells me I'm right."

"What you ought to do is find some distraction and not think about gloomy things."

"Nothing interests me anymore. I'm being serious with you. My history has gone by; my country is a different one; my life is made up of memories. Ever since your mother died I've had no one to talk to. The only consolation I have is that I'm still lucid—if you could have seen the number of women friends who've died in total arteriosclerosis. I want to die with my head on straight; I don't want to be an inconvenient old rag. And inconvenient to whom, besides? I have no children ready to take me on, and it wouldn't be right to burden you people—no, no, Francisco, I've got to die, and soon. If I believed in God I'd ask Him—don't interrupt, I have to tell you something very important. I've been thinking along these lines: your sisters are married, and married well; of the four of you, you're the one who's had the worst luck, or maybe you didn't have the opportunity. I don't know, but I know quite well that you're living on a miserable little salary from that company—your wife told me once you'll never get anywhere there—and you've also been the one who's been closest to me, the one who's loved me most. I'm going to leave you this house and some shares of stock; that's all I have left from Domingo's fortune, a small income that inflation's been eating up and that I've been selling off over the years, but it's more than enough for me even if it's really nothing. I also want to leave you the plantation in Barlovento."

He saw her as aged, crazy, raving; her wrinkles seemed more marked, her hand was quivering, and her voice was getting weak.

"You're talking nonsense, Aunt, getting your times mixed up. The Barlovento plantation belonged to your father in the last century; we're in 1984 now."

"Papa's plantation was expropriated back then, but I believe—I've been told, that is—that you can petition for the property rights through a series of maneuvers I don't understand too well. I can't explain it to you; you'll have to go see this gentleman."

She got up, opened the drawer of a small desk, and handed him a card: *Heliodoro Chuecos Rincón, Lawyer-Historian, Investigator of Legal Traditions. Cola de Pato to Desbarrancado, No. 32.*

"He's a scholar; he knows everything. He thinks the plantation could be mine again—yours, that is, because I'm leaving my share to you. You have to go see Don Heliodoro."

"But where did this Don Heliodoro pop up from? A lawyer-historian who lives on the Cola de Pato block? He's some shyster who's putting you on in order to bilk a few *reales* out of you."

"Young people think they know everything and that we old-timers are incompetent. Don Heliodoro isn't any sharpie. If he told me you should look him up, it's for good reason. I've known him all my life—that is, Domingo knew him, and he came to visit a few weeks ago, and while we were talking, the plantation came up. He gave me the idea, told me he had a lot of old papers. That's his business. What can you lose by going?"

"My time, going there to talk nonsense."

"That plantation can be mine, and therefore yours; it was expropriated from Papa by Joaquín Crespo to build a railroad . . . but they never paid anything. If you don't want to do it, I'll get a lawyer to take it on." Belén was furious.

"I'll go," Francisco said. "I'll go just to please you." And he put the card in his pocket.

But he didn't go, Alejandro. He played dumb when Belén called him to insist and when Silvia, his wife, argued that maybe this was his chance. As he thought back, the plantation of his grandfather, José Francisco, seemed to be part of the family mythology Aunt Belén used to tell him about when he was a child, and all he could foresee in that consultation with Don Heliodoro, on which others laid so much importance, was the waste of an afternoon. As if he had so much to do! From home to office, office to home—that poor fool didn't want to recover his past. Until one fine day, weary of Belén's importuning, he decided to go. He took the subway and started walking through steep alleys he hadn't seen since childhood, on those now-remote visits he'd made with his mother to old friends from other times. The house was in La Pastora, in a row of buildings, pinched between skyscrapers, that preserved the neighborhood's old style; the entranceway showed the remnants of tiles, a floor of damp and cracked mosaics, farther on a small courtyard with straw-bottomed chairs, a plastic-covered sofa, the refrigerator, and a television set. Don Heliodoro Chuecos received him in his slippers, his long tropical shirt open and his undershirt showing.

"You'll have to excuse me; I didn't expect you today. Heliodoro Chuecos Rincón at your service. Have a seat."

Francisco brushed against a cat sleeping under the chair, and Don Heliodoro chased the animal off.

"He's used to sleeping there." Then called to someone who must have been his wife. "Take Don Cipriano away, old girl; I've got a visitor."

"My name is Francisco Villaverde. I'm Belén Sánchez Luna's nephew."

"Of course, of course, your charming aunt Doña Belén spoke to me about you, of course." A parrot began to shriek in its cage. "Carmela, do me a favor and cover up the parrot. So you're interested in the juridical history of the Curiepe Valley. Yes, certainly, it's logical—your family had extensive holdings there. Some time ago, as a matter of fact, I had occasion to chat with your distinguished aunt, a fine lady, no doubt about it. I was a friend of your esteemed uncle Don Domingo—friend is saying a lot, his servant and someone who recognized his generosity would be more exact—and we talked about the plantation her family had in Barlovento. It's a region I'm quite familiar with, particularly interesting for an investigator because it's been embroiled in litigation ever since the colonial period, and today there are more than ten thousand adulterated sales documents in existence, from its beginnings and including successive tracts. You can't imagine the number of mythical rights that have been asserted concerning the Curiepe Valley, with titles superimposed or parallel and treacherous assignees who claim properties with no right to them whatsoever. This is due, my dear friend Villaverde, to a lack of cadastral regulation, but most of all to a lack of honest and scrupulous functionaries and an excess of venal judges. More than one or two registry books have been lost here, and do you know why? You don't, but you can imagine, because corrupt functionaries have caused them to disappear in order to favor one of the litigants. Are you a lawyer? Oh, an engineer; engineering is a profession of great civic responsibility, as is the study of the law. I'm an attorney by profession but a historian by avocation. Carmela, do something about Rafael; he won't let us talk! My wife named the parrot Rafael because she likes to make fun of the politicians, and she says this parrot is as golden-tongued as President Caldera. But where were we? Ah, yes, I was telling you that a lot of registry books have vanished, and that has been an assault on history; but you've probably realized that this country has no interest in history at all. It hates history, I would say. I've put together a work, friend Villaverde, that contains almost the entire story of Venezuela. With the papers I possess, the documentary record from the year 1749 could be written, and to some extent a chronicle from the mid–seventeenth century. You're probably asking yourself how I got hold of them— well, with the patience and tenacity of an Andean transplanted into this valley of Caracas. I was born in El Táchira a whole round of years ago, and I came to the capital when I was very young. It was then that I got to know your distinguished uncle, Don Domingo. I had the temerity to present myself in his office; he was a minister of the Worthy General Gómez at the time. Well, I was bold enough to go and tell him that I was the nephew, grandnephew to be exact, of Mrs. Lucía Chuecos, whom he'd known in other times; and Don Domingo, without asking for any other explanation, granted me a pension—that is, Villaverde, a stipend that allowed me to study for a legal career. You see that I can only recognize and praise his magnanimous gesture, whose only motive was to help the poor boy I was—though I did him a few favors, I wasn't able to pay him back as much as I would have liked. So a while back your distinguished aunt, Doña Belén, crossed my mind, and I thought I would like to pay her my respects because so much time has passed, so much time in everything, Villaverde. I was most pleased to see the ruddy good health that Doña Belén has maintained . . . but you're interested in talking about the Curiepe Valley, and here I am rattling on about memories. Come in and have a look at my files."

Francisco followed him into an adjoining room, evidently the master bedroom because the center was occupied by a bed with sheets in disarray. Against the walls thousands of papers lay on boards held up by towers of bricks.

"See my work. If published, it would amount to more than twenty volumes, but it remains unpublished because of a lack of means. I've made inquiries to a lot of people. I've gone to institutions, but all in vain; they don't recognize me as a true historian. I don't have the degrees that certify me as such, so they place no value on this work. One gentleman, whom I shall not name, answered that I was only an amateur and that the library he was in charge of couldn't take a chance on me." He put on his glasses and rummaged about the boards. "Here it all is, Villaverde; I've got the whole juridical tradition of your family's Barlovento holdings here. The first document we can go back to concerning the Curiepe Valley is the decree that awards title to Captain Juan de Villegas on January 5, 1663, in recompense for the conquest and subjection of the Cumanagoto Indians. Juan de Villegas, it is known, came to the province of Venezuela in the middle of the seventeenth century with his father, who'd been a cooper in Málaga and later married a descendant of Francisco Maldonado de Almendáriz, a family of lineage from Villacastín. The first

controversy arose in 1710 when his daughter, Inés Villegas y Solórzano, solicited, jointly with her husband and cousin, Alejandro Martínez de Villegas, a ruling that those lands were exempt from settlement
on the grounds of having already been settled. They were referring,
naturally, to the 1663 document testifying that said lands were barren
and unpopulated, and in accordance with which her father had paid
67¹/₂ pesos, during the time of Governor Pedro de Porras y Toledo,
for the rights to half its annual income and its settlement . . . but Governor Rojas y Mendoza asked that those titles be presented, and since
Doña Inés couldn't find them, required that they adduce evidence of
Porras y Toledo's authority in order to confirm them. Alejandro Martínez then petitioned to block that investigation of titles, and since he
was a man of note, a council magistrate, he angrily demanded that his
wife's rights be declared quite proper and her claims sufficient, and
insisted on a guarantee that there would be no reason or ground for
doubt in the future of this case, neither for him nor for his heirs. In
his petition he cited all the services his forebears and those of his wife
had given the Crown and argued that if Porras y Toledo awarded the
rights to Alejandro's father-in-law and uncle, it was because he was
making full use of his authority; and if he made use of it, it was because he had it. A cogent bit of logic, don't you think? Well, in that
way Doña Inés was granted the rights to the Curiepe Valley in 1711;
or, rather, the possession granted in 1663 was ratified. These lawsuits
between colonists and governors have filled the Archives of the Indies. It was a confrontation in which the roots of independence can
doubtless be detected, and especially on the part of the magistrates,
who were named from among the most prominent men and who
showed a belligerence that gave the functionaries from the Iberian
Peninsula some very hard times . . . but I'm getting off track. Carmela, would you please bring some coffee for the doctor and me—
you'd like some coffee, wouldn't you? Let's see, where was I? In the
deed of 1711, the property on the banks of the River Curiepe, down
to the point where it enters the sea at Higuerote Cove, was confirmed
as belonging to the Villegas family.

A girl passed through the courtyard and stopped in front of the
television set. Her clumsy movements, her hoarse, unharmonic laugh,

and her childish expressions as she faced the screen betrayed her condition.

"Carmela, take the television inside so the child won't disturb us."

Francisco helped the woman carry the set to a rear room. The girl, grasping his jacket, kept repeating to him, "Let's watch *Happy Afternoons.*"

"You'll have to excuse this embarrassing situation, doctor; we have a serious problem with this daughter. My wife has submitted ever so many petitions to the Ministry of Education to get a special education scholarship, but it's been useless—long waits in anterooms of the offices and bureaus that handle them, but nothing in the end. I don't have the wherewithal to pay for private school; my situation is precarious. That's why I'm telling you, Villaverde, I don't believe too much in democracy. You probably think that therefore I miss the old dictatorships, the all-powerful governments that took care of everything. Well, no, I don't yearn for anything at all anymore, and I don't believe in anything either, I've seen too much already. And that's the bad part of it, when a person has seen too much. The only thing I ask of democracy is a scholarship for that child, and they won't give me one."

Don Heliodoro wiped his eyes with his shirtsleeve.

"I'm probably bothering you with matters that don't interest you. I've dedicated my life to the history of this country, Villaverde. I've invested my efforts and the little I have to dig around in registry offices, in archives, in parishes, and anywhere I've heard that someone has kept old papers. My wife, Carmela—you've met her now—is a wonderful person, a self-sacrificing wife and an outstanding mother, but also, as you've probably noticed, a simple woman, uneducated; she places no importance on these matters, says the study of property doesn't engage her attention because she's never owned any, an ingenuous judgment. Naturally I try to explain to her that we're talking about History, but she threatens to burn all my papers because she wants to rent out the room that serves as my archive; we're living in dire need. From time to time I get a bit of work—somebody interested in recovering a legal transfer, some juridical study pertaining to property—but I don't disdain doing maintenance work either, a little painting, a little plumbing, you understand. Naturally I'm not going to charge you anything; for me it's a great honor to pay Doña Belén back in this way for an unforgettable favor. Well, we were in 1711; in 1715 another dispute starts over the Curiepe Valley; the free man of color Juan del Rosario Villegas, an ex-slave of the family who as was customary bore his owner's surname, initiated a claim before the Crown, alleging that his former master, Don Alejandro Martínez de Villegas, had given him uncleared land where he could set up a plantation and stating that he'd received permission for settlement from Governor Cañas y Merino, a bandit for sure. For over forty years the blacks of Curiepe were enmeshed in litigation with Doña Inés Villegas, with all manner of documents going back and forth and eliciting contradictory decisions from different high courts, and even with appeals to the Council of the Indies. I've enjoyed reading the protesting briefs and affidavits of that lady, Villaverde, and more than once I've imagined that old colonial dame standing behind the scribe, huffing with fury and shouting insults against Juan del Rosario, the governors, and the king himself. Indeed, there's a curious story according to which two blacks from Curiepe traveled to Madrid to plead for the help of Charles III. They obtained a decree that in some way, a little vague, tried to protect them from dispossession—but you know how money talks; the lawsuits raged on without any resolution, lasting over the whole eighteenth century. In 1789, Nicolás, a son of Doña Inés, who'd died at a very advanced age in 1780, was a member of the city council of Caracas, and he petitioned to inherit the land. It's clear that in doing so he committed forgery in the matter of boundaries, taking in a rather larger extent than what had originally been established in the deeds. I hope you won't feel offended by that remark; my intention is to explain as faithfully as possible the intricate matter of the rights of ownership in Barlovento. That forgery led to confusion and fraudulent filings, which multiplied the lawsuits among the purported property owners themselves and between them and the blacks of Curiepe, who hadn't dropped their claims. The last colonial document is from 1793, when the High Court of Caracas handed down a decision supporting the blacks who were settled in the Curiepe Valley and providing a momentary end to the litigation. There were also controversies among the blacks, so many that the lawsuits are heaped one atop another in the archives. Perhaps the most outstanding is the one that charged Juan del Rosario himself. Shortly after his death his son-in-law, the free black Juan Marcos Marín, initiated a complaint against José Miguel de Soto, a black of the Curaçao tribe who, as village captain of Curiepe at the time and owner of land bordering that of Juan del Rosario, decided to annex it. Juan del Rosario's son-in-law sought protection, and, strange as this sounds, when they asked him to present his father-in-law's title, the document in question didn't turn up; from what could be ascertained, it had gone astray during the wrangles with Doña Inés. It's curious that this paper had also been lost to Marín, probably had been misplaced among Juan del Rosario's papers. What is certain in the case is that the attorney for the black Indian Soto said Marín couldn't prove his legal standing through a purely testimonial procedure; he would need authentication. The witnesses testified that Juan del Rosario had founded the village, with title awarded for same, and that he had royal authorization. They said this title had been presented in the legal quarrels with Doña Inés Villegas; they attested that the lawsuit in question had consumed what little Juan del Rosario possessed, including a small house his mother owned in Caracas in the gully of the Anauco; and, lastly, they testified that his only daughter was married to Juan Marcos Marín, from which union several children had been born. And what happened? It was declared corroborating evidence, but they told Marín to take his rights and play his tune elsewhere. But this sidelight doesn't have anything to do with the problem. Would you like another coffee? I used to smoke, but I've given up that bad habit; I'm left with only the vice of coffee. Naturally, the War for Independence brought on a suspension of the legal bickering, and, also, the region was virtually abandoned, you might even say was left in devastation, and it wasn't until after 1830 when cultivation started again. An intriguing story comes up here. During the war, the Martínez de Villegas family came to an end, as happened with so many old colonial aristocratic families. All its descendants had died—some in combat, others during the tragic withdrawal to Oriente, and evidently some few managed to emigrate to the Antilles, but nothing was ever heard of them again. In 1824, in the baptismal registry of the Caracas parish of Altagracia, is an amendment in which a Franciscan, Antonio González by name, confirms the baptism certificate of 1812 for a child named Isabel, a descendant of Doña Inés and Don Alejandro. The priest swore this child had fled Caracas with her family during the withdrawal of 1814 and had been saved by a slave woman who took her to Barlovento for several years; and thus he recognized that the child was the daughter of Francisco Martínez de Villegas whom he had baptized. Naturally, this fact could not be substantiated, because there's no record of the family members who retreated with the child toward Oriente. There *was* word of Francisco Martínez de Villegas; it is known that he died near Valencia in 1812, serving as a captain in the forces of the Marquis del Toro. As a result, then, it became completely impossible to prove the child's identity, and it's most probable that it was a matter of chicanery on the part of the slave woman, who presented the girl in Caracas to Father González in the hope, perhaps, that she might in that way secure herself a letter of freedom. You know that this was a tremendous problem for the slaves after independence; they'd been promised emancipation in exchange for joining the army, but it was all demagoguery—like so many things, friend Villaverde, like so many things in our history. Once the war was over, inexpensive labor was of paramount importance for the landowners, so Bolívar's offer of freedom for the blacks went down the drain. No sir, the aristocrats wouldn't accept that; think of all the time that passed until the Monagas Law was promulgated. But here I am straying from the matter that concerns you. Márquez Brito, in his book *Landowners and Slaves in the Barlovento Region,* states that La Trinidad plantation, founded with the borders of the titles of settlement of 1663 and then deceitfully extended in 1789, was recovered in 1835 by José Manuel Blanco, who presented as documentary proof the Franciscan's addendum declaring that his wife, Isabel Francisca, was the daughter of Francisco Martínez de Villegas and therefore the sole heir to the lands; and Brito comments that the amendment in question, which had no probative force, no confirmation, was accepted as true. The plantation resumed production, though it never attained the splendor of colonial days because the price of cacao was slowly sinking, and coffee was becoming the number one export; the plantations could subsist on their crops, but on a much less grandiose scale than before, and they suffered the scourge of the civil wars that recurred through the nineteenth century. Your family held land in Curiepe until 1884, but cacao export documents show a decrease in production—it dropped to zero in some years, which can probably be explained by the incursions of rebel groups that impeded cultivation. During the seven years of Guzmán Blanco there was relative peace, and your distinguished grandfather, José Francisco Blanco, began planting again . . . though the number of sacks exported was quite reduced, of course, until 1884, when, during the first presidency of General Joaquín Crespo, an expropriation was decreed affecting the plantation's boundaries. The reason was the construction of a rail line linking the whole coast from Carenero to San José de Río Chico, which was to lower the cost of transporting cacao to the sea; so on June 5, 1884, a contract of concession was drawn up between the nation and a Spaniard by the name of Roig for the construction of the Carenero Railway Co., Inc.; the curious thing is that this gentleman, a few years after having obtained the rights, sold it to a Dutch company called the Carenero Railway and Navigation Company. I knew Roig's children fairly well because he left the region and came to Caracas, where he opened a bookstore—a very good one, yes, I used to buy juridical texts there; it stayed in business until just a few years ago. But I'm digressing. In 1889 the Dutch had the trains running, but because of disagreements about the conditions of the concession, they resold their rights to a Corsican named Salini, who acquired them with an obligation to extend the line . . . but no, that gentleman didn't extend anything, and at the turn of the century General Cipriano Castro took it over for unfulfillment of contract. Documents at the Ministry of Public Works tell how Salini appeared in person there, protesting that he'd purchased it in good faith and was now being punished for other people's mistakes, since he knew nothing about the lengthening of the line. He claimed he was really a victim, because he had solicited a renewal of his rights and the necessary articles for the preservation of the railroad and had been refused. That case against Salini bogged down because General Castro was quite ill, and a short time later he left the country. Rumbling and bumbling, the railroad kept functioning until the end of the forties, when it was finally abandoned, partly because it wasn't profitable and partly because it suffered periodic damages from floods and its maintenance costs brought on losses . . . so those gentlemen—I'm referring to the Corsican's heirs, as he was naturally dead by then—turned over their lands to coconut production, which continues even now under the brand name of Saltwater Coconut. And here, finally, Villaverde—I suppose you've been overwhelmed by so many details, but it's been necessary to make a creditable reconstruction in order to help you understand the facts—we come to the present. A resolution by the Ministry of Transport and Communications in 1983 established the reversion of the concessionary lands to the nation, since the contract drawn up in 1884 was for ninety-nine years, but the owners of Saltwater Coconut have ignored this resolution and are dividing up the land with the intention of selling it. What it's all about is the fact that the land has no rightful heirs. Who are the owners? The occupants are a few peasants who till their plots with no titles of ownership that give them anything; that's why I don't believe in democracy. What happened to agrarian reform?—Watch out for Don Cipriano! The cat, Villaverde, the cat you haven't noticed and that's untying your shoelaces. Excuse the rambling, but it makes me think of a tortoise my wife was given; we kept him right here in the courtyard, but one day he escaped, and she posthumously baptized him Rómulo because he was so wily. Well, it so happens that the tenants have gone any number of times to official agencies and demanded the land for collectives, because they need it for building homes and planting, and the municipal council has echoed those pleas. The press has reported the matter, but without results, or, more accurately, with terrible results, because the coconut company has plenty of power, and it isn't rare for the national guard to be used from time to time to drive out the occupants and lay waste to their crops. That's how things are, friend Villaverde. Which leads to your interest in all this: the tract that belonged to your family hasn't been sold yet, and it's one of the most valuable pieces because of its proximity to the shore; it's an ideal spot for a tourist establishment, that's what I mentioned to Doña Belén, and in my modest opinion a claim on your behalf should be presented, allowing that the act of expropriation was done with a social aim, for the welfare of the nation, but arguing that since it's quite well known now, and has been for over forty years, that the goal was the construction of the railroad, which has fallen into disuse, that the current beneficiary is a private enterprise, the coconut company. You could initiate a claim alleging, first, that the aforementioned company is making unlawful use of the land; second, your rights by legal precedent and tradition; and third, the invalidity of the act of expropriation. This last would be the most difficult to establish, but you have a powerful argument in the illegal sale these gentlemen are conducting. I could cite similar cases where the court has handed down a decision that would buttress your claim. Of course, you'll have to have a prestigious lawyer. I, you can imagine, have never had the means to rent an office, or even pay the monthly dues to the College of Lawyers. No, in this case I couldn't help you, but what I can help you with are the original titles."

Don Heliodoro went into the bedroom and, after a long time, emerged to hand Francisco a file with tattered, yellowed edges. "I managed to find this, Villaverde, at a friend's antiquarian book shop in the Romualda block, where he had all kinds of old papers. I gave him a hundred bolívares, one hundred bolívares in those days, and he gave them to me immediately. Do you know how he happened to come by them? It's a strange story. When they began to demolish the houses downtown, a brother-in-law of his, who was one of the masons, found a bundle of papers in an attic, and since he knew about my friend's interests, instead of throwing them away he brought them to the store as a gift. There's the twist of fate, Villaverde; to my eyes it's brought us an utterly unique document. I'm giving you a historical jewel: the founding title for the first settlement of what today is the village of Curiepe. Of course, there's no paucity of conflicting opinions. I can cite García Ocando, who in *Lawsuits of the Villegas Family: Notes for a Juridical History of the Eighteenth Century* asserts that those titles were never granted and lays out the evidence on which he bases his judgment, which is contrary to that of Luis Alberto Rangel, who in his magnum opus *Cacao Production in Colonial Venezuela* confirms the possessions of the Villegas family since 1663. There's also Romero España, the famous historian, whom I went to show the document, and he received me, telling me it was a nineteenth-century facsimile that proved nothing and, furthermore, saying I was a reactionary because I denied the village's founding by Juan del Rosario, a freedman of the family, who was the one who'd really settled it. Carmela says that he makes me, by comparison, a show-off dilettante passing himself off as a historian, but I think you'll appreciate the document and will understand that it's a modest gift I'm offering your distinguished aunt, Doña Belén, to whom I've nothing better to give, since I can't any longer repay your esteemed uncle, Don Domingo. I attended his funeral, you know. No, of course; you were just a small child then. I didn't want to bother the family, either. I am, Villaverde, the nephew of the woman who ran a well-known brothel in Caracas at the beginning of the century. I can tell you these secrets because it's between men; I would never bring up such an inappropriate matter with Doña Belén. Before my Aunt Lucía died, very old then, in Lobatera where we come from, she gave me a letter to your uncle, whom she called Captain Sánchez. Your uncle had been a heroic soldier in those days of uprisings and mutinies, and she told me, *Look up Captain Sánchez, who's a minister now,* and that's what I did—what other recourse could a down-at-the-heels boy arriving in Caracas with a cardboard suitcase have? And your distinguished uncle, Don Domingo, told me—I remember perfectly, I've told it many times to Carmela, but she pays no attention, says she doesn't even want to hear the name *Gómez* mentioned because they arrested her father back then for stealing chickens and he spent ten years building highways. Well, that's a personal opinion, and this is what he said to me: *Look, Heliodoro, I'm going to make restitution to you for a debt I owe your aunt.* I stood there with my mouth open because I'd never heard anything about that, and he told me, *It's a moral debt, a swinish thing I did a long time ago and that has made me lose sleep.* I never found out, Villaverde, what he was referring to, and it never occurred to me to ask him, either; I just let myself be thankful to him. Carmela says thankful for what—do I think the stipend he paid me was from him and not out of government coffers . . . but that's an opinion, Villaverde, and I pay it no heed. If you want, we can go inside; I think it's starting to rain."

When Francisco went out onto the street, it was completely dark already, and he ran to escape the downpour. In the pocket of his jacket he carried a nearly illegible document that his Aunt Belén would like to have.

A facsimile from the nineteenth century that proves nothing, a document with only the power to prick the curiosity of idlers; some old papers a mason discovered in my attic when I, tired and disappointed at not finding them, was weeping over the demolition: my walls smashed by hammers, my floor tiles pounded into bits, my doors and windows pulled apart, my grillwork thrown onto the trash heap, the pavement of my courtyard dug up, the tiles of my roof wrecked, and, finally, my space made to disappear; a few documents that have sentimental value for a half-dotty old woman who's going to stash them away without remembering afterward where—is that, Alejandro, what the titles have become, the titles I've been looking for since 1710, when I wanted to present them to Rojas y Mendoza because you were beginning to clear my lands per the agreement? And what do you think, Juan del Rosario, about the historians' conclusions? You and I fought over those papers for twenty years, and now they're collectors' items. I already knew, I think I told you, that they took away the small plot you left your son-in-law, but I couldn't recall, I have so many things stored away in my memory, that your title as Royal Founder had been revoked; that I petitioned for it to be taken away I have no doubt, but I'll say the same as Alejandro, that if I asked them to strip your authority it must be because you had it—the scoundrel Cañas y Merino gave it to you, it's true, but he was governor and had the power to do so. Remember that now a defender has appeared for you: a certain Romero España says that you were the only founder of Curiepe. But I've also got my champion: a fine gentleman named Luis Alberto Rangel has dedicated two fat volumes to demonstrating our rights. We've even appeared in the newspapers; the municipal council of the Brión district is claiming the lands that Saltwater Coconut stole from both of us. And it was your fault, Joaquín Crespo, because the Corsican's descendants wouldn't have a leg to stand on in this business if you hadn't trumped up that foolishness of expropriation. Our lawsuit has been revived at last, Alejandro, and I'm ready—as I've always told you, Juan del Rosario, my houseboy and freedman—to defend again what's mine and belongs to me. Did you hear that hogwash from Don Heliodoro, that he can't believe my great-granddaughter Isabel was my great-granddaughter? Have you set that down, scribe? A windbag chronologist preserves the titles of Doña Inés and rewrites history in his own way. Well, that's all I needed, to have to wait for Heliodoro Chuecos Rincón's approval in order to be sure of what I saw with my own eyes. Didn't I weep tears of blood for the twenty-two days the withdrawal to Oriente lasted, accompanying Isabel as she went along, dying by degrees, with no hope of reaching Barcelona? Wasn't I witness to how a heroic slave girl stumbled through the jungle carrying that child in her arms, and then took care of her as if she was her own until she turned the girl over to Fray Antonio? And will the word of a Franciscan hold less sway than that of this character who slinks into our story from the back room because Domingo Sánchez owed his aunt a favor from the days of that miserable and disease-ridden Caracas of the nineteenth century? Why didn't Rincón tell Villaverde that the debt Domingo carried was the theft of a girl he delivered to the lust of Cipriano Castro? Why didn't he tell him that Domingo Sánchez was syphilitic, and that's why Belén couldn't have children? Ah, he said nothing about that; he's only the servant, and someone who recognizes the generosity of your distinguished uncle Don Domingo. An accomplice and lackey of Domingo Sánchez is what he is—I say that without ever having seen or heard anything about him; I had too many matters at hand to keep up with every henchman Domingo Sánchez had. So be it. But let's leave these details behind, Alejandro; now the time has come to recover what's ours. You always considered it yours? Yes, Alejandro, because you died in peace . . . but I didn't; I died with the sufferings of history. You haven't had to undergo the humiliation of an afternoon on the Cola de Pato to Desbarrancado block, listening to that idiot twist my tale in any fashion that occurs to him and making my insides churn as he went on spinning infamous lies, like the claim that my son Nicolás extended and adulterated the boundaries or that the slave girl Daría invented the origins of my great-granddaughter Isabel to procure herself a letter of freedom. Enough nonsense! And then that Charles III's decree did little to protect the blacks because he didn't invest it with much importance. It's obvious that Rincón doesn't know about the annoyance they gave me by continually demanding money for the improvements I told Lardizábal I wouldn't pay for and never did. Don Heliodoro, on the other hand, most generously sends Belén the titles to repay an unforgettable favor. Besides, he is misinformed; I didn't die in 1780 but on April 23, 1781. But that's enough of blockheads. There are more important matters now, Alejandro. Let's see who those blacks are who are going about in Curiepe and claiming my plantation in the newspapers.

ERNESTINO'S MEMORY

You're probably thinking, Juan del Rosario, that the weight of the years has distracted me from what's been happening on my land. You don't know me very well if you thought my memory had lapsed. I cursed Joaquín Crespo when he invented his railroad, and I was sure his toy wouldn't last too long. I think it was in 1950—maybe earlier, maybe later—when a heavy rain that lasted several days turned the line into a mudhole; the tracks were covered with dirt, and tree trunks snapped by the wind hit the rails and smashed them. The railroad was left in pieces, its belly ripped open like a snake broken up into its coils, a useless toy tossed aside in the middle of the jungle by some absurd god. The coaches were ruined, overgrown with brush and lost forever, except for a few that were in good shape and were carried off by peasants to serve as homes. That's what remained of Joaquín Crespo's railroad, and though it was late, I got my revenge. But the trains weren't needed anymore, in fact never were; by that time they'd opened a highway that cut through the jungle to Caracas, and over it began to stream miserable peasants attracted by the good life the city promised. It would have pained you to see them, Juan del Rosario, abandoning the land you'd fought so hard for that was of no use at all to them. You would have grieved over their desolation— women loaded down with children who were swollen with parasites, men without futures in a slow exodus that, over the years, was covering the mountains that surround the city. I'm going to tell you some stories, ones I think it will interest you to know.

For example, you would have liked to know Ernestino. He said a spirit had assured him he was your personification, and that's what he explained to José Tomás, his godson. He would lower his voice when he mentioned you: "Don't tell anyone, Joseíto, but an old man who read me tobacco leaves when I was a boy called his spirit, and the spirit spoke just the way I'm talking to you, José Tomás, and it said I come from Juan del Rosario, a rebel black who fought with the Spaniards in order to be free." Not free, because you'd already been freed by me—the spirit must have meant something else—but that's how Ernestino understood it. You know that your people have always been superstitious and ready to believe in the beyond. They gave teaching and parish priests a pretty hard time by putting the Church of Rome's saints and African gods in the same sack, and worshiping Saint John as if he were a live person, getting him drunk and bathing him at the beach during the summer festival—or, if not that, drinking and singing at wakes for infants, which is without doubt a blasphemy. You're not too sure of that descent? He wasn't either; in his besotted memory names and voices were all scrambled. At one time someone must have spoken to him about the days of the founding, when you wrote to the king, or about the blacks rising up in *cumbé* rebel groups; maybe he confused you with Guillermo Rivas, a black who started an uprising in Ocoyta and with whom I was lucky not to be entangled. You gave me suffering enough! Tales that must have got all mixed up in his head, and in solitary moments, when traipsing through the woods among the animals, he thought he was your reincarnation.

As a child, Ernestino peddled cans of water. He would put them in a small cart and pull it along as if he were a mule, winding through the roads between plantations, looking for thirsty workers in the woods who might appease their thirst for a penny. He was a nobody then, a shadow who approached with his cart, offered the water, deposited a few coins in his pocket, and disappeared. The plantation owners, who were still growing cacao, knew him as *the black boy with the water can* and, outside of complaining if he raised the price, had no dealings with him. From those days of roving the forest he got his knowledge of herbs and his ability to cure snakebites, so added to his trade as waterboy was that of witch doctor. "I'm not a witch doctor," he'd argue. "I heal, and that's something else. The only sickness I cure is snakebite; I learned how from an old man who lived back in the woods around here, and he taught me the ancient wisdom." But in 1945 the black boy with the water can was transformed into Ernestino Tovar, the founder of the first branch of the Acción Democrática party in the valleys of Barlovento, and his place became the first district headquarters, where registrations began, very few at first: his mother; his two brothers; a brother-in-law; his close friend; and his lady love, Ramonita Romero. During the three years civilian government lasted until its temporary disappearance under the dictatorship of General Pérez Jiménez, the region's landowners and merchants stopped looking down on him, and instead of his dragging his little cart to visit them, they came to greet him and give him bottles of whiskey, and instead of calling him *the witch doctor with the water can,* they called him "Comrade Tovar." In his youth he'd been or had the reputation of being the most respected man in the village: he'd pleaded with neighbors to let themselves be cured by doctors, had told the women that when the people from the health service came they should get their children vaccinated and not hide them in the woods, had urged the men to join the Peasant Federation and advised that if their farms were invaded they shouldn't go out on the highway and burn cars but rather present a complaint to the Public Prosecutor for Agrarian Matters; he'd explained what Agrarian Reform was, and when any peasant brought him a snakebitten dog, he'd take advantage of the visit to sing the praises of Betancourt. José Tomás would accompany him sometimes when he worked his plot or walked to Capaya to visit an invalid; or, sitting in the shade, they would chat about earlier times, and Ernestino would show off his small private altar. "Here's Our Lady of Altagracia, venerated by all of us because she's been in Curiepe ever since the village has been a village, and Rómulo Betancourt, president of Venezuela, founder of the Democratic Party; and when you come of age I'm going to register you in the party so you can be like me, a rabid Adeco, a member of Acción Democrática, until the day you die." The newspaper photograph, cut out and pasted on a piece of cardboard, presided along with the Virgin over the single room of his cane-and-mud house. "You're going to become a man during democracy," he promised José Tomás. "While that bandit Pérez Jiménez was around, all he did was persecute Adecos and steal money, but that mess is over now, and there's going to be real honest-to-goodness democracy." His faith was unbreakable. Not long ago, when the last elections were held, Ernestino—sickly and declining as he was—put in his appearance to vote for his party. They asked for his identity card; he removed a lot of shreds of paper from a worn and dirty wallet, but the card didn't appear. "Everybody here knows me," he protested. "Just ask them who I am, and everybody will know; ask them, and they'll tell you Ernestino Tovar was the first Adeco here." But he had to return home downcast after walking three hours to get to the polls—without voting for his party, and without establishing when he'd been born, which was hard to find out because all those who could have known had died. He said he remembered all the men born after him and that he'd made love to all the women, but the one he liked best was Vicenta, whose first lover he'd been.

When Vicenta was a child, shortly before she knew Ernestino, the adults would get together on Saturday night after chores, and sitting on the ground, she would listen to their stories, fables, and tales while they drank, and through their narrations she came to understand what life was like and the destiny of men and also heard about the existence of supernatural beings. There were wandering spirits, those angels that remained in the air when Satan fled Paradise and took thousands along with him, and in that exodus of demons there were also the enchanted—the ones who dropped into the water and took refuge in wells and lived in La Reina pond or Loma del Viento—and among these the vile spirits who stole children in order to free themselves from their enchantment, but also the good ones who protected human beings and felt love for them. From the first time she'd made love, she went with her girlfriends to Saint John to see if the mint was in bloom yet, a sign of fertility for the first to find it, and she stopped to peer into the deep wells and pools where the mysteries are, and if a reflection of a face appears on the surface of the water, it foretells life, but if there's a shapeless and dark, confusing swirl, it means death. "Those are old wives' tales," Ernestino told her. "None of that's true; the only thing true is the incantation for snakebite. There's proof of that, the ones who stay and the ones who go. It comes from ancient wisdom, from our ancestors, and it's transmitted from one man to another; women can't make it work, and if you see a man about to do it when there's a pregnant woman around, don't let him, because it's no good then. One learns the prayers and doesn't repeat them; a person who goes around repeating them doesn't cure anything, and the incantations really work only after the old man who taught them to him has died." Vicenta had bought perfumes in the drugstore to allure men and had discovered the secrets of muslin flower and *venamí* extract to get her first lover and also the miraculous use of the water of seven essences (which brings money, a shower of gold), divine water, flower water, rose water, cinnamon water, and cologne water to hold him; but when Ernestino proposed that she go with him, because she seemed lively and well disposed for work, she thought it wasn't good for the shadow always to fall from the same branch, and she went to live with Picafino until she had a little girl she couldn't support, and then she left for Caracas to look for work. She'd had just the one daughter. Over time she stopped believing in spirits, good or bad, but engraved in her open palm still were the fourteen grains of sand from when she'd gone to bathe in the river and had thrown a handful of sand into the air so that when she caught it she could count the grains in her hand as the number of children there would be in her womb. That's why Vicenta wasn't afraid of the witch of Birongo, because only she, they said, really knew how the body and soul could avoid births. When Vicenta began as cook in Doña Cristina's house, Belén and she were roughly the same age; Belén was engaged to Miguel, her first husband, and Vicenta was a girl coming to Caracas in a carter's wagon and leaving a child behind. And she'd lived with them until Belén and Domingo Sánchez went to Europe. Then Vicenta was in a kind of despair: she packed her cardboard suitcase and went off in a bus to Barlovento, the way she'd come, with an empty feeling and no prospects. She was happy to see her daughter, Ignacia, again, to hug her tightly, tearfully, and tell her she was going to stay now, and they would no longer see each other only Easter week, when Missy Belén would give Vicenta time off to travel to Curiepe, where she could greet her brothers and sisters, ask about her friends, about the newly dead, and then dance and sing merry *mampulorios* for them, be first in the Maundy Thursday processions, walk barefoot to Birongo to visit Ernestino and listen to his tales as they sat in the doorway of his house at dusk. Most of the time it was as if Ignacia didn't exist, except for being the recipient, now and then, of a part of Vicenta's savings—when she could send it. On the other hand, Belén, despite the gap in their status, was someone much closer, an intimate she could tell when she had a migraine and needed to spend the whole afternoon lying in the darkness of her room, somebody who would be sympathetically afflicted and wander through the house not knowing what to do, someone full of joy and enthusiasm while preparing for parties and receptions or getting ready to go shopping, someone Vicenta could forgive for an irritated word or an unpleasant gesture when she hadn't followed her orders, someone who liked to laugh and loosen her tongue when she chose to. Someone, in short, whom Vicenta knew well. Ignacia, on the contrary, was a shadow, a daughter whom relatives had brought up, a somewhat sad child, a bit withdrawn, who would silently watch her mother get out of the bus, waiting for her to say something or produce a dress or sash or a pair of white shoes from the suitcase. An adolescent who met her once a year and looked at her mutely, hoping she'd say something, always with the impression that her mother didn't know what to say. A woman who hugged her wordlessly, who wept when she saw her and made her weep too, as much as Vicenta had cried over Belén's departure for Europe—an occasion when she'd insisted on going to the dock to see her mistress for the last time as she disappeared into what seemed to Vicenta the end of the world; Belén's consolations, reassuring that she would be back and would send for her, were useless, and yet, when Vicenta returned to Curiepe with her cardboard suitcase, she quickly changed her mind, and it seemed to her that she had come back because she had to look after José Tomás.

Ernestino's efforts to save Ignacia were in vain. She'd been leaning over the edge of the calm, brownish water, washing a piece of the child's clothing, and had become distracted; had she been more alert she might have been able to leap away and avoid the bite. "An evil critter," Ernestino said; "they don't usually come so close to the water." A snake put there on purpose, some said, but who would have wished evil on Ignacia, a good and simple woman who wasn't coveting anybody's husband? They spent the night by her side, Vicenta and Ernestino, the best enchanter in the region—it was rare that someone didn't come for him to cure a cow stung by a scorpion or relieve a donkey bitten by a spider or save a peasant from a bushmaster; there was not a settlement or plantation nearby where they didn't know and call on him. He was there, not moving, for two days, giving her a drink from his bottle of preparatives from time to time, short sips of finely ground corocillo root and bullweed in cane liquor, applying the antidote to her leg while praying over her: *Most holy sacrament son of the eternal immensity give me your divine aid to cure this sick woman who was bitten by a snake a mad and poisonous animal amen Jesus at her foot I bear a light and by her hand a cross cursed be snakes by the sweet name of Jesus consummatum it is.* He bathed her in the river and emptied the calabash of water over her head, but the leg kept swelling until it turned purple and gangrenous, and then, in agony, lying in the hammock, she died. "Some go, and others stay," Ernestino said. He, who'd saved so many, couldn't save Vicenta's daughter; he disappeared from his house for several days, wandered about swilling cane liquor and betting on cockfights until his grief passed. Vicenta stayed with the little boy, turned his head about as if to nurse him, clinging to two certainties: the child was not going to die of hunger, nor would she turn him over to someone to be taken care of; and so, with José Tomás on her back, she went from plantation to plantation offering her services as ironer, sweets cook, laundress. Where could they find a better recommendation than that of having served in the house of a minister?

She repainted her house's walls a bright yellow and the windows pale blue; she scrubbed and scrubbed the concrete floors Ignacia had neglected, swept cockroaches and scorpions out of the corners, planted geraniums in oilcans to beautify the yard; and when the sun first peeped out, she was already going down the street with a basin on her head, hawking candy and corncakes and picking up clothes to wash and iron. Sometimes she would miss her clean and well-cared-for room in Dr. Sánchez Luna's house; her right to rest in the afternoon and, after dinner was served, listen to comedies on the radio; her high-class position as first cook in a rich house with two kitchen helpers; going out every morning, basket in hand, to do the buying at the market after having set the day's menu with Belén; the long periods when the house was empty, with the other servants in their rooms, when she would sit in the service porchway and enjoy the coolness of the ferns she had planted herself.

Those were times gone by; later she was compensated with the delight of watching José Tomás grow and become an agile and quick-witted little boy who before and after school would help her sell. He was serious, with two notebooks and some pencil stubs, as he recited fragments of national history. A thousand and one times, "When they dragged Vicente Emparan to the council and he asked the people if they wanted him and the people said no, then, Grandmother, he told them I don't want to rule either, and do you know why? Because the priest Madariaga got behind him and did like this to them with his finger." A thousand and one times the beheading of the black man José Leonardo Chirinos: "Why did they kill him, Grandmother, if he was a good man?" A thousand and one times the withdrawal to Oriente: "Grandmother, the Liberator passed by here, through Barlovento, when he was running away from Boves." A thousand and one times the Admirable Campaign carried out by the Liberator for the benefit of the slaves. The boy was enthusiastic about learning and had a good head for figures. "Grandmother, do you know how to add fractions?" "No, child, how would I know, since I count on my fingers? But nobody can trick me; go ask Ernestino, see if he can." But José Tomás got to know more even than Ernestino, and Vicenta went to ask her old confidant what she should do. "There's nothing more to learn here," said Ernestino, "and he's finishing school; send him to Barcelona, to the priests' school." The advice stuck in his throat; he hated priests and felt veneration only for the Virgin of Altagracia and the Christ Child of Curiepe, but he was ruled by an unquestionable pragmatism. "If you send him to a high school in Caracas you'll have to pay for room and board, and I've heard that the priests in Barcelona give them three meals a day and a place to sleep. Send him, because he's got the head for it; if he was stupid I'd let you know."

José Tomás had been Ernestino's pupil, and the child paid attention as if his words were the unvarnished truth of history. He would listen to him tell how the war with Spain spawned a long-lasting desolation and revolt; those were times of hatred and of the slogan "Death to the Whites." With those stories Ernestino tried to arouse the passion of pride and recovery in him, but José Tomás was never satisfied. "I like democracy better, Godfather, where everybody respects and obeys the law," the boy would tell him. Nevertheless, his admiration had no limits as he listened to Ernestino recall events that he, in turn, had heard from others; it seemed to José Tomás that *this,* not the one he'd recited by rote for his schoolteacher, was the true history. Ernestino narrated as if he'd lived the fragments he was describing in person, as if he'd been the main actor in all those events. When his tongue was set to wagging by the effects of cane liquor, he could hark back to the days of Independence and even further back, and in such moods he'd told José Tomás how those lands of Barlovento, ever since the time of the Spaniards, had always been in litigation, since the first cacao was planted and the slaves hacked down the forest with machetes and planted the huge bucare, mijao, and rain trees that shaded my property. Families, he explained, intercrossed by many links, had owned the land and the blacks who worked it; but the blacks had always been rebellious and didn't like dictatorships, and one of those families, the richest of all, the one that owned the most groves, had been in a dispute with the blacks of Curiepe for almost a century. He was very well informed about our lawsuits, as you can see, Juan del Rosario. One fine day José Tomás found himself putting four changes of clothing into his grandmother's cardboard suitcase, getting on the bus, and leaving behind the only landscape he knew. The two of them sat there, bouncing up and down, on the long road to Barcelona; they came to the door of the priests' school and rang the bell, and his grandmother called out the long list of his virtues: a model of discipline, hard work, and intelligence, and almost with the vocation of a saint . . . until Father Manuel said, "Have him come in; let's see if he's ready for secondary school." And he was; he emerged six years later with a high-school diploma, the carpenter's trade, and some rudiments of bookkeeping. During his adolescence José Tomás's only joy was the arrival of vacation, when he would run to the bus station to travel to Curiepe, and the only moments of relief from his imprisonment were Saturday afternoons, when Father Manuel would hitch up his cassock and referee soccer games. "Get me out of this school," the boy asked Vicenta. "I'm bored to death here." But Vicenta remained implacable; she'd wept whole nights over Ernestino's advice, but once decided, she wouldn't be moved. "You'll thank me for it someday, Joseíto; when you're grown up you'll thank me," Ernestino said. He turned into a tutor and swelled with pride year after year as he saw his godson's grades. "The boy can get to be a doctor, Vicenta; he can go to the university and be a glory to his country." Since he'd taken over the young man's political education, he was a little worried by the enthusiasm with which José Tomás reported that he was picked, some Sundays, to be an altar boy at a high mass that was sung; Ernestino was allergic to priests and the Church. "The virgin and the saints are up in heaven," he said, "but down here on earth it's Rómulo Betancourt." He also took charge of his godson's sexual initiation. "You've got to be very careful with women," he advised, "because there's always the danger of a bad sickness. When you have to do what men do, go to Ramonita Romero's house, because I know her, and I know her girls are clean."

Ramonita Romero shared Ernestino's admiration for Rómulo Betancourt and, most of all, gloried in the fact that the party provided a place for those who walked with their feet on the ground, the ones who sold cans of water or who, like her, had been born in the backcountry and been parceled out at random from house to house by their mothers. Ernestino had bestowed upon her the title of a party founder, since she'd been the seventh to be enrolled and was always the first to pay her dues, and because she was without doubt the richest of the first militants. On the outskirts of Curiepe she'd established a house frequented by peasants, small farmers, and fishermen from

Higuerote. It had four bedrooms and a parlor, the latter divided by cardboard partitions into three cubicles, and a backyard that served as a chicken pen and bottle dump. The first girls to serve there had been recruited from neighboring settlements, but a distant event, one far removed, the fall of the Vichy government, came to have a great effect on Ramonita's house (as the business was familiarly known), and was the reason for its enjoying years of splendor. A French collaborator had fled to America and ended up in San José de Río Chico, where he opened a small restaurant whose scant success and meager profitability were a source of great anxiety for him. One day, out of boredom or because he was tormented by his situation, it occurred to him to pay a visit to Ramonita's house, and he got the idea of proposing a partnership with her. She would back his establishment, and he would find some émigrée compatriots of his who shared his adversity. When the first Frenchwoman arrived at Ramonita Romero's house the clientele underwent a dramatic change. Within days word spread throughout the valley, sparking astonishment and curiosity. The place lost its local atmosphere, and Ramonita, full of optimism, undertook its redecoration. She bought a phonograph and some Celia Cruz and Miguelito Valdés records, expanded her drink offerings, cutting back on rum and cane liquor to make room for whiskey; the cots and hammocks were replaced by real beds, and all the rooms enjoyed the luxury of a ceiling fan; the windows were clad with metal screens to deter the clouds of mosquitoes that, at dusk, made the place unbearable. She painted the walls and bought secondhand plastic-covered sofas for the parlor; she got rid of the chickens in the backyard to eliminate the stench that had penetrated every corner, and hired a man who, in addition to cleaning up, had the duty of keeping order if a customer got drunk and unruly or if a row broke out. She revised the prices, setting that of the Frenchwomen at twice that of the indigenous girls, and adjusted the fee to the time of day, restricting the time squandered on small talk, dancing, and telling jokes, which didn't bring any profit. The link between quality and price had the immediate effect of lowering demand for the local women, and their customers, ragged small farmers and truck drivers for whom the enjoyment of imported women was prohibitively expensive, ceased to frequent the place, leaving it to the plantation owners and prosperous merchants. The wives of the new clientele noticed that the Saturday domino games, like the Sunday bowling matches, were getting longer and longer, and also the increased frequency of their husbands' sudden and unexpected trips to take care of business. Nobody was fooled. Ramonita Romero was immediately accused of being the principal cause of the moral deterioration of the region. Contempt for her became widespread, and an icy, blameful silence hung over her name; even pronouncing it was considered an offense against public virtue.

When the most distinguished ladies of the region, along with their husbands, decided that they too wanted to enroll in the party, they had to pass through Ernestino's filter and confess their democratic vocations to him, but they thought this step deserved a condition. Ramonita Romero could not share the same ideals with them: it was either they or Ramonita. Then Ernestino chose, and his reply was definitive: "Ramonita is a whore, but she's a founder of the party, and she stays." The aspiring lady democrats had to put their plans in abeyance for the moment. But I see that I'm losing the thread of one story for that of another. I'll get back on track, Juan del Rosario; I want to give you the antecedents of how things are now on the land we've been grappling over.

When José Tomás got out of the priests' school, his grandmother was aggrieved, for her lecture to convince him to go to Caracas and study to be a doctor was useless; José Tomás wanted to stay in Curiepe and follow Ernestino's example. He set up a small sawmill on the Caucagua road and began to make a lot of money, much more than he ever thought he'd see in one place when he was a child with just a cardboard suitcase and a bag of cassava roots that his grandmother was sending as a gift to Father Manuel. He bought a used jeep, and in it he rode back and forth among the settlements to learn of abuses and attacks against the peasants; he advised them to organize into syndicates, spoke with the women to find out what their needs were, and became a respected and cherished man, head of the party's district headquarters. In every election his name was first for councilman, there was no wake to which he wasn't invited or baptism at which he wasn't the godfather, and on Saturday nights he would gather with his numerous friends and comrades to drink beer and bowl. But one night Cocolo didn't show up.

Cocolo was a black man as strong as a tree trunk; the women said he had enough seed for more than fifty boys, and when soused he would shout at the top of his lungs, *I'm a black man of pure Spanish stock.* Cocolo was always spoiling for a fight, and few were the men who dared cross his path when he lost at bowling or at a cockfight, because they were in fear and trembling that he would go wild and break chairs or take a punch at the most unsuspecting person. But Cocolo was also a friend of José Tomás, had been ever since the local school, where Cocolo never got beyond third grade; ever since the days when José Tomás would come back from the priests' school in Barcelona and Cocolo would be waiting for him to go swimming at Higuerote or fishing in the river; ever since—they couldn't have been more than fourteen—they first visited Ramonita Romero's house. José Tomás was puzzled as to why Cocolo would miss the Saturday get-together, but they started the game without him. *That one's off on a bender somewhere; he'll show up tomorrow,* they thought. And, indeed, Cocolo did show up the following day, in front of his house, with a bullet in a leg and another, fatal, one in the back of his neck. It wasn't hard to figure who the culprits were. The woman who lived with Cocolo told how the police had come by and told him he was trespassing on the property of Saltwater Coconut, that where he was there couldn't be any house or planting, that he had to pack up his things and leave, because the next day they were coming to burn the house down. Cocolo told them that was fine, he was going in to get his belongings; and then he went into the house, picked up his machete, and hurled himself at the policemen.

José Tomás paid for the coffin, and some neighbors donated candles and flowers. As soon as they'd buried him, José Tomás took off for Birongo in his jeep. He found Ernestino rocking in his hammock, barefoot, stripped to the waist, his hat resting on his stomach; the old man, his hair white and with one eyelid drooping, almost closed, from a stroke, was nibbling at pieces of coconut that he was softening with his almost empty gums. His broad shoulders and long arms revealed that this was a man who'd once been strong and muscular.

"Ernestino, they killed Cocolo yesterday."

"Cocolo. He was your friend when you were kids. They killed him a long time ago because he was a communist."

"That was Bernardo, Ramonita Romero's son."

"Yes, that's right. It happens with me sometimes, Joseíto, that I ask my daughters where my hat is and I've got it on my head."

"The police killed Cocolo because he had his farm on Saltwater Coconut land, and I remembered that you'd told me about that land, that the Barlovento railroad used to go through there."

"I remember when there was an earthquake, around 1900, and the houses of the Spaniards and the church of Our Lady of Altagracia, all that came tumbling down, but right now I can't remember whether I saw it or whether my mother told me."

"You told me those lands were part of a grant given long ago."

"During Rómulo's time? Could it have been during Rómulo's time? I remember Rómulo, once when he came to Curiepe and I went to greet him and he said to me, *Well, by God, Ernestino! I sure have heard a lot about you!* And then we went to have pineapple cider at my place."

"Yes, but it's not Rómulo I want to talk about. The railroad business was a long time before."

"That was what my father told me, that it doesn't belong to the Frenchman; my father told me that, but I can't remember what the Frenchman's name was except that my father told me it's a contract General Crespo made with the Frenchman, and when it's up he's got to give everything back—railroad, cars, land. The Frenchman's got to give it all back."

"That concession must be about over; that land's got to be reclaimed, because the coconut people can't keep on with their abuses."

"I remember the train, how I was scared when I watched it run through the woods at full speed, and my father told me how they brought in the cars, the rails, the engines, how they brought all that in; my father worked on the railroad, but one day I didn't see any more of him. He left home or somebody killed him on the road. My mother said he fell off a cliff, that a ghost in the shape of a woman appeared to him and that he started following it and fell off a cliff. But I don't believe in ghosts, Joseíto, only in anointments. Do you remember when a doctor came from Caracas, from the university, and took a picture of my voice with a machine? I was telling him about the anointments and the prayers, but I didn't tell him the prayer because that's something you shouldn't be telling somebody without knowing who he is."

"Yes, I remember that, Godfather, but what I want is for you to tell me when they got the Barlovento railroad, when they gave out that concession."

Ernestino got up from his hammock and went inside. He kept paper and pencil on a small table. He sat down before it and started reckoning. He began with the earthquake, the inaugural date of his memories, and he got as far as the deluge that destroyed the Barlovento railroad; from there he doubled back to his mother's memories. He was writing figures, adding, subtracting, biting the pencil. He asked José Tomás not to interrupt because he was getting mixed up in his calculations. José Tomás was waiting for Ernestino's memory to light up.

"Get me a beer to clear my mind, Joseíto."

After several beers he said: "That was around 1884 or 1885, but who can remember that? Don't they have those things written down, Joseíto?"

José Tomás got into his jeep and said, "Tomorrow I'm going to Caracas to look it up in the *Official Gazette*."

Here we are, Juan del Rosario, linked in a lawsuit again. Had you forgotten the smell of the paper, the shuffling of the pages, the passion of the words? I, who know you, my houseboy and my freedman, am sure you're getting your blood hot and sharpening your teeth as you discover that José Tomás has instigated a battle worthy of being recorded among your briefs. Well, I get my drive back, too, when I see Francisco Villaverde ready to move heaven and earth to reclaim my heritage, and in the same way that I'm relishing that, it must please you to see José Tomás leading a protest over the death of his friend Cocolo. Are we in the times of Portales? No, it wasn't Portales who ordered him killed and his house and crops burned. I wasn't involved—you ought to know that I have no voice to give commands, nor are there any lieutenants to obey my writs. More than eighty people came out with banners and signs—men, women, and children marching through the village, and a sizable group got into a truck and continued on to Higuerote, San José, and the coastal settlements. You would have stood open-mouthed to hear them shouting—sometimes with the help of a megaphone, but most often with their own throats—angry denunciations of Cocolo's death: *We've got the right to plant, government murderers.* Didn't the lieutenant come and arrest them or their owners put them in the stocks? Why, Juan del

Rosario, you're deafer than Alejandro! They're free, and they can shout all they want, even if they're bellowing into empty air. The only ones watching, with startled faces, are the weekend vacationers, whose rest was interrupted as the truck went along weaving its way through the line of cars and buses. The drivers didn't care about the uproar of the angry crowd; they were only bothered by the racket and by the blowing of the truck's horn—this spectacle delayed their arrival at the beach, where they wanted to sunbathe, swim in the cove, toss away empty beer and soda cans, and then go up and down over the water in motorboats that pull (I know you won't believe me) an almost naked man or woman on some sort of enormous feet that skim the waves as if it were the miracle of Jesus walking on water. I never went to the beach, Juan del Rosario. You know that Alejandro never wanted to take me there, nor was I able to visit my far-flung holdings. I never saw how the sea split into a thousand blue channels as it caressed my land, or how it built up, with its sand, a gentle boundary. I never saw the riverbeds shake themselves loose of the underbrush and open up into the immense and solitary water. Now I watch with dismay as thousands of people called tourists spread all over it and make camp only two hours from Caracas. Their jabbering drowns out the voices of the people following the councilman and raising a hue and cry about the murder of a farmer. But you probably want to know more about José Tomás and his claims.

Once he was able, thanks to Ernestino's memory, to determine the exact year in which Joaquín Crespo decreed the expropriation, José Tomás went to Caracas to thumb through documents until he found the *Official Gazette* in which was recorded the resolution of the Ministry of Transport and Communications terminating the concession to the Barlovento railroad because ninety-nine years had passed since that ill-fated June 5, 1884, and the ministry consequently decreed the reversion of all rights acquired by Mr. Emilio Salini, whose current heirs are the company known as Saltwater Coconut. That means, Juan del Rosario—I'm trying to explain it in terms you can understand—that the governor has decided that the lands were without owner and that they belonged to the Crown, and that, therefore, the village council, as the bastard descendant of what we knew as the royal town council, has jurisdiction over them. Do you understand, or should I give you more details to make it clear? The chief magistrate of that council was he: José Tomás, Vicenta's grandson. You didn't know they had black councilmen, and had it been so earlier, it would have been a completely different matter for you? I understand you; in those days the head councilman was Alejandro. Well, then, once José Tomás had the resolution from the *Gazette* in his hands, he undertook to claim the lands as a collective belonging to the village. Don't think that we were the only ones who did any writing; you can see him there, sending reports right and left to the Agrarian Prosecutor, to the state deputies, to the Congress, to the General Prosecutor, and to every other governmental agency, tearing up the highway between Barlovento and Caracas in his ramshackle jeep, and in the same way that you pacified your blacks every time I opposed your briefs and appealed unfavorable decisions, he downplays the disheartening slowness of the process. "These things take a long time," he tells his grandmother Vicenta. "The deputy promised that this would be brought up next month," he explains to Ernestino. "Right now they're discussing a law that has priority," he reassures the members of the council. "Look, comrades," he would go on, "the matter's been like this for years, and we can't hurry it along. The important thing is for it to turn out right, not that it be resolved tomorrow." The blacks complained, "This mess isn't going to be straightened out; they're putting us off." One day Cocolo's woman appeared at the village hall to declare angrily that she had five little children, two of them Cocolo's, and when were they finally going to give her a parcel of land to plant? José Tomás had to send her away firmly. And he kept going back like a donkey to a wheat field, shuttling from one appointment to another, one office to another, one authority to another, pleading with the secretaries of powerful people for a few minutes' parley with their bosses, which request was always denied; he was always on a trip, always taking care of a matter of extreme urgency— only to be informed that Congress was not in session—or, if it was, that it didn't have a quorum, or, if it had one, that his proposal had been shelved because there were others that carried more weight. In short, Juan del Rosario, the same time we spent waiting for the slow crossing of the ships that carried our letters to Santo Domingo and even Seville was lost by José Tomás in the ditherings of politicians who never found a moment to resolve that matter for him, small in comparison to the nation's problems, but in which he was investing his whole life. Even so, he continued the struggle without flagging, and when it seemed as if he was hopelessly mired, a newspaperman came and took pictures of him in the main room of the village hall, sitting beneath the portrait of the Liberator, and the interview enabled him to explain to public opinion the predicament in which the council found itself as it defended lands that were communal and that Saltwater Coconut was fraudulently selling. Would you have liked to appear in the newspapers, Juan del Rosario? A little tribune or chronicle you could have distributed on the streetcorners of Caracas? Even so (I'll tell you, since you've never seen a newspaper), they're so thick and have so many news items that one more or less goes unnoticed; outside of those involved in the lawsuit, I don't think anyone paid any attention to the small piece where José Tomás's statements appeared. In all his exertions—though he'd kept silent so as not to alarm his people—he had learned of the existence of a tourism plan of gigantic proportions, and he'd discovered that the sale of the communal lands, my holdings, had already been agreed upon. But that's a horse of another color.

I don't have much confidence in him, Alejandro; he looks to me like a mediocre lad overwhelmed by circumstances. I watched him grow up in the shadow of an equally middling father, dependent on Belén's fortune, which was really Domingo Sánchez's, because—let's come right out with it—when Belén married him she didn't have a pot to pee in. I watched him play in this house, watched him suffer his sisters' bad manners, saw his mother's silliness as she took care of everything by saying it was raising her blood pressure; and then I watched him studying engineering after secondary school, as had been arranged ahead of time, and afterward going to work for a large construction company, which accepted him out of consideration for the memory of his father, a man about whom I can say that at least, within his great laxity, he was honest, and there Francisco stayed year after year, satisfied in the pedestrian narrowness that separated him from his friends and companions of adolescence, dominated by the wealth of his rich brothers-in-law, who would invite him to events at which he would only waste his time and that underscored in him the feeling of his trifling worth. Francisco had set out to be a humdrum man, discreetly happy, keeping his own counsel; and in the absence of any great preoccupations, seeing the prestigious life of his former classmates at the Jesuits gave him a feeling of the greatest banality. Yet beginning with the day he met Don Heliodoro, a glimmer of doubt had slipped into what till that moment had been secure and consistent for him: his small apartment furnished in good taste but without luxuries, his two weeks of vacation each year, his Saturday nights at the movies and then a small neighborhood restaurant, his retirement plan with the company, the well-being of his family. He began to suffer doubts. It was as if he had willingly accepted his existence or, rather, had made a silent accommodation, had humbly accepted that fate hadn't brought him better chances. But he was discomfited to find himself for the first time at the age of forty-something facing what Silvia, his wife, insisted was an opportunity. She had repeated to him over all those years, twenty to be exact, *You're an intelligent fellow, educated; what's happened is that you haven't had an opportunity.* And without wanting to admit it, he knew he'd been biding his time for that opportunity, and Silvia, also without wanting to say so, had been awaiting its arrival. Maybe his father had been someone without an opportunity too, and now Don Heliodoro Chuecos Rincón, that man who looked like a poor devil to Francisco, had raised the unforeseen possibility that two hours away from Caracas, perhaps, the remnants of what had been a great fortune could be reclaimed, along with the seed of what could restore it to what it had been.

During free moments between his duties as a punctilious and diligent engineer for a large construction company or while waiting in lines of traffic as he traveled the familiar route between home and office, he gave in to daydreams that at first seemed to him distractions as mundane as his person but that little by little were taking on substance in his thoughts. *Dr. Francisco Villaverde moved away,* the concièrge in the old building where he'd lived since his marriage would say; *I'm sorry, Dr. Villaverde is in the United States on business,* the receptionist in his new office would answer. *We're very sorry, but Dr. Villa-verde is on vacation in Europe and won't be back till next month; his assistant can take care of you.* Or, *You'll have to excuse Dr. Villaverde, who's in a meeting and can't be disturbed.* That's how his secretary would talk, and not that irritating, shrill "Francisco, you answer it, fellow, I'm very busy." And Silvia wouldn't tell him, *Tomorrow I'm going to see if I can buy some curtains that are marked down.* No, Dr. Villaverde's wife, with a chauffeur and a Jacuzzi, would no longer be the prudent administrator of two small salaries, and she would leave the banking house where she'd served for eighteen years without interruption except for maternity leaves. Mrs. Villaverde would now have more important things to do than indulge the bad moods of her bosses; Mrs. Villaverde would be part of a very different setup. When the time of the banalities they hoped for arrived, he would surely have better subjects to discuss with his brothers-in-law, and his sisters would find better commonplaces to share with Silvia. And one fine day he left all of us gaping: I was the first to be flabbergasted when his old friends, for whom he was a faint memory from the distant days of adolescence, received an unusual visit from Francisco Villaverde Blanco, who was, having initiated the claim for land belonging to his family inheritance, in search of partners for a tourism project. The bewilderment was greatest for himself, because, though he'd expected they'd slam the door in his face, he found himself suddenly immersed in the bustle and activity of a successful businessman. So you can see now, Juan del Rosario, our dispute has been revived.

"Obviously," the lawyer told him, "there's no doubt about the legal issues concerning the plantation. It is to the heirs of Carlota Villaverde and Mrs. Sánchez Luna, both daughters of the petitioner José Francisco Blanco, that the undivided rights to the former plantation La Trinidad belong. But initiating a claim for these lands, even when the term of expropriation has ended, I consider a waste of time; years would pass before the Supreme Court would decide the case, and time and money would be lost. No, I definitely don't recommend proceeding that way; what looks much more promising to me is the matter of Saltwater Coconut. Along with the district judge, I've made a visual inspection, and the inescapable conclusion is that Saltwater has invaded lands outside the boundaries set by the expropriation. As you know, the contract, originally drawn up in 1884, granted five hundred yards on either side of the rail line; the tracks cut through the precise middle of what was La Trinidad plantation, so that the property was split in two. Your grandfather could have objected at the time that the totality of the property was affected by the expropriation, but he didn't do so; it's to be supposed that the plantation, bisected, was rendered unusable for its purposes, and for reasons unknown to us he chose not to pursue his rights. As it stands now, Saltwater has encroached upon and fenced in much more than those five hundred yards, so it's possible, and I see a very clear right, for a claim to be made to everything that wasn't explicitly set off in the expropriation decree. Nevertheless, you know that the best lawsuit is the one that doesn't get to court. If we let Saltwater know we're going to institute proceedings against them, a restitutory ban, it's quite probable that they'll want to negotiate; there's no assurance that we'll win, but if it's declared that the suit has been filed, the sales campaign they've begun will be interrupted. Do you understand? Then it's likely that they'll prefer to reach some kind of agreement, naturally, and this couldn't be anything else but taking them on as partners in the construction of the development. The headache is the intermediate strip that makes up the original expropriation and that has reverted to the nation; it's land that becomes communal, the property of the village, and unfortunately, it crosses through the tract from one end to the other. That's the thorniest problem to resolve, because nobody's going to put money into a project that will provoke endless claims by the council, which has the power in its hands: if they don't approve the construction permits, nothing can be done. This is more a political than a legal matter because I suspect they haven't thought at all about developing those lands, but in the interest of populism they're going to withhold permission. On the other hand, when I was in the region I had a long talk with the judge, and he was telling me about some problems that have had a great impact on the people there. The owners of Saltwater are powerful people, influential, you understand; there's a lot of money involved, and they seem to have good connections with the government, with all governments. The coconut business is a drop in the bucket in relation to the other interests they have in this country, industrial and financial, so that for them it hasn't been hard to stop incursions by peasants who cross their boundaries and plant crops; they simply call the National Guard and ask their help in getting the trespassers out. Normally the peasants are frightened and leave, but a while back a very serious incident occurred. A man was killed, one very well liked in the village, it seems, and a close friend of the head councilman; this gave rise to strong protests, with demonstrations, accusations before the Agrarian Prosecutor, demands before Congress. It seems to me an auspicious situation for you, because it's to be supposed that the council will prefer to support you people rather than Saltwater, which has become their sworn enemy."

Belén had been listening in solemn silence, and when the lawyer came to this point she interrupted: "But the head councilman is Vicenta's grandson. Don't you remember," she addressed Francisco, "that Vicenta came to Caracas because she had to have medical tests, and she visited me and spent hours telling me about her grandson, what a marvel he was, that he was a politician, that they always elected him head of the council? Francisco, don't you remember that I commented about it to you?" Francisco didn't recall. "What you've got to do is go to Curiepe and talk to Vicenta's grandson; tell him you're my nephew, and he'll know perfectly well who I am."

"You're talking," Francisco answered grouchily, "as if it were a matter of doing public relations work at a cocktail party; it doesn't matter that the head councilman is the grandson of someone who used to be your cook during the time of Gómez, that your cook spoke to her grandson about a lady and a doctor she worked for fifty years ago."

"Francisco, don't be impertinent. I'm sure this gentleman thinks this is important."

Francisco was used to arguments with Belén, quarrels he always lost, in which all he could do was give in honorably. The lawyer intervened discreetly.

"Still, Francisco, in matters like this the people involved count for a lot; if you could approach the councilman from a perspective that's, let's say, more intimate, it wouldn't be negligible."

Our attorneys, Juan del Rosario, were a bunch of pettifoggers of small account who in every instance would purport that it was necessary to consult their big books in which the Laws of the Indies were recorded—if they didn't have to write to the Council to receive an explanation of how to interpret those mincing provisions that governed even the colors slave women should wear and who had the right to carry parasols. How different from these lawyers! If I'd had one like this man, who could explain things so clearly and who had his eyes wide open for business, I assure you, Juan del Rosario, that my lawsuit would have been settled more quickly and we would have wasted less ink. But don't think that it's only Francisco Villaverde who's being expertly advised; you'll find that José Tomás has friends to instruct him too.

Disconcerted by the crowd milling about in the station, he found himself amid a multitude of people getting on and off buses and vans, lining up at ticket windows, or sitting on the floor surrounded by bundles and suitcases. The jeep was in such bad shape now that he'd decided against chancing another trip, so José Tomás had made the journey in a jam-packed van that ran between Barlovento and Caracas. After a long wait at the terminal, he got into another van, which dropped him a few steps from the Plaza Bolívar. The cathedral clock showed noon.

I find the church has become ugly, in poor taste, painted like a pastel—but what can you do, Alejandro? At least it's standing, and the clock keeps good time. The square across from it is beautiful, but I'm reluctant to describe it because I think it might make your head spin. On the benches under the shade trees, a few men are reading newspapers or chatting; they're old inhabitants of Caracas and have little to do, so they get together to pass the time of day; on the streets encircling the square there's a frantic movement of people who seem quite busy as they walk among lottery vendors, the stands selling knickknacks, and urchins with no trade or aid who look avidly at the packages and purses the ladies are carrying. I think what would most captivate your attention is a group of people in short pants, men and women, who are speaking English and taking pictures, trying to catch sight of the sloths that are hanging from the trees and that the guide points out to them. You would like to be wearing your tricorn hat and carrying your staff once more to pass through the arcades Ricardos built and go to your office in government house? Oh, Alejandro, how they'd laugh if they saw you in that getup. Be content to listen while I trace the path of the councilman from the Brión district, to which your plantation belongs.

Waiting for the offices to open, he walked up and down the narrow sidewalks for a while; from time to time among the very tall buildings of the banks, brokerages, and financial institutions would appear an Arab's hardware store, an Italian's shoe-repair cubbyhole, a Spaniard's bar with its smell of fried food; surges of people were coming out of the Capitolio subway station, dodging holes in the sidewalk, the stands of street vendors, and braking buses. José Tomás went into a lunchroom, managed to jostle his way to the counter, and shouted so the Portuguese behind it could hear his order. The place was packed, and arms holding cups of coffee, glasses of juice, corn cakes, and the daily special reached over his head. Somebody bumped against him without noticing and spilled coffee on his pants. José Tomás cleaned himself off slowly and quietly, ate rapidly in order to get to the Congress. It wasn't easy to get past the guard post; they'd asked a lot of questions, he'd shown them his party membership card and his credentials as councilman several times, and the same number of times he'd heard, *Please wait; you can't pass right now.* People with briefcases were going in and out, along with newspapermen and television crews; automobiles were constantly stopping in front and disgorging important people and their bodyguards. It was a very special day; it seemed they were discussing a monumental law or questioning some luminary.

"You picked a bad day, José Tomás," said the deputy from his state, whom he'd luckily managed to spot in a group of people. "It's impossible for me to see you today, but don't be concerned about your matter. It's moving right along, but we've got to wait." Do you see, Juan del Rosario? He was so sad and downhearted that he looked as if someone had died, and he went into a bar and began to drink beer all by himself and was as lonely as a soul in hell until someone came over to help him. It was a mid-level bureaucrat he'd met in one of his many lobbying tries, who couldn't understand the significance of staking a claim to that strip of land, overrun with snakes and mosquitoes, where they'd killed Cocolo. "Look, friend," the man said, putting his hand on José Tomás's shoulder, "just drop it." José Tomás was downing one beer after another and couldn't come out of his funk. How could he drop it, how could he surrender in the most crucial undertaking of his life? He'd entrusted his sawmill to others, had endured the complaints of his wife, who nagged him every night that his wood was rotting and his partner was robbing him; he'd let slide the bits of gossip that reached his ears, whispers that referred to him, saying José Tomás really is a boob, with all that money slipping through his fingers because he stayed there cutting wood. And now the bureaucrat was warning him, "That claim won't get anywhere, I'm telling you." The man ordered two whiskeys and gave José Tomás a cordial hug, which nettled him. "What do you want that little chunk of land for?" the man went on. "The mess it's in now makes it no good for anything. For planting four banana trees and some cassava? Listen, because I know a lot about tangles like this; you've got an opportunity in your hands, do you hear me? A tremendous bit of luck has turned up, and you're pressing on with that dumb business of a claim. A full-fledged tourist complex is planned for that place, the works, understand? Golf course and the whole shebang, because the deal is in dollars, understand? So you think you're going to stop them with the *Gazette* in your hand that says it belongs to the village council? If you keep harassing people, what will happen is that they'll remove you, understand? You'll never win another election. Look, kid, you're misguided. Forget about Congress here; the ones you have to talk to are the guys planning the project, and remember, I'm telling you out of friendship, because there's nothing in it for me, remember that. But I'm going to give you the facts: the one you have to see is Dr. Francisco Villaverde; he's the man." José Tomás checked his watch and thought it was getting late for the last van to Barlovento. With great difficulty he managed to break away, declining the round that his unexpected friend was offering.

Can you imagine their telling you, my houseboy and my freedman, that you should come to my house on the corner of San Jacinto to see if we could reach an understanding in the lawsuit over my possessions? It makes me laugh to think about it, and I think you too would laugh, imagining the houseboy coming to announce that Juan del Rosario Villegas was at the door and wanted to sit with me in the parlor over a cup of chocolate and some sweets as we hammered out an agreement. You know that you were cordially received and that Alejandrito and Nicolás always asked about you after your father sent you to the plantation, but when you returned, rebellious and taking on the airs of Royal Founder, claiming the land that Alejandro, your master and godfather, promised you, I had you stoned off the premises. Nor did my attorneys deign to talk with yours, because that was all we needed, on top of your trying to rob me of my property, which you'd taken such a fancy to and with such pugnacity. But things have changed, Juan del Rosario; now they've invented a word that we didn't know and that they call *negotiation*. Now they're advising Francisco to talk to José Tomás and José Tomás to talk to Francisco, because people come to a settlement by talking. Just look at what ignorance can do. If I had known my lawsuit could be resolved by a conversation, do you think I would have been leaping from lawyer to lawyer, as enraged as a bushmaster, every time I got word that your blacks had settled on my land, and raising holy hell when told they'd had the even greater effrontery to build a church? Why did they have me burning villages and drafting stupid briefs to that labyrinth of a Council of the Indies and to those crooked high courts that answered whatever popped into their heads and whenever they felt like it . . . if everything could be reconciled by means of a discussion? A man who doesn't even know how to talk, and he gets you hopelessly tied up. Talking, Alejandro, talking; that was all. Take a note, scribe, because I'm sick and tired of having history condemn me: Doña Inés ordered Juan del Rosario's village incinerated because she didn't know how to negotiate. You didn't know how either, let it be said. Learn from José Tomás; he thought he should do the same as you, but wise men know how to change, and since asserting his rights turned out to be more grueling for him than it would have been for you if you'd swum to the High Court in Santo Domingo with the briefs in your mouth, he's adapted to the ways of the times.

When he got back from Caracas he went into his house, slammed the door, yelled at his children to lower the volume of the television, took off his shirt, and lay on the bed. He was furious. That the king hadn't handed down the decree? Don't be a jackass, Juan del Rosario. What king are you talking about? Listen to his conversation with his wife and pay attention, because he's a man of few words.

She came over slowly and began to ask questions: "How long has it been since you talked to Avelino?"

"Keep your nose out of my troubles."

"I'm not meddling in your troubles, but the money you've been giving me hasn't covered what we need."

"Haven't you got enough food for those kids?"

"You've abandoned the sawmill, and everybody's saying that Avelino's robbing you."

"That sawmill's a big pain in the ass."

"That's where the money for food comes from."

"That's it, the money for buying food and nothing more."

"I've never asked for anything more."

"Well, I'm going to; I'm going to ask for quite a lot more. I'm going to ask Dr. Francisco Villaverde for what's coming to me for signing that permission, and if they refuse me, they're going to go crazy at the ministry. That guy can't be an idiot; every day that goes by without the permit he loses a few more pennies."

"But this was known . . ."

"What was known? Be careful and don't say anything to Ernestino or my grandmother. Do you hear? Very careful."

"You're going to get yourself in a jam."

"No, girl, this is the easiest thing in the world. All I've got to do is stay calm until he gets desperate, and then he'll come here on his own initiative."

Did you catch that, Juan del Rosario, you who thought you were so clever? Easier than dispatching a petition to the high court or getting the governor to open his door or shipping out to Spain to appeal to the king, like those poor devils Joseph Antonio Colmenares and Juan Barreto. You died waiting for the fulfillment of Alejandro's promise? Oh, my houseboy and my freedman! Everybody here has died waiting for a promise, and José Tomás, since he didn't want to die waiting for his, has opted to take it into his own hands. Here a vow is an everyday miracle. Besides, at this point promises have grown so muddled that there's no way to put them in order, and I no longer know whether Columbus invented democracy or Rómulo Betancourt the earthly paradise or whether liberalism pledged agrarian reform or the Adecos independence. No matter what you were waiting for, you were very much mistaken in your patience. This is a matter more for ingenuity than for perseverance, and let me get back to the proof of that.

End of a Lawsuit

I have a hazy picture of cacao trees in the midst of the undergrowth. The silence and solitude of the road is broken up from time to time when a woman toting a basket filled with the cassava she has gathered crosses followed by barefoot children or when a boy, a machete in hand and his chest bared, walks in the sunlight. Through the vines wrapped around the lampposts, a settlement can be glimpsed in the distance, and a knot of men can be seen lounging in the shade as if waiting for something. Most of the small plantations visible from the highway look neglected, and rare are any cleared and productive patches bordered by shade trees. I can't recognize the region that was the richest in the province for more than a century when its cacao groves extended far and wide and my name was listed among the principal landowners. Curiepe is no longer the two rows of huts that you founded, Juan del Rosario, nor is it the patch of mud that Andrés Cayetano left behind forever. It's a good-sized town now, with streets well laid out along which there are a lot of buildings from the end of the century: through their windows' grillwork one can see the main parlor—evidence of family life—and there's a courtyard or animal pen in the rear. Painted in vivid and varied colors, most of them are in the process of being torn down, and they're gradually giving way to the small white modern homes with two stories that now alternate with the old ones. On the narrow sidewalks, as before, small carpets of cacao beans have been spread to dry in the sun.

At the end of the nineteenth century, the old church of Our Lady of Altagracia still rose up with the single nave from its old construction along with the walls erected for a second one, vestiges of its rebuilding after the War of Independence. But in 1900 the earthquake destroyed it, and all that's left now are remnants of the thick, crumbling walls, in front of which the present-day parish church has risen, built in the first quarter of this century, as were the village hall, the square, and the façade of the cemetery. It would have pleased Bishop Martí, who watched over it so vigilantly, to know that now the church, painted blue and white, for the first time in its history is completely finished, clean, its niches adorned with simple little icons, its pews all aligned, and the vaults with its saints filled with flowers.

Francisco Villaverde pushes open the large door and, weary and hot from walking the street that slowly climbs up to the small square with shaded benches clustered around the inevitable equestrian statue of the Liberator, settles into one of the back pews. Sitting in the empty church—there was nobody around that Sunday with anything else to do but attend the wake of the councilman's grandmother—he observes the ceiling fans, the leisurely turning of blades that barely manages to cool the place; he feels removed and restless, but free at least from the mob and tumult that filled Vincenta's house. The absence of signs had made him get lost at a fork in the road, and he'd strayed off the main highway and followed a local road that was crowded with vacationers heading toward the beach in mile-long lines behind buses and trucks. He finally got to the funeral, and was annoyed to find himself trapped in that interminable ceremony, breathing in the nauseating smell of the corpse that was starting to decompose and made him feel like vomiting—to such a degree that he found himself obliged to go out for a spell; he preferred the solitude of the church to being crammed in the tiny parlor with people who were weeping, keening, reciting poetry, and drinking rum in honor of an aged woman who didn't matter to him in the least. Eventually he'd abandoned the effort at recollection that Belén had imposed on him by insisting that Vicenta had worked in the house for so many years that she was like family. Hard as he tried, those memories eluded him, and he was convinced that Vicenta belonged to a period before he was born, but he acquiesced in a false memory in which her image at the long kitchen table or taking care of his sisters ended up looking like the truth. Reminiscing over old times, Francisco had become a child who'd tasted the best chicken stew ever prepared in Caracas, which Vicenta cooked, and José Tomás was a boy who surely must have been eternally thankful to Missy Belén and Doctor Sánchez for the many kindnesses shown his grandmother. Months before, wary, each watchful of the words and expressions of the other, they'd met by themselves in the village hall at a table over which the portrait of the Liberator and a photograph of the president presided, and they'd shared that fictitious memory. After much coming and going, meetings in law offices, visits to state agencies, appointments with influential people, recourses and documents, only one thing remained clear, Alejandro: the investors—that's what they call those important people who have a handle on things—agreed to the urbanization project Francisco had presented, but not with an intermediate strip under village control. "You've got to persuade the councilman," they told him, "to give up his claims. We can't build on those lands because it would be buying ourselves a problem; there has to be an agreement, you understand, a deal by which the project will mean essential development for the region. The Saltwater people have already said they like the idea. All that's left is for you to talk to that fellow, the councilman, who's a troublemaker."

And so they'd spoken, feeling each other out, both fearful of making a misstep, of giving more than was necessary or asking more than was possible. They'd conferred until they reached an understanding, at the cutting edge, until they found the point that brought them together, until that exact moment when Francisco was able to entice José Tomás to participate as a partner, albeit a minority one, and in turn José Tomás would prevail upon the council to see that developing new sources of employment would benefit most of them.

Francisco has left the church, is headed back to the house. There's more movement outside the door; down the way a large group of schoolchildren, all scrubbed and combed and wearing their Sunday clothes, is trailing the teacher as she leads them to offer sympathies to the councilman. The close, crowded room has a strong smell of smoke and sweat. The women's wailing swells louder as the time to leave for the cemetery approaches; they've spent all night preparing the corpse and setting up an altar, a table draped with a white cloth on which there are a plaster crucifix, a small picture of the Virgin of Mount Carmel and another of the Sacred Heart of Jesus, two aluminum candelabra with lighted candles. At the foot of the coffin is a pewter plate laden with lemon slices to slow the putrefaction of the body; the latter, rubbed with cherry water and lavender flowers, arms and legs tied with bands, her sex, nose, and mouth stuffed with soaked cotton, wearing her best dress, lies enveloped in a white veil tied with a black ribbon. The hands are arranged to hold a wooden cross on her stomach. A woman gets up from time to time to chase the flies that buzz about Vicenta's face. Another approaches in tears and calls out her name. Farther off, a third laments her leaving forever. All the women are huddled among the few available chairs, praising to each other the virtues of the deceased, remembering her goodness, her generosity, her willingness to help anyone in need, her stamina in working right up to the end. They are composing a communal hymn to her life and her memory; some, the oldest, remember her love of dancing and retell how she used to come out during the vigil of the Cross and processions on Saint John's Day; others speak of her resignation when her only daughter died and of how she poured her love onto the child left behind, José Tomás, who, in the middle of the throng, is receiving hugs and condolences.

Neighbor women had come to tell him. One, when she saw Vicenta in such bad shape, wanted to make a potion of aromatic herbs and ran to the drugstore to buy incense and laurel, but José Tomás put his ailing grandmother in the jeep and stepped on the gas until he got to the hospital in Caucagua. It had already been several days since she could get out of bed; her neighbor tended to her and prepared her meals, but all Vicenta would accept were a few drops of water or a little finely ground cornmeal. She rarely spoke, and when she did it was hard to understand her; sometimes she asked them to change her position because all her bones were aching. The doctor who examined her concluded that it was best to let her die in peace. When her grandson came close she said, "Joseíto, the papers, the papers you went to get in Caracas . . ." And he: "Take it easy, Grandmother, sleep a little so you can get your strength back." But she returned to the papers: "Joseíto, don't forget the papers, that stuff in the *Gazette*." The doctor had asked if he knew what she was talking about. "It's her age," José Tomás had replied. "She hasn't known what she's saying for some time now."

The men also pass by the coffin. Ernestino, limping, accompanied by a daughter who acts as his cane, lingers for a moment, concentrating, as if prolonging a casually interrupted conversation, and then shuffles out to join those talking outside and waiting for the procession to leave; sitting on a stool they've brought onto the street, he shoos the flies with his hat, his remaining good eye almost closed.

José Tomás walks over to embrace him. Ernestino came to see him recently, and his godson received him, as always, with two glasses and a bottle of cane liquor. "What can I do for you? Can I give you something?" "No, son, no, when people get old they don't need anything anymore; I've got my daughters to take care of me; I came to get some medication, to see about this eye that's watering up on me." He'd shown him a teary eye. "I came by to say hello and to tell your wife and children that they should all be well. I had one worry. When I went by here I thought, I'm going to ask the boy what happened with the *Gazettes*; that's why I'm bothering you." "You're never a bother in this house." Sitting in the rocking chair, Ernestino drank down what was in the glass. "On my way here I passed that land. It's full of trucks and tractors, raising a lot of dust. And I thought, *How come they're moving earth if the boy put in a claim for all that to Congress?* "Protests were made to the commissions in charge of it, but they think differently there." A spark had slithered out from between the wrinkles around the old man's eyes. "So what's on their minds? I thought there could only be one reason." "It's not a matter of any reason or right, Ernestino; to be right is one thing, but the way things work out is what matters. For us the problem isn't just the land; what we've got to solve is unemployment. That's what's giving us all the problems we have. You're thinking about youth; the young people today don't want to work in the fields, and with every reason, so since there's no work here, they go to Caracas to be unemployed there too, or stay here and get involved in criminal activities. Barlovento today is a very celebrated tourist area. Delinquency isn't for us; people coming to the beach don't want to be held up, and there are a lot who've sold their vacation houses because they keep getting robbed. We have to assure them of honest work and tranquillity. In a democracy we have to consider the benefits for the majority; we can't keep on thinking the way we used to, that what people want is land; we can't keep killing each other over land. Nowadays wealth comes from other kinds of work." "That sounds fine, but this land is ours and the machines are theirs. Why don't we divide up the pork?" Ernestino's cracked voice had asked. "You should be taking into account the construction jobs," José Tomás replied; "that's not farm work. It has social security, medical benefits, child care for the women workers. This was thoroughly discussed in the council; we were looking for what was best for our people, and it was decided to grant the permission that a company requested to develop a deluxe tourist center. We managed to get rid of the Saltwater people, the ones doing us all that harm, killing, burning farms; they owned the useless land that they got nothing out of. What was returned to the nation in the matter of the railroad concession is a slender strip that doesn't have much value, and the council decided to join it to the property around it that the Saltwater people had taken over through their trickery. The tractors you saw are there because the engineer in charge, Dr. Villaverde, has started to clear the land. It's going to be something good and something well done. You'll see how it's going to be a boon for the region."

The priest enters, recites prayers and sprinkles holy water over the corpse and all over the house. The crowd by the door falls silent and forms a line for the procession. Francisco, leaning against a wall, is waiting impatiently for them to leave for the cemetery. Some young men, José Tomás's sons, and José Tomás himself lift the coffin onto their shoulders. The priest is in front, and behind him the casket that the men carry up the street as it sways from side to side; two steps forward, two steps back. Meanwhile, the women stay behind and with grief-stricken expressions and Hail Marys hasten to strip the improvised altar and take away the chairs. At the grave site the priest intones the response, and the diggers discuss among themselves how the coffin should be placed. One asks if there shouldn't be a toast, and José Tomas brings out a bottle of cane liquor and shares it, asking: "Do you want some?" One by one, those present pass it from hand to hand. Francisco, disgusted, also drinks; when the gravediggers throw the last shovelful into the hole along with the flowers, he embraces José Tomás.

"Thanks so much for coming, Francisco."

"Friends are for good times and for bad. Your grandmother was a person who was dearly loved in my family," he says, and he starts his car and is off to Caracas.

The mourners slowly drifted away, and at sunset only a few attenuated shadows were left beside the wooden cross.

So, then, I've recounted the last chronicle of my memoirs. My lawsuits have come to an end, my complaints have ceased, our litigation is over. I don't understand what explanation you want from me, Alejandro, can't imagine what details I can add to what I've already put down, since it's all as clear as cool spring water. My titles weren't needed; they were, as I've told you, an amateur's keepsake, a sentimental gift Don Heliodoro gave Belén in return for favors received. Your title as Royal Founder wasn't needed, Juan del Rosario; consider it lost, and rest in peace. Our disputes have been resolved, our demands have been settled without all that ravening hunger for old papers, without all that ink that was poured out, and everybody's come out happy—or almost everybody. My voice has lost its strength because I need a scribe to make it heard—and now I've reverted to my image as a crazy old aristocrat, spine bent, nails like claws, dirty locks long and white, lost in her memoirs and amid bedsheets that stink of urine, shouting for her slave women and her children, who've already forgotten her. I'm going back to where I came from, to my sheaves of parchment, where I was a paper ghost. But before nothingness swallows me up, I want to make my farewell.

I've come today for the last time to visit what was my landscape,

these four streets where people of my rank lived, whom I complemented and who complemented me; this church I attended, covered
by my mantle as a sign of privileged status and escorted by two slave
women who carried my rug and drove off the insects; this village that
before my village eyes has become the outline of a great city and
where for eighty-seven years, with brief exceptions, my whole existence took place. There's nothing in it to recall my life, it's all a
strange façade, but sometimes, in the peaceful light of afternoon, a
touch of breeze among the trees, a movement of shadows across the
mountain, the persistent sound of birds, or a sudden downpour makes
me feel for a moment that I'm still here. That even today it's a languid
morning of a long day through which time crosses in its leisurely way
while my eyes caress the courtyard flagstones, the floor and wall tiles
I'd had brought from Andalusia, and as I while away the free hours
under the lemon tree in the backyard. I embroider a stitch in a mantle
or take a turn through the kitchen to see that everything will be in
order when Alejandro arrives home and tells me what was discussed
in government house and what the price of cacao was. Then we'll
have a nice long siesta, because the heat is heavy, and I'll pull out the
porcelain plates and gilt-edged glasses I had imported from France as
I prepare to receive properly my friends the Mijares women, my
cousins the Solórzanos, and his cousins the Blancos; and when night
comes on and he pores over the accounts the steward gives him, I'll
play solitaire, since the children are asleep and the crickets can be
heard in the courtyard. Memory is useless, Alejandro; I've come to
understand that. It's sterile, like a male tree; the more memories that
are stored up, the more it's necessary to forget them. In this unmemo-
ried country, I'm pure recall. Do you, at least, remember me? Do you
remember when we were children and played with tops in the corners of the courtyard of my father's house? Do you remember when
you were an adolescent and rode up and down my lands on horseback
or went swimming, your body gleaming, in Higuerote Cove? Do you
even remember your death, or have you forgotten that too? Do you
know that I screamed, denying it, and they had to hold me down and
lock me in the gallery until your funeral procession passed the corner
of San Jacinto? That I thought I was Queen Joan the Mad? No, not

really, but I couldn't resign myself, either. It wasn't just the pain of losing you; it was the fear of forgetting you. All my life I wanted to be abreast of my own feelings, and death seemed to me to pose a terrible danger for memory. Now, dead for a long time, I'm taking leave of my landscape, and as my corpse eyes register the absence of what I loved so much, I know that my whole ambition and energy have been spent to create a useless voice, the voice of a corpse for the ears of a corpse, and perhaps memory is the most pointless of all our attributes. How much weight, Alejandro, how many bundles have I carried on my back from the time when my father landed at Vela de Coro with his father, who was a cooper from Málaga, until today, when Francisco Villaverde signs his agreement? I would like to have known, one by one, all the days that passed since then, and to have read all the documents that vouch for our existence; but there's no scribe who could take on such a task, and, to tell the truth, I've only been able to follow the chronology of my lawsuit . . . and since that's all over, my chronicle is also coming to an end. Now I'm a dead person with no business and no listeners, and the only company I have left is that of my corpses. Everything I've dictated has been for you, my husband, my cousin, my equal, and for you, my houseboy, my freedman, my opponent. Where are you, Juan del Rosario? Hiding as always, up in a tree so I won't send you to buy a quarter of a sugarloaf that's needed in the kitchen? Come and die completely here beside me; come and console me now as I'm shaken by time, which has made me fall to pieces over the years, just like the papers I never found; come, let's fall apart together, because a gust of wind is all that's needed to make us crumble. And you, Alejandro, what are you doing that you don't hug me? I see you sitting there with your dusty jacket, your tricorn hat at a tilt, your shoes unbuckled, your body spongy like a puppet's, and still and all you're my beloved corpse.